The Cambridge Companion to Duke Ellington

Duke Ellington is widely held to be the greatest jazz composer and one of the most significant cultural icons of the twentieth century. This comprehensive and accessible *Companion* is the first collection of essays to survey, in-depth, Ellington's career, music, and place in popular culture. An international cast of authors includes renowned scholars, critics, composers, and jazz musicians. Organized in three parts, the *Companion* first sets Ellington's life and work in context, providing new information about his formative years, method of composing, interactions with other musicians, and activities abroad; its second part gives a complete artistic biography of Ellington; and the final section is a series of specific musical studies, including chapters on Ellington and songwriting, the jazz piano, descriptive music, and the blues. Featuring a chronology of the composer's life and major recordings, this book is essential reading for anyone with an interest in Ellington's enduring artistic legacy.

EDWARD GREEN is a professor at Manhattan School of Music, where since 1984 he has taught jazz, music history, composition, and ethnomusicology. He is also on the faculty of the Aesthetic Realism Foundation, and studied with the renowned philosopher Eli Siegel, the founder of Aesthetic Realism. Dr. Green serves on the editorial boards of *The International Review of the Aesthetics and Sociology of Music*, *Haydn* (the journal of the Haydn Society of North America), and Проблемы Музыкальной Науки (Music Scholarship), which is published by a consortium of major Russian conservatories, and is editor of *China and the West: The Birth of a New Music* (2009). An active composer, he received a 2009 Grammy nomination for his Piano Concertino (Best Contemporary Classical Composition) and a commission offered jointly by 13 of America's major concert wind ensembles, which resulted in his 2012 *Symphony for Band.*

Ellington at the Rainbow Grill, New York City, circa 1970. Courtesy of the Archives of the Institute for Jazz Studies at Rutgers.

Image on the back cover shows (front row, left to right) Fred Guy's guitar, Junior Raglin's bass, Duke Ellington, Sonny Greer; (second row) Otto Hardwick, Juan Tizol, Ray Nance, Harry Carney, Betty Roché, Rex Stewart, Ben Webster, Wallace Jones, Lawrence Brown; (back row) Harold "Shorty" Baker, Johnny Hodges, Chauncey Haughton, Joe "Tricky Sam" Nanton.

The Cambridge Companion to

DUKE ELLINGTON

....

EDITED BY
Edward Green
Manhattan School of Music

ASSOCIATE EDITOR
Evan Spring

CAMBRIDGE
UNIVERSITY PRESS

CAMBRIDGE
UNIVERSITY PRESS

University Printing House, Cambridge CB2 8BS, United Kingdom

Cambridge University Press is part of the University of Cambridge.

It furthers the University's mission by disseminating knowledge in the pursuit of education, learning and research at the highest international levels of excellence.

www.cambridge.org
Information on this title: www.cambridge.org/9780521707534

First published 2014

Printed in the United Kingdom by T. J. International Ltd, Padstow

A catalogue record for this publication is available from the British Library

Library of Congress Cataloguing in Publication data
The Cambridge companion to Duke Ellington / edited by Edward Green.
    pages   cm. – (Cambridge companions to music)
ISBN 978-0-521-88119-7 (hardback)
1. Ellington, Duke, 1899–1974 – Criticism and interpretation.   2. Jazz musicians – United States – Biography.   I. Green, Edward, 1951– editor.
ML410.E44C34   2014
781.65092–dc23
[B]

2014026370

ISBN 978-0-521-88119-7 Hardback
ISBN 978-0-521-70753-4 Paperback

Contents

Notes on contributors

David Berger, a jazz composer, arranger, and conductor, is recognized internationally as a leading authority on the music of Duke Ellington and the Swing Era. Conductor and arranger for the Jazz at Lincoln Center Orchestra from its inception in 1988 through 1994, Berger has transcribed more than 750 full scores of classic recordings, including more than 500 works by Duke Ellington and Billy Strayhorn. The David Berger Jazz Orchestra has performed all over the U.S. and Europe as well as on TV and for movies.

Andrew Berish is Associate Professor in the Humanities and Cultural Studies Department at the University of South Florida. His book *Lonesome Roads and Streets of Dreams: Place, Mobility, and Race in Jazz of the 1930s and '40s* was published in 2012. His essays on Duke Ellington and Tin Pan Alley, Depression-era "sweet" jazz, and gypsy-jazz guitarist Django Reinhardt have appeared in *Musical Quarterly, Journal of the Society for American Music*, and *Jazz Perspectives*. His research focuses on jazz, American popular music, and musical performance as a spatial practice.

Benjamin Bierman is Associate Professor of Music at John Jay College, CUNY. His primary area of scholarly interest is twentieth-century American music, including jazz, blues, R&B, pop, and concert music. He has essays in the books *Pop-Culture Pedagogy in the Music Classroom* and *The Routledge History of Social Protest in Popular Music*, and the journals *American Music Review* and *Jazz Perspectives*. Upcoming publications include the textbook *Listening to Jazz*. In his compositions, Bierman incorporates elements of jazz, blues, Latin music, and the Western art music tradition. Also active as a trumpet player, he has performed with such diverse artists as B. B. King, Archie Shepp, Machito, Celia Cruz, Johnny Copeland, and Stevie Ray Vaughan.

Anthony Brown, a composer, percussionist, ethnomusicologist, Guggenheim Fellow, and Smithsonian Associate Scholar, is Artistic Director of the Grammy-nominated Asian American Orchestra. He has composed music for critically acclaimed, award-winning film documentaries, theater productions, dance companies, and musical ensembles internationally, and has collaborated with Max Roach, Cecil Taylor, Zakir Hussain, Steve Lacy, David Murray, Anthony Davis, and the San Francisco Symphony. Dr. Brown has served as Curator of American Musical Culture and Director of the Jazz Oral History Program at the Smithsonian Institution, and as Visiting Professor of Music at the University of California, Berkeley. His book *GIVE THE DRUMMER SOME! The Development of Modern Jazz Drumming* is forthcoming.

Anna Harwell Celenza is the Thomas E. Caestecker Professor of Music at Georgetown University. She has published on a wide array of topics, from Liszt and Mahler to Scandinavian music and jazz, and is currently completing a book about jazz in Italy between the world wars. In addition to her scholarly work, she has served as a writer/commentator for NPR's *Performance Today* and has published eight children's books, including *Duke Ellington's Nutcracker Suite* (2011).

Bill Dobbins is a professor of jazz studies at the Eastman School of Music in Rochester, New York. From 1994 through 2002 he was principal conductor of the WDR Big Band in Cologne, Germany. As a pianist, composer/arranger, and conductor, he has collaborated with Clark Terry, Chuck Israels, Red Mitchell, Phil Woods, Dave Liebman, Gary Foster, and Peter Erskine. His publications include *Jazz Arranging and Composing: A Linear Approach* and *A Creative Approach to Jazz Piano Harmony*. His books of transcriptions include *Chick Corea: Now He Sings, Now He Sobs* and *Clare Fischer: Alone Together/Just Me*. His recent CDs include *J. S. Bach: Christmas Oratorio*, which he arranged and conducted, with the King's Singers and the WDR Big Band.

Will Friedwald writes about jazz and nightlife for *The Wall Street Journal*. He is the author of eight books on music and popular culture, including *A Biographical Guide to the Great Jazz and Pop Singers*, *Sinatra: The Song Is You*, *Stardust Melodies*, *Tony Bennett: The Good Life*, and *Jazz Singing*. He has written over 600 liner notes for compact discs, received eight Grammy nominations, and appears frequently on television and other documentaries.

Benjamin Givan is Associate Professor of Music at Skidmore College. His publications on jazz history and theory have appeared in journals such as *Musical Quarterly*, *Theory and Practice*, *The Journal of Musicology*, and *Journal of the American Musicological Society*. He is the author of *The Music of Django Reinhardt*.

Edward Green, editor of this volume, is a professor at Manhattan School of Music, and is also on the faculty of the Aesthetic Realism Foundation in New York. A wide-ranging musicologist, with published essays on such diverse figures as Guido d'Arezzo, Gustav Mahler, Stephen Foster, Harry Partch, Anton Reicha, and Jean-Jacques Rousseau, Dr. Green serves on the editorial boards of *The International Review of the Aesthetics and Sociology of Music*, *Haydn* (the journal of the Haydn Society of North America), and *Проблемы Музыкальной Науки* (Music Scholarship), published by a consortium of major Russian conservatories. He is also the editor of *China and the West: The Birth of a New Music*. Well known as a concert composer, he has received – among other honors – a 2009 Grammy nomination for his Piano Concertino (Best Contemporary Classical Composition). His recent commissions include one jointly offered by 13 of America's leading concert wind ensembles – resulting in his *Symphony for Band* (2012).

John Howland is professor of music history at the Norwegian University of Science and Technology in Trondheim, Norway. His research and writings explore arranging traditions across popular music and jazz-related orchestral idioms. He is the author of *"Ellington Uptown": Duke Ellington, James P. Johnson, and the Birth of Concert Jazz* (2009); the former editor and co-founder of the journal *Jazz Perspectives*; and the editor of both the forthcoming book *Ellington Studies* (Cambridge University Press) and an Ellington-focused double issue of *Musical Quarterly* (2013).

Stephen D. James, the son of Duke Ellington's only sibling Ruth, grew up traveling with his uncle and the band. He trained in composition and percussion. As an adult, James helped manage the band, sat in on drums on occasion, and served as vice president of the family publishing company, Tempo Music.

J. Walker James is a writer, researcher and former award-winning journalist who has assisted Stephen James with writing, archiving, and research related to Duke Ellington since 2007.

Jeffrey Magee is Professor and Director of the School of Music at the University of Illinois, Urbana-Champaign. He is the author of *The Uncrowned King of Swing: Fletcher Henderson and Big Band Jazz* (2005), which won the Society for American Music's Irving Lowens Award, and *Irving Berlin's American Musical Theater* (2012). He has published several articles on jazz and popular music in *Jazz Perspectives, Journal of the American Musicological Society, Musical Quarterly,* and other periodicals. He is the founder and co-editor of the book series Profiles in Popular Music.

Dan Morgenstern retired in 2012 after 36 years as director of Rutgers University's Institute of Jazz Studies, one of the world's largest archival collections of jazz materials. He was editor of *Metronome, Jazz,* and *Down Beat*; has won eight Grammy awards for Best Album Notes; and received ASCAP's Deems Taylor Awards for his books *Jazz People* and *Living with Jazz*. Raised in Vienna and Copenhagen, he came to the U.S. in 1947. He remains active as a writer and consultant on jazz.

Marcello Piras, a musicologist and independent researcher born in Rome, has published a book on John Coltrane; dozens of essays for scholarly reviews, books, and periodicals; translations of books by Gunther Schuller, Elijah Wald, and others; and entries for the *Grove Dictionary of American Music*. He has held master classes on black notated piano music performance practice and has lectured in Italy, Germany, Switzerland, the U.S., Canada, Mexico, and Brazil. From 2001 to 2002 he was a visiting scholar at the Center for Black Music Research in Chicago and Executive Editor of the MUSA scholarly edition series. He currently lives in Mexico, studying the black influence on Baroque music and working on an Afrocentric music history from the Stone Age to the present, integrating paleontology, evolution, brain phylogenesis, linguistics, and archaeology.

Brian Priestley is a freelance music journalist and musician, now based in the Republic of Ireland. A contributor to numerous periodicals and reference works, he has published biographies of Charles Mingus, Charlie Parker, and John Coltrane. As a performer he was based in London for many years, and his four albums – the most recent being *Who Knows?* (2004) – have all included adaptations of Ellington material. As far back as 1972 he played piano in the Alan Cohen band, recording one of the earliest recreations of *Black, Brown and Beige,* part of which he was responsible for transcribing.

Evan Spring, Associate Editor, is a freelance editor and jazz historian. In 2003 he became managing editor of the *Annual Review of Jazz Studies* (ARJS), a scholarly journal published by the Institute of Jazz Studies. In 2011 he transformed ARJS into an open-access online publication, the *Journal of Jazz Studies*. He holds an

MA in Jazz History and Research from Rutgers University-Newark, and for 22 years hosted a jazz program on WKCR-FM New York, interviewing over 200 musicians.

Walter van de Leur, a jazz musicologist, received his PhD from the University of Amsterdam in 2002 for his research on Billy Strayhorn, published as *Something to Live For: The Music of Billy Strayhorn* (2002). He conducted extensive research at the Duke Ellington Collection in Washington, D.C., under two consecutive Smithsonian Institution fellowships, and researched and catalogued Billy Strayhorn's musical legacy in the repository of his estate in Pittsburgh. This research led to four CDs by the Dutch Jazz Orchestra with hitherto forgotten works by Strayhorn (Challenge Records). Van de Leur is Research Coordinator at the Conservatorium van Amsterdam, and Professor of Jazz and Improvised Music at the University of Amsterdam.

Trevor Weston's honors include the George Ladd Prix de Paris from the University of California, Berkeley, and a Goddard Lieberson Fellowship from the American Academy of Arts and Letters. He received fellowships from the MacDowell Colony and the Virginia Center for the Creative Arts. Dr. Weston completed his BA at Tufts University and received his MA and PhD from the University of California, Berkeley. His primary teachers were T. J. Anderson and Olly Wilson. Dr. Weston is currently Associate Professor of Music at Drew University in Madison, New Jersey. He served as department chair from 2011 to 2014.

Olly W. Wilson was born in St. Louis, Missouri, where he played jazz piano with local groups. He was a member of several orchestras as a string bass player, including the St. Louis Philharmonic. He has held faculty positions at Florida A&M University, Oberlin Conservatory, and – from 1970 until his retirement in 2002 – the University of California, Berkeley. His compositions, which include chamber works, orchestral music, and works for electronic media, have received awards from the Guggenheim, Koussevitzky, Rockefeller, Fromm, and Lila Wallace Foundations; the National Endowment for the Arts; and the Chamber Music Society of Lincoln Center. Among the symphony orchestras which have commissioned and/or performed his music are those of Boston, Chicago, New York, Moscow, Cleveland, St. Louis, Detroit, Houston, Oakland, and San Francisco. He has been a Visiting Scholar at the University of Ghana, the Fromm Composer-in-Residence at the American Academy in Rome, and a Resident Fellow at the Rockefeller Foundation Center in Bellagio, Italy. In 1995 Dr. Wilson was elected to the American Academy of Arts and Letters.

Acknowledgements

There are many people I want to thank for the coming to be of this book. I am grateful first to Vicki Cooper of Cambridge University Press, its editor in charge of publications in the fields of music and drama, for her enthusiastic support. When I proposed a book of essays to her that would show why Duke Ellington was America's most important composer, she welcomed the idea heartily. I am thankful as well to Fleur Jones, the editor at Cambridge who supervised the production of this Companion. She has been a model of good cheer and thorough professionalism. There are many others at the Press who helped see this book through to publication, and while I do not know most of their names, in behalf of all the authors of this book, I want to express our appreciation for their work.

As readers of this *Companion* will see, the writings in it range widely in terms of style, methodology, and jazz notation. Ellington, who wanted soloists of highly varied temperaments and musical backgrounds to join together in his band, I think would approve! After all, one of the important new things in jazz was this: composers welcoming the spontaneous, creative, musical commentary of others on their work. That, at its best, is the meaning of improvisation, and some of the very best improvisation in jazz history happened within the Ellington band. I invited the many authors of this book to participate in the same spirit – only commenting not through music, but through words with critical insight. The goal was, through their very different perspectives, to bring forth as richly as possible the meaning within Ellington's music. I thank them all for it. There are two others I wish to mention, each of them originally slated to be a contributor to this *Companion*: Annie Kuebler and Michael James. Sadly, both died before they were able to submit their writings. They are, and will continue to be, greatly missed.

I am grateful to Jazz at Lincoln Center, which houses the Frank Driggs Collection, for the photos of Ellington and the band that now grace the front and back covers of this Companion. And the publishers and I particularly thank the Institute of Jazz Studies at Rutgers University for permission to reproduce our frontispiece photo. IJS archivist Tad Hershorn first drew my attention to it: a photo embodying the joy of music-making, and showing the older Ellington still possessed of the gusto and vibrancy of his youth. While every effort was made, here and elsewhere, to identify the sources of all material used in this volume, and to trace all copyright holders, it has not always been possible. If any omissions are brought to our notice, the publishers will be happy to include appropriate acknowledgements in any subsequent edition of the book.

I want to thank my dear wife, Carrie Wilson, for her warm and careful thought about this book – in fact, about all my work, both as a scholar and as a composer. She has made my expression in each field stronger, and I love her for this – and for much more. I am also deeply fortunate in having Barbara Allen and Anne Fielding as my colleagues in the teaching of music at the Aesthetic Realism Foundation. Our many lively, probing conversations about music have been an ongoing joy in my life. They also made many keen and useful suggestions about how to present Duke Ellington's work in the clearest and most honest light. They made this book better.

The greatest thing that happened to me, as man and musician, was learning from Eli Siegel, the founder of Aesthetic Realism, that art and life explain each other. "All beauty," he taught, "is a making one of opposites, and the making one of opposites is what we are going after in ourselves." The first critic of music to explore the meaning of this great principle was Martha Baird, and I was privileged to be her student. I have also had the inestimable honor of studying with Ellen Reiss, poet, critic, and Chairman of Education at the Aesthetic Realism Foundation. To say all the ways her teaching has deepened my capacity to be an honest critic of music and a true scholar would take me far beyond the confines of an Acknowledgements page.

I conclude with this: as a young musician, I was oriented strongly toward the classical European tradition. I liked jazz greatly, but – to be honest – did not think it had the same size of meaning, emotional heft, that I loved in Bach, Beethoven, Prokofiev. Among other great things Eli Siegel did for me was to open up my mind and heart to welcome beauty wherever it happened. He was the first critic to say, clearly, and decades ago, that Duke Ellington is the greatest composer of America. He inspired me to test that statement: to dig into the music, and report sincerely on what I heard.

That was many years ago. It was the early 1970s. This book is a result, and I am glad to say, I think in the writing within it, in all the chapters in their own ways, Ellington's greatness shines through.

Edward Green

Duke Ellington chronology

EVAN SPRING

For the most part, the dates given for specific compositions in "Notable Recordings" indicate the first studio or concert recordings intended for commercial release. For albums, the designation of "LP" or "CD" indicates how the material was first issued commercially. Some of the compositions listed below were written, in whole or in part, by Billy Strayhorn or others in the Ellington band.

Year	Life and Career	Notable Recordings
1899	Edward Kennedy Ellington born in Washington, D.C., on April 29 to Daisy and James Edward Ellington.	
1913	Ellington enters Armstrong High School and studies graphic arts.	
1914	Ellington travels to Philadelphia, is impressed by local pianist Harvey Brooks, and starts teaching himself piano with assistance from his mother. Writes first composition, *Soda Fountain Rag* (possibly in 1915).	
1915	Ellington dubbed "Duke" by a friend for his elegant clothes and piano playing. Ruth Ellington, Duke's only sibling, born July 2.	
1916	Ellington forms a band with school friends.	
1917	Trumpeter Arthur Whetsol and saxophonist Otto "Toby" Hardwick join band, which also plays with local banjoist Elmer Snowden. Duke studies piano with Oliver "Doc" Perry, and begins romance with Edna Thompson.	
1918	Ellington marries Edna Thompson on July 2.	
1919	Ellington forms his first professional band, and also starts a booking agency and sign-painting business. Duke and Edna's son Mercer Kennedy Ellington is born March 11. Duke meets drummer Sonny Greer, and studies harmony with Henry Grant.	
1920	The second child of Duke and Edna dies at birth. Ellington meets James P. Johnson in Washington, D.C., and plays Johnson's composition *Carolina Shout* for him.	
1921	Ellington makes first trip to New York with Sonny Greer, Otto Hardwick, Arthur Whetsol, and Elmer Snowden. There he meets James P. Johnson again, as well as Willie "The Lion" Smith.	
1922	Ellington continues to find success in Washington, D.C., as a dance band leader and booking agent.	

Year	Life and Career	Notable Recordings
1923	Along with Greer and Hardwick, Ellington joins the New York-based band of clarinetist Wilbur Sweatman. In July, Ellington and a band led by Elmer Snowden begin working at Barron Wilkins' Exclusive Club in Harlem. Duke's wife Edna comes to New York and works as a showgirl at Connie's Inn. In September, Snowden's group starts playing at the Hollywood Club on Broadway. In late fall, Snowden breaks with the band, which becomes "The Washingtonians" under the leadership of Ellington and Greer, and features James "Bubber" Miley and Hardwick.	Ellington's first recording, on July 26, is an unissued test pressing by Elmer Snowden's Novelty Orchestra
1924	The Washingtonians continue to perform at the Hollywood Club and also tour New England. Sidney Bechet joins the band briefly.	The Washingtonians record their first disc in November: *Choo Choo* and *Rainy Nights (Rainy Days)*
1925	The band continues to work at the Hollywood Club, now known as the Kentucky Club. Banjoist Freddie Guy replaces George Francis. In May, the revue *Chocolate Kiddies* opens in Berlin, Germany, with a score written partially by Ellington and lyricist Jo Trent. Ellington meets composer/bandleader Will Marion Cook, who becomes a mentor.	
1926	Joe "Tricky Sam" Nanton and Harry Carney join the band, which continues working at the Kentucky Club. Ellington meets Irving Mills, who becomes his manager.	November 29: *East St. Louis Toodle-O* (adopted as band theme), *Birmingham Breakdown*
1927	Wellman Braud and Rudy Jackson join band; Harry Carney rejoins. Ellington's recording career expands dramatically. Engagement at the Cotton Club begins December 4. Barney Bigard joins band.	April 7: *Black and Tan Fantasy* October 26: *Creole Love Call*
1928	Arthur Whetsol rejoins band; Johnny Hodges joins. Ellington separates from his wife, Edna, and his mother moves in with him. Freddie Jenkins joins band.	March 21: *Black Beauty* October 1: *The Mooche*; also first recordings of Duke as solo pianist: *Black Beauty* and *Swampy River* November 22: *Misty Mornin'*
1929	Cootie Williams replaces Bubber Miley; Juan Tizol also joins band, and Otto Hardwick leaves. Likely year for orchestration studies with Will Vodery. At Vodery's recommendation Ellington's band appears in Florenz Ziegfeld's revue *Show Girl* from July to December. In summer they appear in the short film *Black and Tan*. Dancer Mildred Dixon moves in with Ellington and his mother, father, and Ruth.	January 8: *Tiger Rag* (parts 1 and 2), *Doin' the Voom Voom* January 16: *Saturday Night Function, Flaming Youth* March 7: *The Dicty Glide* December 10: *Wall Street Wail*
1930	The band appears in the Cotton Club's spring revue, *The Blackberries of 1930*, and performs for two weeks on Broadway with Maurice Chevalier. The band appears in its first Hollywood film, *Check and Double Check*, and plays at an NAACP benefit on December 7.	June 4: *Jungle Nights in Harlem* August 20: *Ring Dem Bells, Old Man Blues* October 14: *Mood Indigo*
1931	In February, Ellington ends regular association with the Cotton Club and heads on an 18-week tour. On Christmas Day, the band plays a "Battle of Music" with Fletcher	January 8: *Rockin' in Rhythm* January 20: *Creole Rhapsody* (Ellington's first extended work) June 16: *Echoes of the Jungle*

Year	Life and Career	Notable Recordings
	Henderson's orchestra and McKinney's Cotton Pickers in Detroit.	
1932	Ivie Anderson and Lawrence Brown join band; Otto Hardwick rejoins. Tours cover the West Coast, New England, and Midwest. In November they perform for Percy Grainger's music appreciation class at New York University.	February 2: *It Don't Mean a Thing (If It Ain't Got That Swing), Lazy Rhapsody* September 19: *Ducky Wucky*
1933	Band returns to Cotton Club for spring revue, and makes nine-minute short film, *Bundle of Blues*. On June 12 they begin their first European tour at London's Palladium; Duke meets several members of the royal family.	February 15: *Merry-Go-Round, Sophisticated Lady* February 17: *Drop Me Off in Harlem* July 13: *Harlem Speaks* September 26: *Rude Interlude* December 4: *Daybreak Express*
1934	The band goes to Hollywood and appears in the films *Murder at the Vanities* and *Belle of the Nineties*; also tours West Coast. In December Rex Stewart replaces Freddie Jenkins.	January 9: *Stompy Jones, Delta Serenade* January 10: *Solitude*
1935	Wellman Braud replaced by Billy Taylor and Hayes Alvis; for a period the band functions with two bassists. The band appears in a short film, *Symphony in Black*, which includes the young Billie Holiday in her screen debut. Ellington's mother dies May 27, and Duke composes an extended work, *Reminiscing in Tempo*, in her memory.	April 30: *In a Sentimental Mood* September 12: *Reminiscing in Tempo*
1936	Engagements include week-long stays at the Apollo Theater in New York, the Howard Theater in Washington, and the Paramount Theatre in Los Angeles, plus four weeks at the Congress Hotel in Chicago. In December, small-group recordings that feature band members as leaders begin with "Rex Stewart and his Fifty-Second Street Stompers" and "Barney Bigard and his Jazzopaters."	February 27: *Clarinet Lament (Barney's Concerto), Echoes of Harlem (Cootie's Concerto)* December 19: *Caravan* December 21: *Black Butterfly*
1937	Ellington and the band are featured in five numbers in the Hollywood film *The Hit Parade*. They return to the Cotton Club in spring, then continue extensive touring. Ellington's father dies October 28.	April 22: *Azure* September 20: *Diminuendo and Crescendo in Blue, Harmony in Harlem*
1938	Arthur Whetsol and Freddie Jenkins leave orchestra due to illness. In March, the band headlines the *Cotton Club Parade*, scored completely by Ellington. Duke is romantically involved with Beatrice "Evie" Ellis and moves into her apartment. In December he meets Billy Strayhorn in Pittsburgh.	February 2: *The Gal From Joe's* March 3: *I Let a Song Go Out of My Heart* March 28: *Jeep's Blues* June 7: *Pyramid* June 20: *A Gypsy Without a Song* August 9: *Prelude to a Kiss* August 24: *The Jeep Is Jumpin'* September 2: *Boy Meets Horn* December 20: *Wanderlust* December 22: *Blue Light (Transblucency)*
1939	Billy Strayhorn joins band. Crowd of 12,000 hears Ellington perform at NAACP annual ball on February 11. European tour extends from late March to early May. Ellington ends relationship with Irving Mills and signs with new management and publishing company. Jimmie Blanton joins band in October; Ben Webster joins in December, expanding reed section to five.	March 20: *Subtle Lament* March 21: *Portrait of the Lion, Something to Live For, Solid Old Man* April 29: *Serenade to Sweden* August 28: *The Sergeant Was Shy* October 14: *Weely* November 22: *Blues, Plucked Again* (first duets with Jimmie Blanton)
1940	Herb Jeffries joins band, which has engagements in Boston, Chicago, and Los Angeles. Ellington signs exclusive contract with RCA Victor in March. Ray Nance replaces Cootie Williams in October. On	March 6: *Jack the Bear, Ko-Ko, Morning Glory* March 15: *Conga Brava, Concerto for Cootie* May 4: *Cotton Tail, Never No Lament, Bojangles* May 28: *Dusk*

Year	Life and Career	Notable Recordings
	November 7, the band is privately recorded in top form live in Fargo, North Dakota.	July 22: *Harlem Air Shaft, All Too Soon* July 24: *Sepia Panorama* September 5: *In a Mellotone, Warm Valley* October 1: *Pitter Panther Patter, Mr. J. B. Blues* (duets with Jimmie Blanton) November 2: *Day Dream*
1941	On January 1, ASCAP, in a dispute with the radio networks, bans the playing of its music on the radio; Ellington turns to Billy Strayhorn and his son Mercer for new material. On February 9, Ellington delivers speech, "We, Too, Sing 'America'," to a black congregation in Los Angeles, celebrating the contributions of African Americans to the nation's culture. Strayhorn's *Take the "A" Train* becomes (and remains) the band's theme song. In July, Ellington's first full-length stage show, *Jump for Joy*, opens in Los Angeles, closing in September.	February 15: *Blue Serge, Take the "A" Train, Jumpin' Punkins* June 5: *Bakiff, Just a-Sittin' and a-Rockin'* June 26: *I Got It Bad* July 2: *Jump for Joy* July 3: *Things Ain't What They Used to Be, Subtle Slough (Just Squeeze Me)* September 26: *Chelsea Bridge, Bli-Blip* December 3: *Perdido*
1942	Barney Bigard leaves the band in June. Ivie Anderson is replaced by Betty Roché. Jimmie Blanton dies July 30. American Federation of Musicians' strike against record companies begins August 1. In September the orchestra is in Hollywood to film *Cabin in the Sky* and *Reveille with Beverly*. Harold "Shorty" Baker joins band.	January 21: *C Jam Blues* February 26: *What Am I Here For?* June 26: *Main Stem* September 28: *Goin' Up*
1943	The orchestra performs at Carnegie Hall on January 23 in a benefit for Russian War Relief, premiering the long-form work *Black, Brown and Beige*. Rex Stewart and Ben Webster leave band; Taft Jordan and Jimmy Hamilton join. Extended engagement at the Hurricane Club on Broadway. On June 7 Ellington appears at Negro Freedom Rally in Madison Square Garden. Second Carnegie Hall concert on December 11, premiering *New World A-Comin'*.	January 23: *Black, Brown and Beige* December 11: *New World A-Comin'*
1944	Juan Tizol leaves band. Ten-week return engagement at the Hurricane Club begins in March. Al Sears and Cat Anderson join. In December Ellington, for first time since beginning of AFM strike, resumes recording for commercial release. Third Carnegie Hall concert on December 19, premiering *Blutopia* and *Perfume Suite*.	December 1: *I'm Beginning to See the Light* December 19: *Blutopia, Perfume Suite, Air Conditioned Jungle*
1945	West Coast tour from January to March. Series of radio shows for the U.S. Treasury begins in April and extends to October 1946. Three-month engagement at Club Zanzibar (formerly the Hurricane) in New York begins in September. Oscar Pettiford joins band.	July 31: *Esquire Swank* November 24: *I'm Just a Lucky So and So*
1946	Fourth Carnegie Hall concert on January 4. Otto Hardwick leaves band. Joe "Tricky Sam" Nanton dies. Carnegie Hall concerts on November 23 and 24 include *Deep South Suite*. *Beggar's Holiday*, a reworking of *The Beggar's Opera*, opens December 26 on Broadway with score by Ellington and Strayhorn.	January 4: *Magenta Haze* July 10: *Pretty Woman* November 25: *Happy Go Lucky Local*
1947	Ellington signs with Columbia Records in June. Tyree Glenn joins band. Carnegie Hall	December 24: *Liberian Suite* December 27: *The Clothed Woman*

Year	Life and Career	Notable Recordings
	concerts on December 26 and 27 include premiere of *The Liberian Suite* in honor of that nation's centenary.	
1948	Oscar Pettiford leaves band. In July, Ellington, Ray Nance, and Kay Davis travel to England to perform, leaving rest of orchestra behind due to British union restrictions. Wendell Marshall joins band. Sixth annual Carnegie Hall concert on November 13 includes premiere of *The Tattooed Bride*.	November 13: *The Tattooed Bride*
1949	Fred Guy leaves the band. In February they record 15-minute film *Symphony in Swing* in Hollywood. In April they make first TV appearance on CBS program *Adventures in Jazz*.	February: *At the Hollywood Empire* [CD] September 1: *Snibor*
1950	In March the orchestra records in Hollywood for 15-minute film *Salute to Duke Ellington*. European tour from April to June includes France, Belgium, the Netherlands, Switzerland, Italy, West Germany, Denmark, and Sweden. Paul Gonsalves joins band by November.	September–November: *Great Times! Piano Duets* [LP with Billy Strayhorn] November 20: *Love You Madly* December 18: *Masterpieces by Ellington* [LP]
1951	*Harlem* and *Controversial Suite* premiered at New York's Metropolitan Opera House on January 21 in benefit for NAACP. Johnny Hodges, Lawrence Brown, and Sonny Greer leave orchestra; Ellington "raids" Harry James's band to replace them with Willie Smith, Juan Tizol, and Louis Bellson. Later, Britt Woodman joins, followed by Clark Terry and Willie Cook.	January 21: *Harlem, Monologue (Pretty and the Wolf)* December and various dates in 1952: *Ellington Uptown* [LP]
1952	Willie Smith replaced by Hilton Jefferson, and Betty Roché rejoins. November 14 tribute to Duke at Carnegie Hall features Billie Holiday, Charlie Parker, Dizzy Gillespie, Stan Getz, Ahmad Jamal, and the Ellington orchestra.	March 25: *The Seattle Concert* [LP] July–August: *Live at the Blue Note* [LP]
1953	Constant touring continues, with no engagement longer than two weeks. Louis Bellson replaced by Butch Ballard. Charles Mingus fired from band after his altercation with Juan Tizol. Ellington switches record labels, from Columbia to Capitol.	April 6: *Satin Doll* December 3: *Kinda Dukish* December, January 1954, June 1954: *Ellington '55* [LP]
1954	John Sanders joins band. From October 15 to November 8, Ellington's orchestra is part of Norman Granz package tour with Gerry Mulligan, Dave Brubeck, and Stan Getz.	February 8: *In Hamilton 1954* [CDs] April 13: *The 1954 Los Angeles Concert* [CD]
1955	Wendell Marshall replaced by Jimmy Woode. On March 16, Ellington's orchestra premieres *Night Creature* at Carnegie Hall with the Symphony of the Air. With bookings hard to come by, Ellington provides musical background for the "Aquacade" show, with ice skaters and dancing water fountains, in Flushing Meadows, New York, from late June to early August. Sam Woodyard joins band, and Johnny Hodges rejoins. Duke's contract with Capitol Records expires.	March 16: *Night Creature* premiered at Carnegie Hall
1956	In February, the orchestra records for the Bethlehem label. Ellington signs again with Columbia Records. Triumphant	January: *Blue Rose* (with Rosemary Clooney) [LP] February 7–8: *Historically Speaking: The Duke* and *Duke Ellington Presents* [LPs]

Year	Life and Career	Notable Recordings
	performance at the Newport Jazz Festival on July 7 rejuvenates Ellington's career. The orchestra plays concerts at the Shakespearean Festival in Stratford, Ontario, for first time. In August Ellington appears on cover of *Time* magazine.	July 7, 9: *Ellington at Newport* [LP] August 18: *Live from the 1956 Stratford Festival* [CD] September, October, December: *A Drum Is a Woman* [LP]
1957	In March Ellington appears on Edward R. Murrow's TV program *Person to Person*. On April 28 Ellington's *Such Sweet Thunder* suite, relating to works of Shakespeare, premieres at Town Hall, New York. On May 8, his "jazz spectacular" *A Drum Is a Woman* is broadcast nationally on *The U.S. Steel Hour*.	April–May: *Such Sweet Thunder* [LP] June: *Ella Fitzgerald Sings the Duke Ellington Songbook* [LPs] September–October: *Ellington Indigos* [LP]
1958	Ellington participates in episode of educational TV series, *The Subject Is Jazz*, aired March 26. Carnegie Hall concert on April 6 includes Ella Fitzgerald. During a European tour in October and November, Ellington is presented to Queen Elizabeth II at the Leeds Festival.	February 5: *Come Sunday* (with Mahalia Jackson) March–April: *At the Bal Masque* [LP] April 2–3: *The Cosmic Scene* [LP] July 3, 21: *Newport '58* [LP] September 9: *Toot Suite*
1959	Ellington's theatrical show *Jump for Joy* briefly revived in Miami Beach, Florida. Duke records *The Queen's Suite*, presses a single LP, and sends it to Buckingham Palace. Ellington composes his first full-length film score for *Anatomy of a Murder*. In September, he receives Spingarn medal from NAACP for "highest or noblest achievement by an American Negro." Booty Wood joins band. European tour from September 11 to November 3. Clark Terry, Harold "Shorty" Baker, Cat Anderson, Quentin Jackson, and John Sanders leave band.	February 19: *Ellington Jazz Party* [LP] February 20: *Back to Back* [LP with Johnny Hodges] February 25; April 1, 14: *The Queen's Suite* August 9: *Live at the Blue Note* [CDs] September 8: *Festival Session* [LP]
1960	On March 2 the band opens long engagement at the Riviera Hotel in Las Vegas, where Ellington meets Fernanda de Castro Monte, who becomes his mistress. Aaron Bell replaces Jimmy Woode, and Lawrence Brown returns. In November Ellington travels to Paris to compose music for the film *Paris Blues*. On December 29 he records with French musicians for production of *Turcaret*.	May–June: *Nutcracker Suite* May–June: *Piano in the Background* [LP] June 28–30: *Peer Gynt Suite* July 14: *Unknown Session* [LP] July 22: *Hot Summer Dance* [CD] September 24: *Suite Thursday* premiered at Monterey Jazz Festival
1961	Return extended engagement at Riviera Hotel in Las Vegas in January. On March 7 Ellington flies to Paris to resume work on *Paris Blues*. He composes music for TV pilot of *Asphalt Jungle*. In September he cancels concert in Little Rock, Arkansas, when he learns it would be segregated. Ellington and Louis Armstrong appear on *The Ed Sullivan Show* December 17.	March: *Piano in the Foreground* [LP] April 3–4: *Louis Armstrong & Duke Ellington* [LP] July 6: *First Time: The Count Meets the Duke* [LP]
1962	Duke gives solo piano recital at Museum of Modern Art, New York, on January 4. Buster Cooper joins band. Contract with Columbia Records expires. Cootie Williams returns after absence of 22 years. In November Ellington signs with Frank Sinatra's Reprise Records, also serving as the label's jazz A&R man.	January, February, June: *Midnight in Paris* [LP] May 1: *Featuring Paul Gonsalves* [LP] August 18: *Duke Ellington Meets Coleman Hawkins* [LP] September 17: *Money Jungle* [LP with Charles Mingus and Max Roach] September 26: *Duke Ellington & John Coltrane* [LP] December–January 1963: *Afro-Bossa* and *Recollections of the Big Band Era* [LPs]

Year	Life and Career	Notable Recordings
1963	Two-month European tour from January to March, and one-month European tour from late May to late June. Ellington writes music for Canadian production of Shakespeare's *Timon of Athens*. He also presents a show, *My People*, for the Century of Negro Progress Exposition in Chicago. U.S. State Department sponsors the orchestra's tour of the Middle East and India which is cut short by John F. Kennedy's assassination.	February: *The Great Paris Concert* [LPs] February 22: *Duke Ellington's Jazz Violin Session* [LP] February 28, March 1: *Serenade to Sweden* [LP] August: *My People* [LP]
1964	European tour from February to March. First tour of Japan starts in June and lasts three weeks. Ellington receives honorary doctorate from Milton College on November 24. Mercer Ellington joins band as road manager and trumpeter.	January 14: *At Basin Street East* [CD] April: *Ellington '65* [LP] September: *Mary Poppins* [LP]
1965	Four-week European tour begins in January. Pulitzer Prize committee recommends special citation for Ellington, but is overturned by board of directors. The orchestra closes the "Festival of the American Arts" concert at the White House on June 14. Ellington's work *The Golden Broom and the Green Apple* debuts July 30 at Philharmonic Hall, New York. Ellington's *Concert of Sacred Music* debuts at Grace Cathedral, San Francisco, and is performed many times thereafter.	January: *Ellington '66* [LP] April: *Concert in the Virgin Islands* [LP] July 28: *Duke at Tanglewood* [LP] September 16: *A Concert of Sacred Music* [CD] December 26: *Concert of Sacred Music* [LP]
1966	Ellington writes film score for *Assault on a Queen*. On January 23, the band leaves on five-week tour of Europe with Ella Fitzgerald. Ellington receives President's Gold Medal from Lyndon Johnson in Madrid on February 23. In April, the orchestra represents the United States at the World Festival of Negro Arts in Dakar, Senegal. Tour of Japan in May. Ellington writes music for Milton College production of T. S. Eliot's *Murder in the Cathedral*.	May: *The Popular Duke Ellington* [LP] July 18: *The Pianist* [piano trio LP] Late July: *Ella and Duke at the Côte d'Azur* and *Soul Call* [LPs] December 19–21: *The Far East Suite* [LP]
1967	Ellington's wife Edna dies January 15. Two-month European tour begins mid January. In late March the band joins a three-week Jazz at the Philharmonic package tour of the U.S. Billy Strayhorn dies May 31. Ellington receives honorary degree from Washington University, St. Louis.	March 15: *The Intimacy of the Blues* [LP] August, September, November: *. . .And His Mother Called Him Bill* [LP] December 11–12: *Francis A. and Edward K.* [LP with Frank Sinatra]
1968	Ellington's *Second Sacred Concert* premieres January 19 at the Cathedral of St. John the Divine, New York. On March 27 an Ellington octet performs at the White House for President Tubman of Liberia. Jimmy Hamilton leaves band, later replaced by Harold Ashby. Tours of South America and Mexico in September. The orchestra records music for a documentary film, *Racing World*. Ellington is appointed to the National Council on the Arts in November.	January–February: *Second Sacred Concert* [LPs] January 26: *Yale Concert* [LP] November 5: *Latin American Suite* [LP]
1969	Orchestra records music for the film *Change of Mind*. Ellington honored at the White House with a 70th birthday party and presented with Medal of Freedom by President Richard Nixon. Ellington receives honorary doctorate	April 25: *Up In Duke's Workshop* [LP] April 29: *All-Star White House Tribute to Duke Ellington* [CD] November 25, 26: *70th Birthday Concert* [LPs]

Year	Life and Career	Notable Recordings
	from Brown University. Short tour of the Caribbean and Guyana in June. European tour, starting late October, includes first performance in the Soviet bloc (Prague). Lawrence Brown retires from band; Norris Turney, Wild Bill Davis, and Victor Gaskin join.	
1970	Tours of Far East, Australia, and New Zealand in January and February. *New Orleans Suite* is premiered at New Orleans Jazz & Heritage Festival. Johnny Hodges dies May 11. American Ballet Company premieres *The River*, with music by Ellington and choreography by Alvin Ailey, on June 25. Five-week European tour begins June 28. *The Afro-Eurasian Eclipse* premiered at Monterey Jazz Festival September 18.	April 27, May 13: *New Orleans Suite* [LP] May 28: *The Golden Broom and the Green Apple* [on LP titled *Orchestral Works*]
1971	Ellington inducted into the Swedish Academy of Music on March 12. *Goutelas Suite* premiered at Lincoln Center, New York, on April 16. Ellington receives honorary doctorates from the University of Wisconsin, during a residency for the orchestra, and St. John's University in Jamaica, New York. Three-month tour abroad, including first performance in the Soviet Union, begins in September. New band members include Harold Minerve and Johnny Coles.	February 17: *The Afro-Eurasian Eclipse* [LP] April 27: *Goutelas Suite* [on LP titled *The Ellington Suites*] October 22, 24: *The English Concerts* [LPs]
1972	Longest tour of the Far East to date includes Japan, the Philippines, Thailand, Singapore, Indonesia, Australasia, and Fiji. The orchestra continues to tour constantly around the U.S., though Duke has extended gigs at New York's Rainbow Grill in Rockefeller Center with a smaller band.	April 10: *Live at the Whitney* [CD] December 5: *This One's for Blanton* [LP]
1973	Ellington is awarded the *Ordre national de la Légion d'honneur* by the French ambassador in New York on July 8. Ellington receives honorary doctorates from Columbia University and Fisk University. His autobiographical book, *Music Is My Mistress*, is published in the fall. *Third Sacred Concert* premieres at Westminster Abbey, London, on October 24. The orchestra performs in Zambia and Ethiopia, where Ellington receives the Emperor's Star. Ellington's doctor, Arthur Logan, dies November 25.	January 8: *The Big Four* [LP] October 24: *Third Sacred Concert* [LP] December 1: *Eastbourne Performance* [LP]
1974	Ellington continues touring and plays his last date with the band on March 22 in Sturgis, Michigan. Three days later he is admitted to Harkness Pavillion at Columbia-Presbyterian Hospital for treatment of cancer. In the hospital he continues working on an opera, *Queenie Pie*, and ballet, *Three Black Kings*. Paul Gonsalves dies May 15. Tyree Glenn dies May 18. Ellington dies May 24. The funeral service is held May 27 at the Cathedral of St. John the Divine, New York, with over 12,000 in attendance.	

Editor's introduction:
Ellington and Aesthetic Realism

EDWARD GREEN

I am among a large and ever-increasing number of people who see Duke Ellington as America's greatest composer. I also think a good case can be made that, all in all, Ellington, who lived from 1899 to 1974, was the most influential composer of the twentieth century – for jazz, with its various stylistic offspring, has had more impact worldwide than any other form of modern music. And Ellington is acknowledged almost universally as the greatest of all jazz composers.[1]

Jazz is a word inseparable from Ellington; a word he lovingly embraced, but far more frequently disavowed, sometimes fiercely. He wanted his music seen in a wider and more inclusive light, and felt that the term, used casually, would interfere with people listening deeply and truly to what he had to say. Jazz composer, African-American composer, big band composer: these descriptions all highlight important aspects of his musical career. But if we stop there, and don't go deeper, we will miss the fullness of who Ellington was, and the largest meaning his work can have for us.

I learned from Aesthetic Realism, the philosophy founded in the early 1940s by the great American poet and scholar Eli Siegel: art shows reality as it truly is – the oneness of opposites.[2] The greater the work of art, the more that is so. The size of a musical artist is in proportion to how much of the world is present in his or her work: the depth of the world; its variety; its width; its integrity over time. It is the world we are meeting when sounds come our way, and we are looking for sounds that will tell us the truth about that world.

It is in this fundamental principle of Aesthetic Realism: "The world, art, and self explain each other: each is the aesthetic oneness of opposites."[3] Through this magnificent idea – which has widely affected scholars and critics these past decades, though far too often without acknowledgement – one can see the true relation of art and life.[4] I have found it invaluable in my study of Duke Ellington. It is the key to appreciating the greatness of his music, and the meaning of music, as such.

Ellington and the opposites

In Ellington's masterpieces – compositions such as *The Mooche, Harlem Air Shaft, East St. Louis Toodle-O, Jack the Bear* and *Concerto for Cootie* – we meet vibrant energy and deep thoughtfulness, passion, and control. Again and again, his music swings with intensity, yet also with natural ease. Just think, for example, of *Cotton Tail*. Opposites are convincingly, beautifully together – joined in a way we hope they can be in our own lives.

There are, in Ellington's finest works, a true composition of roughness and velvet smoothness; a sense of the orderliness of the world and its confusion. Sounds are heavy, yet also winsome in their lightness. Sounds are wide, but also edgy; painfully thrusting, yet also lovely, suffusing, tender. There is surprise after sonic surprise; at the same time, there is the *beat* and an unshakable continuity of musical design. We hear poise, elegance, sophistication; we are also in the presence of a sincere, "primitive" wildness that comes straight from the gut.

It is honest, stirring music. Duke Ellington, by putting opposites together, gives us the opportunity to have emotions about the world and the human self that are grand and logical and beautiful. I love him for it.

Earlier jazz literature has given illustrations of the presence of opposites in Ellington, though without seeing the large philosophic significance of that fact. Consider, for example, these words by the British critic Vic Bellerby, taken from Peter Gammond's classic 1958 anthology of essays, *Duke Ellington: His Life and Music*. Bellerby describes how we can hear in *Black and Tan Fantasy*, a masterpiece of the 1920s:

> [a] unification of elements, apparently so diverse. The creamy alto of Otto Hardwick and Ellington's dreamy blues piano have little in common with the opening hymn-like chant and the desperate protests of the brass men; but the whole is so fused together that it would be impossible to add or subtract one single note.[5]

When Bellerby says this music is both "desperate" and "dreamy," yet these elements are "fused together," he is pointing to the opposites in Ellington's art. And we can see also in his words evidence for the Aesthetic Realism idea that art has within it the answers to the problems we face in life. How, for example, can we have integrity, even as we experience emotions that are so contradictory – pleasure and pain, anger and love? How can our "protests" and our sense of the world as deserving "hymn-like" praise go together? But that, as we can see through Bellerby's description, is *exactly* what Ellington and his musicians do!

And doing it, they have achieved something big, aesthetically and ethically.

Like of the world

True art satisfies a great need. Eli Siegel was the philosopher who explained that everyone's deepest desire is to like the world on an honest basis. In art, the conflicts we find in ourselves and in the world are resolved. We go deeper into the truth of things; we see the inseparability of opposites; we experience beauty.

Ellington's suavity, his sensuality, his poignant lyricism, his sophistication, his sly and often politically subversive humor, his advocacy of the grandeur, scope and dignity of "Negro" life, even his inspired roughness (a.k.a. his "jungle style") – all of these are put forward as central to his musical personality. They are all there; importantly so. Yet the most pervasive thing in Ellington, in my opinion, and the thing which ultimately matters most, is *joy*.

This joy is philosophic; it is present when the thing we yearn most to see, we *do* see: the profound friendship that is possible between ourselves and the outside world. It is the joy told of, in his own way, by the great English Romantic William Wordsworth in the "Prospectus" to his poem *The Recluse*:

> ... my voice proclaims
> How exquisitely the individual Mind
> (And the progressive powers perhaps no less
> Of the whole species) to the external World
> Is fitted: – and how exquisitely, too –
> ...
> The external World is fitted to the Mind ...

This joy is not limited to bright, happy things; it takes them in but goes further. It has more courage. A true artist – and Ellington was that – proceeds, even in the midst of heartbreak, on the belief that the world will provide the material needed to express oneself sincerely and beautifully. Art is always the victorious discovery of the fittingness Wordsworth proclaimed.

The Mooche

As an example of the power of art to find something joyous in uncomfortable territory – the kind of territory most frequently used by people to hate the world – we can look at the opening measures of what, I believe, is the greatest music from Ellington's early years: *The Mooche*. It is a work filled with sounds that are strange, painful, snarling, disorderly – yet what is its upshot? A thrilling affirmation of life.

Ellington composed *The Mooche* in conjunction with his lead trumpeter, Bubber Miley. The very first sonority we meet, in the famed recording of

October 1, 1928, is harsh and unsettling. That ghostly trio of clarinets in C minor, hovering high above, sinuous and eerie, is a sound at once remote and impinging. There is terror in the vast and empty space separating the clarinets from the weighted tread of the bass four octaves below. All this we hear immediately; and the sense of the world as dissonant and painful is insisted on further when Miley joins in with brassy snarls on *muted* trumpet, adding to the feeling of suppression and struggle.

There is likewise unease in the harmony. In the center of the opening eight-bar phrase, the clarinets, after slithering down chromatically, suddenly pause. They rest on a double whole note for measures 3 and 4, and on another for measures 5 and 6. These held tones are very stable rhythmically. But is stability the message of the harmony? Hardly! We feel disruption, eeriness, a sense of standing on quicksand – and why? Because the piece begins explicitly in C minor, and the first double whole note finds the clarinets resting on a B9 chord, far away from that key. The next double whole note comes on an even more tonally distant sonority: a whole-tone sonority, which, in 1928, would be guaranteed to give a "lost-at-sea" effect.

Just seconds into the composition, our sense of key and of the stability of the tonal universe has been shattered. We have been wrenched off center. But then what happens? Ellington returns us, so gracefully, directly back to C minor, and the lead clarinet settles in measure 7 on the most harmonically solid possible note (the tonic, over an equally firm tonic harmony). We hear the astonishing boldness of the not-yet 30-year-old artist. He is asserting a world at once off-kilter and balanced, a world of confusion and clarity. And he is showing the *coherence* of that world: a world at once wrong and ever-so-right.[6]

Why does this matter? The biggest fight in everyone, I learned from Aesthetic Realism, concerns the question: How much can the world honestly be liked? Does the world, including the world of other people, deserve my contempt or my respect? At any one moment (though we are not ordinarily conscious of it) we are choosing one attitude or the other. Either we are impelled to make less of the meaning of people and things, thinking that by contrast we rise in our self-esteem; or, we base our like of ourselves on our power to be fair to the world not ourselves. The mistake, I learned, made by people throughout history is to try to build a personality for oneself through private victories of contempt. One form this took in me as a young man was not wanting to get too stirred up by things. I was uncomfortable having feeling I couldn't control. That was certainly the case in situations which were in emotional territory like that of *The Mooche*. When things were difficult, and demanded deeper emotional involvement from me, I kept my distance.

At the time I thought this was smart; I hadn't the slightest idea how anti-art my attitude was. In fact, as was then fashionable among conservatory students, I was a devotee of the abstractionist view of music, and associated success in art with cool and impressive technical mastery.

Some years later, in classes I attended taught by Eli Siegel, I began to learn how much this "cool" way of mind held me back, both in music and in life. With much kindness, he asked me in a 1977 class discussion: "Do you think at times the desire to let go, to be as intense as one can be, is sensible?" And he continued: "You like to see yourself as the master of any situation. But is it wise in any way to have a feeling tell you what to do? What do you think inspiration is: the sudden command of a feeling, or letting the feeling tell you what to do?"

These questions were great, and affected me very much. I began to ask whether I was – despite my love for music – harboring attitudes within me that hurt my art. I told Eli Siegel how important I felt these questions were for my life, and how new. He then continued, bringing the discussion even more directly to music: "In 1810, Beethoven had sounds working in him, and he felt they were telling him what to do, and that the first thing was to get them down. Was that sensible?" Yes, I said, it certainly was. "All sincerity," Mr. Siegel then explained, "is yielding to the meaning of something outside oneself. Now, there are some people who feel strength is in *not* having too big a feeling; and if they do have it, to hide it. But when we do that, we become like the weaker moments of any artist – contrived. When we really feel something, reality tells us what to do. In the field of music, if you are really fortunate, the notes will tell you what to do."

That is what, to my ear, happens in *The Mooche*. In this truly inspired work, early in the "Cotton Club" period, Ellington, Miley, and the band as a whole are finding beauty amid the roughness and irregularity of things. They are finding order within disorder; sweetness within what seems, at first, merely harsh and unsettling. They are saying: "You don't have to turn away from the world and have contempt for it in order to take care of yourself. You can be completely honest about the most painful and terrible things, not water them down a bit, and yet have a sense of beauty – a feeling of being alive in a world that honestly can be liked."

Ellington's love for the concrete, visual world

Ellington, who grew up in Washington, D.C., studied the visual arts in high school and was talented enough to earn a full scholarship to

New York's Pratt Institute. As it turned out, he didn't go to Pratt; he made his career in music. But the feeling he had for the beauty and power of the visual world – the world of actual people, objects, and events – never left him. And he wanted his music to convey it.

On jazz terms, he was aiming after what Berlioz, Liszt, Strauss, and Rimsky-Korsakov likewise aimed for. Bach, too, with his *Capriccio on the Departure of His Beloved Brother.* Or, closer to home, Gershwin with his *An American in Paris.* Ellington preferred the term "tone parallel," which he coined, to the European concept of the tone poem, but the idea in essence was the same: to create compositions which hold together well on strictly structural terms, yet express what the world is like, in terms of a specific story or picture.

For a good deal of the twentieth century, especially in academic circles, a cool, structuralist philosophy of music prevailed. The idea that music was impelled by deep, large, and passionate feeling about the world and people was largely put aside. One could read journal article after journal article brimming with technical talk, and find an emotional desert.

Ellington's view was very different. He wanted his music to be in touch with life always; to deal with and express his feeling about the concrete world. "In my writing," he told Richard O. Boyer in a 1944 interview for *The New Yorker,* "there's always a mental picture. That's the way I was raised up in music. In the old days, when a guy made a lick, he'd say what it reminded him of. He'd make the lick and say, 'It sounds like my old man falling downstairs' or 'It sounds like a crazy guy doing this or that.' I remember ole Bubber Miley taking a lick and saying, 'That reminds me of Miss Jones singin' in church'."[7] And as Boyer reports it, Ellington then repeated nearly word for word what he said earlier: "That's the way I was raised up in music. I always have a mental picture." He wanted there to be no doubt where his aesthetic sympathies lay.

Among the compositions which illustrate this point is his *Harlem Air Shaft* of 1940. It is an amazing picture in sound of the sheer diversity of life found in a Harlem apartment building. But what is most noteworthy is not the cataloguing of the diversity of upper Manhattan life; it is how Duke Ellington "composed" it, bringing unity to that diversity through musically coherent form. That, I think, is what this piece is all about, and why it matters. It is his way of saying joyously, through the language of music: "World – bring on your diversity, your disorder. Bring on the way things get tangled up, and ugly with each other. We'll find order there; we'll find the unity; we'll find beauty!"

In the Boyer interview Ellington tells us, "You get the full essence of Harlem in an air shaft." The piece, he says, included musical images of barking dogs, an aerial falling down and breaking a window, "intimate gossip," and energetic jitterbuggers dancing away – "always over you, never below you." There are fights and lovemaking, someone cooking a great meal, and someone else, he noted, "doing a sad job" with a turkey. And, he said, "you can smell coffee."[8]

How colorful this description is! Some of it, admittedly, may be exaggerated for the purpose of entertaining an interviewer. And Boyer himself clearly wanted to write an engaging piece. He gave it a striking title: "The Hot Bach." But as I showed in a 2011 article for the *Journal of Jazz Studies*, what Ellington says is in the music, pretty much *is* there.[9] Ellington was proud of his ability to get the tangible world into his compositions, and was right to be. It was a sign of his imaginative love for reality.[10]

Ellington scholarship, past and present

The Gammond collection of 1958, which includes the Vic Bellerby essay I cited earlier, has a historic place in Ellington scholarship. It was the first multi-author, full-length study of the composer. I am grateful for it; and in various ways, as I set this book in motion, I had it as my model. I wanted the authors to have diverse backgrounds. There are noted jazz musicians; professional critics; and musicologists, both academic and non-academic, including several not from the U.S. – which is fitting, since Ellington is an international figure. There is also a member of his immediate family: a nephew, Stephen James, who was in a position to see Ellington interact with his band in ways never before reported. I want also to take this opportunity to thank my associate editor, Evan Spring, whose keen eye for factual accuracy, and love for and knowledge of Ellington's music, helped the book take form. I am hardly the only contributor to this volume who benefited from his careful observations.

Returning to the Gammond anthology, one of its most important essays is by Burnett James. Titled "Ellington's Place as a Composer," it asks where Ellington stands in relation to certain enduring artistic principles – principles not limited to jazz. Above all, James is dealing with the opposites of logic and emotion: of the need for music to have impersonal structural integrity, and also heartfelt personal feeling:

> What matters in the present context is that Duke Ellington has achieved to an increasing extent throughout his career as a composer the first requirement of all creative artists – that is, the proper solution to the equation between form and content, between feeling and expression. All his best compositions are remarkable for a quite unusual felicity in finding the exact form and texture necessary to bring the inner emotion to life. He habitually surpasses not only other jazz composers but many straight

composers also in the ability to prevent form in music from becoming mere formalism. His music grows out of an internal compulsion that is not dependent on and tied rigidly to a pre-conceived method or formula. Melody, harmony, rhythmic emphasis, and orchestral texture are all of a piece, and a unified part of the creative process.[11]

Notice the use by James of the phrase "all his best compositions." Some fans of Ellington try to show their enthusiasm through blanket approbation. But this is not fair, and not accurate. Ellington toured constantly, performing on the average well over a hundred concerts or nightclub appearances a year, let alone dozens of dances and recording sessions. He had to snatch off-moments on a bus, or on a train at 2 a.m., to write his music. He had to oversee a myriad of complex business details, often on a daily basis. Perhaps no other composer ever worked under such physically demanding circumstances. Let us also remember that this was Ellington's schedule, year-in, year-out, for roughly a half-century. Under these conditions, naturally some of his work falls short of the very highest standards. The extraordinary thing, given that exhausting schedule, is just how often superb music did emerge!

Ellington and rhythm

Rhythm is a key reason why Ellington's best music is exactly that – *superb*! I think he knew it early on. His career-long focus on rhythm is clear enough from the title to one of his most famous songs: "It Don't Mean a Thing (If It Ain't Got That Swing)." It is a focus he shared with nearly all of the world's great musicians. The legendary nineteenth-century conductor and pianist Hans von Bülow, for example, famously said: "In the beginning was Rhythm." Charming words, and, in my opinion, a very respectful gloss on the Bible.

Why does rhythm deserve such intense praise? Because, as Eli Siegel explained in an essay titled "Conflict as Possibility," through rhythm we can see the world as making sense.[12] In a true rhythm, we feel conflict *as conflict*, yet simultaneously as *resolution*.

In Duke Ellington's powerful (and powerfully subtle) rhythms, contradictory qualities are set against each other: slowness and speed, acceleration and drag, jumpiness and glide. We hear momentum and sudden pause; the stop and go of things. We hear sustained sounds, and sounds that embody the fleetingness of things. We hear weighty, accented sounds, and sounds with enchanting lightness. The pace goes on in an unbroken manner, yet there are shocks that take us completely by surprise. There is the groove, whose steady repetitions give us confidence, and there are

Example 0.1. Core thematic motif of Duke Ellington's *Concerto for Cootie*. Publishing rights administered by EMI Robbins Catalog Inc. (ASCAP) and Sony ATV Harmony (ASCAP).

sounds which seem to come straight out of left field – sounds that remain eternally unexpected no matter how often we've heard the music.

An Ellingtonian rhythm can seem perfectly straightforward, yet complexity will nestle within, just waiting for us to notice it. Let me now give a technical example, which I find thrilling. It comes from my favorite work by Ellington, *Concerto for Cootie*, recorded in 1940, about four months before *Harlem Air Shaft*.

The example will be a single musical phrase: the famous seven-bar phrase that begins the trumpet's melody. Incidentally, hardly anyone else in jazz ever used seven-bar phrases, let alone so gracefully.

It is well established that the core idea in this phrase, heard in measures 1 and 2, was a "warm-up" lick invented by Cootie Williams himself. Throughout his career, Ellington, with his keen ears, was quick to recognize the potential for compositional development in ideas percolating among the musicians in his band. Sometimes he gave formal credit to the band member who originated it; sometimes (not so honorably) he did not.[13] At other times he would pay a player for the right to work creatively with his material. That was the case with this lick by Cootie (Example 0.1).

It is a pattern of eight notes which divides naturally into groupings of seven and one. In measure 1, there are seven relatively swift notes that gently swing at a moderate pace. In measure 2, by contrast, there is a single sustained note. What did Ellington hear in this musical design that so intrigued and inspired him? The world as contradiction. Manyness, then unity; motion, then rest. But together we have one beautifully coherent musical phrase.

At first glance the phrase seems fairly simple, but there is a good deal of complexity just beneath the surface. We hear the complexity when we remember that rhythm cannot be isolated from melody; they interpenetrate in our experience of music. As we pay attention to this melody, the rhythm takes on new dimensions of liveliness.

Let's see how. The first four pitches in this eight-note pattern are B♭, G, G♯, A. Then a C. Then – and this is the point to concentrate on – the final three pitches (marked "b" in Example 0.1) cover exactly the same ground as the opening four (marked "a"). As with the "a" notes, the "b" notes start with B♭ and end with A, but with a signal difference: the G♮ is now absent. As a result, there is a subtle "rush" as we push towards the final note in the phrase.

Example 0.2. *Concerto for Cootie*, opening trumpet melody, measures 5–7. Publishing rights administered by EMI Robbins Catalog Inc. (ASCAP) and Sony ATV Harmony (ASCAP).

Remarkably – and this is the art of it – this compact, three-note version of the basic melodic idea (traveling from B♭ to A) is designed so that we experience it not only as an acceleration, but simultaneously as a "stretching out." How does he do this? By making both halves of the phrase end on an A, but the second A is now a whole note, eight times longer than the first A.

So far I have only talked about two measures of music; still five to go! And at first, Ellington's plan for developing that lick seems almost childishly simple. Measures 3 and 4 are in essence a repetition of what we've just heard. Measure 5 makes us feel that yet another simple repetition will be in store. But no – in this third presentation, when the final note arrives, it is not a sustained whole note as before, but passes by as quickly as the seven notes preceding it.

Technically, this short A – marked with an asterisk in Example 0.2 – is an *elision*. It is, at once, the conclusion of one melodic unit and the beginning of another. It is also the last note of one 7+1 rhythmic pattern and the initial note of another.

One further point to notice: this final group of 7+1 has a very different melodic contour than the earlier groups. They travel modestly, in tight circles: C as the highest note, G the lowest. Their compass is limited. By contrast, this fourth and last group swoops boldly down and up, spanning more than a full octave: from high A down to a low G♯. Yet what do we find right in its midst? C, B♭, G♯, A: the same notes in the same order (marked "c") we heard back in measures 1, 3 and 5, only now an octave lower and shifted just a bit in rhythmic placement.[14] It is wonderful, musically and ethically wonderful. Difference, this music tells us, is likewise sameness!

In February, 1925, soon after Eli Siegel won the prestigious poetry prize of *The Nation* magazine, the 22-year-old author was quoted in the *Baltimore Sun* on the subject of jazz, showing a respect for it *as art* without parallel for that time. He spoke of its "metaphysical ecstasy."[15] And in a column for the *Baltimore American* two months later, he continued to affirm the philosophic depth of jazz, pointing in particular to its rhythms, and its important, new, and thrilling junction of the subtle and the elemental.

When rhythm is great, I learned from him, it meets our primal need to see the world as both coherent and surprising. "As you hear sound you either get what you expect or you don't," he once said, "but since happiness is getting both what you expect and what you don't, the best rhythms have both." And in the essay, "The Aesthetic Center," he gave a definition of rhythm that encompasses rhythm as it can be felt anywhere: "Rhythm is any instance of change and sameness seen at once."[16]

The seven-bar phrase I've been considering from *Concerto for Cootie* is just the merest sample of the rich banquet of great rhythms we meet in the work of Duke Ellington. Such rhythms always show technical finesse, in the mathematical sense of the word *technical*. Yet the math is far from cold; great rhythms arise from, and also make for, great emotion. Great rhythms embody our deepest hopes. As Eli Siegel pointed out, to like life we need to find surprise in it, a sense of freshness and discovery; yet we also yearn for continuity, integrity, stability. We suffer when we lack either. The same person who feels bored at 2 p.m. can feel at 4 p.m. tossed around senselessly. He can feel, "When will this ever be over?" – yet moments later, say, as if it were the complete truth about the universe, "Nothing ever lasts."

If this kind of split feeling was all life could provide – contradiction without coherence – a person would be justified in having a fixed contempt for the world. But *Concerto for Cootie*, and all music with true and powerful rhythm, gives the lie to that contempt. It has us experience a world we honestly can applaud. This ultimately is why we care for Ellington, and why we care for music. We want to know the truth about the world, and we want to feel that when we meet the truth, it will have beauty in it. Great composers and performers give us evidence that this is so – evidence we feel with physical immediacy.

The world is present – yet we can diminish it

In the lengthy *New Yorker* portrait of Ellington by Richard O. Boyer quoted earlier, we find evidence that during Ellington's lifetime some people did sense the philosophic importance of his work. For example, Boyer reports how in 1939, during Ellington's second tour of Europe, his music was talked of in Paris as revealing "the very secret of the cosmos" and expressing "the rhythm of the atom." Boyer tells also of how the poet Blaise Cendrars enthusiastically declared: "Such music is not only a new art form, but a new reason for living."[17] Yes, it is! And because Ellington's music has in it a new way to make sense of the world's contradictions – a new way of revealing a structure in the world that we can honestly esteem – then to say it gives us "a new reason for living" is only right.

Composers are not always the best judges of their own work, and sometimes Ellington did not see clearly enough the size of his own creative achievements. For example, at times he reworked masterpieces in ways that weakened them. Not always, of course; I think the 1937 rewrite of *Birmingham Breakdown* is even stronger than the 1926 original. I also think the mid-30s revisions of *Black and Tan Fantasy* and *East St. Louis Toodle-O* are important in their own right, casting valuable new light on the originals.

But what happened to "It Don't Mean a Thing (If It Ain't Got That Swing)" is a different story. In the 1932 Brunswick recording, there is one of the very greatest musical effects in all of modern music. It happens at the coda. Until then, the piece has been hard-driving, edgy, thrusting – sharp and definite. The key rhythmic pattern has been a $\frac{3}{8}$ figure played eight times in a row in a dynamic cross-rhythm that conflicts with the underlying $\frac{4}{4}$ beat: *Doo*-wah, doo-*wah*, *doo*-wah, doo-*wah*, *doo*-wah, doo-*wah*, *doo*-wah, doo-*Wah!* Then at the coda, the brass continue that relentless $\frac{3}{8}$ pulse, but suddenly they are all alone. The rhythm section has dropped out. The brass now pulse 40 times in a row – 5 times longer than before – and on just a single chord: a tonic A♭6. What a difference this makes! What up to now has been edgy and insistent is suddenly transformed into its very opposite, while remaining audibly the same figure. The brass pulse – do they ever! – but simultaneously engage in a smooth decrescendo. As a result, we meet both ongoing energy and the world as yielding, hazy, growing faint. The music seems to spread out horizontally into space, to dissolve into distant memory. Yet, as we are equally aware, it's exactly the same $\frac{3}{8}$ figure!

This is great rhythm. We are experiencing reality, at the same time, as hard and soft, energetic and calm. It is as beautiful, I believe, as anything in Ellington.[18] Unfortunately, nearly all later performances of the composition sacrifice this amazing coda. They push forward loudly to the end. The result is something shallower, more blatant, as that mysterious 40-fold repetition of the tonic chord is no longer to be heard.

To my ear, it is a great loss. We seem to be experiencing a less profound world, a less surprising world, a world with less cohesion among its elements. If I am correct, a question then arises: Why did it happen?

No one fully knows. Certainly the practical, down-to-earth Ellington saw a need to keep up with the times, and mostly these rewrites occurred during a hard-swinging period in jazz history when audiences expected those kinds of driving endings. Even so, perhaps this is not the complete story. We ought to consider whether here, and in some other rewrites,

Ellington, without consciously intending to do so, made decisions which lessened the power of his music.

As I said earlier when I spoke about myself and what I learned from Aesthetic Realism, it is essential for a person to learn about the fight we all have between respect and contempt. "There is a disposition in every person," wrote Eli Siegel "to think he will be for himself by making less of the outside world."[19] Duke Ellington, I believe, could prefer in his weaker moments something smooth over something authentically challenging; the attractive surface to the puzzling and mysterious depths. It is a universal temptation we can all succumb to.

As we honor Duke Ellington, one of the greatest artists ever in the field of music, it is important – and also kind – to ask: Which way of meeting the world and thinking about people supported the best in him, the art in him? Which way impeded it?

Ellington could, at times, have a mechanical way of flattering people – a false kind of smoothness. (There is an honest smoothness.) Often, in his last decades, he told audiences, "We love you madly." Did he really mean it? One can say it was just a necessary part of "show biz." But Ellington was an artist, and art depends on sincerity.

It might seem strange to say of a man who never attended a conservatory, and was largely a self-taught musician, that Ellington in his weakest music could fall into a formalistic manner, at once too stiff and too limp. This manner mars, in my opinion, many of his late suites and Sacred Concerts. In various ways, they can be too smooth, too predictable. Far too often their sonic textures are overly soft, lacking sufficient grip or edge, and there is an insufficient presence of forward-driving rhythmic impetus.

This excessive softness, smoothness, and predictability does not ask enough of an audience. How different are the best compositions of Ellington! As they please us, they simultaneously ask more of us, inspire us. They push against complacent, ego-imposed boundaries.[20] They embody the principle of respect, which, in terms of etymology, means "Look again!" Respect is an inherently critical state of mind; we can always see more meaning in reality. If we don't find it, says the art of the world, it isn't reality's fault, but our own.

One can listen, for example, to *Daybreak Express*, *Ko-Ko*, *The Clothed Woman*, or *The Far East Suite* (a late work collaboratively created with Billy Strayhorn), and feel moment-by-moment on the edge of discovery. Repeated listening does not alter the feeling; it verifies it. The better one knows this music, the livelier and more surprising it grows, and the greater value we find in it.

And Ellington kept searching, with beautiful pride and modesty. Just days after he was honored at the White House on his 70th birthday with the Medal of Freedom, the highest possible civilian honor, he said in an interview for the Voice of America: "I think I am an up-and-coming musician struggling for a new note just like everybody else."

Jazz and the principle of contradiction

As this essay draws to an end, I want to bring our attention once again to that early masterpiece, *Black and Tan Fantasy*, and relate it to one of the most important things ever said about jazz. This statement, which concerns the collective ethical impulsion out of which jazz emerged, is in an unpublished essay by Eli Siegel, likely written in the mid-1960s, titled "The Novel of Our Time and Jazz."[21] The chief thing in his essay is a showing that jazz has the power to bring together in a coherent and pleasing way the most primal opposites in human emotion: our being for and against the world; our respect and our contempt; our YES and NO to reality.

Jazz, the essay indicates, arose from the human need to integrate these opposites, and from the start has accented the idea of contradiction:

> It was smoothness, the expected, the flowing, the recurrent, the easily melodious which was contradicted by jazz as music . . . Syncopation, ragtime, jazz contradicted melody as habit.

Through snarling timbres, off-key blue notes, and melodic phrasing and rhythmic patterns that can never be predicted, jazz says NO! to complacency and a phony sense of comfort. Jazz, as Siegel explains, does this in order to say even more fully YES! to the self that wants to see the world with justice, largeness, surprise, and accuracy. "Jazz at its best," he writes, "contradicts . . . in order to say there is something more." He continues:

> In my knowing of such people as Jelly Roll Morton, Jack Teagarden, Baby Dodds, Duke Ellington . . . when they were most contradictory they had the most sense of something great beyond.
>
> A mess, a clutter, a confusion can be that defiance of false smoothness which is a beckoning to unseen grandeur. Contradiction is needed by man as thoroughly honest and thoroughly lighthearted.

Technically, Ellington's 1927 *Black and Tan Fantasy*, through a welcoming of the principle of NO, comes to an even more powerful assertion of YES. Contradiction pervades this composition, as it does in *The Mooche*, written a year later. The "NO-and-YES" principle, in fact, is present so overtly in four early works of Ellington – *Black and Tan Fantasy*, *The Mooche*, *East St. Louis Toodle-O*, and *Birmingham Breakdown* – that, as Eli Siegel noted, these four compositions could be considered movements of a single symphony.

As *Black and Tan Fantasy* begins, the roughness of the brass, with their B-flat minor blues chorus, is followed by Otto Hardwick's winsome and sweetly flowing solo on alto sax. So different these are, and how dramatic their connection! On the very last beat of the opening 12-bar blues, Sonny Greer crashes, yet immediately mutes, the cymbal. This sudden thrust of percussion separates these two ever-so-contradictory ways of feeling the world – the dark, ominous way, and the charming, brightly yearning way – even as it joins them.

So much happens in the middle of this work, including a bouncy passage for two clarinets and a very humorous solo by Joe "Tricky Sam" Nanton, in which he imitates the neighing of a horse. Then there's the great conclusion, which shows the principle of contradiction in yet another form. This is now a B-flat *major* blues, until it cadences by quoting Chopin's famous "funeral march." Miley's horn, throughout this blues chorus, is at once intense and easy: insisting on the rough blue notes that contradict the major key, but with a rhythm that bounces. His trumpet is in a triumphant register, but played with a mute, so that impediment is simultaneously honored.

And that tone of Bubber's! – sweet and edgy at once, consoling and critical. We sense he's talking to us, and we can ask: "What is Miley trying to tell me and why do I feel so good hearing it?" I think he's saying NO! to smoothness, to our desire to be complacent. And that NO! makes for a great YES! which we hear as the band twice shouts encouragement to continue. It's as if they've gotten more life through his insistent criticism, and they're shouting "Amen" with all the gusto that affirmation can have in African-American churches. Even in the face of a funeral, this is a YES! to life; to the world; to God. And let us not forget, Duke Ellington was a deeply religious man.

Seeing jazz and Ellington truly

In my opinion, Ellington's music, including the contributions of his magnificent band of soloists, is some of the most exhilarating and liberating music ever come to. So it is both astonishing and cautionary to look back a half-century and see how, while Ellington was still alive, his artistic grandeur made many people feel uncomfortable.

To take the most notorious example, consider the very public snub the Pulitzer Committee gave him in 1965 when they denied him their prize, despite the recommendation of their own panel of musical experts. Ellington's response? – one we can all learn from. Said the 66-year-old composer: "Fate is being kind to me. Fate doesn't want me to be famous too young."

I admire Ellington for coming up, apparently spontaneously, with those words. Faced with elitism, he answered with authentic "class" – with the kind of honest smoothness I wrote of earlier. In this statement, Ellington gave a graceful, yet still sharply ironic NO! to the snobbery of the Pulitzer Committee, and in the process affirmed what the art of music really asks of us. Not pursuit of awards and fame, but love for the sheer possibilities of sound – the world of glorious sound not yet heard; a world of new value.

Ellington's anti-snobbism can also be seen in his oft-quoted maxim that there are only two kinds of music: "Good, and the other kind!" It showed too in his happy desire to share the spotlight. What other major composer would program as the theme song of his ensemble a composition by another man – Billy Strayhorn's masterpiece of swing, *Take the "A" Train* – and do so for decades?

Ellington, at various points in his career, did a great deal of coordinated musical composition; for example, early on with Bubber Miley. Meanwhile, in the actual moments of jazz performance there is "spontaneous collective composition" – that is, the principle of improvisation. Everyone in the band is affected by what everyone else is doing: each musician asserting himself while welcoming the unexpected ideas of the others.

This beauty is present in all of world music, but it is particularly obvious in jazz. And it has an ethical meaning: if people dealt with each other on that basis in everyday life, what a different and far kinder world we would have! There is an insistence on public sincerity, and likewise, an insistence on a deep, loving attentiveness to how others wish to express themselves. Jazz depends on reciprocity: on profound and accurate listening joined with a vibrant, personal, expressively just response. And so, the foundations of authentic social justice are to be found in the procedures of authentic jazz.

Ellington called himself "the world's greatest listener." This statement can seem like hubris, and surely some exaggeration is present. Ellington, in a candid moment, would undoubtedly have admitted that he often listened to music more deeply than, in everyday moments, to the people around him.[22] Even so, I think there is in his words something we all can, and *should*, learn from. There's a proud assertion of humility. There's a man saying he's proud to be affected by the world outside himself, including the people he meets and the musicians he works with; happy to yield to that world and have its meaning penetrate him deeply.

Ellington had the power to hear, within specific sounds, what reality-as-a-whole is like. He had the power to organize those sounds into wonderfully coherent structures unfolding in time – enduringly fresh and everlastingly satisfying musical forms.

We are his beneficiaries.

Notes

1 See, for example, Miles Davis' comment to *Down Beat* magazine after hearing Duke Ellington's arrangement of "Stormy Weather" in a "blindfold test": "I think all the musicians should get together one certain day and get down on their knees and thank Duke." Leonard Feather, "Blindfold Test: Miles and Miles of Trumpet Players," *Down Beat*, September 21, 1955.

2 For a fuller description of this philosophy and also a biography of its founder, see the website of the Aesthetic Realism Foundation: www.AestheticRealism.org. For the specific idea that "Music Tells What the World Is Like," see issue 93 of the journal *The Right of Aesthetic Realism to Be Known* (January 8, 1975).

3 Cited in *Aesthetic Realism: We Have Been There – Six Artists on the Siegel Theory of Opposites*, ed. Sheldon Kranz (New York: Definition Press, 1969), 1.

4 See my short essay "On Two Conceptions of Aesthetic Realism," *British Journal of Aesthetics* 45/4 (October 2005): 438–40.

5 New York: Roy Publishers, 162–63. Bellerby's essay is titled "Analysis of Genius."

6 For an analysis of this work in terms of structures of intervallic unity, see my essay "It Don't Mean a Thing if It Ain't Got That Grundgestalt! – Ellington from a Motivic Perspective," *Jazz Perspectives* 2/2 (November 2008): 215–49, particularly 232–36 and 238–40.

7 "The Hot Bach," reprinted in *The Duke Ellington Reader*, ed. Mark Tucker (New York: Oxford University Press, 1993), 233.

8 Ibid., 235.

9 "'Harlem Air Shaft': A True Programmatic Composition?" *Journal of Jazz Studies* 7/1 (Spring 2011): 28–46.

10 The work is also rigorously organized along structural and motivic grounds. See pages 11–17 of my essay "Duke Ellington and the Oneness of Opposites: A Study in the Art of Motivic Composition," *Ongakugaku: Journal of the Musicological Society of Japan* 53/1 (2007), 1–18.

11 Peter Gammond, ed. *Duke Ellington: His Life and Music* (New York: Roy Publishers, 1958), 148.

12 Published in Eli Siegel's *11 Aesthetic Realism Essays* (New York: Aesthetic Realism Foundation, 1974), 11–14.

13 Ellington, himself, was the victim of similar unacknowledged "borrowings." Perhaps the most egregious example was saxophonist Jimmy Forrest's 1952 rhythm-and-blues hit "Night Train," which used an important riff from Ellington's *Happy Go Lucky Local* of 1946. Forrest joined the Ellington band in 1949 and knew the piece.

14 For comments on the motivic unity of *Concerto for Cootie* as a whole, see Green, "Duke Ellington and the Oneness of Opposites," 2–3.

15 February 2, 1925, morning edition, page 16.

16 *Definition: A Journal of Events and Aesthetic Realism*, issue 10 (1962): 3.

17 *Ellington Reader*, ed. Tucker, 215.

18 Nor is this the only reason greatness can be found in this 1932 work; see Green, "Duke Ellington and the Oneness of Opposites," 8–10.

19 Eli Siegel, *The Modern Quarterly Beginnings of Aesthetic Realism: 1922–1923*, ed. Ellen Reiss (New York: Definition Press, 1997), 13.

20 Note this line by Eli Siegel from his 1966 poem "Hymn to Jazz and the Like":

> The Mooche, you come like a procession of right people at twilight saying, This is right, not that; and you walk against walls and the walls run.

From his *Hail, American Development* (New York: Definition Press, 1968), 62–63.

21 The essay can be found in the archives of the Aesthetic Realism Foundation. The passages cited are, respectively, on pages 1 and 5 of the typed manuscript.

22 There's a kind of pain in the autobiography of his son, Mercer Ellington, that points to this; at times Mercer was not truly enough present in his father's mind.

PART I

Ellington in context

1 Artful entertainment: Ellington's formative years in context

JOHN HOWLAND

Duke Ellington's 1927 debut at Harlem's Cotton Club has long been positioned as a landmark moment in his career. During his initial four-year tenure at the club, the bandleader's orchestra rose to national and then international fame. Throughout this period, the growing critical and public interest in Ellington was fueled by both the ever-increasing brilliance of his compositions and his incomparable orchestra, as well as the innovative promotional strategies of his manager, Irving Mills. The building blocks for this unique career, though, were formed in the musical and cultural contexts of Ellington's youth in Washington, D.C.; in his early years as a sideman and bandleader in both Washington and New York; and especially in his educational immersion in the world of Harlem entertainment.

Edward Kennedy ("Duke") Ellington was born in April 1899 and raised in a loving, middle-class household in Washington's thriving African-American community. In Ellington's youth, Washington had the largest black population of any city in the country, and his racial pride and strong self-image were greatly shaped by the mores of this city's significant black middle- and upper-class communities. His Washington years also laid the foundations of his growth and interests as a musician and composer.

Ellington's family had a passion for music, and he loved to listen to his mother, Daisy, play hymns and light-classical / parlor pieces at the piano, including such favorites as C. S. Morrison's 1896 "Meditation" and Ethelbert Nevin's 1898 "The Rosary." Ellington's father, James Edward (known as "J. E."), played both piano and guitar by ear, and favored opera arias and popular songs of the day.[1] When young Edward was around seven or eight, Daisy arranged for him to take piano lessons with a Mrs. Marietta Clinkscales, but as Ellington later noted, "At this point, piano was not my recognized talent."[2] He was also exposed to black church music traditions, with his father attending the local African Methodist Episcopal Zion church, and his mother attending a Baptist denomination. In both, Ellington heard a range of popular hymns and spirituals, such as "Abide With Me" and "Nearer, My God, to Thee."[3] This music was quite important to him and richly informed his later extended compositions, such as *Black, Brown and Beige* (1943) and his three *Sacred Concerts* (1965, 1968, and 1973), as well as numerous smaller works.

Ellington liked to joke that he had two educations – one in the pool hall, and one in school.[4] In Frank Holliday's poolroom, he was able to observe a cross-section of Washington's diverse African-American community and to overhear both talented pianists and conversations between "the prime authorities on *every* subject."[5] By the time he was 13 or 14, Ellington had begun to seek out performances by many of the region's talented ragtime pianists. Of particular importance was a family vacation in the summer of 1913 to Asbury Park, New Jersey, where he was impressed by a young pianist, Harvey Brooks, who taught Ellington a number of elementary ragtime techniques. After this, Ellington was greatly inspired to return to learning the piano. He later said, "I played by ear then," but acknowledged that he "couldn't begin to play the tunes" of the pianists he admired.[6] At the same time, he worked at a soda fountain called the Poodle Dog Cafe. When the cafe needed a new pianist, Ellington offered his services, but quickly realized that "the only way I could learn how to play a tune was to compose it myself and work it up."[7] Ellington thus wrote his first composition, *Soda Fountain Rag* (a.k.a. *Poodle Dog Rag*), and this creative act was intimately entwined with both necessity and his performance aspirations. Other ragtime-influenced piano compositions followed, including *What You Gonna Do When the Bed Breaks Down?* (1913) and *Bitches' Ball* (1914). As the Ellington scholar Mark Tucker has noted, early works like *Soda Fountain Rag* were not fully composed, "set" compositions but instead "consist[ed] of a few musical ideas that serve[d] as a basis for improvised elaboration." The young pianist regularly adapted such materials in new combinations, tempos, rhythms, and styles. In this period Ellington acquired his nickname, "The Duke," when a friend remarked on his elegant clothes and noble demeanor. After he was goaded into playing a number at a dance, Ellington also discovered that "When you were playing piano there was always a pretty girl standing at . . . the end of the piano."[8] Though he was training to become a commercial artist as he began high school in 1913–1914, Ellington had found the key inspirations for his ultimate career as a composer-musician.

The Washington experiences that left the greatest impact on his growth as a musician were the lessons he learned – both directly and through observation – from the city's pianists. In addition, as Tucker has noted, Ellington found lifelong artistic and professional inspiration in the city's black historical pageants, the elder professional musicians who encouraged his early bandleading endeavors, and the so-called "Washington pattern" of black composer-bandleaders.[9] This "pattern" involved the pursuit of multifaceted careers (as bandleaders, performers, composers, and songwriters), a professional demeanor that commanded cross-racial respect, and the active promotion of black vernacular idioms through original compositions. Tucker points to the older musician-bandleaders Will Marion Cook, James Reese Europe, and Ford Dabney – all central figures in both New York and Washington entertainment across Ellington's youth – as the three most likely career models for the aspiring pianist-composer. Following this "Washington pattern" across his career, Ellington pursued a diverse creative life that spanned work as a pianist and bandleader, work in musical theater and nightclub revues, and the composition of vernacular-based concert works.

Among the many musicians Ellington knew in his teens, the two most important were Oliver "Doc" Perry and Henry Grant. Both were generous, intelligent, "conservatory" musicians who took an interest in Ellington and impressed him with their deep respect for both formal (classically trained) and vernacular ("the cats who played by ear") musicians. Perry, a ragtime pianist whom Ellington called his "piano parent," taught the young pianist rudimentary ragtime and popular-music score-reading skills and chord theory.[10] Grant taught music at Ellington's high school and generously gave him private lessons in harmony, a gesture which the budding musician later felt "lighted the direction to more highly developed composition."[11] Ellington's associations with such supportive, older musicians also led to performance opportunities that set him on track for a career in music rather than art.

These early piano jobs further awakened his skills as a businessman, and a notable lesson came during a job as a substitute pianist for a socialite party. Though Ellington provided the actual entertainment, the original pianist, to Ellington's amazement, still collected 90 percent of this engagement's $100 fee. As he recalled, "the very next day" he "arranged for a Music-for-All-Occasions ad in the telephone book," and Ellington-the-entrepreneur was born.[12] His entertainment agency provided both music – which led to the formation of his first band – and advertisement, with Ellington creating posters to advertise events.

In his autobiography, Ellington remarks that in his Washington youth "it was New York that filled our imagination. We were awed by the never-ending roll of great talents there . . . in society music and blues, in vaudeville and songwriting, in jazz and theatre, in dancing and comedy." He adds that "Harlem . . . [had] the world's most glamorous atmosphere. We had to go there."[13] Ellington further recounts a long list of Harlem's entertainers as well as its famous nightclubs, ballrooms, and theaters. While he and his Washington friends were deeply entranced by the seductive folklore of black Harlem, across their teenage years in the 1910s, this world was only just coming into being.

In a 1925 essay, the famous African-American author James Weldon Johnson notes that, in the 1890s, "the center of [Manhattan's] colored population had shifted to the upper Twenties and lower Thirties west of Sixth Avenue." Johnson adds that the black population moved again in the next decade, this time up to an area around West 53rd Street.[14] It was during this latter era that New York's African-American entertainment traditions first took shape in a variety of stage productions. The black pioneers in Broadway musical theater, the nascent recording industry, and the later dance band industry of the 1910s emerged around the West Indian-born comic Bert Williams and his vaudeville partner George Walker. In late 1897, the young composer-violinist (and former Washingtonian) Will Marion Cook approached Williams and Walker with the idea of mounting an all-black musical called *Clorindy, or, The Origin of the Cakewalk*. Cook's hour-long show opened – without Williams and Walker, due to a prior engagement – in July 1898 at the Casino Theatre Roof Garden on Broadway at 39th Street. This production sparked an African-American entertainment renaissance that produced a decade-plus string of all-black musical theater hits. Another member of the Williams-Walker creative team was Will Vodery, who shared duties as musical director, composer, and arranger with Cook. The successes of Williams, Walker, Cook, and Vodery were not alone. In particular, James Weldon Johnson and J. Rosamond Johnson, in partnership with the performer Bob Cole and the conductor James Reese Europe, mounted serious competition.

Ellington was greatly impressed by the business acumen, cross-racial success, and race-oriented artistry of both Cook and Vodery. He gratefully acknowledged on numerous occasions that across the 1920s both men generously provided him with professional advice as well as "valuable" informal lessons in harmony, counterpoint, and orchestration. Even though the precise nature of these "lessons" is unknown, Cook and Vodery were undeniably important professional friends, role models, and mentors for the young composer across his early years in New York. Ellington's emergence as a Washington bandleader in the mid-teens was also shaped by the broader cultural influence of these older musicians.

In 1910, black Broadway's core members formed the Clef Club, the premier New York booking agency and trade union for black musicians. With James Reese Europe as its president, the Clef Club was at the forefront of providing music for a major dancing craze that ran from 1913 to 1919. Though black stage productions on Broadway waned during the mid-to-late teens, these syncopated orchestras maintained a prominent presence of black performers in white entertainment venues up through 1919. This white market demand for black bands spread to other cities with major African-American communities, including

Washington, and provided many young musicians with opportunities both to perform in, and join, established ensembles, and to organize their own dance bands. Ellington was active in both areas, but even during this period of his growing success, he had his sights set on New York.

Ellington's star-struck impression of black New York was centrally tied to Harlem's rise as the epicenter of the black entertainment community. This uptown relocation came at the end of 1913, when Europe and other musicians broke from the Clef Club to found the Tempo Club, a second black booking agency. Whereas the Clef Club was based in Midtown, the Tempo Club was founded in Harlem. This shift was central to the birth of Harlem entertainment proper, and paralleled the influx of African Americans into this neighborhood. New York's top all-black and mixed-race nightclubs similarly moved up to Harlem across the mid-to-late teens.

Ellington's first personal encounter with the world of Harlem entertainment came in Washington in November 1921, after a friend dared him to play his rendition of the Harlem pianist James P. Johnson's virtuosic composition *Carolina Shout* for Johnson himself. Johnson was impressed, and became a friend and supporter of the young pianist. Through similar Washington encounters, Ellington began to associate with other key New York musicians.

New York's black entertainment renaissance of the 1920s took root on Broadway stages following the immense success of the 1921 all-black musical *Shuffle Along*, by the stage duo of Flournoy Miller and Aubrey Lyles, along with the pianist Eubie Blake and his singing partner, Noble Sissle. This production was the catalyst for a second wave of all-black musicals across the 1920s. While *Shuffle Along*'s success increased white interest in black entertainment in Harlem, fashionable white audiences had ventured up to Harlem's black cabarets from the very beginnings of the community's nightclub scene in the mid-1910s. It was in this earlier period that a celebrated virtuosic piano tradition took shape in and around Harlem's new nightclubs. By the early 1920s, James P. Johnson was the chief exponent of this early jazz idiom, which was known as stride piano. Johnson's 1918 and 1921 piano rolls of *Carolina Shout* laid the foundations of jazz piano for a generation of pianists – including Ellington – who learned the work note-for-note from these rolls.

Despite the rising profile of Harlem nightlife, several major setbacks for New York's black entertainment community occurred in the late teens. First, the 1917 New York arrival of the (white) Original Dixieland Jazz Band (the "ODJB") marked the beginning of a nationwide white interest in jazz-related music (as distinct from ragtime). Shortly thereafter, a group of arrangement-heavy, white dance bands rose to prominence and began to distance themselves from the rough-edged, New Orleans-style, improvised "hot" jazz of the many bands that followed the ODJB model. These "sweet" dance orchestras included the bands of Art Hickman and Paul Whiteman, among others. An important turning point in the racial makeup of New York's music scene occurred in 1919 when the Hickman ensemble displaced the black orchestra of Ford Dabney (a Clef Club member) at theater impresario Florenz Ziegfeld's Broadway roof garden restaurant. After this, there were still a number of smaller Midtown/ Broadway nightclubs and dance halls that featured black jazz-oriented bands. By the early 1920s, Harlem nightclubs began to feature both small bands and the aforementioned piano performers. Within time, these bands were also backing ever more elaborate floorshow revues. By the mid-1920s, many of these nightclub revues aspired to be just as lavish as their Broadway stage counterparts, and this ambition led to larger orchestras and the rise of black big band jazz. This is the precise context of Ellington's rise to fame.

Ellington first traveled to New York in February 1923. He and his friends, drummer Sonny Greer and saxophonist Otto Hardwick, had been hired as backing musicians for the clarinetist Wilbur Sweatman's engagement at Harlem's Lafayette Theatre. During their short stint with Sweatman, Greer, Hardwick, and Ellington circulated among Harlem's entertainment community, and most particularly James P. Johnson's social circle. Ellington was soon introduced to several musicians who later joined his first New York bands, including trumpeter James "Bubber" Miley and trombonist Joe "Tricky Sam" Nanton. After their money and gigs ran out, Greer, Hardwick, and Ellington headed back to Washington. By the summer of 1923, however, they returned with the band of banjoist Elmer Snowden. After several minor fiascos and a spot of good luck, Snowden's band landed a prime spot at Barron's Exclusive Club up in Harlem. While Ellington largely played for dancers at Barron's, he had the opportunity to work as a rehearsal pianist for the Connie's Inn revues (also in Harlem), an engagement that launched his education on the workings of Harlem's burgeoning musical revue tradition. By late summer, he had also partnered with the lyricist Jo Trent in a new song-writing venture. In the fall of 1923, Snowden's orchestra relocated to the Hollywood Club (on 49th Street near Broadway), a small Midtown venue popular among white musicians and Broadway celebrities. Ellington quickly assumed control of the band, and the venue's name changed not long after to the Kentucky Club. The Washingtonians, as they were called, soon began to develop a more "hot" sound with the addition of such new band members as Miley and Nanton.

Ellington's early, pre-Cotton Club compositional efforts from this period ideally reflect the entire breadth of mid-1920s black entertainment trends. Through his partnership with Trent, Ellington hoped to break into the lucrative songwriting business of black Tin Pan Alley. The composer was indeed quickly befriended by such influential black songwriters as Maceo Pinkard. Pinkard notably arranged for the Washingtonians' first recording session, which included such early Ellington-penned instrumental compositions as *Rainy Nights* and the train-themed *Choo Choo*.[15] While fairly routine fare for the day, these early recordings do exhibit small innovative details – and the distinctive instrumental voices of his band members – that were later transformed into hallmarks of Ellington's work for the Cotton Club. With this future in mind, it should be noted that the Trent-Ellington partnership contributed several songs – such as "Jim Dandy," "Jig Walk: Charleston," and "Deacon Jazz" – to a new stage revue, *Chocolate Kiddies*. This production was meant to emulate the success of two earlier nightclub revues, the 1922 *Plantation Revue* and the 1922–1923 *Plantation Days*, both of which went on to Broadway stage runs and lucrative European tours (*Chocolate Kiddies* only accomplished the latter). Ellington was equally successful in the dance band realm, and during this initial foray to New York, his Washingtonians even entered the nascent medium of radio through local broadcasts from the Kentucky Club. The band additionally began to pursue vaudeville work. In sum, these various career developments illustrate Ellington's growing abilities to navigate the increasingly fluid boundaries between dance bands, Tin Pan Alley song publishing, the record industry, radio, and New York nightclub and stage entertainments.

In mid-to-late 1926, Ellington began his professional association with Irving Mills, a well-connected white music publisher, impresario, and talent manager.[16] Together they built the Ellington orchestra into one of the top dance orchestras of the day, black or white. Through his diligent and persistent promotion of the bandleader across the late 1920s and 1930s, Mills was able to advance Ellington's career up a ladder of ever more prestigious accomplishments. The end goal of these efforts can be seen in Mills's 1930s advertising manuals, which boldly demand that promoters "sell Ellington as a great artist, [and] a musical genius whose unique style and individual theories of harmony have created a new music."[17] This "musical genius" image had its roots in Ellington's early years with Mills, over 1926 and 1927, when the bandleader was finding his unique voice as a composer. This individuality partially emerged in a number of mid-1926 recordings, but it is with the November 1926 recordings of such instrumental compositions as *East St. Louis Toodle-O* and *Birmingham Breakdown* – and especially the April 1927 *Black and Tan Fantasy* – that his characteristic early voice as an orchestral jazz composer fully blossomed. Notably, these arrangements were recorded more than half a year before these same numbers became cornerstones for the exotic sound of his Cotton Club "jungle music."

In October 1927, the Ellington orchestra joined the Lafayette Theatre's *Jazzmania* stage revue. It was this engagement that caught the attention of the songwriter Jimmy McHugh, who was busy developing a new floor-show revue at the Cotton Club in Harlem. At the encouragement of McHugh (who had ties to Mills), Ellington and his band were hired as the club's new orchestra. As the story goes, the Cotton Club's gangster associates freed Ellington from a conflicting contract by telling a theater owner to "be big or you'll be dead."[18]

With his employment at the Cotton Club, Ellington had moved to the epicenter of 1920s Harlem entertainment. The club's regular radio broadcasts – which were primarily features for the band – soon spread the bandleader's music and name across the country.[19] For the club's glamorous revues, he contributed band arrangements for songs by the club's white composing staff as well as his own distinctive compositions as instrumental background music for select show numbers. The band additionally provided music for dancing. Ellington's new Cotton Club fame led to national and international tours for the band, work in various Broadway and Hollywood musical productions, and many other high-profile opportunities.

Like Cook's and Vodery's work in the teens, Ellington's Cotton Club-era compositions and arrangements drew unusual cross-race critical praise for his abilities as a "serious" composer working in popular entertainment. From the late 1920s forward, this critical literature routinely positioned the 1926 and 1927 recordings of *East St. Louis Toodle-O* and *Black and Tan Fantasy* as both watershed moments for the bandleader and the first true expressions of his unique voice as a composer. These compositions represent ideal early examples of the "Ellington Effect," to borrow the famous phrase coined by Ellington's later writing partner Billy Strayhorn. In this expression, Strayhorn meant to capture both Ellington's habit of composing and orchestrating specifically for the unique musical talents of his band members, and the distinctive greater whole that was produced when these individual instrumental voices sounded together in the performance of his compositions.[20] Both of these early compositions also immerse the listener in the haunting "jungle music" idiom of the Cotton Club era. As heard in these two compositions, the "jungle" idiom owed a great deal to the combination of Ellington's orchestrations, the collective expression and instrumental voices of his performers, and, most especially, the growl-and-plunger brass contributions of Miley (who was credited as a co-composer on both numbers) and Nanton.

When the critic R. D. Darrell first reviewed the April 1927 Brunswick record of *Black and Tan Fantasy*, he commented on its "amazing eccentric instrumental effects," emphasizing that such "stunts" were "performed musically, even artistically."[21] Five years later, Darrell noted that in this first listening he "laughed like everyone else over [the recording's] instrumental wa-waing . . . But as I continued to play the record . . . I laughed less heartily . . . In my ears the whinnies and wa-was began to resolve into new tone colors, distorted and tortured, but agonizingly expressive."[22] This transformation in Darrell's view of *Black and Tan Fantasy* – from "novelty" record to a more culturally elevated "composition" – ultimately laid a major foundation for later critical arguments that held jazz to be an art. This early Ellington criticism – which often provocatively compared Ellington's rich "orchestral technique" to the music of such classical composers as Igor Stravinsky and Frederick Delius, among others – was quickly recycled as promotional fodder by Mills Artists to reinforce Ellington's growing public image as a "respected" composer. The English critic Constant Lambert's 1934 book, *Music Ho!*, also played a major role in the journalistic reception of Ellington as a "serious composer." Lambert notably states here that Ellington "is a real composer, the first jazz composer of distinction."[23] In a related trend, from the late 1920s onwards, there were regular press accounts of Ellington's social and professional encounters with classical musicians – such as his widely reported 1932 invitation from the noted composer Percy Grainger to have the Ellington band perform in a lecture-demonstration in Grainger's New York University music appreciation class. With such favorable publicity, Ellington's music came to be positioned as the very definition of new, culturally elevated "jazz composition."

As Tucker has argued, the originality of a number like *East St. Louis Toodle-O* was only achieved after Ellington's "long experience playing Tin Pan Alley pop songs, hot jazz numbers, and the blues." In finding his own voice, he "had evoked a style that drew upon all these genres, as well as African-American folk music, both secular and sacred . . . But in a way, even before setting foot in the Cotton Club door, Duke Ellington had arrived."[24] As Tucker further emphasizes, the bandleader's early years at the Cotton Club formed the "final important phase of his musical education" through his on-the-job immersion in the production processes of the club's floorshow revues.

Early and mid-century highbrow–lowbrow cultural rhetoric regularly insisted upon rigid distinctions between the spheres of art and entertainment, with the former field retaining great cultural privilege and status, and the vast latter arena being typically viewed (from above) as a cultural wasteland. What is unusual in early Ellington criticism is the readiness of his proponents to characterize him as a "real composer" and to compare his arrangements and compositions to the work of revered classical composers. Such loosely supported comparisons of jazz and classical compositions were key elements in these efforts. While such cultural rhetoric proclaiming the *art* of both jazz and Ellington's music was clearly advantageous for his career, and while his early Cotton Club years were central to his training, growth, and fame as a composer, Ellington himself found earlier models for appreciating the art of black popular music – and ultimately jazz – in the work and professional ideologies of his Harlem entertainment mentors and peers. In this tradition, popular music could indeed aspire to be artful entertainment.

Notes

1 Duke Ellington, *Music Is My Mistress* (Garden City, NY: Doubleday, 1973; reprint, New York: Da Capo, 1976), 20, and Mark Tucker, *Ellington: The Early Years* (Urbana: University of Illinois Press, 1991), 20.
2 Ellington, *Mistress*, 9. There were various spellings for her name. See also Tucker, *Early Years*, 23.
3 Tucker, *Early Years*, 22.
4 Ibid., 25.
5 Ellington, *Mistress*, 30.
6 John Edward Hasse, *Beyond Category: The Life and Genius of Duke Ellington* (New York: Simon & Schuster, 1993), 36–37.
7 Ibid., 37.
8 Ibid., 38–39.
9 See Mark Tucker, "The Renaissance Education of Duke Ellington," in *Black Music in the Harlem Renaissance: A Collection of Essays*, ed. Samuel A. Floyd, Jr. (Knoxville: University of Tennessee Press, 1990), 111–27.
10 Ellington, *Mistress*, 28.
11 Ibid.
12 Ibid., 31.
13 Ibid., 35–36.
14 James Weldon Johnson, "The Making of Harlem," *Survey Graphic*, March 1925, 635.

15 See Tucker, *Early Years*, 103–4.
16 Ibid., 196–98.
17 "Irving Mills Presents Duke Ellington," a Mills Artists advertising manual from early 1934 (New York: Mills Artists, n.d.), 18. From the Schomburg Center, New York Public Library.
18 Tucker, *Early Years*, 210.
19 These broadcasts were band features rather than the club's floorshow revues. See John Howland, *Ellington Uptown: Duke Ellington, James P. Johnson, and the Birth of Concert Jazz* (Ann Arbor: University of Michigan Press, 2009), 127, 315n40.
20 Billy Strayhorn, "The Ellington Effect," *Down Beat*, November 5, 1952, 2; reprinted in *The Duke Ellington Reader*, ed. Mark Tucker (New York: Oxford University Press, 1993), 269–70.
21 R.D. Darrell, writing in the *Phonograph Monthly Review*, July 1927; reprinted in *Ellington Reader*, ed. Tucker, 33–34.
22 R. D. Darrell, "Black Beauty," in *Ellington Reader*, ed. Tucker, 58–59.
23 Constant Lambert, *Music Ho!: A Study of Music in Decline* (1934; republished London: Penguin Books, 1948), 155–57.
24 Tucker, *Early Years*, 258.

2 The process of becoming: composition and recomposition

DAVID BERGER

Nat Hentoff once told me that Duke Ellington often described his music as "in the process of becoming." One of the things we all love about jazz is its *one time only* nature – catching lightning in a bottle. Of course, this is in direct opposition to the formal compositional process where specific notes are rendered onto paper for eternity. Jazz composition thus involves a dramatic tension: the integration of improvisation into a planned format. Even after Ellington had solved this problem in a given composition, he continued to look for new ways to achieve that perfection of musical form which, at the same time, would make for fresh performances.

For most artists the commercial recording of a composition, arrangement, or performance is *the* definitive realization, but for Ellington – and here is the beauty and the frustration – the recording is but one of many performances of an ever-evolving piece of music.

The beauty is in Ellington's conception of art: "Art is dangerous. It is one of the attractions: when it ceases to be dangerous, you don't want it."[1] One potential danger in the performing arts is the possibility of change. We wait for a certain something to happen, but maybe it won't. Maybe something else will be there and change the experience, making it somewhat or even totally different. Maybe we will like it better, or maybe we will like it less. It's a risk we as listeners take. Ellington not only demands this of us listeners, but also encouraged his players to take risks and inspire him.

A frustration many people have with Ellington is that in a 50-year career he wrote and recorded more music than we can ever digest. If only there were some way to limit it. Some recordings appear identical, but on a closer look, we notice details that are changed. Russell Procope said that he played the clarinet solo on *Mood Indigo* every night from 1946 to 1974 and never played it the same way twice.[2] This solo had the same basic pitches and rhythms as the famous Barney Bigard solo on the initial 1930 recording, but as with many of the Ellington set pieces, Procope was always aware that he had the latitude to change it as he saw fit, whether in small or big ways.

Ellington, unlike most of his fellow bandleaders, was loathe to tell the players too much on how to interpret his music. He wanted the individual band members to express themselves through his music. The spirit was more important than the notes. When he gave directions to the band, most often he would be descriptive (e.g., "give me some personality" and "reeds – you are the train whistle"), leaving the musical details to the players. Often he would tell a story to get what he was looking for.

Clark Terry tells the wonderful anecdote about recording "Hey, Buddy Bolden" from *A Drum Is a Woman* with Ellington in 1957. There was no written trumpet part for Clark, who told the Maestro that all he knew about Buddy Bolden was that he was the first great jazz musician in New Orleans long ago and that he played the trumpet. But that wasn't enough information to create a trumpet feature. Ellington told Clark that Buddy Bolden had a sound so big, he could play the trumpet on one side of the Mississippi, and people could hear him all the way on the other shore; that he was the most stylish of dressers and always had all kinds of women following him around; that he would run diminished chords up and down the entire range of his horn like glorious fanfares that would inspire even Gabriel in heaven. Clark said that within a minute or two of hearing Ellington's descriptive prose, "I thought I was Buddy Bolden."[3]

Lawrence Brown, whose early personal dispute with Ellington soured their relationship, but nevertheless didn't stop him from performing with the orchestra for another 25 years, would always say that Ellington's real gift was sales. He was a con man of the highest order – he conned audiences into listening to his music and he conned the players into following him anywhere. Perhaps "conned" is a bit strong. Ellington had the ability to get people to want to do what he wanted.

Ellington would jest that he used a gimmick to keep his personnel – he paid them money. But the truth is that he paid them far less than they could earn elsewhere. As Rex Stewart wrote, "Those of us who have had the privilege of working with Duke are constantly reminded of the debt that we owe him for being allowed to be in his orbit."[4] Once an interviewer asked Harry Carney why he stayed so long (47 years). Harry responded that every day he got to go to work and sit down next to some great musicians, and on his stand would be a new piece of music with his name on it written by Duke Ellington. Why would he ever want to leave?[5]

Process

But what about the actual music? What was the process of composition? In the European classical tradition we tend to think of two opposite processes exemplified by Mozart and Beethoven. In general, Mozart worked quickly with few if any revisions, while Beethoven's music went through numerous rewrites and changes. Each man achieved greatness through his own method.

So which camp does Ellington fall into? Actually both. Some pieces like *Concerto for Cootie* and *Harlem Air Shaft* were performed and recorded nearly as originally conceived. The eight-note motif of *Concerto for Cootie* came from Cootie Williams. Ellington heard it and offered him a small sum of cash. Since Cootie had no particular interest in doing anything with his lick, this seemed like a fair enough deal to him. Jimmy Maxwell, Cootie's subsequent roommate in Benny Goodman's band, once told me that the open horn theme in D-flat major, heard later in the composition, was improvised by Cootie. Since no score or second trumpet part has survived, we can't know for sure.

On *Harlem Air Shaft* Ellington changed the title, added a clarinet solo on the third and fifth choruses, and allowed for trumpet improvisation and rhythm section interpretation. Other than that, the famous 1940 recording is quite like the Ellington handwritten score.

Other pieces contain large sections of music that were created in the recording and never written down. For the first three minutes or so of *Happy Go Lucky Local* (side one of the original 78 record), the original score was scrapped completely and replaced by music created from Ellington's oral description of a rural train ride through the South. The conductor's bell, the couplings banging together, the engineer's whistle, and the other train onomatopoeia are all prelude to the magnificent blues choruses on side two.

Most of Ellington's music falls somewhere between the two poles of composition and improvisation. Each piece is a case of problem solving by a master problem solver. Ellington's lack of formal musical training kept him free of the usual tricks and clichés that many other composers, arrangers, and bandleaders employed. Instead he created his own solutions. One example is when Ben Webster was added to the four-man saxophone section, thus making a five-man section. On many of the preexisting charts, Webster was told to play the lead alto saxophone part down an octave. This would strengthen the lead without disturbing any of the harmonies. No new part would need to be created, nor would any of the original parts need to be rewritten. An interesting situation occurred: on the closely voiced sections, Webster's tenor now sounded a second or third below Carney's baritone. It is uncommon in most bands to put the baritone anywhere but on the bottom of the saxes or brass. Ellington liked this reversal of roles so much that he continued to use it as an alternative color to the normal saxophone order.

The most famous cliché about Ellington is Billy Strayhorn's statement that Ellington's instrument is his orchestra. On a superficial level this can be said about every composer, and certainly about every composer who conducts his own band or orchestra. But in the case of Ellington, it goes much deeper. Ellington wrote not only for a given instrument, but, more specifically, for an individual player with his own particular sound, timbre, personality, and musical sensibilities.

When a player left the band his features were generally retired or rearranged for an entirely different instrument. When new players joined the band, in many cases they would barely solo at all for six months or even a year until Ellington understood their musical personalities and how to integrate them into the sound of the band. Clark Terry's only solo for a long, long time was *Perdido*. He often said, "Duke taught us who we were." Britt Woodman replaced his idol Lawrence Brown in the trombone section. After his first performance with the band (where he played Brown's solos note for note as he had copied them off the original records), Ellington summoned Britt to his dressing room where he told the young trombonist, "I hired Britt Woodman, not Lawrence Brown."[6]

In 1939 three major jazz artists joined the orchestra: Billy Strayhorn (arranger/composer), Ben Webster (tenor saxophone), and Jimmie Blanton (bass). Strayhorn was an enormous help to Ellington, taking on the responsibility of writing nearly all the music Ellington had no time or inclination to write. Blanton revolutionized the way the bass was played in jazz by liberating it from its root functions and making it into a real melodic virtuosic voice. Ben Webster was Ellington's first tenor saxophone star, melding the styles of Coleman Hawkins and Johnny Hodges.

Two Ellington pieces written in 1939 prior to the arrival of Webster and Blanton did not get recorded until March 6, 1940. Ellington had the challenge of figuring out how to integrate these two powerful personalities into already formed pieces: *Ko-Ko* and *Jack the Bear*.

Ko-Ko

Many critics cite *Ko-Ko* as Ellington's greatest composition. One can easily see why it would receive such accolades. Like Stravinsky's *The Rite of Spring* it is at once the most primitive and most sophisticated music in its genre. This basic three-chord minor blues has tom-tom rhythms, plunger growls, and shrieks that go back before slavery all the way to Africa. And yet there is harmonic, melodic, rhythmic, and formal sophistication ten to twenty years ahead of its time.

Little was changed on the recording of this piece from its original conception, with the exception of the two newcomers in the band. Blanton pretty much keeps to the written bass part until the second-to-last chorus, at which point each section of the band plays a scale-wise version of the four-note motif starting at the bottom and ascending to the clarinet at the top. This

Example 2.1. Tenor saxophone part (on bass clef) for Ben Webster on *Ko-Ko* (Duke Ellington), recorded March 6, 1940, and included on *The Blanton-Webster Band*, RCA Bluebird 5659–2-RB (CD, 1986). Transcribed by David Berger. Publishing rights administered by Sony ATV Harmony (ASCAP).

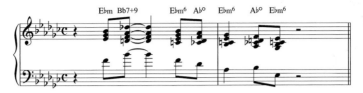

two-measure cascade is answered by a two-bar bass break, which essentially happens three times. Curiously Blanton, who was known for his outrageous technique and rhythmic and melodic invention, chooses to walk quarter notes in each of the three breaks. His sound and rhythmic propulsion are so astonishing that he makes what should be the weakest instrument in the band (and indeed it usually was until then) into Atlas holding up the world on his shoulders. He continues to walk under the shout chorus (the next 12 measures), further energizing the band in a way that no one in 1940 had ever heard.

Ellington's solution for Ben Webster was of a different nature – much more subtle, but no less creative. Since all the reed voicings were already in complete four-part harmony, Ellington could use his normal solution for adding a saxophone part – having Ben Webster double the lead clarinet part down an octave. But in the case of *Ko-Ko* that would not work so well, since it's a much more harmonically adventurous piece and the doubling would sound too conventional. Ellington wanted something wilder, so he wrote Webster a new part. Fortunately this part (in Ellington's hand) has survived.

After resting for the introduction, the reeds enter at letter A, answering the valve trombone in rich four-part harmony. Webster's part adds an extra note to each voicing. His rhythms are identical to the other reeds, but he adds a fifth, and, most notably, dissonant note to each harmony. While skipping from ninths, elevenths, thirteenths, and alterations, he also has an interesting melody of his own. This would be akin to taking a completed crossword puzzle and inserting a letter on each line that would give a deeper meaning to the words. Not just any letters, but odd ones like x, y, z, k, j . . . (Example 2.1).

The climax of this first chorus comes in the ninth and tenth bars, where Webster plays a normal blues melody from the dominant (B♭) to the ♭7 (D♭) of the key (E-flat minor). The genius of this is that at this moment the saxes and rhythm section are playing substitute chords of the ♭VI7 to the V7 (B7 to B♭7), thus making Webster's notes the major seventh on a dominant ♭VI chord and the augmented ninth of the V7 (Example 2.2).

Example 2.2. Tenor saxophone part (on bass clef) for Ben Webster on *Ko-Ko* (Duke Ellington), recorded March 6, 1940, and included on *The Blanton-Webster Band*, RCA Bluebird 5659–2-RB (CD, 1986). Transcribed by David Berger. Publishing rights administered by Sony ATV Harmony (ASCAP).

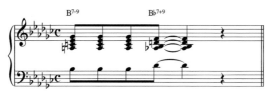

Example 2.3. Arrangement of winds on *Ko-Ko* (Duke Ellington), recorded March 6, 1940, and included on *The Blanton-Webster Band*, RCA Bluebird 5659–2-RB (CD, 1986). Transcribed by David Berger. Publishing rights administered by Sony ATV Harmony (ASCAP).

All this sounds natural due to the blues sensibilities that Ellington has created, but surely no one had ever written anything so daring in all of jazz. Where can we go from here?

The saxes, including Webster, are unison for the next three choruses. The succeeding chorus has the following call and response pattern: the trumpets play an ascending scale-wise four-note motif in unison and are answered by the harmonized reeds and then the harmonized trombones, each playing a repeated two-note motif. For this chorus Webster's added pitches are the fifth saxophone and the first trombone, making each section sound richer. For a little icing on the cake, Ellington gives Webster a sixteenth-note turn on his notes with the trombones (Example 2.3).

In the following chorus of cascading four-note scale motifs, Webster is the fourth saxophone, the first trombone, the fourth trumpet, and finally the mirror of the clarinet, thus making each section a little fuller and richer than they were in the original conception of the piece (Example 2.4).

On the succeeding shout chorus Webster joins Otto Hardwick and Carney in the saxophone unison while Hodges and Bigard are with the dissonant brass voicings. At the end of the coda Webster first is the bottom trumpet, then

Example 2.4. Arrangement of winds on *Ko-Ko* (Duke Ellington), recorded March 6, 1940, and included on *The Blanton-Webster Band*, RCA Bluebird 5659-2-RB (CD, 1986). Transcribed by David Berger. Publishing rights administered by Sony ATV Harmony (ASCAP).

echoes the baritone motif on the dominant, and finally finishes as the fourth reed on the scale-wise four-note motif much as he did in the sixth chorus.

The beauty of Webster's part is its absolute integrity. It is as beautiful horizontally (melodically) as it is vertically (harmonically). Once one becomes aware of this tenor saxophone part, it is difficult not to listen for it throughout the arrangement. What should be a minor detail is written in such an interesting way that the informed listener doesn't want to miss relishing any of it.

Jack the Bear

Jack the Bear presented Ellington with a different set of problems. Whereas *Ko-Ko* was a fully functioning piece that the band just needed more time to learn to perform, *Jack the Bear* lacked compositional focus. Here is a case of a piece that might have never been recorded had Ellington not figured out how to fix the arrangement. In this case both Jimmie Blanton and Billy Strayhorn provided the answer.

Ben Webster merely was given the lead clarinet part to play. The tenor saxophone sounds an octave lower than the clarinet, so with the exception of the clarinet solos (where Webster joins the other saxes in unison background figures), the added fifth saxophone merely serves to support the lead part, without adding any extra harmonic information.

In its original conception, *Jack the Bear* began with an ensemble introduction and used the same material for the coda. Here is where the piece faltered. This material, although not bad in itself, did not introduce or tie up the entire piece in a way that was satisfying. The intro's relationship of loud/ soft and high/low was too blatant. These opposites are explored throughout the piece, but in a much more subtle and integrated way.

Introductions and codas have the heavy responsibility of informing the listener what is about to unfold and then, at the end, summing up what we have heard. These were Ellington's most difficult sections to write. Most often he would work out a piano introduction on the bandstand or in the recording studio. The spontaneity relieved him of thinking about how important this was, and left him to let his subconscious do the work.

Codas were another story. So often they would be added during the recording session (as in *Purple Gazelle* from the LP *Afro-Bossa*) or improvised by band members on the bandstand (*Rockin' in Rhythm* and *The Gal from Joe's*). Ruth Ellington once told me that her brother, Edward, had a great fear of death, and that writing endings symbolized death to him, hence his trouble writing them. There are some famous Strayhorn codas to complete Ellington arrangements (for example, *I Got It Bad* and *Harlem*). But just to be enigmatic, Ellington contributed the coda to Strayhorn's *Take the "A" Train*.

In the case of *Jack the Bear*, Ellington's son, Mercer, told me that Strayhorn came to New York to work with the orchestra in 1939 just as they were leaving on a European tour. The Maestro instructed Mercer to take care of Strayhorn until they got back. Strayhorn ended up staying in Ellington's apartment, where he could look through Duke's scores. One such score was an abandoned piece named *Take It Away*. Strayhorn came up with the idea for the trombone/reed/bass call-and-response introduction, which begins and ends the piece, thus focusing on a virtuoso bass solo like no one ever heard before. Aside from Blanton's mastery of the instrument and huge sound, Ellington's understanding of recording technique led him to have his bassist stand in front of the band – right next to the microphone. Although Ellington had been using this recording setup for years, this was his first recording of a bass feature with the big band, and the results were startling. The bass is a full partner to the rest of the band in terms of volume, intensity, and virtuosity. Furthermore in a mere three minutes Blanton set down the parameters of bass melody and harmony for the next 20 years.

Along with the introduction and coda came a new title: *Jack the Bear*. It's no wonder that Ellington discarded *Take It Away*. Had this piece had something to do with the paring down of the instrumentation (like Haydn's "Farewell" Symphony), then this would have been a fine title. But sometimes Ellington chose working titles hastily just for identification, and after seeing where the piece went, he would come up with something more appropriate. The meaning of *Jack the Bear* is somewhat elusive. There was an expression around that time, "Jack the Bear, he don't care," but that in itself doesn't pack enough meaning to explain this piece, so scholars dug back further to the early part of the twentieth century and

Example 2.5. Unison signal in *Jack the Bear* (Duke Ellington), recorded March 6, 1940, and included on *The Blanton-Webster Band*, RCA Bluebird 5659–2-RB (CD, 1986). Transcribed by David Berger. Publishing rights administered by EMI Robbins Catalog Inc. (ASCAP) and Sony ATV Harmony (ASCAP).

Example 2.6. Piano chord and band tutti answer in original chart of *Jack the Bear* (Duke Ellington) in the Duke Ellington Collection, Smithsonian Institution, Washington, D.C. Publishing rights administered by EMI Robbins Catalog Inc. (ASCAP) and Sony ATV Harmony (ASCAP).

found a New York pianist named Jack the Bear.[7] Not a surprising name for that profession, what with Willie "The Lion" Smith and Donald "The Lamb" Lambert as competitors.

Since Jack the Bear never recorded, we don't know a whole lot about how or what he played, but, most likely, the unison signal that Ellington uses as a transition throughout the piece (Example 2.5) was either a lick of his that Ellington had learned or it was something that reminded Ellington of his predecessor. It may even have come to Ellington from his mentor, Willie "The Lion" Smith. No matter where Ellington got it from, its harmonic roots in the traditional vaudeville chaser cannot be overlooked. It is this lick that inspires Blanton's bass lines for the piece, so when we first hear the signal, we experience a feeling of recognition, having heard Blanton's solo on the new introduction. This is absolutely crucial to the understanding and enjoyment of the piece.

This piece is essentially a 12-bar blues with some 8-bar strains interjected. The 8-bar introduction, which uses the reed responses from the first shout chorus by downwardly terracing the dynamics while lowering the octaves on successive statements, was definitely an afterthought. The original chart began on what is now the ninth bar. However Ellington's piano part in this call and response with the band is new. What he originally conceived was a high loud whole-note chord that resolved to a soft unison quarter note on the downbeat of the second bar. Then the band tutti answer would stay soft for two more bars. This pattern is basically repeated twice, making slight alterations to fit the blues chord progression (Example 2.6).

Example 2.7. Piano and band tutti answer in recording of *Jack the Bear* (Duke Ellington), recorded March 6, 1940, and included on *The Blanton-Webster Band*, RCA Bluebird 5659–2-RB (CD, 1986). Transcribed by David Berger. Publishing rights administered by EMI Robbins Catalog Inc. (ASCAP) and Sony ATV Harmony (ASCAP).

Now here's the tricky part: Ellington removes the loud chord and its resolution from the original chart and replaces it with a blues motif that arpeggiates the vi minor seventh with half-step chromatic lower neighbor grace notes to the C (Example 2.7).

The odd thing is that on the fifth bar Ellington repeats this figure almost verbatim instead of using a C♭ to imply the ♭7 on the IV chord of the blues. It could be a IVmajor9, except that Blanton clearly stays on the tonic for the entire eight bars, never even hinting at the D♭ chord. Bars 9–12 do the traditional V to I cadence. They are then followed by the aforementioned unison signal for four extra bars.

The rest of the chart follows as planned until the recapitulation. When the blues chorus without the IV chord returns, it is Blanton who provides the calls to the band instead of Ellington. He also stays on the tonic for eight bars. Following this 12-bar chorus Blanton plays a spectacular chromatic four-bar break ending with an ascending scale up to the tonic. The band plays a tonic thirteenth chord to end the piece.

These are the most famous four measures in all jazz bass playing. Charles Mingus transcribed Blanton's solos from this piece and kept that sheet of music his whole life. Modern bass playing starts here. But it is not just Blanton's playing that makes this such a wonderful moment. This cadenza is the logical extension and conclusion of the little four-bar signal that inspired this whole three minutes of music.

If we look at the original score, in place of the final bass solo in the coda there are two bars of ensemble. Then there is some blank space on the paper followed by three alternative A♭7 voicings – none of which wound up being used on the recording. The blank space on the paper shows that

Ellington was unsure how he would end this piece. Along comes Jimmie Blanton, and the puzzle is solved.

Coda: an American way of composing

Early in Ellington's career, Will Marion Cook gave the young composer-bandleader some informal composition lessons while riding in the back of taxicabs. At least two pieces of sage advice became crucial pillars of Ellington's relationship with pencil and paper.

It was the European-trained Cook who explained the basic processes of musical development – retrograde, inversion, truncation, diminution, and so on. Ellington quickly became a master of these techniques and constantly invented new and wonderful-sounding combinations.

A related tidbit of advice from Cook was not to look to Europe for musical inspiration, but rather to mine the American folk and popular music traditions so that he could create truly American music. And further, Cook advised that when Ellington faced a musical problem, he should figure out how others solved it and then find his own way.

Ellington's creative problem solving fed on itself year after year, but always in deference to the band's performance. Once a new piece was composed and arranged, and parts copied, it was placed on the individual music stands where it became the musical property of the musicians. Ellington would let the musicians find themselves in the music, and would gently encourage them to tell a story and to play together nicely. He defined himself as a creator of settings for his great soloists. He saw his job as inspiring his musicians to be great. This generosity created one of the greatest symbiotic relationships in all of Western music.

Notes

1 This quote is widely attributed to Ellington, but its source is unclear.

2 Interview in *Memories of Duke* documentary (1980), directed by Gary Keys.

3 From the *Duke Ellington: Reminiscing in Tempo* documentary on PBS television, in the American Experience series.

4 Rex Stewart, *Jazz Masters of the 30s* (1972; New York: Da Capo Press, 1982), 102.

5 Bill Coss, "An Evening with Harry Carney," *Down Beat*, May 25, 1961.

6 Britt Woodman conversation with the author.

7 According to Eubie Blake, Jack the Bear's real name was Wilson: "*He* had a lot of tricks. You could learn a lot from *watchin'* him. He didn't have to work because he always had women keepin' him. He was always dressed to kill. Diamonds, everything." Al Rose, *Eubie Blake* (New York: Schirmer Books, 1979), 148.

3 Conductor of music and men: Duke Ellington through the eyes of his nephew

STEPHEN D. JAMES AND J. WALKER JAMES

Duke Ellington had synesthesia, a neurological condition characterized by a merging of the brain's sensory circuitry. He heard sounds as colors and saw colors as sounds. The flight pattern of a bird would occur to him as a musical phrase. The approach of a rumbling train could form a bass line in his head. To him, baritone saxophonist Harry Carney's "D" was dark blue burlap. Johnny Hodges playing a "G" on his alto sax came across as light blue satin. As a synesthete, Duke experienced the world in a way that was very uniquely his own, a quality reflected in the way he functioned as both a bandleader and a composer. He saw people, situations, and art from a different angle and through a different lens. The lifelong, overriding theme he always harkened back to was one of connectedness and of finding harmonies and beauty where they might not be immediately obvious.

Duke Ellington, my uncle, was my father figure. After the departure of my father, we shared a uniquely intimate relationship. The two of us traveled together all over the globe, sleeping in the same hotel rooms, sharing transport and meals. I also worked as a manager for the band on major tours, and was the impetus behind some of Duke's historical collaborations. It is from that vantage point that I discuss Duke's career, with particular focus on his relationship with his band, his partnership with co-composer Billy Strayhorn, and his artistic vision and endeavors in his latter years. Based on my experience with my uncle, a portrait emerges of a bandleader who deftly managed the antics and unbridled egos of his musicians for the greater good of music; of a composer who eschewed conventions; and of a deep thinker who through his music tried to spread a message of unity and commonality to a world divided by politics, religion, and race.

Duke and his men

Given his synesthesia, it is not surprising that Duke referred to his band as his palette. He likened his stage performances to creating a new painting every night. He even conducted with a visually artistic flair, using his up-down, side-to-side strokes to trace the shape of a treble clef in the air. Duke viewed his band as his greatest instrument, but unlike a piano made of inanimate keys, strings, and pedals, each member of the band had a personality attached. And as is often the way with great artists, the personalities behind the Duke Ellington Orchestra were often difficult, headstrong, and temperamental. Part of Duke's genius was in how he managed the men in his band, creating beauty out of the chaos, and forming what is arguably the most brilliant ensemble in American musical history.

Duke had an exceptionally high tolerance for bad behavior, substance abuse and ill temper from his band. If he valued a player's talent, Duke – unlike Count Basie, an orderly disciplinarian who managed his musicians in an almost military fashion – would often overlook whatever personal foibles and flaws might come along with the man. Lateness, drunkenness, and personality conflicts were commonplace in the orchestra. Violence between the musicians was known to erupt. Duke worked around whatever problems came his way, especially with his longer-term players, and consistently managed to evoke masterful performances out of his musicians. Once Duke had cultivated a certain sound and sensibility in a player he was loathe to let him go. Additionally, Duke's complicated chromatic and contrapuntal harmonies often proved disconcerting to uninitiated or strictly traditional players, who would doubt what was written on the staves in front of them at first and second blush.

But that is not to say Duke turned a blind eye to the trouble his musicians stirred up. Newcomers who created issues could be summarily dismissed, as when a young Charles Mingus was fired in 1953. After less than a week with the band Mingus had an altercation with trombonist Juan Tizol. Tizol claimed Mingus tried to attack him with an iron curtain rod after Mingus disagreed with Tizol's musical instruction. Mingus counterclaimed that Tizol came after him with a knife. While Tizol habitually carried a blade on him, there was no evidence that he came at Mingus, beyond the bassist's claim. Tizol, an elder statesman of the Ellington orchestra, was deferred to in that episode and Mingus was fired by Duke on the spot. While Duke recognized Mingus as a great talent, and even worked with him a decade later on the album *Money Jungle*, he did not hesitate to axe the new bassist for the greater good of the band and the security and well-being of an established member, Tizol.

Duke was also known to pink-slip a musician if he didn't mesh with the rest of the band musically. In the 1960s, at my behest, Duke hired bebop drummer Elvin Jones. Elvin's reputation and résumé were stellar. A master of percussion, he had worked as a sideman for Mingus and Miles Davis, and was a member of John Coltrane's quartet. Elvin did not cause any ripples in the band personality-wise. But his playing was too avant-garde for the old guard. So despite Elvin's great talent and prestige, Duke very politely let him go.

In general, the band's antics and misbehaviors were dealt with without firings. A skillful reader of people and situations, Duke would let the band members stretch out and follow their impulses right up until the disorder spilled over into their performance. At that point, Duke would intervene. And when that time came, he did not lead through fear or intimidation. Mediation and psychological manipulation were his most commonly used tools for dealing with other human beings. Two to four times a year, the band would reach a point where their wanton ways translated into terrible performances. Duke would wait until a particularly shoddy performance, until the men had boarded the bus with all their instruments packed and stowed away. Then word would begin to spread that Duke wanted to speak with the band.

The idea of Duke setting foot on the bus was cause for alarm. Duke never rode on the band bus, preferring the quiet, calm presence of his driver, baritone saxophonist Harry Carney, to the raucous noise of the bus. So when word got out that Duke would be boarding the band bus, everyone knew it wasn't good. The band would fall into an uncharacteristic silence, as Duke climbed the steps of the bus. The stillness continued as Duke would begin pacing between the driver's seat and the back of the bus. Then Duke would speak to the band. Although he never lost control, his anger was evident and his voice was raised.

The speech he would give was always a variation on the theme of togetherness. Duke would tell the band he had worked hard to get himself in this position, and that the band had worked alongside him to put themselves where they were. Duke would tell the band they were not holding up their side of the deal by embarrassing themselves on stage, and if they wanted to remain in their position of prestige they needed to maintain a higher level of performance. Duke would also, in his way, subtly invoke race, reminding the band that they represented black American culture and had a duty to represent their people in a positive light. Then Duke would return to his chauffeured car, leaving the band to ruminate on his words in silence.

These speeches would typically have an instantaneous – though not permanent – effect on the band, causing them to improve upon their musicianship and performances for at least a couple of months. Then, inevitably, the backward slide would begin again, resulting in another subpar performance and another visit by Duke to the band bus. This cycle could not be ended. It was a dilemma inherent in Duke's formula of choosing the best talent and the best musicians for his artistic vision, despite the problems they might bring with them. The train would inevitably run off the tracks; Duke could only learn to cope and right the course.

Duke's most effective weapons in corralling his band were his words, which he used in wide range and with great fluidity. He could gently coax, intelligently argue, or slice to the heart of someone's weakness. The only commonality in his usage is that he was hardly ever direct, always preferring insinuation and suggestion. In the 1960s, the band was playing at jazz impresario George Wein's club Storyville in Cape Cod, Massachusetts. Backstage, trumpeter Willie Cook was waiting to go on, projecting his usual arrogant attitude and the cool aloofness of a hipster. Willie, a handsome, fine-featured man, was a heavy drug user and known to cause trouble. Not long before the Storyville gig, Willie had been among a group of band members arrested for narcotics while the orchestra was in Las Vegas. The arrest caused Duke professional embarrassment. As Duke rushed on to the stage at Storyville, he accidentally stepped on Willie's feet. Willie puffed up in anger and shouted at Duke: "Hey man, you stepped on my foot." Duke stopped and stared Willie directly in the eye. "You stepped on my life," Duke said abruptly, and without apology, before he turned on his heel and kept on going.

But Duke did not like to have bad words with people. He tended to mediate disputes, again using the idea of togetherness and a common goal to bring warring musicians around. Cat Anderson was one of the most volatile personalities, a prickly man who had to be handled with a delicate touch. Cat was known for playing extremely high notes on his trumpet that would shrill above the rest of the band. An orphan from South Carolina, he was mercurial and could shift from a back-slapping good mood one moment to extreme fits of rage the next. His temperament, combined with the trying schedule of the road, often resulted in fights. In the late fifties, during a concert at an outdoor amphitheater in Detroit, drummer Sam Woodyard hit his cymbal, which loosed and flew across the stage, hitting Cat in the back of the head. Cat, convinced this was a personal affront, launched into a screaming fit and stormed off stage. Duke kept on playing as if the entire scene had never occurred, finishing the number before smoothly calling for an unplanned intermission. Cat needed a great deal of handling and cajoling to be convinced to rejoin the band after the break. But somehow Duke assuaged Cat, who agreed to finish the show and to temper his accusation that Woodyard had tried to kill him.

More typically, conflicts within the band were of a more mundane nature. Musicians would come into Duke's dressing room with grievances about their pay, or the music, or another band member. Duke would usually be in his typical rest position, legs up on the wall, silk kerchief covering his eyes. Or he would be writing away, already rethinking the previous performance for the next day. Duke would calmly defuse the complainants' concerns, redirecting their thoughts with his verbal gymnastics, or coolly assuring them that they would be taken care of.

Most of the major eruptions and misadventures in the band were sparked by volatile personalities like Cat, or by the heavy drinkers and drug users, such as Paul Gonsalves, Ray Nance, Sam Woodyard, and Willie Cook. Johnny Hodges, the alto saxophonist whose signature smoothness of tone became synonymous with the Duke Ellington orchestra, was not of that ilk. Johnny was among the band members who seemed to be constantly perturbed about one thing or another. Senior in status and superior in talent, Johnny harbored a condescending attitude. He would come up to Duke, tap his arm repeatedly, and then launch into a lengthy speech about how Duke should be running the band. Johnny would also constantly threaten to leave the orchestra, although he actually ventured out only once to form his own group. Johnny was gone from 1951 to 1955, before returning to both Duke and his old petulant ways. Duke composed songs for Johnny, such as *Jeep's Blues*, to feature his unmistakably silky tones and the uncanny timing of his phrasing. Duke based the songs on riffs that Johnny had played for him. But Johnny felt entitled to royalties for the music he inspired, and would rub his thumb and forefinger together when these songs were played to display his dissatisfaction.

But in truth, while Duke might have based *Jeep's Blues* on a riff or some noodling, he was never one to deny an enterprising musician his due as a composer. Duke was sensitive to giving musicians credit for their work. Before he formed his own publishing company – Tempo Music – in 1941, publishers such as Irving Mills and Jack Robbins routinely attached their names to Duke's work. It wasn't until Duke formed Tempo that he had complete control over attributing credit where it was due. Duke encouraged his musicians to take advantage of the publishing opportunities that Tempo offered and gave broad play, both on stage and in the recording studio, to the songs of his musicians. Billy Strayhorn's *Take the "A" Train* is perhaps the most famous example of this, followed by Juan Tizol's *Caravan* and *Perdido*. But lesser-known pieces abound, such as Johnny Hodges' *Squatty Roo* and Cat Anderson's *Trombone Buster*, a piece written to feature Buster Cooper, whose trombone playing mirrored his speech pattern, which was marked by a series of sputtering stutters followed by energetic bursts of exclamatory phrases. And if Duke contributed to another band member's piece, he would regularly grant attribution to both parties, as in his collaborations on *Air Conditioned Jungle* with Jimmy Hamilton and *Rent Party Blues* with Johnny Hodges. For Duke, musical credit was not a zero-sum game. He was secure in his reputation and status, and felt there was enough credit, glory, and stage time to go around.

Duke did not have much patience for haggling over financial matters, nor did he have much respect for musicians who used offers from other bands to leverage a higher paycheck. When trumpeter Cootie Williams left the band for a better-paying position with Benny Goodman in 1941, Duke did not counteroffer or try to convince him to stay. This remained a lifelong offense to Cootie despite his deep admiration for Duke as a composer and musician. Duke wasn't pleased with the thought that his players were thinking of leaving him, and while he handled day-to-day gripes about money with aplomb, he found it particularly distasteful that someone would leave his orchestra for the sake of money.

Duke could be very personally generous with his musicians. Paul Gonsalves, the tenor saxophonist whose solo brought the 1956 Newport Jazz Festival to its feet, had the smooth sound of more traditional players, such as Coleman Hawkins and Ben Webster, with some of the bebop stylings of Charlie Parker. Paul was known for his great affability. He was equally known for his extreme drunkenness – a trait that Duke disliked, but tolerated. Duke called him "The Ambassador," a reference to his ability to charm and disarm everyone he met on the road regardless of their background. Duke would position Paul front and center during tours sponsored by the U.S. State Department, since Paul was sure to win over whatever dignitaries were in front of him. But Paul was also a constant source of trouble to Duke and the band due to his alcoholism. He once disappeared on the road in Japan after missing our stop on the bullet train. But in quintessential Paul Gonsalves fashion, he somehow commandeered a crew of rice paddy workers to drive him back to the city where the band was performing. Paul's long-term alcoholism and substance abuse eventually resulted in his suffering from seizures. On one occasion, Paul began seizing during a flight over Europe and we had to get special emergency clearance to land in Greece during a military *coup d'état*.

Late one night, after playing a gig in Las Vegas, Paul decided he would go into Duke's dressing room to complain about his pay. Paul had been fulminating for a couple of days after realizing that he was the only man in the band who did not own his own home or car. So Paul shored up his nerve, gathered his thoughts, and began ferociously banging on Duke's door, expecting an argumentative retort from Duke. "Door's open," Duke responded calmly, diffusing Paul before he even came in the room.

Paul entered to find Duke deep into a composition, pen and paper in hand. "Paul, it's good to see you, but I'm writing," Duke said. Paul persevered, saying he wanted more money so he could get a house and a car like the rest of the band, and that he wanted to talk about it right that minute. Paul's wife, Joanne, was living in Rhode Island and had grown tired of not seeing her husband, who was spending his time in New York and on the road. Upon hearing Paul's complaint, Duke wearily got up from his seat, put his arm around Paul, and launched into a speech, which began, "Paul, you and I are both artists, so I know you understand I need this time to get things done." Somehow, Paul soon found himself in the hallway, alone with no answers and not a cent more in his paycheck. In fact, Paul claimed that after Duke's brain twisting, he had forgotten why he even went to see Duke in the first place. Paul managed to pull himself together enough to broach the topic again the next day, and Duke told him that they would be back in New York in eight days and would deal with it then. Duke then conveyed the situation to my mother, Ruth Ellington, and his son, Mercer, back in New York. My mother and Mercer went about making arrangements for Paul and Joanne to purchase a house in Long Island. Two days after the band got back to New York, Duke had Paul picked up in a chauffeured Cadillac. The car took Paul to Long Island, right to the doorstep of his new home. This incident is very indicative of Duke's generosity as well as his indirect, often unexpected way of dealing with his men.

But Duke did not have such a warm relationship with everyone in his band. He was almost as notorious for his skills of seduction as he was for his music, but he rarely kept the same woman around for long. Such was the case with actress Fredi Washington, who had a short-lived affair with Duke. But while Duke lost interest in her, she always carried a torch for him, even after her marriage in 1933 to Lawrence Brown, a trombonist with the band. Lawrence was aware of his wife's unrequited yearning for Duke and harbored a quietly simmering animosity towards him. Lawrence stayed with the band, aside from venturing off with Johnny Hodges in the early 1950s, for the steady paycheck. While Duke was aware of Lawrence's negative attitude and grumblings, he was immune to their impact. Such personal pettiness barely pinged on his radar. He employed Lawrence for his ability as a player and his musical contribution to the band, despite his sourness.

Music was the metric by which Duke Ellington made his decisions – not ego, not personality, and not what was most easy or conventional. In Duke's world, the music always came first. This is how he led his life and his band, and how he managed to overcome an almost insurmountable degree of chaos and conflict to bring an assembly of the greatest players of his time together on a near-nightly basis.

Duke and Strays

Duke's relationship with my godfather, Billy Strayhorn, was one of the most pivotal and influential of his life, professionally and personally, musically and emotionally. Duke and Strayhorn first crossed paths in

Strayhorn's native Pittsburgh in 1938. Strayhorn had had a couple of months of classical training at the Pittsburgh Musical Institute and had been working at a drugstore as a soda jerk and delivery boy. After an Ellington concert, Duke heard Strayhorn perform a song that he had composed and set lyrics to, and immediately sensed a great talent and a sympathetic intellect. Duke was so impressed he hired the 23-year-old on the spot as a lyricist, and soon moved him in to live with his only child, Mercer Ellington, and my mother, his only sibling, Ruth Ellington.

Duke's initial impression of Strays proved prescient. Very early on, Duke began to cultivate Strayhorn's prodigious talent in both composing and arranging. Duke did not believe in coddling great talents, and his initial methods for training Strayhorn were very much "sink or swim." One of Strayhorn's first assignments with Duke was to arrange two pieces, "Like a Ship in the Night" and "Savoy Strut," for Johnny Hodges in a small-group session. In addition to similar trials by fire, Duke worked closely with Strays, teaching him the particulars of his inner world as a composer. In the early years of their collaboration, Duke spent a great deal of time teaching Strays the fundamentals of the harmonies that he was trying to achieve with the band, and how he wanted to layer the instruments within a composition. Strays readily absorbed Duke's ideas and eventually contributed his own artistic vision.

Strayhorn came into his own as a composer in part thanks to a radio industry boycott against the American Society of Composers, Authors and Publishers (ASCAP) in 1941. Duke was an ASCAP member, so his material was off-limits on the radio for the duration of the strike. Mercer and Strayhorn were not ASCAP members, so Duke commissioned them to compose a new band book. But Duke's compulsion to compose could not be quelled. On the sly, he had more than a little hand in Mercer's and Strayhorn's work during this period; for example, "Things Ain't What They Used to Be" is attributed to Mercer but came more from Duke's mind. But Strayhorn showed marked development during that period, composing *Passion Flower* and *Chelsea Bridge*.

Ever subdued and reserved, Strays hated the limelight, preferring the comfort of his home and the company of his friends to the rigors of the road. On the rare occasion that Strays would attend a performance, my uncle would unfailingly call him up to the stage to sit in and play something – often *Take the "A" Train*. Strays would trudge up to the stage with palpable reluctance. When Strayhorn was not around, Duke would make every effort to credit him as the composer of whatever Strayhorn material was performed.

While Strayhorn was an undeniable genius as a composer, he did not have the best temperament for tangling with the rough and difficult personalities of the band. He was gentle, intellectual, and soft-spoken, an anomaly in the hard-charging, often odious, sometimes violent world of jazz musicians. But that does not mean Strayhorn always remained in the background. In 1956, I witnessed Duke and the orchestra recording the Ellington songbook with Ella Fitzgerald. Duke and Strayhorn collaborated on the 16-minute, four-movement *Portrait of Ella Fitzgerald*, in which Duke and Strays took turns at the piano and in a semi-scripted verbal tribute to the great songstress. The recording is a prime example of Duke's willingness to share the stage with Strayhorn on major projects, and also highlights the marked difference between them as pianists – Duke playing with rawness and the sensibility of an arranger, and Strayhorn showing his classical, more restrained bent.

One consistent exception to Strayhorn's tendency to skirt the edge of the action was when his song "Lush Life" was performed. This melancholic song of lost love was extremely personal for Strayhorn, and he was very exacting and demanding about the way it was sung. He invariably became very emotional about the phrasing and emotional timbre of those who dared to sing it in his presence. In addition to being the song closest to his heart, "Lush Life" is the prototypical example of how Strayhorn's style differed from Ellington's. Strayhorn had an openness and emotional vulnerability that was all his own. The melancholia, earnestness and bittersweet longing of "Lush Life" is a contrast to Duke's raw sensuality and his tongue-in-cheek approach to both life and musical composition.

But at times, it was hard even for Duke and Strayhorn to know where one began and the other ended. Duke and Strays shared an uncanny closeness in terms of thought process. They would often collaborate on the phone due to Duke's demanding touring schedule. Duke would call Strays late at night after the day's gig was over, and their methods of communication knew no bounds. Sometimes one or both would be on the piano. Other times words were the medium. And still yet, one would hum, sing or otherwise vocalize a melody to the other. At times, it was as if mental telepathy was at play. In 1958 Duke and Strayhorn were communicating via telephone about a piece for the Great South Bay Jazz Festival on Long Island. Duke asked Strayhorn to compose a movement, which Duke received from Strays minutes before going on stage. Strayhorn himself said he was astounded to find that his piece had been a seamless development of what Duke had written, even though Strayhorn had not known what Duke had composed beyond their hurried telephone conversation. This phenomenon was not uncommon with the two men. On more than one occasion, Duke and Strays would come up with the same melodic line simultaneously without the other knowing it. This is perhaps not surprising, since Duke was highly instrumental during Strayhorn's formative period as a composer.

Had Duke Ellington not spotted and cultivated his talent early on, Strays very well could have languished, struggling for recognition in a world where – as a black, gay man – he was a double minority. By taking Strays into his life and his family, Duke provided him with the space to be himself artistically as well as a place where he could truly be himself as a person, finding love and acceptance with no prejudice against his sexual orientation. As time went by, Strays and Duke became more in synch with each other. Duke would sketch out a basic melody and Strays would take it and fill in the right harmonies. But Duke's style never drowned out Strayhorn's musical voice. The haunting melancholy of *Lush Life*, *Lotus Blossom*, and *Passion Flower* is as unmistakably Strayhorn's as his own fingerprint.

Strayhorn and Duke also shared an emotional closeness. After Duke separated from his first and only wife, Edna Ellington, he became guarded, especially with women. His relationship with his only son, Mercer, was not very warm, and often strained. He was very close to my mother, and his best friend Bob Udkoff was also a confidant. But Billy Strayhorn filled an emotional void in Duke, with a kind of love that was undefinable, beyond category, as Duke would say.

Duke took it hard when Strayhorn passed away after battling cancer. It was almost as if the intrinsic sadness of Strayhorn's music was a sort of omen, as if something in his psyche foretold his own tragedy. The beginning of the end came in April, 1964. Strays and I decided to surprise Duke on his birthday with a custom-made white vicuña coat that we had special-ordered from Duke's tailor in Chicago. We traveled to Montreal where the band was performing, checked into our hotel, and ordered room service. Strays ordered a Heineken, and when he took his first swig he complained of difficulty swallowing. I urged him to have it checked out, which he did upon our return to New York. The doctors discovered the esophageal cancer that would eventually claim his life.

Strays died in late May, 1967. I was with Duke and the band in Reno for a gig at Harrah's Casino. We held an impromptu memorial there, and interrupted the casino gig to go back to New York for the funeral. I saw Billy cremated, flames licking the outside of his coffin as he disappeared in darkness. After his funeral, as he had requested, a small group of his closest friends – including my uncle, myself, and my mother – gathered at the 79th Street Boat Basin in Manhattan where we scattered his ashes along with handfuls of rose petals into the Hudson River. We continued to gather there on the anniversary of his death for many years to come, scattering roses into the waters and watching the currents take them away from us, out to sea.

Church and State

As bebop reshaped the jazz world in the 1950s, the big band sound began to be something of an anachronism. My uncle, however, always found a way to ride out the changes of time. He kept his band working at a breakneck pace, traveling around the world to expose other cultures to American jazz. Later in his career he also began a new focus on religious music, an undertaking that he said was the most important of his life.

No matter his age or popularity, Duke never stopped touring. A favorite saying of his was: "Name the town, and I'll get you the morning paper." He liked to stay on the move for a number of reasons. He claimed that sitting still would stagnate his creativity. And creativity was nearly impossible if Duke was in the same place for too long, since word of his whereabouts would leak, followed by an inevitable scrum of admirers, spurned lovers, sycophants, and mooches. Duke also felt the band would get lazy and stale with too long of a hiatus. But perhaps the most important reason for the perpetual motion of Duke and his band was that he liked to play for the people. The band was his palette, the music was his canvas, and he wanted to paint a new portrait for a new audience every night. Playing live gave Duke instantaneous feedback on his new pieces in a way that composing on paper or recording in a studio could never replicate.

The State Department tours provided a breadth of travel opportunities for Duke and band. It was like being in a time capsule, arriving in a new country every day with 23 band members and 64 pieces of luggage. Duke had a vivid interest in other cultures – evidenced musically by such works as *The Afro-Eurasian Eclipse* (1971) and *Latin American Suite* (1968). He was also a keen observer of the world. Although he never went to China, the main thing he tried to impart to me from his travels was that he felt the Chinese would one day rule the world. He would often prod me to learn Mandarin, in a half-joking way that usually indicated there was serious-ness behind his words.

The State Department tours also gave Duke the opportunity to perform his *Sacred Concert*s to an international audience. After the premiere of *A Concert of Sacred Music* in 1965 at Grace Cathedral in San Francisco, Duke's main goal was to play his sacred music to as many people in as many places as possible. Wherever we went, domestically or abroad, Duke made an effort to book a venue for a *Sacred Concert* performance. He considered his religious works to be his magnum opus. Duke was not stridently religious or evangelical, although my mother and my maternal grandmother were more of that vein. He didn't regularly attend church. He didn't speak much about God. But he considered himself a Christian and believed in a Supreme Being. Through his *Sacred Concerts*, Duke was trying to impress the idea of unity and oneness upon the various religious, political, and ethnic groups of the world, much like he used the idea of commonality and shared goals to motivate his band.

The timing of Duke's religious turn in his twilight years resulted in speculation that fears about mortality prompted him to look heavenward. Duke never spoke much about death. In fact, our entire family avoided issues of death to the point that no one – Duke, my mother, and my brother included – ever made out a will. The belief was that talking about death or acknowledging it in any way was a jinx. My uncle was oddly superstitious. He refused to launch lawsuits, even when they were clearly merited, saying it was bad karma. After he received news of his mother dying while he was wearing a brown suit, he banished the color brown from his wardrobe. Whenever one of Duke's superstitions came into play, he would acknowledge it in his own inimitable way, by leaning over and saying: "You know we're not superstitious, but why tempt fate?"

Duke and bebop

Duke wasn't an artist who dealt in time and trends. He artistically dwelt almost entirely in his own head. While he might look to the world around him for inspiration, he never looked to other musicians, believing a sort of artistic isolation would evoke greater creativity. So not surprisingly, he had rebuffed my efforts to play John Coltrane for him. But thanks to a pneumonia scare, Duke was confined to a hospital bed and at my mercy. I lugged a record player into the hospital room, and began playing Coltrane for Duke. He looked askance at me, but readily recognized the genius and great skill of Coltrane. Later, in 1962, I approached producer Bob Thiele of Impulse! Records about the possibility of a Duke–Coltrane collaboration. It took a lot of engineering, but my uncle finally agreed to the project, resulting in the 1962 album *Duke Ellington & John Coltrane*.

Most of the pre-session planning was simply getting both Duke and Coltrane at the same place at the same time. Duke waited until he spoke with Coltrane in person to decide what would go on the album. Such spontaneity was typical of Duke, who had reams of music jotted down on paper and even more stored in his head. He would merge and mesh his unused material with previous compositions, flavoring the result with whatever occurred to him musically in the moment. The result was a mix of old Ellington standards revamped for Coltrane's style, along with the Coltrane song "Big Nick" and two new Ellington compositions: "Take the Coltrane" and "Stevie," a song composed during the recording session as a nod to my role in the album.

Duke's bebop stint didn't end with Coltrane. Also in 1962, he recorded *Money Jungle* on the United Artists label, with Max Roach on drums and Charles Mingus on bass. *Money Jungle* includes two Ellington classics ("Warm Valley" and "Solitude") and – as a tribute to Mingus's forgiven but not forgotten bout with Juan Tizol – the most warlike rendition of Tizol's "Caravan" ever recorded. The remainder of the material was written specifically for the album, most of it composed in the studio session. With more than a hint of mirth, Duke again referenced the Mingus–Tizol showdown in an original composition entitled "Switch Blade." Duke also featured Mingus's unique manner of fluttering notes on his bass to beautiful effect in the haunting piece "Fleurette Africaine."

However, the dulcet tones of music were not the only sounds emanating from the *Money Jungle* recording session. Mingus and Roach loved each other but had an ongoing friction that frequently spilled over into their professional collaborations. During the session, the two began to argue over a musical point, and the heated discussion soon grew personal. Soon, Mingus and Roach were up from their seats, face to face in aggressive stances toward one another. Once again, Duke had to intervene, once again invoking his message to put petty differences aside for the sake of the greater good, or what to Duke's mind was the greatest good of all: Music.

4 Ellington abroad

BRIAN PRIESTLEY

The musical value of Ellington's work, as opposed to its entertainment value, was recognized by a minority of observers quite early in his career. In the second half of the 1920s and the early 1930s, when his activities were focused mainly on New York, he was generally discussed in the context of his nightclub and theater associations. But those who responded to his radio broadcasts, heard widely across the United States, and his records, many of them released internationally, soon began modifying the reception of his music. It thus fell to relative outsiders to focus on the uniqueness of the actual sound produced by the Ellington band.

Significant contributors to this process were the Boston-based "classical music" reviewer Robert Donaldson (R. D.) Darrell, from as early as 1927, and Anglo-Irish bassist-arranger-composer-critic Spike Hughes, writing from 1931 onwards under the pseudonym "Mike."[1] In 1932 the Australian Percy Grainger, as Dean of Music at New York University, became the first composer of what was called "serious" music to introduce his students to the Ellington band in person, and to the idea that its music was also worth considering seriously.[2]

However, researcher Bertil Lyttkens has noted that Ellington's music arrived in Europe in 1925, long before any recordings of his band.[3] At least five songs by Ellington and lyricist Jo Trent – four of them specially created for the all-black revue *Chocolate Kiddies* – were heard in several European cities such as Berlin and Moscow, performed by the Sam Wooding band and the show's singers, including Adelaide Hall.[4] Despite a confident press prediction of recordings by the cast members, it's unlikely that any such recordings were made, let alone released.[5] Yet during the 1920s, cover versions made in Europe of these Ellington songs actually outnumbered those made in America.[6]

Not until Duke's first major tour in 1931 did he step out beyond the USA, with his first one-week appearance at Toronto's Imperial Theatre. In some ways Canada was not so different from the States, and Ellington played opposite a movie that, despite an unenthusiastic review in the *Toronto Telegram*, got six times as much column space as the band. But the journalist

Thanks for their invaluable assistance to Bjarne Busk, Bill Egan, Bertil Lyttkens, Arne Neegaard, Ken Steiner, Alain Tercinet, and also to Andrew Homzy – B.P.

did make an artistic point: "When they play *Liza* in one dance number accompaniment they demonstrate that they can serve up sweet music of a high order, but they waste too much of the rest of their time trying to get hot on the high notes. We would rather hear some music."[7] Already, his manager Irving Mills was ensuring that Ellington was widely interviewed on this tour, and the first article under Duke's byline appeared the same year in another English-speaking country, namely England.[8]

The major change in the evaluation of Ellington's music came about when his band first went to Europe in 1933. Otto Hardwick, a saxophonist and clarinetist who left Ellington's band in 1928 to spend a year in Europe, took retrospective credit for this development: "In 1929 you couldn't get him to cross the Hudson river! ... I told Duke when I got back [from Europe], it was a terrific field for him. It took a couple of years to soak in, but it did eventually, once Mills got wind of it."[9] Thanks to Mills and U.K. bandleader-impresario Jack Hylton, Duke was booked for an eight-week tour of Europe. Also thanks to Mills, no doubt, the tour was noted in a *Time* magazine article of more than 700 words:

> Europe in the past few summers has heard smooth, suave jazz played by Paul Whiteman, Rudy Vallee, Guy Lombardo. It has also heard Negro syncopators who scorn sweet stereotype melodies and easy orthodox rhythms. But this summer Europeans will have a chance to hear hot, pulsing jazz played as they never have heard it before. Last week on the S. S. *Olympic* Negro Edward Kennedy ("Duke") Ellington sailed with his 14-piece all-Negro band to play in London, Liverpool, Glasgow, later on the Continent ... Ellington's arrangements, apparently tossed off in the approved hot, spontaneous manner, have been carefully worked out at rehearsals beginning often at 3 a.m. after his theatre and night-club engagements, which gross as much as $250,000 a year.[10]

The piece is mostly accurate and highly enthusiastic, but tame compared to the fever that gripped local writers and audiences in the run-up to this historic visit. Articles in both the specialist and general press culminated with the weekly *Melody Maker* (mainly aimed at British musicians) beginning its front-page coverage with: "Well! He's here! We have been reading about the Duke this last four or five years; he has become an almost legendary figure; it seemed impossible that we should ever see him in the flesh, or hear those amazing sounds other than via a gramophone. Yet, unbelievably, he is here."[11]

That gives a flavor of the anticipation that fueled audience reaction on the opening night of the band's two-week vaudeville booking at the London Palladium. In 1955 a newspaper gave Ellington's elaborated account:

"Terrifying experience. That audience kept a steady applause for 10 minutes.
Did you ever stand on a stage with nothing to do but this" – here he bowed and
smiled and bowed and smiled – "for 10 minutes. Terrible. Especially the way the
British do things. First they clap. Then they go 'Wooooooo!' Finally they stamp
their feet. You don't know whether they like you or are trying to run you off the
stage. Ruined the whole show. We all were shaking like a leaf."[12]

Duke was impressed too by a reception at Jack Hylton's Mayfair home
and, at a subsequent private party, by the presence and active interest of
members of Britain's royal family. On another occasion he was welcomed
by classical composer Constant Lambert. Ellington also socialized with
less renowned musicians, such as the BBC Symphony's harpist Sidonie
Goossens and her husband, composer-conductor Hyam Greenbaum, who
was part of Spike Hughes's circle.[13] Band members also encountered the
British version of racism, with difficulties over hotel bookings, while
Ellington himself stayed at the prestigious Dorchester Hotel, which had
previously hosted Paul Robeson.[14]

Some fans and journalists harbored doubts as to whether Duke's
Palladium slot was tainted by his instincts as an entertainer, which were
underlined by the presence of vocalist Ivie Anderson, the tap-dance duo
Bailey and Derby, and "snake-hips" specialist Bessie Dudley, who danced to
Rockin' in Rhythm. Spike Hughes arranged for *Melody Maker* to promote
Sunday performances, first at the Palladium and then at the Trocadero
cinema, billed as "musicians' concerts" and intended to feature Ellington's
"pure" jazz repertoire.[15] Hughes's program notes even instructed the audience not to applaud individual solos, but when Duke noticed audience
laughter at the wah-wah style of the brass, he inserted some of his popular
repertoire after all. Most interestingly, in a recorded interview with Percy
Mathieson Brooks, editor of *Melody Maker*, Ellington was asked whether
"rhythmic music" would ever migrate from the ballroom to the concert hall.
His answer may have been pre-scripted in a style uncharacteristic of his
speech patterns, but he said: "Yes, inevitably, perhaps not in this generation;
it is the youngsters of these days who will make the audiences of tomorrow,
and they have no prejudices of which they must rid themselves."[16]

The enthusiastic response of local players immediately increased the
number of cover versions, most remarkably seven tracks by Madame
Tussaud's Dance Orchestra; despite being the in-house band of a wax
museum, it achieved some very lifelike impressions. European fans too
gained a huge boost from this Ellington visit. As for Ellington himself, he
did not expect such wild acclaim, or to find so much knowledge of his
work displayed by the more aware listeners and commentators. As he
wrote in 1940, "The main thing I got in Europe was *spirit*, it lifted me out

of the groove. That kind of thing gives you courage to go on with a lot of things you want to do yourself."[17]

The careful choice of words seems in retrospect designed to counter accusations, which began flying in 1934 and 1935, that Ellington's head was fatally turned by comparisons made in Europe between his work and that of Ravel, Stravinsky, Delius, and even Bach. The first three were named no doubt because of Duke's developing harmonic language, although when the name of Delius was first mentioned to him (in fact, by Percy Grainger) Ellington had never heard of this rather unique Anglo-German composer. More meaningful, and more fraught, was the comparison between Ellington and George Gershwin, which has since been made more explicitly by several writers.

A recent writer summarizes the possible influence on Duke of the Gershwin comparison: "Evidently this figuring of Ellington as a more righteous and authentic Gershwin had an effect on Ellington, who in 1935 controversially attacked *Porgy and Bess* for its inauthenticity, and produced a string of his own serious, extended compositions such as *Reminiscing in Tempo* (1935), *Symphony in Black* (1935), and *Diminuendo and Crescendo in Blue* (1937), whose titles deliberately glossed that of *Rhapsody in Blue*."[18]

The content of these Ellington compositions is discussed elsewhere in this volume, but the increase in ambition, compared to the 1931 *Creole Rhapsody* (another pseudo-Gershwin title), suggests the "things you want to do yourself." *Reminiscing in Tempo* aroused particular hostility from Spike Hughes, despite his earlier comment that *Creole Rhapsody* was "the first classic of modern dance music,"[19] and from the producer and critic John Hammond, who in 1933 had talked of funding an Ellington musical show. Hammond and Hughes were both advocates of jazz drawing strength from its African-American roots, as opposed to writers who saw jazz as raw material for Europeanized composition. The latter group included some of Ellington's African-American contemporaries, such as the writer-educator Alain Locke and composer-arranger William Grant Still.

The band's tremendous reception in Europe, then, should be understood as providing vindication of Ellington's direction, and of his compositional leanings, rather than any specific musical inspiration. The song *Best Wishes*, which he claimed to have written "since I have been in England," was recorded a year earlier in New York.[20] Similarly, a piece with the Swedish title *Smorgasbord and Schnapps*, co-credited to Duke, Rex Stewart, and Stewart's friend, arranger-guitarist Brick Fleagle, was recorded shortly before the band's 1939 visit there. A seemingly more plausible dedication, *Serenade to Sweden*, was premiered during this visit, but nevertheless had its genesis in the 1934 Ellington recording of *Moonglow*.[21]

This second trip to Europe in 1939 again made a huge impression on audiences. Stewart, one of the few additions to Ellington's notably stable personnel since the 1933 tour, gave a graphic description of what European appreciation meant to the visitors, despite the occasional racial stereotyping in some of the newspaper coverage: "You have to be a Negro to understand. Europe is a different world. You can go anywhere, do anything, talk to anybody ... You are like a guy who has eaten hot dogs all your life and is suddenly offered caviar. You can't believe it."[22]

Unlike the 1933 tour, in which most appearances were on vaudeville bills, the majority of the 1939 dates were concerts, with the band as the sole attraction. This applied not only to engagements in Paris, Belgium, Holland, Denmark, and Norway, but also to two weeks in Sweden, where the band played small towns such as Huskvarna as well as three dates in Stockholm. The third date coincided with Ellington's fortieth birthday, which found him woken in his hotel room by the Swedish Radio band, and later serenaded on stage by ten young girls singing "Happy Birthday" in English, with the impromptu addition of teenage singing star Alice Babs, who happened to be in the audience.

As when Duke was interviewed live on the BBC evening newscast in 1933, this birthday concert was broadcast live – both unheard-of departures for European national radio networks at the time. He also spoke at length to a Swedish interviewer, incidentally making a diplomatic endorsement of local polka and schottische music. ("Well, it is different from our swing, of course, but it's very beautiful and very graceful.") Not too much should be read into his inclusion at several concerts of a contemporary Swedish pop song, *En Rød Liten Stuga*. As Rolf Dahlgren pointed out in 1994, "The company that handled the concerts was mostly a music publisher [Reuter & Reuter], so they wanted him to play one of their tunes ... Duke wrote [arranged] it in a few minutes and his manager, Irving Mills, wrote the English lyrics."[23]

The 1939 tour included no appearances in England, because of conflict between the U.S. and U.K. musicians' unions. This was brewing as far back as 1933, when Jack Hylton was not allowed to play in the States, and then English bandleader Ray Noble had to form a U.S. band with only two sidemen from his English outfit, to which the British union replied with a total ban on visiting instrumentalists. Unlike in other European countries, this impasse continued in Britain until the mid-1950s, with the exception of players perceived as vaudeville performers, such as Fats Waller and Art Tatum (both in 1938) and pianist-singer Hoagy Carmichael in 1948.

Thus it was that, also in 1948, Ellington's first postwar trip abroad involved putting the whole band on notice, apart from vocalist Kay Davis and vocalist-violinist-trumpeter Ray Nance, who could boost Duke's credentials as a vaudeville attraction. A return visit to the London Palladium was followed by a tour of theaters in the U.K. and a brief trip to the Continent, all accompanied by a British trio. But the only audio documentation of this venture was a London recording of Nance backed by the quartet of British-Caribbean musicians led by drummer Ray Ellington; naturally, the records were billed as "Ray Nance and the Ellingtonians."[24]

By contrast, Ellington's three-month-long 1950 tour of the Continent was with the full band, augmented by saxophonist Don Byas (who was already resident in Europe) and second drummer Butch Ballard, hired to cover for an increasingly unreliable Sonny Greer. Interestingly, critical reaction to the opening Paris concerts was so divided – between those who thought Ellington should provide all new material and those who craved the earlier classics, with added dissension between devotees of the 1927 repertoire and the 1940 repertoire – that he asked *Jazz Hot* magazine to print the following statement:

> If I go to a French restaurant . . . I expect to read a menu written in French. If I can't understand everything, I ask for a translation. By analogy, there's a lot of things you can't express about jazz except with "jive language" [in English in the French original], and that's why I asked a friend to translate this: "Jazz can't be limited by definitions and rules, jazz above all is total liberty of expression. If a single definition of this music is possible, that indeed is it."[25]

Ellington's 1950 European concert program included a recent extended work, the excellent *The Tattooed Bride*, which, incidentally, a contemporary commentator claimed was written or at least begun in Paris in 1948.[26] The 1950 tour also produced a number of small-group recordings led by Ellington's alto saxophonist Johnny Hodges and others but without any participation by Duke, doubtless precluded by his Columbia recording contract. But apart from the expected adulation, little specific inspiration came from the trip, and it was an already existing commission from the NBC Symphony that enabled Duke to work on the extended composition *Harlem* during his return passage to New York.

In the postwar period, however, the inspirations and commissions started to come from further afield. A keen student of black history, Duke was honored by a request in 1947 from the Liberian government for a piece commemorating the establishment of the republic one hundred years earlier; the half-hour *Liberian Suite* was first performed at Ellington's Carnegie Hall concert that year. In the summer of 1956, shortly after his popular triumph at the Newport Jazz Festival, he appeared at the annual Shakespeare Festival in Stratford, Ontario, which led to the commission for *Such Sweet Thunder*, an album-length suite on Shakespearean characters and themes. Although this premiered in New York the following May, he duly played it at the 1957 Shakespeare Festival, which led to another return engagement in July 1958 before Britain's Princess Margaret, for whom Ellington had composed the ten-minute *Princess Blue*.

In October 1958, the Leeds (England) Music Festival invited Ellington to contribute to its first-ever jazz concerts. (The organizers of the festival, one of whom was related to the royal family, were probably unaware of the existence of *Princess Blue*.) This provided the excuse for a full English and European tour, and afforded me among many others a first opportunity to see Duke in action. Too inexperienced to appreciate the finer points, I have an abiding memory of Hodges being featured on "Half the Fun" (from *Such Sweet Thunder*), and its closing rhythm-section vamp coinciding with the stage-lights fading to black as a spotlight picked out Strayhorn, who came on stage just to play a single low piano note.

What Ellington specifically recalled was his official presentation to Queen Elizabeth II, along with her husband and her sister Princess Margaret. The result was his creation of *The Queen's Suite*, recorded in spring 1959 as a gift to Her Majesty and never released or even performed publicly until 1976, except for Duke's piano solo "The Single Petal of a Rose." Although an autumn 1959 European tour excluding the U.K. provided no such direct inspiration, the winter of 1960–1961 did find Ellington and Strayhorn spending several weeks in Paris working on the film *Paris Blues*. During this stay Duke was also commissioned to record incidental music for the revival of a 250-year-old comedy by Alain-René LeSage, *Turcaret*.

With the new decade Ellington abandoned his beloved transatlantic liners for the inevitability of air travel, and from 1963 to 1973 undertook concert tours of Europe every year but two, despite the increasingly changed tastes in the music business. Other aspects of the European experience were less quick to change, as witnessed by journalist Steve Voce at a 1963 Liverpool concert. Before going on stage, Ellington switched on a dressing-room TV set, to be confronted by the hugely popular *Black and White Minstrel Show*. While Voce squirmed with embarrassment, "Suddenly the Minstrels went into *Caravan*, and [trombonist] George Chisholm came on. 'Well produced show,' said Duke."[27] On the plus side, the amount of coverage in both the general and specialist press was considerable, despite Liverpool's Beatles beginning their bid for world domination.

From now on, Europe became just part of the band's itinerary. In the autumn of 1963, seven years after first using jazz musicians for cultural missions, the U.S. State Department finally called on Ellington. The tour, intended to last several months, included the Indian subcontinent and various Middle Eastern countries before being terminated in the wake of President Kennedy's assassination. (Ellington biographer John Edward Hasse notes that other ongoing State Department tours were not cancelled.[28]) The important point is that this trip had an artistic outcome, as Ellington knew it would. "From my perspective, I think I have to be careful not to be influenced too strongly by the music we heard . . . I don't think that is the smart thing to do. I would rather give a reflection of the adventure itself," he told Stanley Dance. "Later on, something musical will come out of it, in its own form."[29]

Europe, of course, still provided an audience of knowledgeable and appreciative listeners, for whom *Harlem* was revived on the 1963 tour. The four initial movements of *Impressions of the Far East*, inspired by the State Department tour, received probably their first public performance at London's Royal Festival Hall in February 1964, along with a preexisting Strayhorn composition renamed "Isfahan." These compositions were played nightly throughout Europe before their U.S.A. unveiling two months later. This was soon followed by the band's first tour of Japan and the Far East proper, which inspired *Ad Lib on Nippon*, another composition debuted in Europe, during the 1965 trip. Noting that "the choice of material for this year's tour was even better than last year," my concert review devoted 400 of nearly 1200 words to the 20-minute version of *Black, Brown and Beige*, which Ellington would record for his personal "stockpile" on his return to the U.S.[30]

From 1958 onwards, Europe's national television stations began taping concerts and documentaries of Ellington's music. After Duke introduced his first *Concert of Sacred Music* in San Francisco in 1965 and repeated it in various locations including Coventry Cathedral early the following year, the Coventry performance was broadcast on TV throughout the U.K. at Easter 1966, 15 months before the San Francisco version was aired on U.S. public television. Even the genesis of Ellington's Sacred Concerts may have a European connection, as biographer Derek Jewell reports Ellington's debut appearance in church taking place in Paris on Christmas Eve, 1960, before an estimated 100,000 listeners, with his solo piano rendition of *Come Sunday*.[31]

The January–February 1966 European tour was also significant for introducing a new composition called *La Plus Belle Africaine*, prepared in advance of the band's April trip to the first World Festival of Negro Arts in Dakar, Senegal. Among other American participants was pianist-composer Randy Weston, not only a musical descendant of Duke but for a while published by Tempo Music, the Ellington family imprint. (It was in Switzerland, though, that Duke first met, and produced a recording by,

South African pianist Abdullah Ibrahim, another Ellington disciple.) As well as endorsing his position as a symbolic leader of the African diaspora, this festival had symbolic meaning for Duke himself; his stage announcements refer to this first performance on African soil coming "after writing African music for 35 years."[32] While there, he also insisted on playing for America's ambassador to Senegal, Mercer Cook, son of bandleader-songwriter Will Marion Cook, who mentored Duke back in 1920s New York.

In 1967 Europe saw the band again, but with fewer noteworthy new compositions apart from *The Shepherd*, which was later incorporated in the *Second Sacred Concert* of 1968. Another revival of an extended work (say, *Reminiscing in Tempo*) might have compensated for this lack of new material, although the previously revived *Harlem* did appear at some 1967 concerts. But one notable aspect of the *Second Sacred Concert* was the use of Swedish singer Alice Babs, whom Ellington had officially met (apart from her presence at his fortieth birthday concert in 1939) on his 1963 tour. He not only recorded an album with her then, but resolved to employ her special talent again, making her the only European musician featured with the band (apart from last-minute stand-ins such as saxist Tubby Hayes and occasional guests such as pianist Raymond Fol).

In lieu of any European visit in 1968, Ellington undertook his debut tour of Mexico and South America, his first experience of the southern hemisphere. South America was such virgin territory that the Buenos Aires audience reception was comparable to that in London 35 years earlier, according to Stanley Dance and Harry Carney, who were each present on both occasions.[33] A pre-tour piece captured on film and disc as *Mexicanticipation* led to the post-tour studio recording of a *Latin American Suite* that developed the same material, plus further movements. Its content parallels Ellington's *Far East Suite*, the 1966 recording that developed from *Impressions of the Far East*, in reflecting the increased tendency of recent jazz toward a less harmonically oriented, more "modal" approach. The *Latin American Suite* complements that by picking up the 1960s interest in fusing jazz improvisation with Latin rhythms, a development foreshadowed by Ellington and Juan Tizol's *Caravan* as far back as 1936.

By autumn 1969, after a gap of two-and-a-half years, European demand was still high and in many cities the band performed two long concerts in a single evening. Thus a fan could observe deities like Lawrence Brown and Cootie Williams not only walking the earth, but also grabbing a snack between shows at the funky diner across the road from London's Hammersmith Odeon. For this writer, this image is irresistibly brought to mind by the so-called *70th Birthday Concert* album, which, compiled from two British appearances, is short on major works but has the last authorized live recordings of Johnny Hodges.

Within a matter of months, Hodges was dead and Brown retired from music. As the pace of international touring increased, the remaining seniors in the band and even younger members must have experienced it all as a blur. Europe in the summer of 1970 was preceded by a visit to the Far East and Australasia, where at one of his endless press calls Ellington declared, "This is the life for me. I'm a wandering minstrel. I go around the world making noises and listening to noises."[34] The suite that emerged from this last experience, *The Afro-Eurasian Eclipse*, may be compared to *The Far East Suite* for its conversion of exotic experiences into Ellington noises, just as the 1971 *Togo Brava Suite* (dedicated to Togo, the African state that first put his image on a postage stamp) bears an ideological similarity to *La Plus Belle Africaine*.

The peak of the overseas touring schedule was achieved in 1971, with five weeks in the U.S.S.R., followed by five weeks in Europe, followed by three weeks in Latin America. The Russian venture, organized by promoter George Wein rather than the State Department, was successful as propaganda as well as on musical grounds. Given the strings of one-nighters elsewhere Duke was almost surprised at the gaps between performances. He said when interviewed in London, "Do you know I only had to do two concerts a week there? Man, that was *easy*. So easy, I had to find something for the band to do. So I called rehearsals!"[35]

The next year saw the longest tour yet of the Far East, while in 1973 the only international trip – and Ellington's final overseas tour – was a mere six weeks concentrated on Europe with a brief side trip to Ethiopia and Zambia. Opening and closing in London, the tour included Ellington's *Third Sacred Concert* in Westminster Abbey and participation in the Royal Command Performance at the London Palladium.[36] Although some rehearsals of the sacred music took place before leaving for England, the band's only tryout with Alice Babs, who once again took a leading role, was on the day of the concert itself.

The band was now without Cootie Williams too and, sadly, Paul Gonsalves was hospitalized shortly after arriving in London. As one of the half-dozen outsiders who sneaked into the Abbey for the rehearsal, I was able to witness Babs and Carney running through the bewitching *My Love*, while Ellington himself looked almost as ill as he must have been, seven months to the day before his death. It cannot have helped his equanimity that, nine days later at the high-minded Berlin Jazz Festival, vocalist Tony Watkins was greeted with such booing that Duke terminated the concert, allegedly suffering a minor heart attack. Once again, a spotlight was thrown on the relative proportions of creativity and entertainment Ellington deployed in order to please all the sections of his audience.

Perhaps I may be allowed to draw attention to one new development during the last years of Ellington's life. The repertory movement devoted to recreating his classic works was already under way, given a boost by London's Alan Cohen band (of which I was a member) performing and recording in 1972 a complete version of *Black, Brown and Beige*. This preceded the live album of the New England Conservatory Repertory Ensemble under Gunther Schuller, including *Reminiscing in Tempo*, and the George Wein-sponsored New York Jazz Repertory Orchestra, which performed the works of Duke and others at the Newport Jazz Festival–New York from 1974 to 1976.

Clearly such activity, which continues to the present day, is somewhat secondary to the huge achievement of Ellington and his sidemen in creating the music in the first place. But the reception which that repertory music received in Europe, and eventually the world, was far from insignificant in inspiring musical developments and in underlining the respect with which the original music deserves to be treated.

Notes

1 Examples of Darrell's writings on Ellington between 1927 and 1932 and a Hughes article from 1933 are included in *The Duke Ellington Reader*, ed. Mark Tucker (New York: Oxford University Press, 1993), 33–40, 57–65, 69–78.
2 In an uncharacteristic slip of the pen, Stanley Dance names the organizer of the New York University concert as Porter Grainger, who was the pianist and writer of "Tain't Nobody's Business If I Do." Dance, *The World of Duke Ellington* (New York: Da Capo Press, 1981), 295.
3 Bertil Lyttkens, panel discussion "Duke Ellington in Sweden 1939," *Ellington '94* conference, Stockholm, May 19–22, 1994.
4 Mark Tucker, in *Ellington: The Early Years* (Urbana: University of Illinois Press, 1991), 120–21, mentions five Ellington-Trent songs in *Chocolate Kiddies*; John Franceschina, in *Duke Ellington's Music for the Theatre* (Jefferson, NC: McFarland, 2001), 14, writes that another Ellington-Trent tune, "Skeedely-Um-Bum," was included in some productions of the revue.
5 Tucker, *Early Years*, 134.
6 Bjarne Busk, "Duke Ellington Material Recorded by Other Artists in the 1920s and 1930s," *DEMS Bulletin* 5/3 (December 2005–March 2006).
7 Ted Reeve, "First Nights at The Theatres," *Toronto Telegram*, June 2, 1931.
8 Reprinted in *Ellington Reader*, ed. Tucker, 46–50.
9 Interview by Helen Oakley Dance in Dance, *World of Duke Ellington*, 59.
10 "Hot Ambassador," *Time*, June 12, 1933; much of this text was reproduced, with its opening 200-plus words replaced by a new introductory paragraph, in a piece datelined "London, England, June 23, 1933" for the *Chicago Defender* (city edition), June 24, 1933, page 8, as partially shown in Ken Vail, *Duke's Diary, Part One: The Life of Duke Ellington 1927–1950* (Lanham, MD: Scarecrow Press, 2002), 82. It seems likely that both journals were adapting copy supplied directly by the Mills office.
11 "The Duke at the Palladium: Long Awaited Debut to Packed Houses," *Melody Maker*, June 17, 1933.
12 *Kingsport News*, Kingsport, Tennessee, September 23, 1955.
13 Author's conversation with Sidonie Goossens, *c*.1999.
14 Largely omitted from most accounts, such incidents are alluded to by biographers Barry Ulanov, Don George, and John Edward Hasse.
15 Duke agreed to include one of Hughes's own Ellington-tinged compositions, *Sirocco*.
16 This interview was produced on a 78 rpm record, presented to retail customers who purchased a sufficient number of Ellington discs during his visit.
17 *Swing*, September 1940, 24.
18 George Burrows, "*Black, Brown and Beige* and the politics of Signifyin(g)," *Jazz Research Journal* 1/1 (2007): 52.
19 Quoted in Derek Jewell, *Duke: A Portrait of Duke Ellington* (New York: W. W. Norton, 1977), 51.

20 *Ellington Reader*, ed. Tucker, 89. The fiction succeeded presumably because the record had not been issued in Europe.

21 Barney Bigard recalled that the popular Mills-published song by Will Hudson, "Moonglow," leaned heavily on *Lazy Rhapsody* ("I believe Mills arranged a big settlement with Duke over that"; Dance, *World of Duke Ellington*, 85). But Bigard failed to note that Ellington also borrows from himself: the intro to his 1934 "cover version" of *Moonglow* becomes the opening phrase of *Serenade to Sweden*.

22 *Ellington Reader*, ed. Tucker, 244. Barry Ulanov and John Edward Hasse mistakenly attribute this comment to Ellington himself.

23 Rolf Dahlgren, panel discussion "Duke Ellington in Sweden 1939," *Ellington '94* conference, Stockholm, May 19–22, 1994. The interview and the Swedish Radio concert recording of the song translated as *In a Little Red Cottage by the Sea* were first released commercially in the 1970s.

24 Issued on the specialist label Esquire, the four sides listed the local performers under pseudonyms because the popular Ray Ellington Quartet was signed to another label.

25 Charles Delaunay, *Jazz Hot*, May 1950, 21. The Ellington quotation has been re-translated from the French by the present author.

26 André Hodeir, *Jazz Hot*, May 1950, 23.

27 Steve Voce, *Jazz Journal*, March 1963, 12.

28 John Edward Hasse, *Beyond Category: The Life and Genius of Duke Ellington* (New York: Simon & Schuster, 1993), 354. For further background on this tour, see Harvey G. Cohen, *Duke Ellington's America* (Chicago: University of Chicago Press, 2010), 411 *et seq.*

29 Dance, *World of Duke Ellington*, first three sentences from page 17, last from page 23.

30 *Jazz Monthly*, April 1965, 23.

31 Jewell, *Duke*, 109.

32 The same conceit was employed for subsequent performances, for instance on *The English Concert* (United Artists, 1971).

33 Dance, *World of Duke Ellington*, 266.

34 Jock Veitch, "The Duke and His Secret Concert," *Sydney Morning Herald*, February 8, 1970. Incredibly, advertisements reveal that one of the stage attractions competing with Ellington in Sydney was the touring version of England's *Black and White Minstrel Show*.

35 Jewell, *Duke*, 157.

36 The tradition of an annual Command Performance, attended by the general public as well as royalty, dates back to 1912 and traditionally features a motley variety of performers from all branches of show business. In 1973, Ellington's set topped a bill that included 11 other acts.

5 Edward Kennedy Ellington as a cultural icon

OLLY W. WILSON AND TREVOR WESTON

At the beginning of the prologue of his autobiography, *Music Is My Mistress*, Edward Kennedy Ellington described his parents and his childhood in the following insightful and fanciful narrative:

> Once upon a time a beautiful young lady and a very handsome young man fell in love and got married. They were a wonderful, compatible couple, and God blessed their marriage with a fine baby boy (eight pounds, eight ounces). They loved their little boy very much.
> They raised him, nurtured him, coddled him, and spoiled him. They raised him in the palm of the hand and gave him everything they thought he wanted. Finally, when he was about seven or eight, they let his feet touch the ground.[1]

Ellington's pride in discussing his family, early childhood, and adolescent development reveals much about his personality and sense of privilege and destiny. He obviously perceived himself as a proud member of a family that was upwardly mobile and actively involved in the pursuit of an economically stable and socially fulfilling life, aspirations that were shared by many middle-class African Americans in Washington, D.C., during the first 20 years of the century. The famous photograph of the four-year-old Ellington – in which he stands regally, dressed in what appears to be a military uniform, with his right arm resting on a chair, and his left arm placed behind his back – reveals volumes about his early childhood as a boy of self-confidence and promise.

Much of *Music Is My Mistress* describes Ellington's idyllic childhood and gives us an insight into his complex personality. He discusses his family in the first chapter, including details of his father's entrepreneurial skills and means of making a living.

> My father had a job working as a butler for Dr. Cuthbert at 1462 on the south side of Rhode Island Avenue. I believe the house is still there. The cook and the maid were under him, and he was the fellow who made the decisions around the house. The doctor was rather prominent socially, and he probably recommended my father for social functions, because my father also belonged to what you might call a circle of caterers. When he or one of his cronies got a gig, all the others would act as waiters. They hired good cooks and gave impeccable service. They even had a page, I remember,

because one day something happened to the page and I had to stand in for him . . .

During World War I, he quit the butler job and rented a big house on K Street, in the fashionable area where all the suffragettes were. He rented out rooms, and continued as a caterer until he went to work on blueprints in the Navy yard. He kept at that till he had trouble with arthritis in his knee.

J. E. always acted as though he had money, whether he had it or not. He spent and lived like a man who had money, and he raised his family as though he were a millionaire. The best had to be carefully examined to make sure it was good enough for my mother. Maybe he was richer than a millionaire? I'm not sure that he wasn't.[2]

Ellington also commented on his father's penchant for speaking effectively and effortlessly in flattering poetic terms, particularly to women.

He was also a wonderful wit, and he knew exactly what to say to a lady – high-toned or honey-homey. I wrote a song later with a title suggested by one of those sayings he would address to a lady worth telling she was pretty. "Gee, you make that hat look pretty," he would say. He was very sensitive to beauty, and he respected it with proper gentility, never overdoing or under-doing it. He would never scratch a lady's charisma or injure her image.[3]

It is plausible that Ellington's ability as a man of verbal eloquence had its origin in his father's utterances. In support of that assertion, one need only cite Duke Ellington's convincing assessment of his father's persuasive and expressive verbal fluency:

While my mother had graduated from high school, I don't think my father even finished eighth grade. Yet his vocabulary was what I always hoped mine would be. In fact, I have always wanted to be able to be and talk like my pappy . . . Whatever place he was in, he had appropriate lines. "The millions of beautiful snowflakes are a celebration in honor of your beauty," he declared in Canada. Complexions were compared to the soft and glorious sunsets in California. In the Midwest, he saw the Mississippi as a swift messenger rushing to the sea to announce the existence of a wave of unbelievably compelling force caused by the rebirth of Venus. In New York and on the East Coast, he spoke about "pretty being pretty, but not that pretty." Sometimes he would attempt to sing a song of praise, and then apologize for the emotion that destroyed the control of his voice.[4]

What Ellington reveals here are the sensibilities of a proud man whose values were profoundly shaped by the optimism of the emerging, urban African-American middle class of the first two decades of the twentieth century. As the eminent historian John Hope Franklin states:

The two world wars had a profound effect on the status of Negroes in the United States and did much to mount the attack on the two worlds of race.

The decade of World War I witnessed a very significant migration of
Negroes. They went in large numbers – perhaps a half million – from the
rural areas of the South to the towns and cities of the South and North. By
the thousands they poured into Pittsburgh, Cleveland, and Chicago.
Although many were unable to secure employment, others were successful
and achieved a standard of living they could not have imagined only a few
years earlier. Northern communities were not altogether friendly and
hospitable to the newcomers, but the opportunities for education and the
enjoyment of political self-respect were greater than they had ever been for
these Negroes. Many of them felt that they were entirely justified in their
renewed hope that the war would bring about a complete merger of the two
worlds of race.[5]

Duke Ellington was an extraordinary creative artist whose brilliant contributions to the world were rooted in his profound understanding of the
broader African-American music tradition. His particular genius was the
ability to create a new paradigm that celebrated and reinforced the characteristic elements of that tradition while simultaneously introducing
significant innovations to it. As such, his work was shaped fundamentally
by aesthetic principles and conceptual processes of music-making derived
from African music and altered to conform to the realities of the African-
American experience. Although he visited Africa on concert tours several
times during his fabulous career, there is little evidence that he was directly
influenced by specific African music. On the other hand, there is abundant
empirical evidence that his musical universe was centered in the concepts
that collectively comprise the African-American music tradition, and that
his basic sources were African-American manifestations or transformations of modes of musical thought and practice shared with West African
cultures and the African diaspora. As Henry Louis Gates, Jr. states in
discussing the nature of the relationship between African and African-
American culture, and refuting the notion that African-American culture
has nothing to do with African culture:

> Common sense, in retrospect, argues that these retained elements of culture
> should have survived, that their complete annihilation would have been far
> more remarkable than their preservation. The African, after all, was a
> traveler, albeit an abrupt, ironic traveler, through space and time; and like
> every traveler, the African "read" a new environment within a received
> framework of meaning and belief. The notion that the Middle passage was so
> traumatic that it functioned to create in the African a tabula rasa of
> consciousness is as odd as it is a fiction, a fiction that has served several
> economic orders and their attendant ideologies. The full erasure of traces of
> culture as splendid, as ancient, and as shared by the slave traveler as the
> classic cultures of traditional West Africa would have been extraordinarily
> difficult. Slavery in the New World, a veritable seething cauldron of

cross-cultural contact, however, did serve to create a dynamic of exchange and revision among numerous previously isolated Black African cultures on a scale unprecedented in African history. Inadvertently, African slavery in the New World satisfied the preconditions for the emergence of a new African culture, a truly Pan-African culture fashioned as a colorful weave of linguistic, institutional, metaphysical, and formal threads. What survived this fascinating process was the most useful and the most compelling of the fragments at hand. Afro-American culture is an African culture with a difference as signified by the catalysts of English, Dutch, French, Portuguese, or Spanish languages and cultures, which informed the precise structures that each discrete New World Pan-African culture assumed.[6]

Research into the relationship between African and African-American music certainly concurs with the basic viewpoint stated above. This viewpoint is also consistent with the published work of Robert Farris Thompson, who studies the relationship between African and African-American art, and Albert Raboteau, who studies African and African-American religion. Moreover, Duke Ellington, in an interview with Carter Harman in 1964, stated unequivocally: "My strongest influences, my inspirations, were all Negro."[7]

To paraphrase a passage I wrote in 1974, the relationship between African and African-American musical traditions consists of the common sharing of a core of conceptual approaches to the process of music-making, and hence is not basically quantitative but qualitative. The particular forms of African-American music that evolved in the New World are specific manifestations of this shared conceptual framework, which reflects both the unique nature and specific contexts of the African-American experience. As such, the essence of their "Africanness" is not a static body of something that can be depleted, but rather, a shared conceptual predisposition, the manifestations of which are infinite. The common core of this shared cultural affinity consists of ways of doing something, not simply something that is done.[8]

The African influence on African-American music and, by extension, Duke Ellington, has been reflected historically in shared or similar conceptions regarding (1) the fundamental nature of the musical experience; (2) principles of musical organization – specific approaches to musical form, patterns of continuity, and syntax; and (3) performance practices – the processes involved in actively making music.

Many fundamental aspects of the musical experience are shared by African and African-American music. One of the most salient of these shared concepts is the view of music as a communal activity in which there are no detached listeners, but rather a communion of participants – a view which expects and encourages the active interaction of all participants. The notion of "inclusion" in the music-making process becomes an important dimension of performance in both African and African-American music.

Duke Ellington's extensively documented method of working with his band members is an excellent example of this practice. Ellington developed an exceptionally fruitful collaborative relationship with his band. As Gunther Schuller states:

> A unique musical partnership, truly unprecedented in the history of Western music, developed in which a major composer forged a musical style and concept which, though totally original and individual, nevertheless consistently incorporated and integrated the no less original musical ideas of his players. No such musical alchemy had ever been accomplished before, with the possible exception of Jelly Roll Morton's *Hot Peppers* recordings of 1926. Miraculously, the Ellington imagination fed on the particular skills and personalities of his players, while at the same time *their* musical growth was in turn nurtured by Ellington's maturing compositional craft and vision. This process of cross-fertilization was constant and, given the stability of personnel, self-expanding.[9]

The Ellington band was shaped by the unique artistic symbiotic relationship between Ellington and individual artists like Bubber Miley, "Tricky Sam" Nanton, Sonny Greer, Otto Hardwick, Arthur Whetsol, Lawrence Brown, Johnny Hodges, Barney Bigard, Paul Gonsalves, Cootie Williams, Ben Webster, and Clark Terry, to name a few. Each of these artists had a distinct musical personality, and Ellington created the precise musical framework to enhance and expand that personality by challenging the artist to explore new musical forms and contexts in which to achieve even greater heights of sublime artistry. In a broad sense, Ellington's approach both reinforced a traditional African/African-American ideal and created an innovative means of doing so. He was a composer because his overall conception shaped the final result, but he also worked within the received framework of communal collaboration.

At the end of the nineteenth century, Paul Laurence Dunbar wrote "We Wear the Mask," a poem that captured with exceptional insight an important aspect of the African-American experience:

> We wear the mask that grins and lies,
> It hides our cheeks and shades our eyes, –
> This debt we pay to human guile;
> With torn and bleeding hearts we smile,
> And mouth with myriad subtleties.
>
> Why should the world be over-wise,
> In counting all our tears and sighs?
> Nay, let them only see us, while
> We wear the mask.

We smile, but, O great Christ, our cries
To thee from tortured souls arise.
We sing, but oh the clay is vile
Beneath our feet, and long the mile;
But let the world dream otherwise,
We wear the mask!

The metaphor of the mask also invokes *minstrelsy*, the nineteenth-century entertainment tradition based on the crude caricature of African-American culture by white men in blackface – a tradition that provided ideological support for the institution of slavery. Simply put, minstrelsy was a white distortion of African-American culture for commercial gain. Minstrelsy was not only the first indigenous American popular music, but also established norms of show business practice, some of which are still part of American popular entertainment today. As an entertainer entering the field at the beginning of the 1920s, Ellington – like many before him, including composer Scott Joplin, comedian Bert Williams, and George Hicks, founder of the Georgia Minstrels, the first African-American minstrel troupe, in 1865 – all had to accommodate the expectations of this tradition. Ellington wore the mask in the 1920s as his mentor, the erudite violinist and composer Will Marion Cook, had worn it almost two decades earlier. That is, although Ellington was always regal, urbane, and sophisticated in his public appearance and demeanor – a credible exemplar of the scholar Alain Locke's "New Negro" – his work at the Cotton Club in Harlem was influenced very much by remnants of the minstrel tradition. The cover page of *Jig Walk*, one of his earliest piano compositions, written in 1925 for the musical revue *Chocolate Kiddies*, clearly displays the stereotyped images of the minstrel show.

The Cotton Club patrons were almost exclusively white and the entire theatrical ambiance was based on the image of either the "old southern plantation" or the "primitive" jungle. The titles of many of the compositions designed for the Cotton Club revues invoke the image of the African jungle (*Jungle Blues, Jungle Jamboree, Jungle Nights in Harlem*, and so on). The suave, tuxedo-clad Ellington band played beside these minstrel show-like tableaus, and here we have Ellington cast in the role of the music creator of "fantasy land" revues based on stereotypical images of "darkies" on the southern plantation or the exotic, erotic mysteries of Africa.

There is no question that the smashing success of Josephine Baker's appearance in *La Revue nègre*, which opened in Paris in October 1925 and catapulted her into instant stardom, had an influence on the subsequent New York Cotton Club revues. Major figures of European "highbrow" culture were fascinated by the *Revue nègre*. Glenn Watkins, in his astute study of the development of modernism, tells us:

Fernand Léger, Blaise Cendrars, and Darius Milhaud all attended the opening night performance, as did Jean Cocteau, Janet Flanner, and Jacques-Émile Blanche. Colette, F. Scott Fitzgerald, and Erich Maria Remarque caught later ones, and Cocteau, who totally succumbed to her charm, attended six times. Man Ray photographed her, and she posed repeatedly for Picasso, who called her the "Nefertiti of now." F. Scott Fitzgerald speaks of her in *Babylon Revisited*; Hemingway was dazzled by her and later claimed to have danced the night away with her; Alexander Calder's first wire sculpture of 1926 attempted to capture the vitality of her figure; in 1928 the Viennese architect Adolf Loos designed a house for her that seemed to conjure up the stripes of an African zebra more than the black and white marble striations of Siena's Cathedral; and in 1929 aboard the *Lutetia* on their way back from South America, the architect Le Corbusier honored her, and in the process created something of a stir, by appearing at the costume ball in blackface and with a circle of feathers around his waist.[10]

The cultural context of this adulation must be taken into consideration. The early twentieth-century emergence of "modernism" in art, music, and dance was fueled by a strong attraction to "primitive," "exotic," and presumably "pure" non-European models, and Africa – as expressed by African and African-American music, dance, and art – was central among these. The concept of absolutely pure "primitive" expression was highly attractive to many of the intellectual elite of the post-World War I "Jazz Age," who were seeking new models of human expression in the wake of what appeared to be the "end of the century decadence" of European culture.

Duke Ellington's Cotton Club revues were an American manifestation of this phenomenon, and Carl Van Vechten, George Antheil, George Gershwin, and others were interested in these developments as well. The notion of Duke Ellington as a wearer of the mask relates to the supreme irony of this extraordinarily creative man producing music that was "pseudo-African" on the surface, but in reality was the manifestation of new approaches to the creation of African-American music. The Cotton Club revues enabled Ellington to experiment with new ideas, establish a band with a distinctive style built upon the musical personalities of his specific performers, and expand his compositional skill within a tradition in which improvisation was vital. Behind the mask of an entertainer was a superb creative artist who defined much of what is best in African-American and American culture.

In a broader sense, Ellington was a pivotal agent in effecting an extraordinary (and perhaps inevitable) change in the perception of African-American music by the American public in general and the intellectual elite in particular. During the 1920s and 1930s, most popular depictions of African Americans were still dominated by minstrelsy's image of "black folk" as crude, ignorant, and childish. Ellington's music, his "suave persona," and his scintillating, disciplined, and musically superb orchestra fundamentally altered American society's impressions of African Americans. This dynamic music encompassed urban sophistication, postwar optimism, an unquenchable zest for life, and the ability to capture the essence of multifaceted human emotions suggested by such titles as *Black and Tan Fantasy*, *Mood Indigo*, *Sophisticated Lady*, *Solitude*, and *It Don't Mean a Thing (If It Ain't Got That Swing)*.

Ellington's music reflected a more nuanced, subtle, and complex reading of African-American culture, and, ultimately, projected a sophisticated and realistic understanding of African-American life. Duke Ellington used his music to communicate the complexity, depth, joy, and beauty of the contemporary African-American and American experience.

The European perception of people of sub-Saharan Africa and the African diaspora as inferior human beings is centuries old, and was expressed in the most direct terms even by some of America's most eminent champions of egalitarianism, democracy, and liberty. In 1785, Thomas Jefferson's *Notes on the State of Virginia* was first published in France and included the following:

> But never yet could I find that a black had uttered a thought above the level of plain narration; never seen even an elementary trait of painting or sculpture. In music they are more generally gifted than the whites with accurate ears for tune and time, and they have been found capable of imagining a small catch [meaning a "round," usually at the interval of a unison, as in the popular "Are You Sleeping?"]. Whether they will be equal to the composition of a more extensive run of melody, or of complicated harmony, is yet to be proved.[11]

If Jefferson (1743–1826) had lived in Newport, Rhode Island, given his intellectual curiosity, he might have heard of the music written and published by the African-American former slave and singing-school master Newport Gardner (1746–1826). Eileen Southern's comprehensive study of African-American music, *The Music of Black Americans*, quotes a contemporary writer, John Ferguson, from 1830:

> Newport Gardner . . . early discovered to his owner very superior powers of mind. He taught himself to read, after receiving a few lessons on the elements of written language. He taught himself to sing, after receiving a very trivial initiation into the rudiments of music. He became so well acquainted with the science and art of music, that he composed a large number of tunes, some of which have been highly approved by musical amateurs, and was for a long time the teacher of a very numerously attended singing school in Newport.[12]

And if Jefferson, late in life, had visited Philadelphia and paid close attention to the formal band music of that time, he would have heard of Francis Johnson (1792–1844), who was described in a popular book published in 1819 as the "leader of the band at all balls, public and private."[13] Eileen Southern writes of Johnson:

> Johnson was indeed a celebrity of all times! During his short career he accumulated an amazing number of "firsts" as a black musician: first to win wide acclaim in the nation and in England; first to publish sheet music (as early as 1818); first to develop a "school" of black musicians; first to give formal band concerts; first to tour widely in the nation; and first to appear in integrated concerts with white musicians. His list of achievements also included "firsts" as an American, black or white: he was the first to take a musical ensemble abroad to perform in Europe and the first to introduce the promenade concert to the United States.[14]

Francis Johnson was followed by a long line of musically literate African-American composers who were active in the nineteenth century as concert bandleaders, dance bandleaders, and publishers of sheet music that reflected the musical taste of their time. These musicians were active in major cities such as Philadelphia, where composers Aaron J. R. Connor (d. 1850), James Hemmenway (1800–1849), and William Appo (c.1808–c.1878) were among the leading composers and bandleaders; St. Louis, where Joseph Postlewaite (1827–1889) directed at least four bands and published dances and marches that became well known; and Boston and Cleveland, where Justin Holland (1819–1887) published music that was also well known in the United States and Europe. By the end of the nineteenth century, African-American composers in the written tradition of minstrel music, such as James Bland, were internationally acclaimed, and by the end of the first decade of the twentieth century, the "kings" of published classic ragtime were musical giants like Scott Joplin and Tom Turpin.

Duke Ellington's emergence as a major figure in American music occurred during his tenure at the Cotton Club, which began in 1927. In this context, Ellington catapulted his band into the first rank, as a result of the musical excellence of its members, the brilliance and imagination of his original music for revues at this venue, and the new image he and the band projected to the American public, as superb artists of the highest order. Between the time he first published a piano solo piece and the time he left the Cotton Club, Ellington had become one of the most popular and influential musicians in the country. One reason for Ellington's emergence was his major role in changing the general public's view of his music, from signifying the sensibilities of a shuffling, indolent minstrel show character to demonstrating the power of a creative artist whose ideas were compelling as music and influential as agents of social change. Ellington was a cultural icon during his lifetime, and as an icon continued to shine even more brightly long after his death.

The distortion of African-American culture associated with the nineteenth-century minstrel show enticed the audience to laugh at the antics of crude, ignorant, and inferior black people as depicted by white blackface performers with large red lips. The thousands of African-American people who fled from the stifling "neo-peasant trap" of share-cropping and other institutions of "slavery by another name" in the post-*Plessy v. Ferguson* (1896) legal environment of the South were entranced by their exodus to the bustling, dynamic life of the northern cities, where at least some "people of color" appeared to be living exciting lives. The powerful, authentic music of the 1920s "Jazz Age" enticed black and white people to participate in the exuberant celebration of life that this music both reflected and demanded. This dramatic shift in the perception of African-American culture in the United States resulted from many important and diverse social, political, and economic factors, as with any such major transformation in the cultural values of any society. Nevertheless, an undeniable quantum shift of cultural values occurred in the United States in the first three decades of the twentieth century, and the fundamental nature of the American spirit was indelibly transformed by the emergence of jazz and blues as a phenomenal expression of the American experience. Edward Kennedy Ellington was a major force in making this change happen.

Duke Ellington's first original extended work, *Creole Rhapsody*, recorded in 1931, reveals his early compositional concerns. The work is over eight minutes long and required both sides of a 78 rpm disc. The title makes reference to "Creoles of color" or people of African, French, and/or Spanish descent.[15] In any case, Ellington seems to clearly connect this music to its ethnic identity. Musically, *Creole Rhapsody* represents the diversity of Ellington's musical output. The piece begins with minor-mode "exotic" jungle music, which after 16 measures moves to a brief piano cadenza, before the next contrasting section in a major mode, organized into 12-measure phrases. What becomes obvious very soon is that this piece is not intended to support dancing. The steady tempo and regularity necessary for dancing are interrupted often throughout the piece, sometimes symbolically thwarted by Ellington's piano cadenzas. The music at the end of the first part evokes the mellow calmness of Ellington's mood pieces. It becomes more obvious in the second part that Ellington is developing prior material from the piece and elaborating elements of his compositional voice. The short piano cadenzas continue to "call" or direct the music into different sections as if the piece were improvised. The soloists help define various sections of the piece by their instrumental timbre, and Ellington, like a master drummer of a traditional West African music ensemble, shapes the piece by redirecting the mood with interrupting cadenzas. This connection between timbre and form is very important in this piece and in Ellington's music generally, and *Creole Rhapsody* is an important example of his efforts to develop jazz within the tradition of African-American music.

Ellington clearly states his objectives as a composer in the important essay "The Duke Steps Out," published in 1931 in *Rhythm*, a British magazine. The trajectory of his artistic vision seems to stem from ideas and opinions expressed in this essay, which articulates his approach to composition and a musical vision rooted in originality.

> Always I try to be original in my harmonies and rhythms. I am not trying to suggest that my tunes are superior to those of other writers . . . I put my best musical thoughts forward into my tunes, and not hackneyed harmonies and rhythms, which are almost too banal to publish.[16]

While Ellington generally did not attack or belittle the work of other musicians, he was aware early in his career of the qualitative difference between his compositional goals and the general field of popular music in the early 1930s. Continuing Scott Joplin's and James Reese Europe's legacy of innovation, Ellington was more concerned with defining African-American music through his art than with being pigeonholed by commercial expectations. *Creole Rhapsody* may have been the first extended work to literally break the conventional mold of recorded African-American music by requiring both sides of a 78 rpm disc, but this composition also revealed Ellington's musical direction and concerns as stated in "The Duke Steps Out":

> But I am not content with just fox-trots. One is necessarily limited with a canvas of only thirty-two bars and with a strict tempo to keep up. I have already said that it is my firm belief that what is still known as "jazz" is going to play a considerable part in the serious music of the future. I am proud of that part my race is playing in the artistic life of the world.[17]

Reminiscing in Tempo (henceforth referred to as *RIT*) was Duke Ellington's first truly controversial composition. Composed after the devastating loss of his mother in 1935, *RIT* allowed Ellington to cope with this emotional nadir by placing his brooding thoughts in this composition. Reaching almost 13 minutes in length, *RIT* required four sides of two 78 rpm discs, exceeding the logistical requirements of *Creole Rhapsody*. *RIT* also broke the mold of aesthetic expectations of "jazz" music. Similar to *Creole Rhapsody*, *RIT* is not designed for dancing and is definitely meant for listening. *RIT* is not an example of Western classical art music collaborating with jazz, nor is it an example of a jazz composer collaborating with Western classical music. *Creole Rhapsody* could have been mistaken for a long jazz piece, but in writing *RIT* at 12′ 55″, Ellington was clearly expanding a genre of African-American music within its own musical syntax and forms of expression. Four years after writing "Duke Steps Out," Ellington created in *RIT* a non-foxtrot, non-32-bar, non-strict-tempo work of "serious music of the future."

Musically, *RIT* is an example of Ellington's mood/blue pieces where a melody seems to float over an ostinato accompaniment. The orchestral writing fits firmly within the aesthetics of big band arrangements, and the sections of the orchestra have their assigned roles. The rhythm section establishes the original ostinato, and then brass and wind instruments enter as soloists or as a soloing section. The opening muted trumpet solo is an alternating minor third over shifting parallel harmonies in the ostinato; in general terms, this is a blues riff without a blues progression. This melody can also be heard as a distillation of the important contribution of field hollers, cries, spirituals, blues, and gospel music to the tradition of African-American melody. Beginning *RIT* with the constructive material of a blues riff, Ellington firmly roots the work in the tradition of big band music and the African-American musical tradition. The use of instruments with fixed rhythmic elements against other instruments with changing rhythmic elements is fundamental to African-American musical expression.[18]

Development throughout the work comes from the changing combinations and timbres of the solo instruments. The music becomes most intense soon after the ninth minute of the piece, when the four-chord ostinato becomes a more complex dissonant chord against the moving woodwind countermelody and the riff melody. The organic growth of the piece is all intrinsic, similar to Ravel's *Bolero*. What are missing, to those listeners expecting a conventional jazz recording, are the harmonic and formal signposts associated with the popular music of the time. Although the length of *RIT* is in itself significant as an expansion of standard recording practices, Ellington's composition of a work outside the limitations of commercial popular music is more important. Ellington not only extended the duration of his individual works, but he also expanded the definition of African-American music.

Duke Ellington used his music to document African-American culture, and the titles of his works reveal a commitment to recording elements of African-American life. In his 1933 essay "My Hunt for Song Titles," Ellington declared, "It will not, therefore, surprise the public to know that every one of my song titles is taken from, and naturally principally from, the life of Harlem."[19] Understood, but not stated in this quote, is that Harlem was the cultural center of African-American life in the 1930s. Harlem encompassed the diversity of African-American society, as reflected in Ellington's music. The titles of his works also incorporated the African-American vernacular, including "dicty," "jive," "rent party," and other words and phrases that were common to the denizens of Harlem. Similar to the titles of bebop songs in the 1940s and hip-hop songs of the 1980s, Ellington's titles give an added stamp of cultural authenticity to his music. These titles also have a didactic quality by revealing to the general public unique elements of African-American culture. Teaching the world about African-American society was an important goal of Ellington's work; he also stated in "My Hunt for Song Titles" that "it is through the medium of my music that I want to give you a better understanding of my race."[20] And in "The Duke Steps Out" he wrote:

> I am therefore now engaged on a rhapsody unhampered by any musical
> form in which I intend to portray the experiences of the coloured races
> in America in the syncopated idiom. This composition will consist of
> four or five movements, and I am putting all I have learned into it in
> the hope that I shall have achieved something really worth while in
> the literature of music, and that an authentic record of my race *written
> by a member of it* shall be placed on record.[21]

Although the didactic intent of his artistry seemed to be missed by many critics and some of his fans, Ellington's nine-minute film *Symphony in Black* and his extended work *Black, Brown and Beige* were important ballasts to the imagery and import of the music of African-American artists. Released in 1935, *Symphony in Black: A Rhapsody of Negro Life* helped to cultivate a serious understanding of African-American music among the general public. The film presents four sections or movements, the traditional number of movements in a classical symphony, entitled "The Laborers," "A Triangle," "Hymn of Sorrow," and "Harlem Rhythm." *Symphony in Black* tells the history of African Americans through music as dictated by Ellington in "The Duke Steps Out."

The first movement is an obvious documentation of the hardships African Americans endured during slavery. Reminding his public of the legacy of slavery and the mistreatment of African Americans in the United States, Ellington opens *Symphony in Black* with an example of one of the first documented forms of African-American folk music: the work song. The second movement eventually reveals a blues performed by Billie Holiday. As one of the most important genres of the African-American musical tradition, the classic blues, as performed by Holiday in "A Triangle," also symbolically represents the great migration of African

Americans to northern urban centers. "Hymn of Sorrow" uses slow, melancholy music to support scenes of devout African Americans in church at prayer or listening to a sermon. This third movement of *Symphony in Black* pays homage to the centrality of the church in African-American culture.

The last movement, "Harlem Rhythm," ends the rhapsody with music and images associated with what could be scenes from a revue at the Cotton Club. The Ellington orchestra's tenure at the Cotton Club represented the epitome of the new artistic developments in African-American music that inspired pilgrimages to Harlem by white jazz enthusiasts living in other parts of New York City, and the film ends with music evoking these exciting advancements.

Duke Ellington did not direct the filming of *Symphony in Black*, but the images of African Americans in general, and Ellington specifically, are culturally significant for 1935. A year later, the Warner Brothers film *The Green Pastures* was released, depicting "a story of heaven and of earth as it might be imagined by a very simple, devout people," according to the trailer. Presenting a common, patronizing view of African Americans as simple folk with a confused understanding of the world and heaven, *The Green Pastures* promoted the popular stereotypes of black life in America. In stark contrast to *The Green Pastures* and similar depictions of African Americans, *Symphony in Black* begins with Duke Ellington composing a new commissioned work at a piano in his studio. After writing down his music, he then performs it. We see him thinking about his work in a reflective manner. This is an uncommon treatment for any African American on the silver screen in the 1930s. Eight years after the release of *The Jazz Singer* starring Al Jolson in blackface, Duke Ellington is represented as an authentic recorder of the history of his race in America in *Symphony in Black*.

The culmination of Ellington's musical historiography of African-American culture is the monumental composition *Black, Brown and Beige*, premiered at Carnegie Hall in 1943. The title alone reveals a desire by Ellington to write music that represents all people of African descent, regardless of their hue. *Black, Brown and Beige*, which Ellington subtitled *A Tone Parallel to the History of the Negro in America*, presents a history of African Americans, but in more detail than *Symphony in Black*. Ellington announces each of the three movements in the live Carnegie Hall recording to give a detailed description of the music. "Black" starts with a work song, similar to *Symphony in Black*'s beginning, but Ellington here also includes a spiritual section to round out the important forms of African-American music before the end of slavery. The second movement, "Brown," represents the migration of West Indians into the African-American community, emancipation, and the development of the blues in response to continued hardships. Ellington's description of the last movement, "Beige," balances a fine line between patriotism and suffering in the African-American community. The revolutionary moment in the piece, one might say, occurs in Ellington's discussion of the suffering in the last movement. Ellington proclaimed from the stage:

> The first theme of our third movement is . . . the veneer that we chip off as we get closer and find that all these people who are making all this noise and responding to the tom toms are only a few people making a living, and they're backed really by people who, many don't have enough to eat and a place to sleep, but work hard and see that their children are in school. The Negro is rich in education. And it develops until we find ourselves today, struggling for solidarity, but just as we are about to get our teeth into it, our country is at war and in trouble again, and as before, we, of course, find the black, brown, and beige right in there for the red, white, and blue.[22]

Rich in history and complicated social and political debates, Ellington's eloquent introduction to "Beige" is a soliloquy parallel to his music in general, and *Black, Brown and Beige* specifically. Ellington also makes an important connection between his orchestra and the plight of all African Americans – or, as he put it, the people backing him and his band members. In other words, the "Maestro" is telling the audience that if you support our music-making, then you need to know that we are no different than our families and loved ones who struggle and work hard to make sure that the next generation receives a good education. Or, even more poignantly, Ellington seems to be saying, "We, the Black, Brown, and Beige community, are not shiftless or lazy, but are focused on improving our future through education and hard work, while continuing to help defend America in every war, despite social and institutional barriers to our progress."

Ellington's final statement on *Black, Brown and Beige* summarizes the ideas and goals of the piece, without literally describing the musical organization of this movement, thereby enabling the musical experience of the work itself to achieve his artistic objective of expressing "an authentic record of my race *written by a member of it*."

Notes

1 Duke Ellington, *Music Is My Mistress* (New York: Doubleday, 1973; reprint, Da Capo Press, 1976), x.

2 Ibid., 10.

3 Ibid., 12.

4 Ibid.

5 John Hope Franklin, *Race and History: Selected Essays 1938–1988* (Baton Rouge: Louisiana State University Press, 1989), 144.

6 Henry Louis Gates, *The Signifying Monkey: A Theory of African-American Literary Criticism* (New York: Oxford University Press, 1988), 4.

7 Duke Ellington interview by Carter Harman, May 30, 1964, from the Carter Harman collection, Archives Center, National Museum of American History, Smithsonian Institution, Washington, D.C.

8 Olly W. Wilson, "The Significance of the Relationship Between Afro-American Music and West African Music," *Black Perspectives in Music* 2/1 (1974): 3–22; the original passage is on page 20. See also Alan P. Merriam, *The Anthropology of Music* (Evanston, IL: Northwestern University Press, 1964).

9 Gunther Schuller, *The Swing Era: The Development of Jazz 1930–1945* (New York: Oxford University Press, 1989), 48.

10 Glenn Watkins, *Pyramids at the Louvre: Music, Culture, and Collage from Stravinsky to the Postmodernists* (Cambridge, MA: Harvard University Press, 1994), 135.

11 Thomas Jefferson, *Notes on the State of Virginia*, ed. Frank Shuffelton (New York: Penguin Books, 1999), 147.

12 Eileen Southern, *The Music of Black Americans: A History*, 3rd edn. (New York: W. W. Norton, 1997), 69.

13 Robert Waln, *The Hermit in America on a Visit to Philadelphia* (Philadelphia: M. Thomas, 1819).

14 Southern, *The Music of Black Americans*, 107.

15 Two important studies of Creole identity and culture in Louisiana are Gwendolyn Midlo Hall, *Africans in Colonial Louisiana: The Development of Afro-Creole Culture in the Eighteenth Century* (Baton Rouge: Louisiana State University Press, 1992) and Carl A. Brasseaux, Keith P. Fontenot, and Claude F. Oubre, *Creoles of Color in the Bayou Country* (Jackson: University Press of Mississippi, 1994).

16 Duke Ellington, "The Duke Steps Out," *Rhythm*, March 1931, 20–22. Reprinted in *The Duke Ellington Reader*, ed. Mark Tucker (New York: Oxford University Press, 1993), 46–50; the quote appears on pages 48–49.

17 Ibid., 49.

18 See Olly W. Wilson, "Black Music as an Art Form," *Black Music Research Journal* 3/2 (1983): 1–22.

19 Duke Ellington, "My Hunt for Song Titles," *Rhythm*, August 1933, 22–23. Reprinted in *Ellington Reader*, ed. Tucker, 88.

20 Ibid., 89.

21 *Ellington Reader*, ed. Tucker, 49–50.

22 Ellington's stage remarks appear on the CD *The Duke Ellington Carnegie Hall Concerts: January 1943* (Prestige 2PCD-34004–2).

PART II

Duke through the decades: the music and its reception

6 Ellington's Afro-Modernist vision in the 1920s

JEFFREY MAGEE

If, as an older man, Ellington placed high value on music "beyond category,"[1] then his first decade in New York proved the musical and social value of that notion and established career patterns that extended to the end of his life. The categories that both challenged and spurred Ellington were jazz and race. By 1930, he had made the first in a series of claims about striving to develop a new kind of race music. "I am not playing jazz," he said, "I am trying to play the natural feelings of a people."[2] In the later 1930s he noted that his aim had "always" been to develop "an authentic Negro music."[3] He insisted that he did not play jazz because when he began his career, he recalled, "jazz was a stunt."[4]

Such insistence served as an antidote to persistent stereotypes about both jazz *and* African Americans, and the further we get from its original context, and the more the discourse about jazz (from textbooks to television documentaries) treats Ellington's music *as jazz*, the more difficult it becomes to fully engage with Ellington's stated vision. By saying he wanted to cultivate a kind of music that was more than jazz, "more than the 'American idiom'," and "definitely and purely racial," Ellington articulated a broad vision that implicitly defied the narrow frames of the era's racial discourse.[5] As a musician who strove both to develop the idioms associated with African Americans, especially the blues, and to cultivate a sophisticated, cosmopolitan artistic persona, Ellington was an early exemplar of Afro-Modernism and the New Negro project of redefining the black experience in American life, as a southern and largely rural population migrated en masse to the urban north.[6] And beginning in the 1920s, Ellington proved again and again that he could at once fulfill and foil the expectations that audiences placed on black musicians.

Race in Ellington's New York

By emphasizing his music's racial dimension, Ellington demonstrated a savvy mix of idealism and realism. The idealism took root in Washington,

Thanks to Holly Holmes for making the transcriptions and preparing the musical examples; to Katy Vizdal for research assistance; and to James Dapogny for sharing his knowledge as well as scores and parts from his own transcriptions and stock arrangements of the period.

D.C., where Ellington's family instilled a strong sense of racial pride.[7] He took that pride to New York, where, in the real, everyday experience of his musical career as bandleader and composer, his professional milieu placed race in the foreground and reminded him of it at every turn.

To recover the texture of Ellington's early career, its racialized musical contexts are worth reviewing. The recording industry segregated its products into "general" and "race" series. Record company managers forced black bands to play styles associated with "race" musicians, especially "hot" jazz and blues, and they discouraged, or even forbade, the musicians from playing other dance music, such as waltzes. Fletcher Henderson's band, which Ellington admired above all others when he first came to New York, excelled at playing waltzes, but was never allowed to record them. Rex Stewart, a trumpet player with Henderson for a few years before joining Ellington in the mid-1930s, recalled "an unwritten custom among record people that no negro orchestra should be allowed to record anything that wasn't blues or hot stuff."[8]

Race also informed Ellington's public appearances. Nightclubs, ballrooms, and theaters routinely segregated their audiences, whether by allowing African Americans into just a small, dedicated space of a venue (such as a balcony or a roped-off portion of the dance floor), by admitting them only if they were celebrities, or by not admitting them at all. Other venues cultivated black clientele. The rare nightclub that catered to all races was known as a *black and tan*. But a band could not be "black and tan." In public, groups of musicians performed with their own race, and light-skinned members of black ensembles sometimes even had to don blackface makeup, as did the New Orleans Creole clarinetist Barney Bigard and Puerto Rican trombonist Juan Tizol when they appeared on film in Ellington's band in 1930.[9]

Racial coding saturated musical life. Names of New York nightclubs in the early-to-mid 1920s revealed a fad for conjuring the Old South – a savvy way to herald black entertainment. The Club Alabam near Times Square featured Fletcher Henderson in 1923–1924, and soon thereafter Ellington's band played at the downtown Plantation Café and the Kentucky Club before landing uptown in Harlem's Cotton Club in December 1927. The décor and floorshows at such venues tended to trade in the familiar racial tropes of idyllic plantation nostalgia or primitivist exotica – or both, as in the Cotton Club. Cab Calloway famously recalled the Cotton Club's bandstand as "a replica of a southern mansion, with large white columns and a backdrop painted with weeping willows and slave quarters … like the sleepy-time-down-South during slavery."[10] The Cotton Club shows also trafficked in Africanist primitivism. Songwriters Dorothy Fields and Jimmy McHugh wrote original material for the Cotton Club shows during much of

Ellington's tenure, and their tune "Diga Diga Doo," which premiered at the Cotton Club in a show called *Blackbirds of 1928* and which Ellington recorded later that year, typifies the primitivist vein, with its African allusion ("Zulu man is feeling blue . . .") and provocative lyrics in which the ersatz-scat title phrase becomes a euphemism for sex.

Racial language permeated Ellington's world in yet other ways. Journalists commonly referred to "negro" and "colored" bands and used sly synonyms such as "indigo," "sepia," "dusky," and "chocolate."[11] (Many of those terms would show up in titles of pieces that Ellington wrote and played.) Through the 1920s and into the 1930s, black bands adopted names that advertised or implied racial distinction, such as the Jungle Band and the Harlem Footwarmers: two pseudonyms, on competing record labels, for the band that usually recorded under the more dignified name of Duke Ellington and his Orchestra. Among Ellington's early recordings, too, may be found many titles conjuring the primitivist, plantation, and urban tropes of the period's black soundscapes, including *Black and Tan Fantasy, Creole Love Call, Creole Rhapsody, Jungle Jamboree, Echoes of the Jungle, Harlem Flat Blues, Saturday Night Function,* and *Hottentot* (a Dutch term that entered the English language to describe the most "primitive" Africans), to name just a few.

Such titles, however well they may have fit into the restricted racial discourse of 1920s Manhattan, nevertheless mask a musical style that continually challenged stereotypes by its variety and sophistication. Gunther Schuller aimed to emphasize that variety when he identified five types of pieces in Ellington's repertoire in the Cotton Club years: dance numbers, jungle-style or production numbers, "blue" or "mood" pieces, pop tunes, and "abstract 'musical compositions'."[12] These categories have proven durable in the jazz literature, despite their mix of stylistic and functional qualities and Schuller's own caveats about them.[13] But as Schuller was the first to acknowledge, the categories do not tell the whole story. And Ellington, of course, resisted categories even as he sometimes accepted them when they proved beneficial to his ambitious goals.

So with Schuller's framework as a reference point, we might consider a more holistic view of Ellington's early career as it developed in a milieu in which variety and sophistication stood for more than just practical musicianship.[14] For black musicians they marked the intersection of racial politics and commercial viability in a music industry that reinforced the stylistic stereotyping of "black" music as blues and "hot" jazz.[15] In the musicians Ellington hired, in the music he played, and in the ways he and his band were presented to the public in the media, Ellington developed, highlighted, and exploited variety and *contrast* in ways that resisted easy categorization.

Tonal personalities

Ellington has always been well known for hiring a musician for his unique
tone; he referred to his sidemen as "tonal personalities." More than that,
however, we can see in Ellington's early choices a tendency to favor
contrasting approaches within each section, so that no one player embodied a typical Ellingtonian sound. For example, in 1928, Ellington's first full
year in the Cotton Club, his trumpet section featured James "Bubber"
Miley for his growling plunger-mute style and Arthur Whetsol for his
sweet, poignant lyricism. Miley was the band's first original voice, and
Ellington's style owes a lot to Miley's brief and erratic tenure. When Miley
left in early 1929, Ellington replaced him with Cootie Williams, who,
without being asked, gradually realized he needed to learn the growling
style from trombonist Joe "Tricky Sam" Nanton. Nanton, too, had a
unique tone, unlike any trombonist in the instrument's history. He had
a way of using mutes, with the plunger alternately covering and uncovering the straight mute to convey an eerie, distorted vocal quality – like a
soulful singer with a powerful tone and affect but whose language eludes
clear understanding. In contrast to Nanton, Ellington also had the singing,
"legitimate" sound of valve trombonist Juan Tizol, whose soaring tone
would grace many Ellington compositions (and some of his own) from the
late 1920s onward. Moreover, by the late 1920s Ellington had in place a
unique reed section that included the deep, burly baritone saxophone
sound of Harry Carney, the sensuously lyrical alto saxophone style of
Johnny Hodges (who did not read music very well), the sweet melodic
lines of alto saxophonist Otto Hardwick (who did), and the versatile
clarinetist Barney Bigard. Along with Ellington's elegant, stride-based
piano style, the rhythm section boasted the fine banjo player Fred Guy,
an expert showman in drummer Sonny Greer ("like a high priest, or a king
on a throne," according to Ellington),[16] and Wellman Braud, whose pro-
pulsive string bass notes (sometimes *bowed*), four to the bar, mark him as a
rarity in the 1920s, when most bands had a tuba player pumping out the
bass on beats one and three.

Certain members of the band held musical dualities within themselves.
Bigard, with his uniquely "woody" tone, would alternate between high-
range obbligato filigree and a rich broad tone in the clarinet's low, or
chalumeau, register.[17] Williams claimed that playing with a plunger mute
and playing "open" were his "two ways of being," and that "both expressed
the truth."[18]

Another duality embedded in the Ellington band was its blend of
urbane New York sophistication and the traditional New Orleans influence. Wellman Braud and Barney Bigard both hailed from the Crescent

City, and at least three other Ellingtonians – Bubber Miley, Cootie Williams, and Johnny Hodges – were heavily influenced by New Orleans players: Miley by King Oliver's use of mutes, Williams by Louis Armstrong's majestic virtuosity, and Hodges by Sidney Bechet's uniquely singing tone and improvisational fluency. Ellington had heard and admired Bechet even before coming to New York, and hired him briefly in 1925.[19] As Stanley Dance put it, "Ellington was probably more strongly aware of the importance of the New Orleans idioms – rhythmic and otherwise – than any other bandleader in the city [of New York], but he would characteristically utilize it over the years in an extremely individual manner."[20]

Most of the musicians who joined Ellington in the late 1920s and early 1930s stayed in his band for many years, even decades, and they comprised the compositional palette for what Billy Strayhorn would call "the Ellington Effect" – a unique style developed out of the tonal personalities of the band members. These band members were not just colors added to – or just interpreters of – Ellington's compositions, since, for Ellington, composition was more like supervision of a group project than a solitary act of artistic creation. Williams noted that collaboration was the norm: "Everyone made suggestions," he recalled, "it was a family thing."[21]

Toward jungle style and beyond

With these men at the fabled Cotton Club, known as the "Aristocrat of Harlem," Ellington cultivated his first distinctive style, a merger of his band's unique tonal personalities and the demands of creating evocative music for a stage show featuring scantily clad young women billed as "tall, tan and terrific." The style was known as *jungle music*, and it comprised all or most of the following: the muted, growling horns of Miley (or a surrogate) and Nanton; slithering chromatic melodies and harmonies cast in a minor mode; low and murky sonorities; and a heavy four-beat tread in the bass and drums. Why such sonic markers came to stand for the jungle (especially the *African* jungle) in 1920s America may be attributed partly to well-established patterns of musical exoticism (in which a musical device such as chromaticism signals something distant and unfamiliar), partly to the primitivist African scenes in the Cotton Club shows, and partly to the Ellington band's unique timbres.

The sound itself was in place before Ellington entered the Cotton Club, in the first strain of *East St. Louis Toodle-O*, a 1926 piece that stands out as the earliest Ellington standard. It stayed in his book after its premiere, became the band's signature theme until *Take the "A" Train* replaced it in the early 1940s, and was performed and recorded by Ellington many times until his death almost half a century later.[22] It is also perhaps the most discussed piece in the early Ellington repertoire.[23]

Most commentators single out the piece as a prime early example of the "Ellington Effect," especially in the unique sonorities of the principal theme. That theme, which became the band's calling card through the 1930s, combines Bubber Miley's trademark growling trumpet melody with a recurring countermelody whose "ominous undercurrent," as Mark Tucker aptly calls it, arises from its minor mode and a "bottom-heavy scoring" that includes a baritone saxophone, a bass (tuba or bowed string bass, depending on the recording), and a single line of left-hand piano.[24] Tucker observes other qualities that make the piece exceptional and anticipate several later Ellington works: the unusual delay of the secondary theme; the "linear" piano accompaniment instead of the standard rag-derived "oom-pah" style; and an "overall architectural balance."[25]

East St. Louis had yet something else that caught the ear of perceptive listeners. The writer Ralph Ellison remembered hearing it on radio during the Depression and found that "our morale was lifted by something inescapably hopeful in the sound," something both "triumphant" and "moody."[26] Ellison here captures something that so many Ellington commentators explore: a contrast of musical moods that has the power to summon a richly complex feeling.

Another pre-Cotton Club piece that summons elements of the jungle style, but likewise reaches beyond it to evoke a complex affective alloy, is *Black and Tan Fantasy*, first recorded in the spring of 1927 and revisited many times after that. The title itself conjures contrast – the *racial* contrast unique to the "black and tan" nightclubs that catered to a mixed-race clientele. The piece has attracted commentary on the marked *musical* contrasts between the two strains: one, an earthy but subtle blues chiefly featuring Miley's growl style, and the other, a sweet and lyrical song featuring Otto Hardwick's alto saxophone. And the final cadence based on Chopin's "funeral march" from the Piano Sonata No. 2 in B-flat minor has been heard variously as a dark and dour conclusion and as an unexpectedly witty musical wink. Indeed, few commentators agree on the artistry or meaning of the piece's contrasts. Gunther Schuller, for example, singles out Miley's "great contribution" in the blues sections, but he hears the songful interlude (presumably written by Ellington, not Miley) to be "slick trying-to-be-modern show music" and "quite out of character with the rest of the record."[27] Mark Tucker brought a more balanced approach to the piece, noting the dominance of Miley's theme and tone but also eloquently describing Hardwick's "silky alto" melody and the rich harmony that begins on a flat-VI chord as "evoking the illicit pleasures and over-ripe atmosphere of a 'black and tan' cabaret."[28] In the end, despite the piece's stylistic variety, Tucker hears the piece as a creative "compound" unified by Ellington's alchemy.[29] Between Schuller's insistence on the piece's irreconcilable disparities and Tucker's claims for its unity stands Ralph Ellison's vivid, affect-driven description of the piece's "blues-based tension . . . [that] warned us not only to look on the darker side of life but also to remember the enduring necessity for humor, technical mastery, and creative excellence."[30] More recently Scott DeVeaux and Gary Giddins have staked out another position that finds a more specific scenario. They argue the stark musical contrasts in *Black and Tan Fantasy* support a satirical program. In this view, Ellington intended the contrasts to be unsatisfactorily resolved, because the racial coexistence encouraged by a black-and-tan nightclub can only be a fantasy whose brief existence leads inevitably to the death knell tolled by the Chopin funeral march.[31] The notion that Ellingtonian unity comes through uneasily reconciled contrasts recurs in later pieces, as we'll see.

If *East St. Louis Toodle-O* and *Black and Tan Fantasy* stand out as Ellington's most original pre-Cotton Club pieces, then *The Mooche* shows how some of their elements could be harnessed for service at the Cotton Club. Like the earlier pieces, *The Mooche* – whose title Ellington borrowed from a slow, southern African-American dance[32] – would become a staple in Ellington's repertory after its initial recording in 1928, and is often cited as an exemplar of jungle style for its haunting introduction and first strain. R. D. Darrell, a young critic who wrote the first substantive commentary on Ellington's music, called the piece "a mighty lament that is as expressive and sinewly constructed as anything Ellington has ever written."[33] Darrell's awkward neologism "sinewly" shows a writer reaching for unusual language to describe the musical density of Ellington's pieces, packed with call-and-response, harmonic richness, and colorful surprise, as in the opening of *The Mooche* (Example 6.1, from the October 17, 1928 recording).

Ellington recorded *The Mooche* many times. On an April 1930 recording, it begins with a moody vamp whose dynamic swell evokes a menacing deep breath on two sonorities: a C-minor chord and a G-augmented chord (G–B–Eb), whose added sharp-fourth (C♯) and seventh (F) suggest a whole-tone aggregate (G–[A]–B–C♯–Eb–F). These two chords form important pillars in the ensuing first strain, an unusual 24-bar AAB structure and one of the most memorable passages in Ellington's Cotton Club period. A trio of close-harmony clarinets plays the piercing principal phrase, heard twice starting high and slithering down almost an octave. Miley's restless, growling trumpet responds to both phrases, filling out the 16-bar strain. The chromatic harmony, in which each chord shares at least one pitch with its predecessor and the other voices move just a step away, suggests the sensibility of a pianist using

Example 6.1. *The Mooche* (October 17, 1928), beginning. (See end of chapter for permissions and publishing information.)

his fingers to find the next chord, and indeed, pianistic chord voicing was an Ellington calling card.[34] After the first strain, in another typically Ellingtonian move, the sinister mood evaporates and the second strain offers a contrast in mode, harmony, form, and texture. An oddly perky 12-bar blues in E-flat features a brass trio playing the main idea: a three-note syncopated figure borrowed from the end of the clarinets' chromatic slides in the first strain (Example 6.2).

In the October 17, 1928 recording, another blues strain assumes an entirely different character with a call-and-response between two of Ellington's great soloists with strikingly dissimilar styles (Example 6.3). Miley's bluesy trumpet chatter strains against the harmony with A♮s over A-flat minor (mm. 6–7) and over a B♭ seventh chord (mm. 10–11). Johnny Hodges injects contrast on alto saxophone with sweeter and shapelier melodic curves that hew closer to their respective chords.

These examples typify Ellington's use of the blues. He wrote few pieces that offer a straightforward sequence of 12-bar blues choruses, but he wrote many that embed the blues in an interior section of a larger form. There he changes the mood, harmony, and melody of the piece to avoid predictability and to highlight contrast.

Example 6.2. *The Mooche* (April 3, 1930), second strain, beginning.

Example 6.3. *The Mooche* (October 17, 1928), Bubber Miley and Johnny Hodges call-and-response.

Musical "pictures" beyond category

Contrasts within pieces helped Ellington insure that variety foiled easy typecasting – racial and musical. For Ellington these contrasts may reflect an effort to translate into music the "mental picture" he claimed to have "always" needed to fuel his musical imagination.[35] As in *Black and Tan Fantasy*, we can only hazard educated guesses as to what pictures Ellington had in mind for individual pieces. Titles may help but may also be deceptive. A case in point is *Saturday Night Function*, recorded three times in 1929.[36] The title suggests a boisterous party, but the piece maintains a measured poise throughout. Moreover its formal structure juxtaposes two contrasting ideas: secular and sacred. The four grinding 12-bar blues choruses at the work's core conjure a humid, sultry late-night dance, but the two plagal, hymn-like 16-bar strains that frame the blues section summon an entirely different mood of religious solemnity.

The overall shape and sound of the piece inspires speculation about a possible "picture," program, or concept: the framing 16-bar strains have an unmistakable churchy quality to which the interior blues choruses form a gritty, and decidedly secular, foil, as if the Saturday night function required a kind of opening blessing and a benedictory conclusion. Even if the story or picture behind *Saturday Night Function* remains elusive, it is instructive to reflect on how such contrasts between the blues and hymn-like or quasi-spiritual themes served more overt programmatic ends for the later Ellington. A similar contrast informs his extended work of 1950, *Harlem*, with its recurring blues motif and its quasi-jungle music passage that yields to a contemplative spiritual theme.[37] Ellington's pieces *Beggar's Blues* (recorded May 28, 1929) and *Lazy Duke* (recorded November 20, 1929) likewise feature a blues-based structure concluding on a hymn-like plagal cadence.

In *Immigration Blues*, an earlier work (recorded December 29, 1926) that Mark Tucker has called "Ellington's first important piece using the blues form," we can hear the seeds of these ideas. Tucker highlights the contrast between the non-blues first strain, with its "folk-like melody" and its "plagal cadences and hymn-like solemnity," and the blues-based second strain, and he goes on to suggest a possible "picture" that Ellington had in mind: "The opening section," writes Tucker, "suggests the folk culture of the southerner, steeped in religion and expressed through the spiritual. The second section might have represented the southerner after relocation – now with a case of the blues."[38] The notion that Ellington deployed blues and spiritual (or hymn) styles as antithetical means toward programmatic ends throughout his career deserves closer and more systematic scrutiny.

Mood Indigo (1930) is neither blues nor spiritual, yet it is suffused with a quiet pathos and reveals Ellington's gift for working expressively within standard pop-song structures. Its signature sound featured an instrumental trio drawn from different sections of the band: muted trumpet, muted trombone, and clarinet (Example 6.4). Such a combination of instruments was rare in early big-band jazz, which favored the clear separation of brass and reeds. But the trio sonority was unusual not only for its timbre mixing. It was unusual, too, for its voicing, with the brass moving in thirds on top, while Bigard played the bottom of the triad in his clarinet's chalumeau register. The overall effect was intimate and melancholy.[39]

Mood Indigo exemplifies what Ellington referred to as a "plaintive" style he began to cultivate in the late 1920s.[40] Two other, lesser-known gems in this style are *Black Beauty* and *Awful Sad*, both featuring trumpeter Arthur Whetsol, whose "poignant" tone Gunther Schuller called "the

Example **6.4.** *Mood Indigo* (December 11, 1930), beginning. (See end of chapter for permissions and publishing information.)

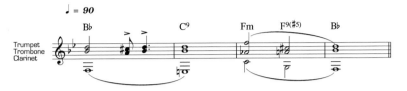

Example **6.5.** *Black Beauty* (October 25, 1928), first strain, beginning. (See end of chapter for permissions and publishing information.)

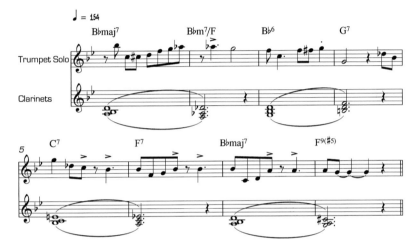

perfect melodic vehicle" for Ellington's subtle "mood vignettes."[41] Dedicated to the memory of Florence Mills, a dancer who died at 32 and whose funeral attracted a throng of more than 100,000,[42] *Black Beauty* represents the first in a series of musical "portraits" that Ellington would create for great African-American artists and leaders throughout his career, including Bert Williams, Bill "Bojangles" Robinson, and Martin Luther King. Both *Black Beauty* (Example 6.5) and *Awful Sad* (Example 6.6) show Ellington's penchant for tight, block-chord voicing moving chromatically (even pianistically) under a solo. (Ellington also recorded *Black Beauty* as a piano solo on October 1, 1928.) Both pieces also demonstrate a built-in paradox of musical contrast: even Ellington's most poignant ballads had a syncopated current.

The stylistic range of Ellington's early work goes even further, and in many cases Ellingtonian ideas resonate in other music. *Birmingham Breakdown* (1926), for example, features a jerky, syncopated rhythm that would reappear in popular songs, as Ellington ruefully noted in a magazine article he published in 1931.[43] A repeated figure in a trumpet solo of *Hot and Bothered*

Example 6.6. *Awful Sad* (December 20, 1928), first strain, beginning. (See end of chapter for permissions and publishing information.)

(1928) – a hard-charging piece itself based on the old standard *Tiger Rag* – became the riff on which Fletcher Henderson's band based its out-chorus on *Honeysuckle Rose*. Meanwhile, it seems hard to believe that the same composer wrote *Creole Love Call* (1927) and *Old Man Blues* (1930), for example, yet both take existing tunes and remake them almost beyond recognition. *Creole Love Call*, based in part on King Oliver's 1923 recording of *Camp Meeting Blues*, features a haunting wordless vocal by Adelaide Hall; here the voice becomes another tonal personality in Ellington's palette. *Old Man Blues* is not a blues at all, but an exuberant dance-band arrangement of Jerome Kern's "Ol' Man River." Another Ellington standard from this period was *Rockin' in Rhythm*. Heralded by a signature Ellington piano solo, the piece has a memorably perky main tune and a relaxed swing – "as close as an arrangement gets to sounding spontaneous," Ellington himself claimed – that kept it in the band's book for decades.

Rhapsody in race

In 1931, toward the end of his Cotton Club residency, Ellington ventured into new creative territory with his first effort at an extended original composition that filled both sides of a 78 rpm record: *Creole Rhapsody*. The title itself suggests a spirit of dialogue with musical issues and landmarks of the 1920s, as if Ellington is creating a racially marked response to George Gershwin's *Rhapsody in Blue*; this issue has been explored in depth by John Howland in a book that perceptively integrates musical and social issues.[44] Although the piece features sonorities and forms that Ellington

Example 6.7. *Creole Rhapsody* (Duke Ellington), Part 1 (January 20, 1931), beginning. Publishing rights administered by EMI Mills Music Inc. (ASCAP).

had used before, it is like nothing else he had ever conceived, and more importantly, it shows how Ellington wanted to create music beyond category – specifically beyond the racial and musical categories in which his music tended to be placed. *Creole Rhapsody* is, as Ellington called it, "the seed from which all kinds of extended works … later grew." Ellington recorded the piece twice in 1931; the following analysis is based on the first recording in January. In both versions the piece sounds rhapsodic indeed, and the listener's principal reference point is a recurring, syncopated three-note motif in block chords. This motif launches the piece, recurs throughout Part I, and reappears slightly altered in Part II – often in call-and-response textures as in the opening bars (Example 6.7).

The January 1931 version makes perhaps the clearest case for a programmatic reading of the piece. Repeated listenings reveal a clear overall form in Part I, which, once grasped, makes audible Part II's formal truncations, extensions, and departures (see Figure 6.1). Those formal anomalies, moreover, raise once again a strong sense of a programmatic impulse. Indeed, coming to terms with the work's unusual structure brings us close to grasping its larger programmatic goals and leads us back to familiar Ellingtonian contrasts and paradoxes.

In the January 1931 version, Part I comprises a large-scale ternary (ABA) form in which the first and third sections present the principal theme in a 32-bar a-a-b-a popular song form. Yet the theme is chiefly rhythmic and harmonic in nature and avoids the easy tunefulness of a pop song, and its outlines become obscured through timbral variations. The pop-song structures frame the interior "B" section, comprising a pair of blues choruses featuring solos by clarinet and trumpet in turn. Also emerging in the blues section is a sonority that will reappear in Part II and haunt the piece: a tight snare roll on the backbeat.

PART I

0:00	a (8 bars)	brass play three-note motif with clarinet obbligato
	a (8 bars)	as above
0:32	b (8 bars)	piano solo
	a′ (8 bars)	piano solo
1:06	c (12 bars)	clarinet melody over brass chords
1:32	c′ (12 bars)	open trumpet solo over sax chords and emerging snare roll on backbeats
1:57	a (8 bars)	brass, with alto sax obbligato and snare-roll motif
	a (8 bars)	as above
2:32	b (8 bars)	saxes lead, with brass reinforcement
	a (8 bars)	brass and alto sax, with snare roll growing softer, ending with cymbal crash

PART II

0:00	a (8 bars)	unaccompanied piano solo, slow, rubato, like an introduction, featuring three-note motif rhythmically altered ("Part II rhythm")
0:21	c (12 bars)	unaccompanied piano solo
0:48	x (4 bars)	saxes and brass
0:56	c″ (16 bars)	extended blues form (5+5+6) featuring trombone soli melody with soft snare roll
1:32	c′ (12 bars)	muted trumpets
1:59	a (8 bars)	saxes play theme (in Part II rhythm), with trumpet obbligato
	a (8 bars)	open trumpets (in Part I rhythm) with baritone sax obbligato
2:33	x (8 bars)	strange transitional section, slows down, seems to lose direction, then animated piano heralds final section
2:50	a (8 bars)	full ensemble (Part II rhythm), loud blaring
	coda	full ensemble continues on two-note cadential motif as snare roll continues

Figure 6.1. Formal outline of *Creole Rhapsody*, first version (January 20, 1931, Brunswick recording)

Part II is like a distorted-mirror reflection of Part I, suggesting that, as in his later masterpiece *Diminuendo and Crescendo in Blue* (1937), Ellington aimed to exploit the structural dictates of the 78 rpm record, which required the piece's division into two parts lasting a little over three minutes each. Whereas in *Diminuendo and Crescendo* Ellington creates a *dynamic* contrast between the record's sides, in Part II of *Creole Rhapsody* Ellington takes Part I's themes and forms and effectively dismantles their orderly presentation, while truncating and elongating the parts. Part II begins with Ellington's unaccompanied piano solo based on the principal theme's "a" section, but the solo alters the rhythm of the three-note motif, and its ruminating rubato style has an introductory quality. That quality gets confirmed when Ellington launches into the blues section, at tempo, after only eight bars. The interior blues choruses thus come "early" and are then altered, the first alteration featuring trombone soli in close harmony playing an irregularly phrased extension to 16 bars (5+5+6), and the second alteration featuring the muted trumpets in a standard 12-bar form, with the increasing prominence of Sonny Greer's tight snare roll on the backbeat.[45] Now the principal theme at last returns in what promises to be its full 32-bar original form, but at the point where we expect the bridge (the "b" section of the a-a-b-a song form), the music gradually slows and seems to lose direction in a strange transitional section, until Ellington's animated piano heralds the final section: a full ensemble fanfare on the principal theme yielding to a brief, soft coda featuring a two-note cadential motif supported by Greer's snare rolls.

A listener cued to Ellington's claim that he "always" had a "mental picture" when creating his compositions hears tantalizing hints of a program in *Creole Rhapsody*. In Part I's juxtaposition of pop-song and blues forms Ellington brings together, in what amounts to a *segregated* ternary form, white Tin Pan Alley and a black folk idiom. (Just four years earlier, in the song "Can't Help Lovin' Dat Man," Jerome Kern and Oscar Hammerstein II had used the same two forms together – a blues verse and an a-a-b-a refrain – to signal the dramatic significance of their troubled heroine Julie's mixed-race status in *Show Boat*.) In Part II's anomalies one might hear a portrayal of confusion, or perhaps a challenge to the established order, when the lines between and within these forms become blurred – in the rubato piano "introduction" that segues directly into the blues; in the extension of the blues form; in the insinuating presence of Greer's snare roll; and, particularly, in the near breakdown of musical progress, which Ellington's piano rescues with an energetic and heraldic lead-in to the final, fanfare-like restatement of the main theme. Certainly the rubato passages in Part II show that Ellington had more than dance music in mind. What exactly he did have in mind remains hard to define. Ellington withheld a verbal explanation of the piece's meaning, but he left plenty of palpable musical clues for anyone seeking to imagine the "picture," or concept, that informed the unusual trajectory of *Creole Rhapsody*.

Irving Mills and Ellington's public persona

The musical contrasts and anomalies that Ellington wrote into pieces such as *Creole Rhapsody* – and into the shorter, more formally conventional compositions that preceded it – also played out in his public persona. Ellington consistently strove to present a dignified, sophisticated image to a public that was saturated with stereotyped images of African Americans as primitive or happy-go-lucky or "natural" musicians. The key figure in helping to shape that persona was Ellington's manager Irving Mills, beginning in late 1926 or early 1927. Mills's impact upon Ellington's career was immediate and long-lasting, even though their contractual association lasted less than a decade. Mills strove to present Ellington as an original, high-class artist. He recognized that crafting an image of Ellington as a dignified artist – a "genius," as his advertising repeatedly emphasized – could yield commercial success.[46] In this aim, Mills was preceded by the white publisher John Stark, who during the heyday of ragtime promoted rags by Joplin and other black composers as classy, sophisticated works, helping to break down popular prejudice against the music, and, by extension, against African Americans in general.[47] In both cases the publishers mixed commercial and idealistic impulses not easily disentangled. Ellington, who had learned the importance of management and good publicity in Washington, D.C., backed up Mills's advertising with his band's dignified image, dramatic stage presence (including lighting effects that other bands did not use), and original compositions in a variety of styles.[48] The band's Cotton Club residency, begun within a year after Mills joined forces with Ellington, enhanced its image. Ellington remembered the club as "a place that commanded more respect . . . than any I've ever heard of."[49]

Mills's agency projected Ellington and his music not just in advertising, but through every available medium: radio, records, sheet music, theater, and film. Under Mills's auspices Ellington won his Cotton Club job in the very year that the Columbia Broadcasting System began carrying music from the venue on network radio. Under Mills, too, Ellington began making more records, writing and playing more of his own compositions (instead of pop tunes by others as most bands did), and publishing sheet music and arrangements of his work. Theater and film work brought an aura of prestige and good pay.

It should be noted that Ellington had written for the theater before Mills came along. In 1925, Jo Trent convinced Ellington to write songs for an all-black revue called *Chocolate Kiddies*. The staging, typically, portrayed plantation and Harlem scenes. The songs ranged from the lyrical ballad "With You," to an old-fashioned ragtime number "Jim Dandy," to the up-tempo, Charleston-inspired dance tune "Jig Walk," which continued to be played by jazz musicians into the 1940s.[50] Although *Chocolate Kiddies* never came to Broadway, it toured the European continent for two years (with Sam Wooding's band, not Ellington's, playing the music). As Tucker notes, the show thus "played a vital role in introducing Europeans to black-American performers and musical styles."[51] The sustained popularity of *Chocolate Kiddies* increased Ellington's appetite for theater music, and thus helped pave the way for his work at the Cotton Club.

As many commentators have noted, playing regularly for the slick and sexy Cotton Club revues stoked Ellington's musical imagination, but that experience also led to more theater work, which won further prestige and renown. In 1929, the band got a huge break when it appeared onstage in the Florenz Ziegfeld-produced Gershwin musical *Show Girl*, a job that Ellington called "valuable in terms of both experience and prestige."[52] The next year saw a string of high-profile appearances: at the Fulton Theatre with the French actor-singer Maurice Chevalier in a revue produced by Charles Dillingham; at Harlem's Lafayette Theatre in another revue; and, for a two-week stint, at the Palace, Manhattan's premier vaudeville theater.[53] Mercer Ellington recalled the band's unusual "flair for dramatic accent" and "greater sense of theater" than other bands.[54] This made good artistic and commercial sense in a time when Broadway and Harlem mingled freely. Barney Bigard recalled that Sunday night at the Cotton Club was "'Professionals' Night,' meaning all the Broadway stars would come because there were no shows on Sundays on Broadway."[55] Harlem went to Broadway, too, when the revue *Blackbirds of 1928* (with songs by Jimmy McHugh and Dorothy Fields) was brought downtown after its successful run in the Cotton Club.

It may strike later observers as painfully ironic that most of Ellington's stage appearances in the late 1920s, in the Cotton Club and beyond, took place amid the persistent tropes of minstrelsy. In what Ellington called the "valuable" experience in Ziegfeld's *Show Girl*, for example, the band, smartly clad in red uniforms, played Gershwin's "Liza" on a terraced minstrel-show platform as 45 young women in minstrel costume sat on the steps below.[56] But in fact, Ellington and his band's dignified bearing and creative musicality (and its ability to *read* music) subverted minstrel clichés for all who watched and listened.

Minstrelsy also framed Ellington's film appearances, even as his on-camera presence actually reinforced his sophisticated stage persona. That points to another Ellingtonian contrast. The 19-minute short *Black and Tan* (1929), with its all-black cast, evokes the exotic, sexualized atmosphere of the Cotton Club shows as it tells the story of a romance between a handsome, dignified bandleader (Ellington) and a dancer (Fredi Washington) that ends tragically when the dancer collapses on stage and later dies to the strains of *Black and Tan Fantasy* accompanied by a wailing chorus. The plot also occasioned the use of *Black Beauty*, further blurring the lines between fantasy and reality, as dancer Florence Mills had died not long before the film was made. Krin Gabbard has noted how one scene offers contrasting images of African Americans. It begins with a well-dressed Ellington and Arthur Whetsol playing their instruments in the act of composing (in this case, *Black and Tan Fantasy*). Two black comedians then show up as piano movers to repossess Ellington's instrument. Gabbard observes that the "illiterate, shiftless" stereotype acted out by the piano movers serves to remind the viewer how far Ellington and Whetsol stand from them.[57] In the full-length feature

Check and Double Check (1930), Ellington again appears very much as himself, as he and his tuxedoed sidemen perform on a bandstand in a posh Long Island estate. Although very much the smiling entertainer in his only scene, Ellington's sartorial elegance, pianistic virtuosity, and musical leadership stand in sharp contrast to the benighted bumbling of the blackface main characters, Amos and Andy, then at the peak of their popularity on radio. Moreover, as Gabbard notes, the film marked a first: a black band given a credited role in an otherwise all-white film.[58] Both films place Ellington's dignity and sophistication in the foreground as racial caricatures surround him within and beyond the cinematic frame. It remains a contradiction of the era that Ellington was able to achieve such prominence only with the help of a powerful white agent.

In his public persona and above all in his music, Ellington devoted his entire career to challenge what Ralph Ellison called Americans' "inadequate conceptions of ourselves."[59] While the racial assumptions of 1920s New York certainly restricted black musicians, they reflected a larger trend that also benefited the musicians: a surge of interest in all things African American. The historian Ann Douglas has written that "the 1920s were the decade in which the Negroization of American culture became something like a recognized phenomenon,"[60] and few musicians showed a savvier sense of how to use that phenomenon to their advantage – and to forge an artistic synthesis from its unresolved tensions – than young Duke Ellington.

Acknowledgements

Cambridge University Press thankfully acknowledges the following sources for providing the rights to publish the Ellington excerpts in this chapter:

Awful Sad
By Duke Ellington
Copyright © 1929 Sony/ATV Music Publishing LLC in the U.S.A.
Copyright renewed
All Rights Administered by Sony/ATV Music Publishing LLC, 8 Music Square West, Nashville, TN 37203
Rights for the world outside the U.S.A. controlled by EMI Mills Music Inc. (Publishing) and Alfred Publishing Co., Inc. (Print)
International Copyright Secured All Rights Reserved
Reprinted by Permission of Hal Leonard Corporation

Black Beauty
By Duke Ellington
Copyright © 1928 Sony/ATV Music Publishing LLC in the U.S.A.

Notes

1 John Edward Hasse, *Beyond Category: The Life and Genius of Duke Ellington* (New York: Simon & Schuster, 1993), 18–19.

2 *The Duke Ellington Reader*, ed. Mark Tucker (New York: Oxford University Press, 1993), 45.

3 Ibid., 135.

4 Ibid., 255.

5 Ibid., 49, 135.

6 In the chapter "Jazz and African American Modernity" from his book *What Is This Thing Called Jazz? African American Musicians As Artists, Critics, and Activists* (Berkeley: University of California Press, 2002), 35–39, Eric Porter explores Ellington's "New Negro vision." While focusing chiefly on post-World War II generations, Guthrie P. Ramsey Jr. uses the term *Afro-Modernism* to connote the creative tension faced by black musicians in a variety of idioms from the 1920s onward, in *Race Music: Black Cultures from Bebop to Hip-Hop* (Berkeley: University of California Press, 2003), 27–30 and chapter 5.

7 Tucker, *Ellington: The Early Years* (Urbana: University of Illinois Press, 1991), chapter 1.

8 Rex Stewart, *Boy Meets Horn*, ed. Claire P. Gordon (Ann Arbor: University of Michigan Press, 1991), 113. See also the comments of Ellington's erstwhile colleague Elmer Snowden, who reported that Victor Records demanded a specific style of "Negro music," in

Stanley Dance, *The World of Swing: An Oral History of Big Band Jazz* (1974; reprint, New York: Da Capo, 2001), 53.

9 Tucker, *Early Years*, 290n11.

10 Cab Calloway and Bryant Rollins, *Of Minnie the Moocher & Me* (New York: Thomas Y. Crowell, 1976), 88.

11 Writing on Ellington regularly featured such monikers. See, for example, *Ellington Reader*, ed. Tucker, 23 and 51, for articles from 1925 and 1931 that use such words in reference to Ellington, his music, and other black performers.

12 Gunther Schuller, *Early Jazz: Its Roots and Musical Development* (New York: Oxford University Press, 1968), 339.

13 Schuller, *Early Jazz*, 339. Among textbooks, a recent one by Frank Tirro adopts Schuller's categories. See Frank Tirro, *Jazz: A History*, 2nd edn. (New York: W. W. Norton, 1993), 222–23. Eric Porter also reiterates the five categories in *What Is This Thing Called Jazz?*, 35.

14 As Porter has put it, Ellington's "New Negro vision depended upon access to multiple forms of musical knowledge," in *What Is This Thing Called Jazz?*, 36.

15 For how these forces affected Fletcher Henderson's early career and how they may be seen as a kind of Harlem "renaissancism," see Jeffrey Magee, *The Uncrowned King of Swing: Fletcher Henderson and Big Band Jazz* (New York: Oxford University Press, 2005), 5–6, 28–33.

16 Quoted in Mercer Ellington, *Duke Ellington in Person: An Intimate Memoir* (Boston: Houghton Mifflin, 1978), 66.

17 "Barney had that woody tone that Pop always adored," wrote Mercer Ellington, *Duke Ellington in Person*, 65.

18 Stanley Dance, *The World of Duke Ellington* (1970; reprint, New York: Da Capo, 1981), 106.

19 For details on Ellington's early links to Bechet, and their mutual admiration, see Tucker, *Early Years*, 75, 111, 113.

20 Stanley Dance, liner notes to *The OKeh Ellington* (Columbia C2K 46177), 9.

21 Dance, *World of Duke Ellington*, 102.

22 On the term "Toodle-O," which connotes a kind of dance, and its pronunciation ("todalo"), see Tucker, *Early Years*, 250–51.

23 See, for example, Schuller, *Early Jazz*, 326–29, and Tucker, *Early Years*, 248–58. Tucker, acknowledging Schuller's effort, provides the most in-depth exploration of the piece and its history; Schuller's analysis has proven the most influential, and it stands

behind the brief discussion of the piece in Ken Rattenbury, *Duke Ellington: Jazz Composer* (New Haven: Yale University Press, 1990), 18–19.

24 See Tucker's transcription from the Victor recording of December 1927, judged by Schuller as featuring an "improved format" compared to the three earlier recordings. Tucker, *Early Years*, 253 (Schuller's claim quoted on page 251).

25 Tucker, *Early Years*, 255.

26 Ralph Ellison, "Homage to Duke Ellington on His Birthday," in *Going to the Territory* (New York: Vintage Books, 1987), 218.

27 Schuller, *Early Jazz*, 330–31.

28 Tucker, *Early Years*, 245.

29 Ibid., 247.

30 Ellison, "Homage to Duke Ellington," 218.

31 Scott DeVeaux and Gary Giddins, *Jazz* (New York: W. W. Norton, 2009), 135–37.

32 Hasse, *Beyond Category*, 140.

33 Darrell article of December 1928 quoted in *Ellington Reader*, ed. Tucker, 35.

34 See Schuller, *Early Jazz*, 343, and Rattenbury, *Jazz Composer*, 24.

35 *Ellington Reader*, ed. Tucker, 233.

36 The following discussion is based on the post-Miley Ellington band's May 28, 1929, recording under the pseudonym of Sonny Greer and his Memphis Men.

37 For a thoughtful analysis of the piece, see Mark Tucker, "Ellington, Edward Kennedy (Duke)," in *The International Dictionary of Black Composers*, ed. Samuel A. Floyd, Jr. (Chicago: Fitzroy-Dearborn, 1999), I: 421–22.

38 Tucker, *Early Years*, 233.

39 For a fuller discussion of *Mood Indigo*, see Tucker in *International Dictionary of Black Composers*, ed. Floyd, I: 419–20.

40 Quoted in ibid., 420.

41 Schuller, *Early Jazz*, 341.

42 Hasse, *Beyond Category*, 141.

43 See *Ellington Reader*, ed. Tucker, 49.

44 John Howland, *Ellington Uptown: Duke Ellington, James P. Johnson, and the Birth of Concert Jazz* (Ann Arbor: University of Michigan Press, 2009), especially 167–71.

45 Sonny Greer featured this distinctive percussion sonority on at least two earlier recordings: *Big House Blues* and *Rocky Mountain Blues*, both in October 1930.

46 Harvey G. Cohen, "The Marketing of Duke Ellington: Setting the Strategy for an African American Maestro," *The Journal of African American History* 89/4 (Autumn 2004): 301.

47 Jeffrey Magee, "Ragtime and Early Jazz," in David Nicholls, ed., *The Cambridge History of American Music* (Cambridge University Press, 1998), 396–97.

48 Mercer Ellington repeatedly notes his father's early and persistent belief in the power of good management and publicity, and traces it to a Washington, D.C., character named "Black" Bowie whom "you could call a schemer, an idea man, a dreamer, or a hustler." Mercer also notes that his father "had been coached by Irving Mills, one of the all-time masters" in shaping a public persona and manipulating the media in maintaining it. See *Duke Ellington in Person*, 14, 78.

49 Quoted in Cohen, "The Marketing of Duke Ellington," 297.

50 For a discussion of the *Chocolate Kiddies* music, see Tucker, *Early Years*, 120–35. See also John Franceschina, *Duke Ellington's Music for the Theatre* (Jefferson, NC: McFarland, 2001), 11–15.

51 Tucker, *Early Years*, 120.

52 Quoted in Hasse, *Beyond Category*, 122.

53 Hasse, *Beyond Category*, 125–27. For a sense of the central and consistent role of theater in Ellington's career, see Franceschina, *Duke Ellington's Music for the Theatre*.

54 Mercer Ellington, *Duke Ellington in Person*, 66.

55 Barney Bigard, *With Louis and the Duke* (New York: Oxford University Press, 1986), 46–47.

56 Hasse, *Beyond Category*, 122, quoting Mercer Ellington.

57 Krin Gabbard, *Jammin' at the Margins: Jazz and American Cinema* (Chicago: University of Chicago Press, 1996), 163.

58 Ibid., 167.

59 Ellison, "On Initiation Rites and Power: Ralph Ellison Speaks at West Point," in *Going to the Territory*, 42. Thanks to Richard Crawford for drawing my attention to this statement.

60 Ann Douglas, *Terrible Honesty: Mongrel Manhattan in the 1920s* (New York: Farrar, Straus and Giroux, 1995), 77.

7 Survival, adaptation, and experimentation: Duke Ellington and his orchestra in the 1930s

ANDREW BERISH

Historical accounts of Duke Ellington and his orchestra gravitate toward a handful of iconic moments in the band's long career: their time at the Cotton Club in the late 1920s, for instance, or the concerts at Carnegie Hall in the early 1940s (it was at the band's January 1943 appearance that Ellington introduced his epic musical history of African-American life, *Black, Brown and Beige*). The years from 1931, when the band ended its run at the Cotton Club, through 1939, when Billy Strayhorn, Ben Webster, and Jimmie Blanton arrived, have not received nearly the same attention. The era lacks a defining event to focus historical understanding. What we have, instead, is a patchwork of stories.

Some accounts focus on the band's successful European tours, particularly its first trip to Britain and France in 1933. These tours were extremely important, and helped establish Ellington's stature as an international star. For other writers, the decade was defined by the death of Ellington's mother in 1935, a signal tragedy that fundamentally altered his life (and generated the creative spark for one of his most ambitious extended works, *Reminiscing in Tempo*). These events, important as they were, do not do justice to the complex trajectory of the band during the Depression. The successes of the early 1930s, including that first European tour, were followed by financial struggles, even at the height of the "swing" phenomenon. During these commercial ups and downs, Ellington reconfigured his band several times by adding dynamic new musicians: Lawrence Brown, Ivie Anderson, and Rex Stewart. And even as Ellington struggled through several personal crises, his public persona grew more defined and confident. Through a carefully developed image, Ellington became a brand synonymous with elegance and sophistication. He became an icon not only of American popular music but also of African-American life.

The twists and turns that Ellington and his band faced during these years were closely tied to the social upheaval triggered by the nation's historic economic crisis. The Great Depression upset nearly every stratum of American society and nearly every public and private institution in the nation. Most pertinent for a commercial dance band was the near-collapse of the popular music industry – the combined workings of Tin Pan Alley,

Hollywood, theaters, dance halls, radio, and recording. Approaching the precipice in the early 1930s, the industry rebounded mid-decade and experienced massive national growth and consolidation, spurred on in large part by the commercial phenomenon of swing.

Navigating this rapidly changing cultural landscape required flexibility, and Ellington had to define and then redefine his organization and his approach to music several times. When the orchestra left the Cotton Club in 1931, it was a traveling dance band, a recording phenomenon, a New York City show band, and a purveyor of "authentic" black American music. By the end of the decade, the band was also an international concert hall attraction. No single term or "moment" can sum up this era. As for so many Americans, the 1930s were years of survival, adaptation, and experimentation.

Travel

The Ellington orchestra would spend most of the Depression years on the road, though in generally much better conditions than most bands, black or white. Once their gig at the Cotton Club ended in February 1931, the orchestra began an aggressive touring schedule that lasted for months. Radio broadcasts had served the group particularly well, helping to spread their music across the continent. This, in turn, led to more broadcasting and performance opportunities. "By early 1933," historian Stuart Nicholson writes, "forty-five radio stations across America were broadcasting Ellington's live performances."[1] This was especially impressive given that Ellington could not secure a corporate sponsorship – a common and lucrative way of funding such frequent radio appearances. Ellington and his orchestra rode through the worst years of the economic collapse, 1931 and 1932, relatively secure in their bookings and commanding high fees from promoters and venues. Ironically, it was with the revival of the music industry and the emergence of swing that their fortunes changed.

Unlike the many black "territory" bands that plied the theater and dance halls across specific regional areas, the Ellington orchestra traveled all across the country. In 1934 Ellington hired private railroad cars (two sleepers and a baggage car), a luxury that became his preferred mode of transportation. The railroad cars provided lots of privacy and solved the difficulties of locating overnight accommodations – a problematic task for African Americans in many parts of the country. Later, when wartime requisitions of trains forced the band on to buses, many members complained of the reduced circumstances.

New York City was their ostensible base of operations, and they would return to the Cotton Club (relocated downtown to West 48th

Street after 1936) several times during the 1930s, but only for one-off musical revues, including the "Cotton Club Parade" in April, 1933 (featuring Ethel Waters), another "Cotton Club Parade" in 1937 (also with Ethel Waters), and a third the following year (this one featuring an all-Ellington score). These return trips were brief and they were soon back out on the road, playing one-nighters for dancers interspersed with longer engagements at theaters in major cities such as Chicago and Detroit.

Setting what would become a predictable pattern, the band's first tour after leaving the Cotton Club lasted 18 weeks and included stays in Boston, Chicago, Detroit, Peoria (Illinois), Joliet (Illinois), Omaha, Minneapolis, Des Moines, Denver, Kansas City, St. Louis, Indianapolis, Buffalo, Toronto, and Philadelphia.[2] Many of the shows were theatrical revues similar to those at the Cotton Club. But they also played for the dance-hungry patrons at the Savoy Ballroom in Harlem. Taking what gigs they could, the band tailored the shows for their audiences, offering stage shows as well as music for dancers.

In 1932 Ellington took his band for its first trip to the West Coast, with important extended stops in San Francisco and Los Angeles. While in southern California the band played a small part in the Amos 'n' Andy feature film *Check and Double Check*, performing a bit of *East St. Louis Toodle-O* and then *Old Man Blues*. The band received a film credit, an unprecedented occurrence for a black band in an otherwise all-white production (the "black" characters of Amos and Andy were played by white actors Freeman F. Gosden and Charles J. Correll) and an indication of both manager Irving Mills's negotiating power and Ellington's growing reputation.

Given Hollywood's influence and power in American culture, film appearances were a logical avenue for promotion.[3] A year after *Check and Double Check*, the band appeared in two more films: a Paramount Pictorial and a short film titled *Bundle of Blues*. In 1934 they returned again to Los Angeles for guest spots in *Murder at the Vanities* and *Belle of the Nineties*, the latter a feature for Mae West. In March of 1935 Mills signed a deal for a nine-minute short devoted exclusively to Ellington and his band. Titled *Symphony in Black: A Rhapsody of Negro Life*, the film was one of the first realizations of Ellington's longstanding desire to tell in music the history of black life in America, an artistic impulse that historian Mark Tucker believes was rooted in the black pageants and theater productions a young Ellington saw growing up in the vibrant, historically conscious black community of Washington, D.C.[4]

In consultation with director Fred Wall, Ellington created a complete score for the short, combining three previously recorded pieces with new material.[5] The film's episodic structure is organized around a narrative frame that has Ellington fulfilling a commission for a "symphony of

Negro Moods." After showing Ellington at the piano in the midst of composing, the film cuts back and forth between the bandleader, the full orchestra at the symphony's "premiere," and elaborate dramatizations that chronicle different aspects of day-to-day black life. This fascinating and unusual document testifies to Ellington's desire to create complex musical compositions that push the bounds of the three-minute Tin Pan Alley popular song. Less significant movie appearances followed in the low-budget production *The Hit Parade* and another Paramount Pictorial showing the band recording *Daybreak Express.*

In the summer of 1933 the orchestra embarked on its first overseas tour for concerts in Great Britain, the Netherlands, and France. The trip was a major success, and they played to full houses on all their stops. Fans came out in force, and the critics were overwhelmingly positive, praising the band for its dynamism, virtuosity, and distinctive sound. The band even found it had a royal fan: at a private party hosted by Lord Beaverbrook, a starstruck Prince of Wales sat in for Sonny Greer and played drums. The heir to the British throne even tried to join the band during a London recording session (Scotland Yard forbade it for security reasons). For Ellington the trip was a revelation: "The main thing I got in Europe," he told *Swing* magazine in 1940, "was spirit. That kind of thing gives you courage to go on. If they think I'm that important, then maybe I have kind [of] said something, maybe our music does mean something."[6] For the band, the tour was a heady experience, a whirlwind of new sights and sounds. Britain and France were hardly racial utopias – English bandleader Jack Hylton, who organized the visit, found it difficult to lodge the entire band together in London because no hotel would permit so many black guests.[7] Still, the band members were treated with a level of respect and admiration that was rare in their home country.

For the remainder of the decade the band kept up an intense touring schedule. In the fall of 1933 Ellington initiated his first tour of Southern cities, presenting his musicians with a new set of challenges. Over a two-month span they played in Dallas, San Antonio, Oklahoma City, and a host of theaters scattered across Texas, Louisiana, Alabama, Georgia, and Tennessee. The decade ended, not surprisingly, with another grand tour: a return visit to Europe in 1939. A labor dispute scuttled plans for performances in Britain, so the band spent just over a month playing dates in the Netherlands, Belgium, France, Norway, and Sweden.

The centrality of travel to Ellington is best captured by his love for – even obsession with – trains. As many scholars have pointed out, the train has been a longstanding trope in black music, both lyrically and instrumentally. Trains formed a key part of Ellington's personal mythos and provided him with subject matter for his music and literary writing. Even when his musical work was not explicitly about trains, he spoke and wrote about their influence on his composing. In the autobiographical sketches collected in *Music Is My Mistress*, he recalls the central role of train travel in the creation of *Reminiscing in Tempo*, an extended composition written soon after his mother's death: "I found the mental isolation to reflect on the past. It was all caught up in the rhythm and motion of the train dashing through the South, and it gave me something to say that I could never have found words for."[8]

His best-known train composition of the 1930s – and one of the band's most striking tunes during this time – is *Daybreak Express* (1933). The recording, issued along with *Dear Old Southland*, is programmatic: the band mimics a train as it pulls out of the station, gathers momentum, and eventually slows down, coming to a complete stop. Horns and reeds sound train whistles while the rhythm section mimics the slow gearing up of the giant steel wheels. After reaching traveling speed, the band plays the song proper, a melody using the chords of the jazz standard *Tiger Rag*. To end the performance, the band reverses the introduction, gradually slowing the orchestral train to a complete stop. *Daybreak* was a daring, highly original work for its time, featuring unusual harmonizations and timbres; but it was also a "conventional" 32-bar popular song. From small works to large ones, Ellington nearly always constructed his original compositions using the forms, procedures, and aesthetics of commercial popular song (and, of course, the blues).

Scholars and critics have justly celebrated *Daybreak* as a showpiece of Ellington's original writing skills. Yet what we *hear* is much more than a single composer's voice. *Daybreak* features little improvisation, but includes many of the band's most distinctive solo instrumentalists. About a minute into the performance, alto saxophonist Johnny Hodges plays two dazzling eighth-note runs over a chromatically descending chord progression. In the middle of the piece, trumpeter Arthur Whetsol plays a string of dramatic high E-flats. Trumpeter Cootie Williams closes the performance with a virtuosic display of half-valving. *Daybreak* evokes travel and mobility – defining aspects of the orchestra's life at the time. But the work also embodies the push-and-pull between instrumental virtuoso and ensemble composer: a characteristic tension of the band, and a primary aesthetic engine of its creativity.

Duke and the band

Though it changed personnel many times over the course of its nearly 50-year existence, the Ellington orchestra always remained the primary vehicle and inspiration for its leader's musical compositions. Ellington is inexplicable without reference to his band, especially during the peak years of his commercial success in the 1930s and 40s.

Critics during the era and later historians have pointed out again and again that the band was unique in its depth of instrumental talent. Many of these musicians contributed compositional ideas as well as improvised solos, and several members complained that their compositional contributions were never fully acknowledged by Ellington.[9] During the 1930s Ellington self-consciously adopted the mantle of composer as well as bandleader, a development closely allied with Irving Mills's marketing strategy. From this point on, Ellington would present himself as *the* central creative force in the band. According to banjo and guitar player Freddy Guy, "[Irving Mills] wanted Duke to be a star, not the band. The men were just rank and file. But I could see through him, man, and [Mills] hated me for it."[10]

Despite this development, Ellington was a remarkably hands-off manager, avoiding conflict when he could. Such a leadership style created some awkward situations. In the fall of 1934, Ellington hired a second bass player, Billy Taylor, to join Wellman Braud, Ellington's bassist since 1927. Scholars still debate why the bandleader did this. Hiring a second bass player was not exactly a vote of confidence for Braud, a New Orleans native whose "slap-bass" style was sounding increasingly out of date. In fact, Mills tried to get Braud's salary cut in half when Taylor joined. The rest of the band threatened to quit en masse, but despite this show of support, Braud soon departed. If Ellington indeed hired a replacement without telling the original employee there was a problem, this would cast the bandleader's much-noted discretion and politeness in a more negative light.

Biographer John Edward Hasse believes there were aesthetic reasons for the duplicate bass players. Ellington was always in search of new orchestral sounds, and a second bass player allowed new arranging possibilities, freeing at least one of the bassists to add melodic or rhythmic counterpoint. There is undoubtedly some truth in Hasse's assessment; hiring Taylor in 1934 broke new ground for ensemble instrumentation. Later, other bandleaders such as Charlie Barnet would also experiment with two simultaneous bass players. Still, it is unclear whether Ellington considered the aesthetic possibilities before or after he found himself with two bassists.[11]

Despite this drama, Ellington's band was relatively stable over the decade as he added several new, enduring members. In 1931 Ellington hired vocalist Ivie Anderson, and then, a year later, trombonist Lawrence Brown. Listeners today tend to encounter Ellington's music as entirely instrumental, but during the 1930s the band recorded many popular songs showcasing Anderson's smooth, swinging, and precise singing, including *It Don't Mean a Thing (If It Ain't Got That Swing)* (1932),

Stormy Weather (1933), *Truckin'* (1935), *Kissin' My Baby Tonight* (1936), *It Was a Sad Night in Harlem* (1936), and *Rose of the Rio Grande* (1938).

Lawrence Brown's presence made the Ellington group the first dance band to permanently feature three trombones. Brown's warm, full, and clear sound and his impressive solo skills (listen to 1938's *Rose of the Rio Grande*) provided the trombone section with a dramatic new voice and a sharp contrast to both Joe "Tricky Sam" Nanton's plunger-muted, "wah-wah" style and Juan Tizol's distinctive valve trombone sound. Brown, writes Gunther Schuller, "combined lyricism, 'hot jazz,' swing and consummate technical command in a synthesis that no other trombonist at the time could muster."[12]

Of the other personnel additions during the decade, one of the most significant was trumpeter Rex Stewart in 1934, replacing Freddie Jenkins, who left because of illness. Stewart's presence helped stabilize a section that saw many personnel changes.[13] As with his other star instrumentalists, Ellington wrote specific works to feature Stewart and his innovative half-valve playing. The first of these, *Trumpet in Spades*, was recorded in 1936.[14] The second and more celebrated work was *Boy Meets Horn* (1938). In 1936 Ellington created an unusually large number of these concert features: besides *Trumpet in Spades*, there was *Echoes of Harlem* for trumpeter Cootie Williams; *Clarinet Lament* for clarinetist Barney Bigard; and *Yearning for Love* for Lawrence Brown. Many of Ellington's songs were designed as solo instrumental features, even if they were not presented as such by the titles.

Ellington also permitted (and participated in) small-group recording sessions that featured his band members in different settings.[15] Perhaps the most famous recording to come out of these sessions was *Jeep's Blues*, issued under Johnny Hodges' name in 1938. The record became a big jukebox hit, and featured Hodges on soprano saxophone (not his customary alto sax) supported by Cootie Williams, Lawrence Brown, Harry Carney, and the Ellington rhythm section.

For all his original compositional activity of these years, Ellington was often engaged in adapting and reworking commercial Tin Pan Alley songs. Sometimes, as with his version of Harold Arlen and Ted Koehler's *Stormy Weather* (1933), these were hits; other times they flopped. In 1938 Ellington recorded an original titled *La De Doody Do*, which according to biographer Barry Ulanov was inspired by the popular cartoon strip *Barney Google* and tried to capitalize on the mainstream fascination with the "hip" lingo of swing fans. The up-tempo tune featured Anderson singing "La De Doody Do / This funny phrase / La De Doody Do is now the craze," a wishful prognostication given its anemic sales.[16]

Irving Mills and Ellington both knew the importance of a hit song, but finding one could be elusive. A few original compositions – *Mood Indigo*

(1930), *Sophisticated Lady* (1933), *Moonglow* (1936), *Caravan* (written by Juan Tizol, 1936), and *Prelude to a Kiss* (1938) – turned out to be surprise hits for the band. However, many of Ellington's original pop songs became hits for other orchestras. Ellington's beautiful 1936 ballad *In a Sentimental Mood* was a big earner for the Benny Goodman and Ozzie Nelson bands. Ellington also spent a great deal of time re-recording older compositions. New versions of *Creole Love Call*, *Black and Tan Fantasy*, *East St. Louis Toodle-O*, and *Birmingham Breakdown* all featured significant changes from the originals, and provided opportunities to feature the band's new instrumental voices on familiar and well-rehearsed material.

The 1930s closed with the addition of three new members that would dramatically change the Ellington orchestra's sound and approach. During a stay at Pittsburgh's Stanley Theatre in 1938, Ellington first met a 23-year-old pianist and composer named Billy Strayhorn. A year later Strayhorn joined the group as a backup pianist, though he soon developed into something much more significant: Ellington's trusted musical confidant and a composer in his own right. Tenor saxophonist Ben Webster joined in December 1939, making the reed section five members strong. Plunger expert Cootie Williams left the band in 1940 and was soon replaced by Ray Nance, a musical jack-of-all-trades. Hired as a trumpet player, Nance was also an accomplished singer, dancer, and violinist. Arguably the most significant hiring was bassist Jimmie Blanton in October 1939. The young bassist had a tremendous sound and driving rhythmic sense that fundamentally changed the group's sense of swing. Blanton's virtuosity would play a defining part in the band's late 1930s and early 1940s recordings.

The end of the decade saw one final personnel change, though it did not involve musicians. In 1939 Ellington ended his relationship with Irving Mills, and signed with the William Morris Agency for management and Robbins Music for publishing. And when his contract expired with Columbia Records, he signed with a competitor, Victor. The break with Mills was a turning point for Ellington and reflected, among other things, his growing confidence and desire for control over his musical career. From the beginning Mills had made sure his fingerprints marked anything and everything produced by the band – even claiming writing credit on many tunes. William Morris saw Ellington differently than Mills had, and encouraged the bandleader in his desire to write extended, often socially conscious compositions.[17] The 1940s would see an explosion of politically oriented musical works, many featured at the Carnegie Hall concerts of the 1940s.

As Hasse writes, "Ellington's players now came from Boston, New York, Washington, Alabama, New Orleans, California – even the West Indies. Part of the contribution that each made to the orchestra was his or her regional accent."[18] A once local phenomenon centered in New York

City had, through radio, recordings, and traveling, become truly national in scope. From this vantage point, the band's position in American society, particularly African-American society, was unique: a regional phenomenon, nationalized through technology, now represented a diverse cross-section of black American life in terms of geography and class. This diversity of people and talent was reflected not only in the unique solo improvisations of the instrumentalists, but also in their highly distinctive timbres. The Ellington band offered listeners an innovative and highly influential ensemble sound that reflected its abundance of distinctive instrumental voices and personalities.

Confronting swing

The 1930s saw profound shifts in public musical taste. The decade began with the music industry in crisis, as record sales plummeted in the first years of the Depression. During these years, public taste in jazz and dance band music shifted away from the "hot" sounds of the 1920s and toward a "sweet" sound that emphasized less improvisation and more moderate tempos, toned-down rhythms, and familiar timbres. Bandleaders such as Guy Lombardo who specialized in this sound did very well, while other bands such as Paul Whiteman's moved away from "hot" jazz arrangements and performing styles. Midway through the decade, however, sweet dance band music rapidly lost mainstream popularity to a new big band style – swing – that was decidedly "hotter" and much more obviously indebted to African-American musical practices. The swing dance band sound featured sharp antiphony between instrumental sections; a more even, driving, four-beats-to-the-bar rhythm; and hotter soloing. By mid-decade this youth-oriented version of dance band music became a national cultural phenomenon. Ironically the Ellington orchestra, which had played a major part in the style's creation – their 1932 recording *It Don't Mean a Thing (If It Ain't Got That Swing)* was a musical and lyrical ode to the style's characteristic groove – struggled for a commercial foothold.

Ellington's artistic inclinations and his desire to be a composer of serious music coexisted with an equally strong drive to be commercially successful. Throughout his career, Ellington was never aloof from broader trends in the popular music world. When sweet jazz held sway in the early 1930s, Ellington obliged with ballads in that style. And when swing took hold, he adapted his band again, recording many pieces in the mainstream swing style practiced by Glenn Miller and Tommy Dorsey. In interviews from the era, Ellington was often critical of the media hype surrounding swing and frequently distanced his band from the musical and business practices of the swing industry. But his criticism was tempered by a strong desire to be a part of this lucrative juggernaut that had energized millions of young and often fanatical listeners. Pieces such as *Buffet Flat, Hip Chic, Battle of Swing*, and *Steppin' into Swing Society* (all 1938) – with their fast, four-to-the-bar dance tempos, riff-based melodies, unison sax solis, and rapid, sectional call-and-response – epitomize swing-era arranging and performing practices. With these songs, the orchestra tried to meet the phenomenon head-on. Yet as Gunther Schuller points out, these recordings still reflected Ellington's approach to harmony and timbre, especially his penchant for highly chromatic and disjunct melodic lines and unexpected chords.[19] These traits may have been partly responsible for the relatively poor sales of these "swing" tunes.

Though he was reportedly reluctant to participate, Ellington also took his group to several "Battle of the Bands" contests, which became a major part of the swing culture. Not surprisingly, the Ellington orchestra more than held their own, allegedly "defeating" such hard-driving black dance bands as Chick Webb's and Jimmie Lunceford's. They also participated in one of the larger popular music events of the late 1930s: the "Carnival of Swing," held May 29, 1938, on Randall's Island in New York City. Close to 25,000 people attended the festival, and the group received an intensely positive reception, playing beyond their allotted time to satisfy the enthusiastic crowd. The growing cultural importance of the new hot dance band jazz was highlighted when Benny Goodman played Carnegie Hall in January 1938. Although Ellington was not invited to perform, he generously allowed Cootie Williams, Harry Carney, and Johnny Hodges to participate in the historic performance.

While navigating this commercial landscape, Ellington was also working on compositions that challenged the formulas demanded by the musical marketplace. He had long harbored a desire to create larger, more ambitious musical compositions than the standard three-minute popular song. This desire received a noticeable boost from the growing number of critics writing about Ellington as a "serious" composer. Interest in Ellington among the classical music intelligentsia grew rapidly in the early 1930s. In 1932, at the invitation of composer and teacher Percy Grainger, Ellington spoke to and performed for a composition class at New York University. Grainger's subsequent comments comparing Ellington to Delius and J. S. Bach sparked a cross-Atlantic debate on the aesthetic importance of the black bandleader's compositions.[20]

Ellington experimented with larger forms in the 1920s, but in the 1930s produced a series of lengthy and ambitious works: *Creole Rhapsody* (1930), *Symphony in Black* (for the 1935 film), *Reminiscing in Tempo* (1935), and *Diminuendo in Blue / Crescendo in Blue* (1937). For all their originality, these works were not without precedent; as John Howland has shown, they were rooted in the "symphonic jazz" and musical theater traditions developed by white bandleaders such as Paul Whiteman and African-American composers such as Will Marion Cook, as well as the chorus-based arranging common to dance band elaborations of Tin Pan Alley song.[21] However, their larger scope and synthetic nature gave Ellington new ways to explore the relationship between improvisation and composition and the formal possibilities inherent in popular song form and the blues. For instance, *Diminuendo in Blue / Crescendo in Blue*, originally issued on two sides of a 78 rpm disc, offered a radical decon-struction and then reconstruction of the familiar 12-bar blues. The opening 12-bar blues choruses – loud and melodically dense – are extended and elided in disorienting ways. The formal instability is matched by a harmonic restlessness: *Diminuendo* modulates five times in just under two-and-a-half minutes. True to its name, the first half ends quietly with just piano and bass. The second half, *Crescendo in Blue*, works in reverse, starting from a bare-bones, *pianissimo* statement of the 12-bar blues and then building increas-ingly complicated ensemble variations in one long, 3-minute crescendo.

An icon of black life

It was during the 1930s that Ellington's public persona – his celebrity – became fully realized, the result of his growing confidence and Irving Mills's intense publicity machine. Ellington was deeply admired not only by music fans, but also by cultural and intellectual leaders in black communities across the country. His most direct political statements (and these were hardly ever direct) would come in the following decade, but in the 1930s the bandleader was frequently involved in many timely social issues, particularly those specific to the African-American community.[22] In 1933 the band played a week's engagement at Harlem's Lafayette Theatre to raise money for the neighborhood's poorest residents. In March 1935 the band was part of the "Scottsboro Ball" held at the Savoy Ballroom to raise awareness and finan-cial support for the "Scottsboro boys," nine young men being held in Alabama on rigged charges of raping two white women.

Even when not part of public political events, Ellington was widely admired in the African-American community. Young men such as pho-tographer Gordon Parks were profoundly impressed and influenced by Ellington's public demeanor of elegance, dignity, and sophistication.[23] The legacy of blackface minstrelsy, "coon songs," and other demeaning popular representations of African Americans still permeated American cultural life. Ellington's dapper, cosmopolitan image was a profound challenge to the predominant representations of black Americans in the entertainment industry.

The explosion of interest in the 1930s for "indigenous" American folk cultures, inspired in part by a powerful Leftist populist movement, drew many artists and intellectuals toward previously ignored cultural materials. A diffuse group of intellectuals and musicians, mainly white, eagerly sought out various forms of black music as proof of the nation's rich store of authentic art. The ethnographic work of John and Alan Lomax is perhaps the most famous example, but many artists were swept up in this search for authentic American folk traditions. Gershwin's 1935 opera, *Porgy and Bess*, combined elements of black folk music (Gershwin spent time visiting the black Gullah community in the Georgia Sea Islands), Tin Pan Alley song-style, and modernist classical forms and techniques. *Porgy and Bess* was promoted as an honest-to-God American opera constructed in part from the nation's musical vernacular. Ellington – who was working out his own compositional synthesis of American vernaculars – spoke out candidly (and uncharacteristically) about Gershwin's opera, claiming it was not "true to and of the life of the people it depicted."[24] Ellington's comments here and in many other interviews show how self-conscious he was of his position straddling musical cultures. With this in mind, we can understand Ellington's unhappiness when John Hammond criticized his dalliances with the elite world of classical composition. From a distance of 70-plus years, Hammond's attacks seem naïve and myopic, but they reflect the intense, fiery debates that played out not just among jazz critics but also in the larger left-wing intellectual circles that Hammond was part of.

The public Ellington visible on theater stages or in interviews was never exactly the same person as the private man. He came from a middle-class background, and never experienced the grinding poverty that was so prevalent in many black communities throughout the nation. During the early 1930s, when the worst of the Great Depression sent unemployment rates close to 25 percent, Ellington was making a healthy income, though not in the range of white bandleaders such as Paul Whiteman or Abe Lyman. In his book *Duke Ellington in Person: An Intimate Memoir*, Ellington's son, Mercer, remembers being keenly aware of his family's financial comfort during these hardest of hard times. He recounts moving to a much bigger house and having new, fashionable clothes: "When I went to school in a brand-new pair of flannel pants and a turtleneck sweater, of whatever was the extreme style then, it makes for differences with the other kids and I had to face a new kind of animosity." At the same time, Mercer testifies that his family's wealth "tended to elevate Pop even more" in the eyes of the black community.[25] Through intelligence, talent, and ambition, Ellington had achieved financial success in a white man's world. The image of Ellington's wealth, though, sometimes outran its reality. He had his share of financial crises over these years – once right after the stock market crash in 1929, and later from 1935 to 1937, when on the heels of his mother's death the music industry experienced a profound realignment around the white swing bands of Goodman, Shaw, and the Dorseys.

Ellington's public face – the dapper, even-tempered voice of black music – came under great strain after the personal tragedies of mid-decade. The most significant was without doubt the death of his mother, Daisy, on May 27, 1935. The bandleader was devastated and completely incapacitated for several weeks, unable to lead the band or write music. Once back at work and on the road, Ellington composed *Reminiscing in Tempo*, which he described as "a detailed account of my aloneness after losing my mother."[26] Sadly, Ellington's father, James Edward ("J. E."), died two years later in October 1937.

Ellington's love life was also turbulent. Having separated from his first wife Edna (Mercer's mother) in 1928, Ellington began an affair with singer Mildred Dixon a year later. Sometime in early 1938 he met Beatrice Ellis (known as "Evie"), a showgirl at the Cotton Club. An affair developed quickly, and Ellington moved in with Ellis, leaving behind Mildred, Mercer, and his sister Ruth in the Harlem apartment at 381 Edgecombe Avenue. According to Mercer, he and Ruth realized that to be with Duke they would have to move, because their father "didn't want to come back and face Mil[dred]." Not long after Ellington moved in with Ellis, Ruth and Mercer left Mildred and the apartment for new lodgings nearby.[27] Ellington's relationship with Ellis soon turned stormy, in part because Ellington still refused to divorce Edna.

Despite these personal upheavals, the 1930s saw Ellington emerge as both a national and international celebrity – fulfilling Irving Mills's marketing dreams. Fittingly for an international musical phenomenon, Ellington celebrated his fortieth birthday (on April 29, 1939) in Stockholm, Sweden. The Swedes' warm reception reflected not only his international stature, but also the deeper transformations of his band during the 1930s. From a local act, impressing New York audiences with its "jungle" sounds and strange harmonies, the band emerged at the end of the decade as a highly respected jazz orchestra with an international reputation. Such cultural standing did not always translate into commercial success, and the 1930s saw the band struggle to maintain its position as a top-draw and top-grossing band. Through the turbulence of the early years of the Depression and the halting recovery of the New Deal, the Ellington orchestra, along with millions of other Americans, survived through adaptation, experimentation, and a little bit of luck.

Notes

1 Stuart Nicholson, *Reminiscing in Tempo: A Portrait of Duke Ellington* (Boston: Northeastern University Press, 1999), 131.
2 Ken Vail, *Duke's Diary: The Life of Duke Ellington, 1927–1950* (Lanham, MD: Scarecrow Press, 2002), 46–51.
3 The movie industry was largely centered in Los Angeles, though Ellington and his band filmed at studios in New York City too.
4 Mark Tucker, *Ellington: The Early Years* (Urbana: University of Illinois Press, 1991), 12–13.
5 Gunther Schuller, *The Swing Era: The Development of Jazz 1930–1945* (New York: Oxford University Press, 1989), 72–74. The previously written and recorded pieces were *Ducky Wucky*, *Saddest Tale*, and *Merry-Go-Round*.
6 Nicholson, *Reminiscing in Tempo*, 149.
7 Barry Ulanov, *Duke Ellington* (New York: Da Capo, 1972), 133–34. First published 1946.
8 Nicholson, *Reminiscing in Tempo*, 86.
9 In an oral history interview for the Smithsonian, longtime trombonist Lawrence Brown described Ellington, somewhat bitterly, as more a "compiler" than a composer of original material. Saxophonist Johnny Hodges – one of Ellington's longest-serving musicians – claimed he would mentally count his "lost" royalty money every time Ellington played one of "his" songs. Other musicians such as clarinetist Barney Bigard have made similar accusations about Ellington's treatment of their alleged musical contributions. Lawrence Brown interviewed by Patricia Willard, July 1976, Jazz Oral History Project, accessed at Institute of Jazz Studies, Rutgers University, Reel 4, transcription pages 35–36; James Lincoln Collier, *Duke Ellington* (New York: Oxford University Press, 1987), 144, 185; Barney Bigard interviewed by Patricia Willard, July 1976, Jazz Oral History Project, accessed at Institute of Jazz Studies, Rutgers University, Reel 2, transcription pages 12–17. Harvey Cohen's new book *Duke Ellington's America* provides a useful and critical summary of these debates over authorship and writing credits in the band. Harvey Cohen, *Duke Ellington's America* (Chicago: University of Chicago Press, 2010), 148–53.
10 Nicholson, *Reminiscing in Tempo*, 159.
11 Ellington deployed this strategy again and again. In 1935 he hired Hayes Alvis as a partner for Taylor. In 1938 Alvis finally decided that two was one too many bass players and left the band. Taylor had just over a year to enjoy the bass duties on his own, because as soon as Ellington discovered Jimmie Blanton, he almost immediately hired the young turk as Taylor's companion. Blanton would have intimidated any bass player at the time, and Taylor soon cracked. In a 1964 interview, Ellington himself tells how Taylor quit in the middle of a gig at the Southland Theatre in Boston – just stopped playing, packed up his bass, and walked out, saying, "I'm not going to stay playing up here with this young boy playing all that bass!" (Nicholson, *Reminiscing in Tempo*, 215). After Blanton died in 1942, Ellington again found himself with two bassists. He hired Junior Raglin as Blanton's replacement, but then added the brilliant Oscar Pettiford in late 1945. Raglin, not surprisingly, soon left.
12 Schuller, *Swing Era*, 54. In his 1976 interview with Patricia Willard for the Jazz Oral History Project, Brown explains how he carefully worked out his solo statements ahead of time because he feared making mistakes. Recordings from later decades show that Brown played nearly the same solo every time he played his signature musical feature, *Rose of the Rio Grande*. His career is a reminder that jazz musicians then and now value consistency, tone, and rhythmic feel as much as innovation or "newness."
13 Along with Bubber Miley's departure in 1929 and Jenkins's in 1934, trumpeter Arthur Whetsol, suffering from a brain tumor, left the band permanently in 1937. Whetsol had been with Ellington since the beginning, and his mental and physical decline, and subsequent death in 1940, deeply affected the bandleader. Once Rex Stewart was aboard, Ellington filled out the section, first with Charlie Allen and then (when Allen left) with Wallace Jones, who would stay with the band until 1944. From the mid-1930s on, Ellington had the three-man trumpet section of Cootie Williams, Rex Stewart, and Wallace Jones.
14 In his book *The Swing Era*, Gunther Schuller, seconding André Hodeir's earlier assessment, describes the tune as an "empty display" of "mindless virtuosity" (84–85). He also lambasts the title for its "unforgivable pun." Spade was a (usually) derogatory term for blacks. Of course the title could also be read as a playful and knowing wink at racist stereotypes.
15 In 1936 Irving Mills acquired the Brunswick company's old music studios and started his own recording labels, Master and Variety. For the "full-priced" Master label, Mills wanted to feature star acts such as the Ellington orchestra. But what to record on the budget Variety label, a line to be marketed to black audiences? A jazz writer and promoter,

Helen Oakley, ultimately convinced Mills to use the Variety label to feature small groups drawn from the Ellington orchestra; John Edward Hasse, *Beyond Category: The Life and Genius of Duke Ellington* (New York: Simon & Schuster, 1993), 205.

16 Ulanov, *Duke Ellington*, 198.

17 Collier, *Ellington*, 195; Cohen, *Ellington's America*, 206.

18 Hasse, *Beyond Category*, 159.

19 Schuller, *Swing Era*, 101–3. From the late 1920s through the 1930s, critics often employed the term "weird" to make sense of Ellington's unusual harmonizations and timbral combinations.

20 The comparison to Delius in particular took on a life of its own, allegedly inspiring Ellington himself to seek out the music of the English modernist composer; *The Duke Ellington Reader*, ed. Mark Tucker (New York: Oxford University Press, 1993), 95. Aside from Grainger's comments, reported in newspaper accounts of Ellington's visit to NYU, American critic R. D. Darrell made similar comparisons to classical composers in "Black Beauty," a lengthy analysis of Ellington recordings published in 1932 in *disques* magazine; *Ellington Reader*, ed. Tucker, 57–65.

21 John Howland, *Ellington Uptown: Duke Ellington, James P. Johnson, and the Birth of Concert Jazz* (Ann Arbor: University of Michigan Press, 2009).

22 Despite this activity, Ellington came under fire from leaders in the black community. Activist Adam Clayton Powell, Jr., later a congressman, criticized the bandleader as a "musical sharecropper" who maintained – seemingly voluntarily – an unjust and unequal creative and business relationship with the white Irving Mills. Such public criticism by a major civil rights leader must have stung Ellington and might partially account for the dissolution of his partnership with Mills in 1939; Collier, *Ellington*, 193–97.

23 Hasse, *Beyond Category*, 216–17.

24 *Ellington Reader*, ed. Tucker, 117. Tucker challenges the veracity of Ellington's comments, claiming the reporter, Edward Murrow, might have exaggerated the bandleader's criticism of the opera. According to Tucker, Ellington himself felt he was misquoted in parts. Tucker still thinks that the underlying voice – and sentiment – is Ellington's.

25 Mercer Ellington with Stanley Dance, *Duke Ellington in Person: An Intimate Memoir* (New York: Da Capo, 1979), 49–50.

26 Duke Ellington, *Music Is My Mistress* (New York: Doubleday, 1973; reprint, Da Capo Press, 1976), 86.

27 Hasse, *Beyond Category*, 219.

8 The 1940s: the Blanton-Webster band, Carnegie Hall, and the challenge of the postwar era

ANNA HARWELL CELENZA

On November 7, 1940, two college friends named Jack Towers and Richard Burris set up their Presto portable turntable in the Crystal Ballroom in Fargo, North Dakota, and made a private recording of the Duke Ellington Orchestra. Both Ellington and the venue's manager had given the men permission, and no one suspected how significant the recording would one day prove to be. Towers and Burris documented an important chapter in jazz history that fateful night in Fargo. Their recording captured a rare glimpse of the ensemble playing in a dance hall setting, where Ellington and his musicians were free – both physically and technologically – from the confines of the recording studio. The recording includes lengthier versions of some of the band's most popular tunes and impressive solos by Ellington, Barney Bigard (clarinet), Harry Carney and Johnny Hodges (alto saxophone), Rex Stewart (cornet), Joe "Tricky Sam" Nanton and Lawrence Brown (trombone), and newcomers Jimmie Blanton (bass) and Ben Webster (tenor saxophone) – the core of what scholars now refer to as the "Blanton-Webster band."

Ellington once stated: "My music talks about the new people I keep meeting, especially the new men who pass through my band and sometimes stay. I use their particular ways of expressing themselves, and it all becomes part of my own style."[1] Although Ellington was attentive to his musicians' individual strengths at every stage of his musical career, the Blanton-Webster years marked a breakthrough in Ellington's output as a composer and a high point in the ensemble's overall cohesiveness.

Jimmie Blanton joined the Ellington organization in 1939, a month shy of his twenty-first birthday. Originally trained on violin, he began playing bass as a student at Tennessee State University, where he performed with the Tennessee State Collegians during the 1936–1937 academic year, and with Fate Marable during summer vacations. Blanton left university in 1938 to work full time with the Jeter-Pillars Orchestra in St. Louis, where he transformed the role of the double bass in jazz, using pizzicato and bowing techniques acquired from playing classical repertoire.[2] In Blanton's hands, the bass became as much a solo instrument as part of the rhythm section, and his hard-swinging virtuosity spurred his colleagues to greater excellence. Ellington first heard Blanton play in 1939 and later admitted, "I flipped like everybody else ... we didn't care about his [lack of] experience. All we wanted was that sound, that beat, and those precision notes in the right places, so that we could float out on the great and adventurous sea of expectancy with his pulse and foundation behind us."[3]

Mesmerized by Blanton's playing, Ellington didn't wait long to get his new prodigy into the recording studio. On November 22, 1939, they cut two sides, *Blues* and *Plucked Again*, the first piano and bass duets ever recorded commercially. More duets came the following year, including the virtuosic showcase *Pitter Panther Patter*. Blanton was also featured on two recordings with the full orchestra, *Jack the Bear* and *Sepia Panorama*.

Ben Webster was invited to join the orchestra in 1940, after Ellington heard him perform during a stop in Boston. Webster had always dreamed of playing with the Ellington organization, and when he took his place next to Johnny Hodges, his longtime idol, magic happened. Webster was the band's first regular tenor sax player, and the driving pulse of his warm, lyrical strains infused the ensemble with fresh energy. Perhaps because of their youth, Blanton and Webster connected right away and their rapport left its mark on the music. Terry Teachout notes that the "closeness of their mutual understanding" can be heard in the live Fargo recording of "Stardust," where "Webster all but whispers Hoagy Carmichael's melody as Blanton accompanies him with self-effacing simplicity."[4]

Trumpeter Ray Nance was a third addition to the Ellington ensemble. Trained in a conservatory setting, Nance was also an accomplished violinist, adding this new timbre to the Ellington compositional toolbox, as in the original 1942 version of *C Jam Blues*. Nance also sang, and is best known as a vocalist for his version of *It Don't Mean a Thing*. Because of his numerous talents – he was also an excellent dancer – Nance quickly earned the moniker "Floorshow."

With the Ellington Orchestra at its peak performance level, 1940 proved to be an epic year. In addition to *Jack the Bear* and the unremittingly intense E-flat minor blues *Ko-Ko* – both astounding three-minute works encompassing the full breadth, vitality, and ingenuity of Ellington's compositional achievements to date – the band laid down a prolific display of new compositions in just a few months. These included *Concerto for Cootie* – a showcase for trumpeter Cootie Williams that André Hodeir called "a bouquet of sonorities" – and *Cotton Tail*, a reference to African-American folklore. Additional tunes included *Dusk*, with its rich sonorities and haunting solos; *Bojangles* and *A Portrait of Bert Williams*, both tributes to preeminent African-American performers; *Harlem Air Shaft*; the dreamy ballad *All Too Soon*; *Sepia Panorama*; *In a Mellotone* – a showcase for inventive call-and-response patterns; *Across the Track*

Blues; and *Warm Valley*, a sensual masterpiece inspired by the landscape of a reclining woman's body.[5]

As band member Rex Stewart recalled, "the band started hitting on all cylinders like a wonderful musical juggernaut."[6] These recordings set a new standard for jazz, and everyone in the ensemble, especially Ellington, realized it. Today, the recordings of the Blanton-Webster band are considered by many to be the pinnacle of the Ellington orchestra, a perfect balance of virtuosity, lyricism, and drive. As English music critic Raymond Horricks noted, the band had "a lust for life" during those years; "it hit harder musically, bit deeper emotionally and swung more animatedly … than any Ellington band that preceded it."[7]

This new, energized sound wasn't simply the result of inspiring performers. A young composer, Billy Strayhorn, joined the Ellington ensemble around the same time, and within a matter of months proved himself invaluable. It was Strayhorn, more than anyone else, who got Ellington thinking about new approaches to writing music. In his autobiography, *Music Is My Mistress*, Ellington admitted Strayhorn's importance in his life:

> [Strayhorn] was my listener, my most dependable appraiser, and as a critic he would be the most clinical, but his background – both classical and modern – was an accessory to his own good musical taste and understanding, so what came back to me was in perfect balance … We would talk, and then the whole world would come into focus. The steady hand of good judgment pointed to the clear way that was most fitting for us. He was not, as he was often referred to by many, my alter ego. Billy Strayhorn was my right arm, my left arm, all the eyes in the back of my head, my brainwaves in his head, and he in mine.[8]

Strayhorn was classically trained and introduced Ellington to modernist works and new ways of thinking about composition. As John Lewis noted upon hearing Strayhorn's vocal arrangement of *Flamingo*, "It had nothing to do with what had gone on in jazz at all before. It sounded as if Stravinsky were a jazz musician." Similar comments were made by Gerry Mulligan: "When Strayhorn came on the scene, he just blew us away … To bring all that complexity to bear and have it be so beautiful was something incredible to everybody who knew anything."[9] Most importantly, Strayhorn reawakened in Ellington an intellectual curiosity that had first taken root during Ellington's formative years.

As Mark Tucker explained in his seminal study *Ellington: The Early Years*, Ellington's privileged upbringing in a middle-class African-American community in Northwest Washington, D.C., instilled his appreciation for a well-rounded education, which included European and American literature, African-American history, and the fine arts.

Ellington also benefited from the role models he found among his parents' friends, who included doctors, lawyers, successful businessmen, and professors at Howard University. Confident in his ability and promise, Ellington never felt excluded from intellectual discourse during his formative years. And even though he avoided the role of political activist, and rarely took a public stand during the 1920s and 30s against policies and practices that offended him, it would be a mistake to categorize him as apolitical or anti-intellectual. Ellington was well aware of the dangers lurking in the shadows of the changing world around him, and as we will see, his creative pursuits during the 1940s were grounded in a lifelong fascination with African-American history and a struggle to break down the categorical boundaries that he believed superficially separated white from black, classical from jazz, and high culture from low culture.

Facing adversity and rising to the challenge

Ellington once said, "I always consider my problems opportunities to do something."[10] This statement was put to the test on January 1, 1941, when Ellington's music was banned from the radio because of a dispute among music industry leaders. The American Society of Composers, Authors and Publishers (ASCAP) had demanded more money from radio networks for the broadcasting rights to works by their members. In response, the networks set up a competing organization, Broadcast Music, Inc. (BMI), and stopped airing ASCAP-registered music. Ellington was an ASCAP member, so he asked his son Mercer and right-hand man Strayhorn – neither of whom belonged to ASCAP – to compose new works for the airwaves.

"Overnight, literally, we got a chance to write a whole new book for the band," said Strayhorn. "It could have taken us twenty years to get the old man to make room for that much of our music, but all of a sudden we had this freak opportunity. He needed us to write music, and it had to be in our names."[11] Strayhorn's *Take the "A" Train* became the Ellington Orchestra's signature tune in 1941. And by the time the ASCAP ban was lifted, Strayhorn had established his role as an invaluable contributor to the Ellington sound.

While Strayhorn worked on writing tunes for radio broadcast, Ellington turned his attention to a new challenge: composing his first full-length stage show. *Jump for Joy: A Sun-Tanned Revu-sical* opened at the Mayan Theatre in Los Angeles in July 1941.[12] As Ellington explained to a reporter, his goal in taking on the commission was

> to give an American audience entertainment without compromising the
> dignity of the Negro people. Needless to say, this is the problem every Negro

artist faces. He runs afoul of negative stereotypes instilled in the American mind by whole centuries of ridicule and degradation. The American audience has been taught to expect a Negro on the stage to clown, and "Uncle Tom," that is, to enact the role of a servile, yet lovable, inferior.[13]

Ellington reflected on these issues again in the Prologue he wrote and performed in *Jump for Joy*:

Now, every Broadway colored show
According to tradition,
Must be a carbon copy
Of the previous edition,
With the truth discreetly muted
And the accent on the brasses.
The punch that should be present
In a colored show, alas, is
Disinfected with magnolia
And dripping with molasses.
In other words,
We're shown to you
Through Stephen Foster's glasses.[14]

Ellington later wrote that *Jump for Joy* was intended to "take Uncle Tom out of the theatre, eliminate the stereotyped image that had been exploited by Hollywood and Broadway, and say things that would make the audience think."[15] Some scholars have wondered if his commitment to the show reflected far-left political sympathies, since most of his collaborators had ties to the Communist Party. Ellington was never an overt left-winger, but like most of the Harlem intellectual-artistic community of the late 1930s and early 1940s, he appreciated the American Communist Party's efforts to fight racism in the Deep South. Ellington was never one to forcefully project his political views, and he kept his cards close to his chest. "We included everything we wanted to say without saying it," he explained when asked why he wrote *Jump for Joy*. "Just to come out on stage and take a soap box and stand in the spotlight and say ugly things is not entertainment."[16]

To put these comments into context, it is useful to remember that Billie Holiday's "Strange Fruit" – an anti-lynching protest song based on a poem by Abel Meeropol, a Jewish school teacher in the Bronx with connections to the Communist Party – had appeared in 1939, and by 1941 it was a million-seller. The song drew mixed reviews from the black community; some praised its powerful visual imagery, while others objected to its portrayal of blacks as victims and claimed its angry, graphic references would only inspire more violence. In 1940, a reporter for the *Baltimore Afro-American* reviewed a performance of "Strange Fruit" in

Washington, D.C., and reflected, "Miss Holiday recently sang the ballad at the Howard Theatre ... and speculation became rife as to whether it actually will incite or condemn mob action."[17] In a public letter to Holiday published in the *Pittsburgh Courier*, Walter White of the NAACP praised the song, but as Frank E. Bolden, a reporter at the paper, explained, White's letter had an ulterior purpose: "What he was really trying to do was to get people like Duke into the game."[18]

Perhaps *Jump for Joy* was Ellington's response. He had a message, no doubt, but his approach was markedly different. Creating engaging entertainment was Ellington's ultimate goal. As he openly admitted to friends and colleagues, he hoped for a box-office success, a show that could carry him and his orchestra all the way to Broadway. Unfortunately, *Jump for Joy* didn't deliver. Although audiences were enthusiastic, most critics were not. Ticket sales slumped, causing *Jump for Joy* to close in just under three months, after 101 performances. The show reopened in November for a week-long run in San Francisco, and in 1959 it was briefly revived in Miami Beach, but it never reached Broadway, as Ellington had hoped.[19]

Ellington tried his hand at writing a musical again in 1946 with *Beggar's Holiday*, an updated version of John Gay's *The Beggar's Opera* (1728). The production opened at New York's Broadway Theater on December 26 but ran for only 111 performances. The cast included both black and white actors, and the prominent depiction of an interracial romance resulted in nightly picketing outside the theater.[20] Ellington struggled to stay on task during the show's production period, so Strayhorn ended up composing most of the music and leading rehearsals.

The failure of *Jump for Joy* and *Beggar's Holiday* disappointed Ellington, but he had bigger concerns. After the U.S. entered World War II, life on the road became increasingly difficult. As Barney Bigard explained:

> Silly things like sleeping bad, eating bad, traveling in crowded trains ... We used to have such bad accommodations on account they took the Pullmans away for the war effort. We traveled on the regular trains and it seemed like the whole country was on the move to someplace or another.[21]

One by one Ellington lost members of his band, either to illness (Blanton died from tuberculosis in July 1942), fatigue (which led to the departures of Bigard, Ivie Anderson and Herb Jeffries) or better contracts elsewhere (Cootie Williams, Juan Tizol). Added to these troubles was the recording ban mounted on August 1, 1942, by the American Federation of Musicians (AFM), which forced the Ellington Orchestra to stop making records for sale to the public. Although the ban was eventually lifted in October 1943, war rationing had raised the cost of shellac, which led to higher production costs and shrinking profits for musicians and bandleaders. Still, Ellington was not disheartened. The hardships he faced simply pushed him towards new challenges, most notably the creation of an extended "symphonic" work suitable for Carnegie Hall.

Composing for the concert hall

Ellington made his Carnegie Hall debut on January 23, 1943. This was a momentous occasion for the composer, a culminating step toward his long sought-after status as a serious musician. Over the previous few years he had established his own publishing business, Tempo Music, and signed with a new record label, RCA. The William Morris Agency, which took Ellington as a client in 1939 after his break with Irving Mills, arranged the Carnegie Hall event and promoted it aggressively, declaring the days leading up to the concert "National Ellington Week." Magazines and newspapers across the country ran features on the historic concert, and tickets became a hot commodity. The list of those lucky enough to secure a seat reads like a who's who of the nation's cultural elite: Marian Anderson, Benny Goodman, Langston Hughes, Alain Locke, Glenn Miller, Eleanor Roosevelt, Frank Sinatra, and Leopold Stokowski, to name just a few.

The highlight of the evening was the premiere of Ellington's *Black, Brown and Beige: A Tone Parallel to the History of the Negro in America*. Ellington described the concept behind the work's title and structure in his spoken commentary from the stage, as well as the printed concert program, which relied on Ellington's press materials for its passage on *Black, Brown and Beige*:

> In this "tone parallel to the history of the American Negro," three main periods of Negro evolution are projected against a background of the nation's history. "Black" depicts the period from 1620 to the Revolutionary War, when the Negro was brought from his homelands, and sold into slavery. Here he developed the "work" songs, to assuage his spirit while he toiled; and then the "spirituals" to foster his belief that there was a reward after death, if not in life. "Brown" covers the period from the Revolution to the First World War, and shows the emergence of the Negro heroes who rose to the needs of these critical phases of our national history. "Beige" brings us to the contemporary scene, and comments on the common misconception of the Negro which has left a confused impression of his true character and abilities. The climax reminds us that even though the Negro is "Black, Brown and Beige" he is also "Red, White and Blue" – asserting the same loyalty that characterized him in the days when he fought for those who enslaved him.[22]

Much has been written about this composition, its connection to Ellington's unfinished opera *Boola*, and his interest in composing a large-scale work that might serve as a corrective to Gershwin's *Porgy and Bess*.[23] As Ellington himself noted shortly before the premiere, "I wrote it because I want to rescue Negro music from well-meaning friends ... It's time a big piece of music was written from the inside by a Negro."[24]

Ellington saw the premiere of *Black, Brown and Beige* as a vital step toward the future of African-American music. The concert itself went well. Ellington and his orchestra played to a sold-out audience. But the following day, when reviews appeared in the press, Ellington's problems began. Critics of all types rejected *Black, Brown and Beige*. They were perplexed that Ellington's new composition did not fit neatly into their preconceived idea of distinct musical genres. Classical critics saw *Black, Brown and Beige* as a flawed attempt at European symphonic form, while jazz critics attacked him for abandoning his origins in dance music and deserting jazz for the concert hall. The collection of news clippings preserved in Ellington's scrapbooks confirms that the controversy over *Black, Brown and Beige* raged for quite a while.[25] Yet for all the debate, few listeners appear to have paid much attention to the composition's social content. According to Ellington, it was this lack of interest in the work's historical perspective that brought about its negative reception in the press.

Ellington wrote a 32-page typescript titled "*Black, Brown, and Beige* by Duke Ellington," which he never published. Now housed in the Smithsonian's Ellington Collection, it is a fascinating read that reveals a great deal about Ellington's knowledge of African-American history and his thoughts about race relations in the U.S. The typescript mixes declamatory prose and poetry that relates the history of blacks in America – a painful history, full of anger and resentment.[26] Scholars who have read the typescript often comment on how different it is from Ellington's more measured public comments about race. After recently reading the script, I was reminded of another luminescent African-American intellectual from roughly the same time period – the historian John Hope Franklin (1915–2009). In his 2005 autobiography, *Mirror to America*, Franklin describes how on countless occasions, when he had been slighted or treated unfairly, he resisted the urge to air his resentment in public. Instead, he vented his anger in a letter, which he then placed in his desk drawer and never sent. Franklin's personal feelings were never made public, but confronting them in this private manner enabled him to draw on them and react to them in what he believed to be a more positive, productive manner. Perhaps this is what Ellington did with his script text for *Black, Brown and Beige*. Although he clearly put great care and effort into the writing and at one point contemplated publishing it, in the end he never did.[27] "You can say anything you want on the trombone," he told a reporter in 1944, "but you gotta be careful with words."[28] Throughout his career, this was one of his guiding aesthetic principles.

At his second Carnegie Hall concert (December 11, 1943), a benefit for Russian War Relief, Ellington played only a few excerpts from *Black, Brown and Beige*. As he told the audience, "We thought we wouldn't play it in its entirety tonight because it represents an awfully long and very important story. And in that I don't think too many people are familiar with the story, we thought it would be better to wait until that story was a little more familiar before we did the whole thing again."[29] At this concert Ellington also premiered the 15-minute *New World A-Comin'* for piano and orchestra. He named the piece after Roi Ottley's 1943 book by the same title. The book, like *Black, Brown and Beige*, tells the history of African Americans before concluding with a look forward into the possibilities of a better future.[30]

After the premiere of *Black, Brown and Beige* journalists queried Ellington constantly about where he stood musically. Was he a musician of jazz or classical music? Ellington responded each time by rebuking preconceived notions of categorical distinctions. Responding to a 1945 article arguing against the idea that Ellington's compositions represented "a growing affinity between jazz and serious music," Ellington had this to say:

> I guess *serious* is a confusing word. We take our American music seriously. If *serious* means European music, I'm not interested in that. Some people mix up the words *serious* and *classical*. They're a lot different. Classical music is supposed to be 200 years old. There is no such thing as modern classical music. There is great, serious music. That is all.[31]

Ellington saw his music as original, modern, and crucially American. This is perhaps most clearly seen in his discussion of "Beige" in a 1947 interview published in *Etude*:

> [T]he Negroid element in jazz turns out to be less African than American. Actually, there is no more of an essentially African strain in the typical American Negro than there is an essentially French or Italian strain in the American of those ancestries. The pure African beat of rhythm and line of melody have become absorbed in its American environment. It is this that I have tried to emphasize in my own writings. In *Black, Brown and Beige*, I have tried to show the development of the Negro in America; I have shown him as he is supposed to be – and as he is. The opening themes of the third movement reflect the supposed-to-be-Negro – the unbridled, noisy confusion of the Harlem cabaret which must have plenty of "atmosphere" if it is to live up to the tourist's expectation. But – there are, by numerical count, more churches than cabarets in

Harlem, there are more well-educated and ambitious Negroes than wastrels.
And my fantasy gradually changes its character to introduce the Negro
as he is – part of America, with the hopes and dreams and love of freedom
that have made America for all of us.[32]

Ellington learned from *Black, Brown and Beige* that the large symphonic
form was not conducive to what he was interested in saying with his music.
So from that point on he turned to a new genre, the suite, when composing
large-scale, programmatic works. For example, at his third Carnegie
concert (December 19, 1944) Ellington performed the four-part *Perfume
Suite*, a collaboration with Strayhorn that attempted to capture the moods
of a woman under the spell of various fragrances. The fourth Carnegie
concert (January 4, 1946) offered the classically inspired suite *A Tonal
Group* as well as the haunting vocalise *Transblucency*, featuring singer Kay
Davis. Ellington's fifth Carnegie program, performed twice on November
23 and 24, 1946, treated audiences to the *Deep South Suite*, a biting
commentary on Jim Crow race relations in the southern states. At his
sixth program, presented on December 26 and 27, 1947, Ellington and
Strayhorn unveiled their *Liberian Suite*, a 27-minute composition commissioned by the nation of Liberia in celebration of its centennial.
Ellington's final Carnegie concert on November 13, 1948, included Billy
Strayhorn's theatrical art song *Lush Life* as well as Ellington's complex
programmatic work *The Tattooed Bride*.[33]

What is a musical score?

An overview of Ellington's most significant compositions in the second
half of the 1940s reveals that he followed two basic rules. First, he turned to
a new genre: the suite. Second, he didn't worry about writing out a
definitive score in the traditional sense. Ellington looked to his band as
his instrument, and he used it much as other composers might use a
keyboard when composing his large-scale works. In general, he tended
to work out the rough draft of a composition in manuscript and then
complete the writing process using the musicians in his band. Manuscript
drafts now held in the Smithsonian's Ellington Collection confirm this
two-stage compositional process, which many Ellington scholars have
described as an *improvisational* method that blurred the line between
his identity as a performer and his aspirations as a composer. There
seems to be a sense of regret in the scholarly community that Ellington
never took the supposed final step of publishing definitive scores of his
serious, large-scale compositions. Gunther Schuller in particular has
described the absence of definitive scores as a weakness separating

Ellington from the likes of contemporaries such as George Gershwin, William Grant Still, and Aaron Copland.

Such denigration of Ellington's efforts is troubling, especially in light of his hard-won stature in American musical culture. Therefore I propose we broaden our conception of "the score" and embrace the technology of recorded sound when discussing Ellington's postwar compositions. Like composers of *musique concrète*, and other twentieth-century avant-garde musicians, Ellington *did* preserve definitive versions of his concert works – not through the opaque and in some respects uncommunicative method of score writing, but rather through the technologically advanced recording process. Simply put, the record was Ellington's score. It was his ideal medium, enabling him to capture the specific timbres, phrasing, and articulations he had cultivated so meticulously on his instrument, the band. As Ellington himself noted in his autobiography under the heading "Dramatis Felidae":

> The cats who come into this band are probably unique in the aural realm . . . because we are concerned with a highly personalized kind of music. It is written to suit the character of an instrumentalist, the man who has the responsibility of playing it, and it is almost impossible to match his character identically. Also, if the new man is sufficiently interesting tonally, why insist upon his copying or matching his predecessor's style?[34]

The recordings Ellington made throughout his career enabled him to capture, definitively, the characteristic voices of his music as he intended them to sound. Consequently, when changes in the music industry during the postwar years – namely a preference for solo singers and small combo groups – caused many big bands to disband for economic reasons, Ellington tapped his own financial resources to keep the ensemble together. Although the second recording ban instigated by the American Federation of Musicians towards the end of 1947 was a blow to him, both artistically and financially, Ellington persevered. Working with the orchestra was the most vital element in his creative process, and he refused to let it go. When the recording ban was lifted in 1950, Ellington concluded the decade that marked his entry into the realm of serious concert music by going into the studio and recording his first long-playing record – an album appropriately titled *Masterpieces by Ellington*.

Notes

1 Nat Hentoff, "The Incomplete Duke Ellington," *Show: The Magazine of the Arts* 4/7 (July/August 1964), no page numbers.
2 According to Barney Bigard in his memoir *With Louis and the Duke* (New York: Oxford University Press, 1980), 74: "When he [Blanton] left St. Louis to join us his professor gave him a list of all the symphony bassists in the towns around the country and a letter of introduction to them . . . Jimmy would go look them up and go take his lesson." As Terry Teachout notes in *Duke: A Life of Duke*

Ellington (New York: Gotham, 2013), 204, Karl Auer, the longtime principal bassist of the St. Louis Symphony Orchestra, served as Blanton's "professor" during his time with the Jeter-Pillars Orchestra.

3 Duke Ellington, *Music Is My Mistress* (Garden City, NJ: Doubleday, 1973), 164.

4 Teachout, *Duke*, 207.

5 John Hasse, *Beyond Category: The Life and Genius of Duke Ellington* (New York: Simon & Schuster, 1993), 267.

6 Rex Stewart, *Boy Meets Horn*, ed. Claire P. Gordon (Ann Arbor: University of Michigan Press, 1991), 189.

7 Peter Gammond, ed., *Duke Ellington: His Life and Music* (London: Phoenix House, 1959; reprint, New York: Da Capo Press, 1977), 96.

8 Ellington, *Mistress*, 156.

9 David Hajdu, *Lush Life: A Biography of Billy Strayhorn* (New York: Farrar, Straus and Giroux, 1996), 86–87.

10 Ralph J. Gleason, *Celebrating the Duke, and Louis, Bessie, Bird, Carmen, Miles, Dizzy and Other Heroes* (New York: Da Capo Press, 1995), 167.

11 Teachout, *Duke*, 221.

12 In recent years, several excellent assessments of *Jump for Joy* have appeared in print: John Franceschina, *Duke Ellington's Music for the Theatre* (Jefferson, NC: McFarland, 2001), 28–45; Gena Caponi-Tabery, *Jump for Joy: Jazz, Basketball, and Black Culture in 1930s America* (Amherst: University of Massachusetts Press, 2008), 175–86; and Harvey Cohen, *Duke Ellington's America* (Chicago: The University of Chicago Press, 2010), 187–94.

13 John Pittman, "The Duke Will Stay on Top," unidentified clipping, probably from a San Francisco newspaper, August or September 1941. Reprinted in *The Duke Ellington Reader*, ed. Mark Tucker (New York: Oxford University Press, 1993), 149.

14 Quoted from an unpublished typescript for *Jump for Joy*, Smithsonian Archives of the National Museum of American History, Ellington Collection, 301, series 4B, box 6, folder 1.

15 Ellington, *Mistress*, 175.

16 Henry Whiston, "Reminiscing in Tempo: An Edited Talk," *Jazz Journal* 20/2 (February 1967): 4–7.

17 Cited in David Margolick, *Strange Fruit: The Biography of a Song* (New York: The Ecco Press, 2001), 74.

18 Ibid., 75.

19 Despite these failures, Ellington himself never lost sight of the show's importance. As David Brent Johnson noted in a radio feature he produced for Indiana Public Media, when a young San Francisco protester confronted Ellington in the early 1960s and asked "When are you going to do your piece for civil rights?" Ellington replied, "I did my piece more than 20 years ago when I wrote *Jump for Joy*." David Brent Johnson, "*Jump For Joy*: Duke Ellington's Celebratory Musical," http://indianapublicmedia.org/nightlights/jump-for-joy-duke-ellingtons-celebratory-musical/ posted February 6, 2008; accessed October 17, 2013.

20 For a detailed description of the production and reception of *Beggar's Holiday*, see Franceschina, *Duke Ellington's Music for the Theatre*, 59–73.

21 Bigard, *With Louis and the Duke*, 77.

22 See "Program for the First Carnegie Hall Concert" in *Ellington Reader*, ed. Tucker, 162. The concert program was attributed to Irving Kolodin.

23 See for example George Burrows, "*Black, Brown and Beige* and the Politics of Signifyin(g): Towards a Critical Understanding of Duke Ellington," *Jazz Research Journal* 1 (May 2007): 45–71; Cohen, *Duke Ellington's America*, 203–36; Kevin Gaines, "Duke Ellington, 'Black, Brown, and Beige,' and the Cultural Politics of Race," in *Music and the Racial Imagination*, ed. Ronald Radano and Philip V. Bohlman (Chicago: University of Chicago Press, 2000), 585–602; Hasse, *Beyond Category*, 261–65; John Howland, *Ellington Uptown: Duke Ellington, James P. Johnson, and the Birth of Concert Jazz* (Ann Arbor: University of Michigan Press, 2009), 179–93; and Teachout, *Duke*, 236–46.

24 Alfred Frankenstein, "'Hot Is Something about a Tree,' Says Duke," *San Francisco Chronicle*, November 9, 1941. Cited in Cohen, *Duke Ellington's America*, 204.

25 Smithsonian Archives of the National Museum of American History, Ellington Collection, 301, series 8, boxes 1, 3, 9, 11, 13, 16.

26 Smithsonian Archives of the National Museum of American History, Ellington Collection, 301, series 4, box 3, folder 7.

27 As Terry Teachout explains in *Duke: A Life of Duke Ellington*, 237, *Variety* reported in June 1943 that Ellington was writing a book about *Black, Brown and Beige*, and that "[He] feels that detailing the thoughts which motivated the work will help toward a better understanding of it."

28 Richard O. Boyer, "The Hot Bach," reprinted in *Ellington Reader*, ed. Tucker,

238. Boyer's article was originally published in three parts in *The New Yorker* in June–July 1944.

29 Cited in Andrew Homzy, "*Black, Brown and Beige* in Duke Ellington's Repertoire, 1943–1973," *Black Music Research Journal* 13/2 (1993): 89.

30 It should be noted that unlike Ellington's music, Ottley's book was against Western imperialism, so much so that it actually included a partial justification of Japanese foreign policy.

31 Anonymous, "Why Duke Ellington Avoided Music Schools," *PM*, December 9, 1945. Reprinted in *Ellington Reader*, ed. Tucker, 253.

32 Gunnar Askland, "Interpretations in Jazz: A Conference with Duke Ellington," *Etude*, March 1947, 134, 172. Reprinted in *Ellington Reader*, ed. Tucker, 257.

33 Hasse, *Beyond Category*, 298–302, gives effective and succinct descriptions of Ellington's Carnegie Hall compositions.

34 Ellington, *Mistress*, 214.

9 Duke in the 1950s: renaissance man

ANTHONY BROWN

Biographers, historians, and journalists writing about Duke Ellington tend to regard the 1950s as the nadir of his career; until of course his triumphant rebirth at the 1956 Newport Jazz Festival, when his closing night concert sent thousands of fans into a dancing frenzy. Ellington himself proclaimed, "I was born at Newport in 1956," and the recording of that performance remains the Ellington orchestra's biggest-selling record ever. The adversities he encountered en route to Newport began with the 1951 departures of his key soloist, Johnny Hodges, his longtime companion and drummer, Sonny Greer, and his star trombonist, Lawrence Brown. He signed with four record labels in as many years, and had largely frustrating dealings with label executives, producers, and publishers. He had to negotiate the absence of his longtime co-arranger/composer Billy Strayhorn during his 1953–1955 hiatus away from the fold. All the while he struggled to keep a big band working on salary (primarily paid with royalties from his earlier successes) when most others had disappeared with the war. Each trial and tribulation seemed truly insurmountable at the time, and none presaged the redemption to come in July 1956.

In light of these challenges and setbacks, a studied listening of Ellington's recordings from the first half of the decade reveals a remarkably consistent quality of inspired sophistication and pathos in his and Strayhorn's compositions and arrangements, performed both live and in the studio. Several recordings from the early 1950s remain among the important documents of Ellington's career, in the company of the decade's later masterful achievements, which include *Such Sweet Thunder*, *Black, Brown and Beige* (featuring Mahalia Jackson singing "Come Sunday"), *The Queen's Suite*, the motion picture soundtrack *Anatomy of a Murder*, and several others.

Most every person of great achievement has had to overcome major obstacles to create, discover, or explore something wondrous and new. In Ellington's case, the scenario of his "darkest hour before the dawn" leading to his "Newport renaissance" – Ellington rising from the brink of economic abyss and "has-been" status to his rightful place as celebrated, reigning jazz royalty – has not yet justly recognized the artistic caliber of his music during those hard times. Like a seasoned prizefighter, Duke fought his way back from the ropes, sticking and moving, steadily blocking punches and throwing blows to deliver the knockout at Newport. Despite the hardships that beset him, Ellington created great music all along the way. His prolific musical legacy was fueled by an idiosyncratic work regimen, a protean imagination, and deep inspiration, both corporeal and spiritual. This chapter reviews a selection of Duke Ellington recordings from each year of the decade as a representation of his artistic excellence, a gauge of his evolving musical methodologies and sensibilities, and a sonic index of his recording career. Twenty-first-century listeners and researchers are invaluably indebted to the release over the past 20 years of previously unavailable Ellington orchestra recordings from international concert tours that document this inspired music performed live before appreciative audiences. This arching survey of Ellington's music in the time of the Red Scare, the Race for Space, and the Atomic Age in white-bread America will be presented within the context of Ellington's career, the impact of technological advancements in popular media, and the sociopolitical and cultural forces informing his life's work at the dawn of the Civil Rights era.

The 1950s actually started out quite well for Ellington and his orchestra. In spring 1950 they returned to tour Europe, their first time overseas since 1939, and Ellington had a major commission from the NBC Symphony to premiere within weeks following the tour. The 2007 CD release of *Live in Switzerland* (TCB Records TCB 43062) documents the Ellington orchestra in fine form performing a set from a concert program in Zurich on May 2, 1950. Musical highlights from an inspired band performing for an engaged audience include the opening salvo of intricate ensemble interplay, brilliant solos and screaming shout choruses in "Suddenly It Jumped" and "Ring Dem Bells," and a revamped "Creole Love Call" vocally caressed by Kay Davis. An impressive rendition of "Air Conditioned Jungle" featuring Jimmy Hamilton's pyrotechnic clarinet follows with bebop overtones that are authentically reprised in a cameo appearance from expatriate tenor saxophonist Don Byas on "How High the Moon." Other highlights include rousing extended versions of "Rockin' in Rhythm" and "Frankie and Johnny" with drummers Sonny Greer and Butch Ballard swinging hard; Johnny Hodges' gorgeous reading of "Violet Blue"; a stellar version of "The Tattooed Bride"; and an always welcome performance of Billy Strayhorn at the piano for his composition "Take the 'A' Train."

Despite their increasing differences during this period, Ellington and Columbia Records continued to produce excellent recordings with a notable watershed in December 1950 titled *Masterpieces by Ellington*, his first ten-inch long-playing disc. Ellington exploited this new medium, which allowed over 15 minutes of recorded music per side, by featuring three of his most beloved works, "Mood Indigo," "Solitude," and "Sophisticated Lady," in new extended arrangements conceived by Strayhorn, and the Duke's own recent tripartite tour de force, "The Tattooed Bride." Ellington had extensive experience with concert presentations of his extended compositions, beginning with the 1943 Carnegie Hall debut of his seminal *Black, Brown and Beige: A Tone Parallel to the History of the Negro in America*. With this recurring concert experience and expectation, Ellington consistently produced a supply of extended works, usually as suites, a concerto, or another musical structure. With Strayhorn contributing lush, entrancing arrangements that breathed new life into golden chestnuts – the non-remarkable vocal contributions from Yvonne Lanauze on the first two selections notwithstanding – the recording fully lives up to its title. Also of note is that tenor saxophonist Paul Gonsalves had formally joined the Ellington orchestra earlier that month, and would play a pivotal role for the rest of the decade and thereafter.

The departure of Hodges, Greer, and Brown in late January 1951 to form another band under Hodges' leadership was remedied in part by what became known in the press as the "Great James Robbery," with Ellington luring drummer/composer Louis Bellson, alto saxophone star Willie Smith, and former Ellington orchestra valve trombonist/composer Juan Tizol from the Harry James orchestra to replace his defecting bandsmen. The James band was working intermittently at the time so the musicians were eager for a steady paycheck, even though their Ellington contracts were just for a year.[1] Ellington's recorded output for Columbia Records that year consisted mostly of new tunes and arrangements of popular songs of the day. Among the standout originals from the May 1951 sessions are "Pretty and the Wolf (Monologue)" and Strayhorn's *Brown Betty*, which only became publicly available in the U.S. with the issue of *The Essential Collection 1927–62* (Columbia/Legacy C3K 65841) honoring Ellington's centennial in 1999. "Pretty and the Wolf (Monologue)" is a rare gem featuring Ellington in the role of raconteur par excellence, spinning an urban tale of the game of love with urbane wit and wisdom. The clarinet quartet accompaniment composed by Jimmy Hamilton adds colorful commentary. In Strayhorn's inimitable portraiture, "Brown Betty" leaves a lasting impression of a warm, sophisticated, and self-assured woman.

"Once again, Duke Ellington and his Orchestra present a full-length program of concert arrangements of some of their most popular numbers." This opening sentence of the liner notes by producer George Avakian for the original LP of *Ellington Uptown* states the artistic objective of Ellington's tenure with Columbia Records at that time. This 1951–1952 recording refurbishes three of his classics, "The Mooche," "Take the 'A' Train," and "Perdido," and presents a recently composed suite, *Harlem*.

Ellington Uptown also features his new orchestra members in the spotlight, beginning with "Skin Deep," a drum feature written by Bellson for himself, his new band, and his new employer. This composition includes a solo showcasing his swinging orchestral musicality and technical prowess behind his signature percussive arsenal outfitted with double bass drums. Originally a "jungle music" soundtrack for a Cotton Club show, "The Mooche" is recast as suave and smooth, extended to include new piano interludes and accompaniment settings for his soloists – clarinetist Russell Procope, alto saxophonist Hilton Jefferson, and trombonist Quentin "Butter" Jackson – all building to a bitonal, screaming coda. "Take the 'A' Train" is an exquisite reinvention of the band's theme music as a concert vehicle for three soloists. An extended trio introduction spotlights "the piano player," as the Maestro (the moniker bestowed upon him by Bellson) often referred to himself, followed by the orchestra's statement of the melody to launch the swinging, agile scatting and caressing inflections of Betty Roché's creamy voice. The tenor saxophone feature by Paul Gonsalves convincingly demonstrates a mastery of ballads akin to his predecessor Ben Webster, and even supersedes his own famed hard-driving blues marathons.

A Tone Parallel to Harlem (later known simply as *Harlem*) was commissioned by conductor Arturo Toscanini and the NBC Symphony and was premiered at New York's Metropolitan Opera House by the two orchestras on January 21, 1951. Ellington began composing *Harlem* aboard the *Ile de France* on his return voyage from the preceding year's European tour. A single-movement symphonic suite, *Harlem* stands among the greatest and most satisfying extended compositions by Ellington. Within 13 minutes, *Harlem* reflects a kaleidoscopic portraiture of the beloved uptown New York neighborhood, cast in the myriad stylistic variations comprising the work's varied episodes, and artfully represented in Ellington's nonpareil blending of sonorities textured with dramatic improvised solo passages. Particularly inventive are his rhythmic and harmonic permutations of the introductory thematic minor-third signature motif throughout, and the shifting cultural references, both sacred and profane, captured musically through statement, impression, or nuanced gesture.

"Perdido" is retooled as a medium-tempo showcase for the entire ensemble, with remarkable solos from trumpeter Clark Terry and the brass quartet, plus Woodman trading fours to stoke the shout chorus closing out the original *Ellington Uptown* LP. Recorded in December 1951, *Controversial Suite* (along with the epochal 1948 *Liberian Suite*) is included on the 2004 CD issue of *Ellington Uptown* (Columbia/Legacy CK 87066). This two-movement composition, comprising "Before My Time" and "Later," begins with a pastiche homage to the Crescent City, New Orleans – the birthplace of jazz – including an honoring bow to the archetypal clarinetist Sidney Bechet. In ultimate contrast, a pan-tonal, "tick-tock" clock motif bookends "Later," which takes the listener on a four-minute trip through Ellington's fascinating sonic landscape of music now and to come.

Ellington's tenure at Columbia had thus far not produced a hit single that made him popular again with the public or the press, and this contributed to his decision to switch to Capitol Records in the spring of 1953. By April the orchestra had undergone personnel changes, beginning with the departure of Ellington's "first chair percussionist," Louis Bellson, with Butch Ballard taking his seat. Alto saxophonist Hilton Jefferson, who had replaced Willie Smith, also left, and Rick Henderson was filling Hodges' original seat. Most poignant and possibly most deleterious to Ellington were Strayhorn's extended absences until 1955 to pursue outside projects. Perhaps serendipitously or even miraculously, "Satin Doll," a catchy tune recorded at Ellington's first Capitol session, became the most popular of his career. His recorded output for Capitol consisted mostly of new tunes and arrangements of popular songs; a ten-minute version of "It Don't Mean a Thing" is the only extended work. Ellington's Capitol sessions were predominantly three-minute singles, mostly attempts to repeat his success with "Satin Doll." He recorded several vocal features, occasionally gave sway to musical fad and fashion, and even explored playing electric piano in his vain attempts to score another hit.

With *Piano Reflections*, Ellington undertook the task of recording an entire LP featuring his piano playing as the central focus in duet and trio settings with his rhythm section, Wendell Marshall on bass and Butch Ballard on drums. Mostly recorded the week after the "Satin Doll" session, *Piano Reflections* is the most satisfying LP from the Capitol era, introducing new pieces among revamped versions of some of his most beloved tunes, including "In a Sentimental Mood," "Prelude to a Kiss," his early, almost innocent "Dancers in Love," Strayhorn's "Passion Flower," and "Kinda Dukish" in its entirety, a rarity since it was abridged to serve as the introduction to "Rockin' in Rhythm." He begins the collection with mostly new works that are fresh and revealing in their titles, moods and emotions. "Who Knows?" is the opener, and contains a solo displaying Ellington's keyboard mastery in full measure. "Retrospection," "Reflections in D," and "Melancholia" are early manifestations of the introspective impressionism Ellington would mine in his spiritually inspired *Sacred Concert* features, "Heaven," "Meditation," and "T.G.T.T."

Recordings of the Ellington orchestra's live dance concerts are especially gratifying for their daringly spontaneous forays into improvised passages often designed to spur on the audiences, as heard on *Duke Ellington in Hamilton, Ontario* (Music & Arts CD-1051). For the loud front row of Canadian dancers that evening of February 8, the orchestra's repertoire ranged from the "The Mooche" (from his Cotton Club days) to popular songs and show tunes of the day, plus the obligatory "Ellington medley" of his crowd-pleasing hits. The recording, albeit of poor fidelity, captures the band in fine form. The leader starts the proceedings in a programmatically unorthodox manner with the stylistically stark juxta-position of "The Mooche" followed by a blistering bebop chart of Charlie Parker's "Ornithology" (incorrectly listed as "How High the Moon," which the tune "Ornithology" is based on harmonically), sounding very much like a Gil Fuller arrangement pulled from the Dizzy Gillespie orchestra's book. The band invests "The Mooche" with the full panoply of timbres and textures characteristic of Ellington's early "jungle swamp music," and then adroitly executes the asymmetrical phrasing and rhyth-mic complexities of modern jazz with confident dexterity and velocity.

The title notwithstanding, *Ellington '55* was recorded at three sessions from 1953 to 1955 but released in 1955. It was the first 12-inch LP recorded by his orchestra, and Ellington capitalized on this extended format (permitting up to 25 minutes of music per side) by presenting new expanded arrangements of his earlier favorites, and also paying tribute to his fellow big band leaders and composers with arrangements of their signature hits. The recording, captured in high fidelity, transports the listener inside the studio where the rhythm section is already vamping on the introduction for "Rockin' in Rhythm"; the band enters sounding fresh and forceful. The following track, an update of "Black and Tan Fantasy," is a remarkable recasting of this 1927 classic featuring Ray Nance's personalized extrapolation of Bubber Miley's original growling plunger-muted trumpet virtuosity. The fraternal tributes – "Stompin' at the Savoy" for Chick Webb, "One O'Clock Jump" for Count Basie, "Flying Home" for Lionel Hampton, "Honeysuckle Rose" for Fats Waller, and "In the Mood" for Glenn Miller – comprise the noteworthy homage performed by an ace ensemble in complete command of the various stylistic demands of the date. The CD issue of *Ellington '55* (Capitol 7243 5 20135 2 4) contains two bonus tracks, both extended selections in keeping with the rest of the album. "Body and Soul" is an especially welcome addition, showcasing an exciting solo outing by Paul Gonsalves. This version begins in a tempo similar to the definitive 1939 recording by Coleman Hawkins, whose groundbreaking performance states the melody's first eight measures before launching into a solo improvisation over the tune's chord progression. Gonsalves begins his version by imme-diately improvising over the chord changes, and then leads the band on a double-time romp over the next three minutes; his extended soloing expertise would become a flashpoint for the band's resurgence in the near future. The collection closes with a rousing, swinging, ten-minute version of "It Don't Mean a Thing (If It Ain't Got That Swing)," with solo features reaffirming the magnificence of the artists Ellington assembled together.

In late 1955 Ellington signed with Bethlehem Records, an independent company that would become known through the popular success of singer and pianist Nina Simone's recordings on the label. Ellington's entire output for Bethlehem was captured during a two-day recording session in Chicago on February 7 and 8, 1956. The first LP released, *Historically Speaking: The Duke*, features ten updated arrangements of some of his classic works from the first three decades of his career. The second, *Duke Ellington Presents . . .*, includes five more Ellington-Strayhorn originals and six newly arranged popular tunes of the day, resembling the programmatic mix on his last Capitol release, *Ellington '55*. The first collection contains several of the most satisfying updated renditions of his early works, including "East St. Louis Toodle-O" and "Creole Love Call"; revamped favorites from the 1940s, "Ko-Ko," "In a Mellotone," "Midriff," and "Stomp, Look and Listen"; and new works "Lonesome Lullaby" and "Upper Manhattan Medical Group." "Ko-Ko" and "Stomp, Look and Listen" are taken at faster tempi, whereas "East St. Louis Toodle-O" and "Creole Love Call" are slower and much more relaxed than the original recordings.

The Duke Ellington Reader, Mark Tucker's collection of literature on and by Ellington, includes a 1958 article by French composer/writer André Hodeir excoriating Ellington for these recordings, particularly his reinvention of "Ko-Ko," long recognized as among his most masterful miniature works. One of the truly invaluable contributions of the Ellington legacy is how his and Strayhorn's rearrangements of earlier works provide a chronological yardstick of their evolution as well as the maturation of the band, with shifts in their sensibilities often informed by national and world events. Ellington's early recordings capture his arche-typal music fueled by youthful exuberance and daring that excited every-one who heard it. These later reinterpretations reflect his life and the world in the fifties, providing a portrait of a seasoned professional and his orchestra at the top of their game: smooth and brash, but always resource-ful, cool, and confident. Hodeir was 20 years younger than Ellington when he wrote his critique, and possibly had not yet come to appreciate the Maestro's reinvention of his active repertory informed by life's élan at a middle-age pace.

Duke Ellington Presents . . . begins with an upbeat Latin-tinged rearrange-ment of "Summertime" that switches to swing time and soars with Cat

Anderson's stratospheric trumpet feature. "Cotton Tail" is taken at a brighter tempo than the original and showcases the ensemble's honed precision and command, framing tenor saxophone soloist Paul Gonsalves, with his bebop articulations and show-stopping cadenza, as a more than worthy successor to the great Ben Webster. On the ballad "Laura," Gonsalves again demonstrates his versatility and rightful place with Webster and Johnny Hodges as a primary purveyor of the trademark lush, sensuous, saxophonic sonorities featured throughout the ensemble's history. The rhythm section, comprising new recruits Jimmy Woode on bass and Sam Woodyard on drums, propels the band with a driving swing through the most intense passages of "Cotton Tail," and buoys the orchestra with a subtle momentum on its most intro-spective numbers, such as "Day Dream," a gorgeous alto saxophone showcase for Hodges. Billy Strayhorn, back on board full time, contributed the arrange-ments to "Laura," "My Funny Valentine," "Deep Purple," and his own "Day Dream," as well as the extended, rousing closing composition, "Blues," which gives everybody a chance to solo, with drummer Woodyard displaying his prowess as both a big band drummer and a modernist influenced by Max Roach.

Newport

By all accounts, the night of July 7, 1956, was truly a transformative, transcendent experience for Duke Ellington, his orchestra, and over 7,000 dancing fans at the closing concert of the Newport Jazz Festival. Ellington and his band had earned their true redemption by swinging and rocking their way back into the hearts and minds and feet of America's youth. The original LP, *Ellington at Newport*, captured by producer George Avakian – often in challenging situations, including the riotous crowding of the stage – documents the magic of that night forever. How Newport, Rhode Island, an exclusive summer resort enclave, became host to the world's most prestigious and longest-running outdoor jazz festival is a story unto itself, and one affectionately told from its beginning up to Ellington's shining (two) hour(s) that fateful night in John Fass Morton's 2008 book, *Backstory in Blue: Ellington at Newport '56*.

The earlier events of the day did not portend how gloriously the night would end, with several incidents that could have derailed the show. The band's initial concert was interrupted after two numbers, and they were required to wait backstage for hours before assembling on stage for their closing set. Tensions were also mounting because some of the orchestra members did not show up in time or were not in condition to perform, causing an initial delay. But as the consummate professionals they were, when it was time to deliver, the band came out swinging. By the time they launched into *Diminuendo and Crescendo in Blue*, featuring Paul Gonsalves's marathon 27-chorus saxophone solo, Ellington had the crowd in the palm of his hand. Gonsalves, already a featured soloist in the orchestra, became a bona-fide star following his extraordinary performance at Newport.[2]

Chroniclers of the event credit various people as the spark that ignited the wildfire sending thousands of fans onto their feet, clapping and dancing while Ellington's orchestra with Gonsalves stoked the flames. Avakian's original liner notes cite a blonde woman in a black dress (actually brown) who danced passionately in front of the stage as the inspiration. Count Basie's drummer "Papa" Jo Jones was stage right keeping time by slapping the stage with a rolled-up newspaper, while egging the band on with encouraging exclamations. Of course the band was roaring with Sam Woodyard's solid backbeat keeping steady time for the band and the dancers, with everyone caught up in the magic of the moment. When the number was over and the frenzied crowd threatened to riot if the concert were halted, Ellington managed to restore order and continue the concert; a true episode of "veni, vidi, vici" if ever there was one. Ellington was featured on the cover of *Time* magazine the next month (although the article was planned before his Newport appearance), his Columbia recording of the event was a smash hit, and Ellington resumed his rightful place as the King of Swing and the King of Jazz, to remain a formidable and influential force in the course of jazz for the rest of his life.

Ellington's next major composing project was for a television show depicting a fanciful telling of the origins of jazz. Recorded in late 1956, *A Drum Is a Woman* is a musical suite in four parts, a narrated allegory about the journeys of jazz in the persona of "African chantress" Madam Zajj. An expanded theatrical version – a light-hearted, pastiche quiltwork of music, songs, and dance – was produced as a CBS television show broadcast on May 8, 1957, on *The U.S. Steel Hour*. As narrator, Ellington reprises his raconteurial role that he first introduced in "Pretty and the Wolf (Monologue)." Several sections of *A Drum Is a Woman* are noteworthy for their inspired solos, including trumpeter Clark Terry's commanding stylistic portrayal of the architect of jazz in "Hey, Buddy Bolden," the saxophone features for Johnny Hodges ("A Drum Is a Woman, Part 2") and Paul Gonsalves ("Congo Square"), and the fine vocals of Margaret Tynes, Joya Sherrill, and Ozzie Bailey throughout. Strayhorn's signature orchestrations range from Caribbean expressions and jungle impressions ("Carribee Joe," "Congo Square") to celestial projections in the quixotic "Ballet of the Flying Saucers" and "Zajj's Dream."

By late 1957, the "race for space" was raging between the U.S.A. and the U.S.S.R. after the latter successfully launched the first satellite, Sputnik, into orbit around Earth. At the same time, the struggle against racial inequality – the Civil Rights Movement for black Americans to achieve full citizenship in the United States – was gaining momentum and international attention through boycotts, sit-ins, and the charismatic leadership of a young Baptist minister, Dr. Martin Luther King, Jr. The African-American community was dispirited, some outraged by white political leaders who stonewalled and refused to follow the rule of law, particularly when federal troops were forced to intercede so that black children in Little Rock, Arkansas, could attend racially segregated schools.[3] In late 1957 Ellington wrote an article, "The Race for Space," that candidly revealed his thoughts on both subjects. This cogent, insightful critique was presumably commissioned, but remained unpublished until its inclusion in *The Duke Ellington Reader*, after editor Mark Tucker located it in the Smithsonian Institution's Duke Ellington Collection in 1988. In his essay, Ellington echoes the prevailing attitude of the black community that America's misdirection and resultant failures – as characterized by its lag in aerospace innovation – were due to the encumbrances of de rigueur racial discrimination and legislated subjugation. He recognizes the inclusive nature of jazz, and draws parallels between the disciplines of science and music, noting the shared impulse of inspired creativity in both endeavors:

> The field of jazz has not yet become an arena of the sort of racial conflicts based on color, national origin and the like that I sincerely believe along with many other Negroes is pinning the United States to the earth . . . In jazz, as in the sciences, I am in a medium for creators . . . Musicians, physicists, mathematicians, geneticists, biologists, geologists, astronomers, atomic researchers – are motivated by the same burning urge to create . . . Because so many Americans persist in the notion of the master race, millions of Negroes are deprived of proper schooling, denied the right to vote on who will spend their tax money and are the last hired and first fired in those industries necessary for the progress of the country . . . It seems to me that the problem of America's inability so far to go ahead of or at least keep abreast of Russia in the race for space can be traced directly to this racial problem which has been given top priority not only throughout the country but by Washington, itself.[4]

Ellington was among the first to truly recognize and clearly articulate the foundational role of freedom in jazz: to identify the democratic ideal as realized in jazz performance. His closing paragraphs underscore his conviction in the necessity of cooperation within the collective creative process to succeed in both science and music.

Put it this way. Jazz is a good barometer of freedom . . . In its beginnings the USA spawned certain ideals of freedom and independence through which, eventually, jazz was evolved and the music is so free that many people say it is the only unhampered, unhindered expression of complete freedom yet produced in this country . . . It has been proven that teamwork required for success in scientific endeavors takes in all kinds of combinations of people . . . And there are jazz bands which achieve that so essentially different sound made up of a polyglot of racial elements . . . for they have freed themselves from the suspicions of racial differences and dedicated themselves to the business of discovering, arranging and playing of that different sound. The sound of harmony. So, this is my view on the race for space. We'll never get it until we Americans, collectively and individually, get us a new sound. A new sound of harmony, brotherly love, common respect and consideration for the dignity and freedom of men.[5]

Such Sweet Thunder

Ellington first conceived of a suite inspired by Shakespearean characters after receiving a warm reception from the Canadian audience during his July 1956 appearance at the Stratford Shakespearean Festival in Ontario. A recording of this historic performance and the enthusiastic crowd is available on the 1989 CD release *Ellington Live from the 1956 Stratford Festival* (Music & Arts CD-616). Completed after *A Drum Is a Woman*, *Such Sweet Thunder* received its first full performance at the "Music for Moderns" concert at Town Hall, New York, on April 28, 1957. This suite is recognized as among Ellington's most masterful, a stunning collection of varied musical portraits, evocative of a full palette of moods and emotions realized through a brilliant casting of orchestral colors, textures, and rhythms. Although Ellington can justly take credit for this work's compositional greatness, Strayhorn's contributions – particularly "Up and Down, Up and Down (I Will Lead Them Up and Down)," "The Star-Crossed Lovers," and "Circle of Fourths" – are jewels in the gold crown. The opening, "Such Sweet Thunder," begins with a bold, bluesy, swinging swagger, then adds a sophisticated balance of softer dynamics and solo textures, and ends with the full-blown blues that began the proceedings. The contrasting "Sonnet for Caesar," composed with a musical structure inspired by the sonnet form, is a slower-paced showcase for the lithe clarinet of Jimmy Hamilton. "Sonnet to Hank Cinq" is a trombone chops workout custom-composed for Britt Woodman. "Lady Mac" is a contrapuntal portrait of Lady Macbeth in waltz time. A piano feature introduces "Sonnet in Search of a Moor," which becomes a vehicle for Jimmy Woode's pizzicato bass solo supported by a bed of woodwinds. The

Space Age surprise comes with the glissando slide trombone fanfare announcing "The Telecasters," which settles into a strolling stop-time feature for the baritone saxophone of Harry Carney with horn support and Sam Woodyard sliding along with brushes until the climactic recapitulation. "Up and Down, Up and Down" is dedicated to Puck, the whimsical wood sprite from Shakespeare's popular comedy *A Midsummer Night's Dream*. Strayhorn's signature contrapuntal composing predilections are masterful in this alternately romping and reposing gem, despite Ray Nance's challenged violin intonation. Katherina from *The Taming of the Shrew* is portrayed in "Sonnet for Sister Kate" as a soulful song played on slide trombone by Quentin Jackson, supported with a thick saxophone cushion. The most popular and undeniably the most beautiful work of the suite, Strayhorn's "The Star-Crossed Lovers" is a breathtaking ballad played to sublime perfection by the unparalleled alto saxophonist Johnny Hodges. This romantic ode seemingly captures exquisite love in full bloom in the ultimately doomed lives of Romeo and Juliet. Surprisingly, Strayhorn composed the piece prior to the suite, and originally titled it "Pretty Girl." "Madness in Great Ones" is Ellington's astounding rendering of Hamlet as he tried to act crazy. This composition is a concise example of Ellington's more adventurous writing – and his personalized interpretation of "crazy" – with contrasting textures, moods, and virtuosic obbligatos, capped with an unbelievable supersonic showcase for trumpeter Cat Anderson. According to the original LP liner notes, "Half the Fun" is a North African musical fantasy, and "an exotic setting and a sensuous musical feeling provide the Nile, the barge, an ostrich fan and – Johnny Hodges." The high-velocity "Circle of Fourths" is a harmonically sophisticated vehicle that launches Paul Gonsalves into a breathtaking saxophone improvisation to close the suite, toot suite. The title references the piece's harmonic structure as well as the "four dimensions of Shakespeare's artistic contribution: tragedy, comedy, history and the sonnets," as Ellington's producer Irving Townsend writes in the expanded CD notes.

The 1957 Columbia album *Ellington Indigos* remains among my favorite Ellington recordings of all time. Whenever I am asked to recommend a Duke Ellington album as an introduction to his music, I readily suggest this album. I feel anyone can appreciate *Ellington Indigos* as much as I do, because it is as near to a perfect record album as any I can imagine in its superior stereo fidelity, the sequencing of the tunes, the fresh new arrangements of Ellington originals balanced with popular standards, and performances that are timeless in their exquisite beauty. Whether or not Ellington ever intended to create a soundtrack for romantic engagements, this collection of sumptuous ballads is without parallel.

Black, Brown and Beige

One of Ellington's most remarkable recordings of the decade – of his entire career – was created during the February 1958 sessions of his orchestra with Mahalia Jackson. A native of the wellspring of America's music, New Orleans, Mahalia Jackson delivered the depth of spiritual reflection and invocation that Ellington sought to breathe life into his sorrow song, "Come Sunday." She brings a majestic presence to the proceedings, and the recording is a triumphant collaboration that remains a classic reinterpretation of his earliest symphonic-length work.

Black, Brown and Beige was originally composed by Ellington to inaugurate his annual concert series at Carnegie Hall, New York's premier music venue, on January 23, 1943. Ellington created history with this multi-movement extended work, subtitled *A Tone Parallel to the History of the Negro in America*. Despite his ambitious blending of various African-American musical genres and traditions, his idiosyncratic and unorthodox treatment of thematic development, functional harmonic conventions, and textural modulations was ill-received by the classically predisposed critics of the day. Affected deeply by this, Ellington scrapped the original version and crafted a shorter version, with the 1958 recording also introducing sung lyrics to "Come Sunday," originally a feature for Johnny Hodges on alto saxophone. The 1958 recording of the *Black, Brown and Beige* suite is deeply indebted to the brilliant reorchestrations of Billy Strayhorn; his backgrounds for Jackson's unique rendition of the spiritual are transcendent, with lush horns in emulation of a hushed gospel choir.

The Queen's Suite

Duke Ellington and his orchestra were invited to give a command performance for Queen Elizabeth II at the Leeds Music Festival in October 1958, after which Ellington and other representatives of the arts from Europe were presented to Her Majesty and the Duke of Edinburgh. Ellington was so impressed with the experience that, at his own expense, he composed, recorded, and pressed one copy of a dedicated suite, which he arranged for delivery to the Queen at Buckingham Palace. Despite repeated requests to make the recording public, Ellington refused, knowing this music was something that only they shared (with the exception of one movement, "The Single Petal of a Rose," which he performed in concert). In 1976, after Ellington's death, *The Queen's Suite* was made public on jazz impresario Norman Granz's Pablo Records label.

The opening title, "Sunset and the Mocking Bird," signals the sublimely poetic music that only Ellington and Strayhorn could compose to evoke such imagery. Like most of the titles in this six-movement suite, this piece has a story behind it: Ellington was inspired by an evening bird call that he transcribed and composed the piece from. Jimmy Hamilton's clarinet solo captures the bird in flight, and Hodges' obbligato statement of the theme is heavenly. In his autobiography, *Music Is My Mistress*, Ellington explains the evening experience that inspired "Lightning Bugs and Frogs." Driving along the Ohio River, the orchestra came upon the sight of "millions of lightning bugs, dancing in the air. It was a perfect ballet setting, and down below in a gully, like an orchestra pit, could be heard the croaking of frogs."[6] "Northern Lights" was inspired by another of Ellington's terpsichorean interpretations of natural wonder; the composer was Strayhorn, who did not witness the celestial splendor, but was inspired by Duke's telling of it. Ellington's piano feature dedicated to the Queen, "The Single Petal of a Rose," remains a precious gem in the Duke's crown jewels.

Anatomy of a Murder

In early 1959, filmmaker Otto Preminger entreated Ellington to compose the musical score for his new production, *Anatomy of a Murder*. A film noir murder mystery wound up in a tense melodrama of rape and revenge, *Anatomy of a Murder* featured an all-star cast led by Hollywood's all-American humble hero, James Stewart (*Mr. Smith Goes to Washington*, *It's a Wonderful Life*), with rising young stars Lee Remick as the sultry, victimized wife, Ben Gazzara as her jealous Army officer husband, and George C. Scott as the big-city prosecutor whom Jimmy Stewart faces in the courtroom showdown.

German-born Preminger already had proven successes with his productions of *Porgy and Bess*, *Carmen Jones*, *Laura*, and *The Man with the Golden Arm*, which clearly document his fascination with American subcultures and their concomitant music. Nominated for seven Academy Awards including Best Picture (1959), *Anatomy of a Murder* was hailed by the Los Angeles Times as "one of the most extraordinary films ever made."

The score Ellington and Strayhorn composed for the film is brilliant, and is among the most entirely satisfying works of their shared career. Ellington and Strayhorn's music captures the full range of the intrigue, passion, suspense, and sexuality of the movie. The dramatic episodes are buoyed with rhythmic propulsion or driving agitation, while other scenes and characters are given introspective accompaniment or dressed in flowing romance and sensuality.

The music set to the opening credits is a tour de force; the first 30 seconds of the main theme alone are worthy of study. This kaleidoscope of sonorities and moods serves as a microcosmic overture capturing the myriad emotions and intensity of the film before settling into a driving groove with horns providing pointillistic punctuations to the title sequence, which then seamlessly segues into the opening scene of Stewart cruising in his automobile. Ellington's "Flirtibird" is an indelible portrayal of the gorgeous young Army wife, with Hodges' alto providing the leitmotif – his signature finesse, beauty, and allure a perfect match for Remick's character. The constant in its ever-changing recurrence is Ellington's trademark treatment of romantic ballads. Strayhorn's "Haupe" (a.k.a. "Polly's Theme"), for Stewart's character, the protagonist Paul (Polly) Biegler, is equally memorable and appears in various guises throughout the movie. Their individualized mastery of thematic variation, extrapolation, and modulation is evident in the shifts in moods and styles of each accompanied appearance by the respective characters throughout the film. Their incomparable attention to detail, a hallmark of their craft, is easily evident in the copiously varied backgrounds for the soloists. The last track on the recording, "Upper and Outest," is a recap of the main theme and accompanies the closing credits. Cat Anderson finishes off the proceedings with his ultrasonic trumpet acrobatics.

Ellington and some members of his band make cameo appearances in the film as performers in a small nightclub. Ellington's character, "Pie-Eye," is even featured in a piano duet with Stewart, whose character is a jazz aficionado of every style from "Dixieland to Brubeck." As satisfying as it would seem to see Duke and his men on the big screen, Ellington's character, his few spoken lines, and their delivery are woefully stereo-typical, and his obligatory "hip" lingo feels uncomfortably forced despite his irrepressible charisma. The orchestra's brief film characterization notwithstanding, the recording alone of *Anatomy of a Murder* stands as a true testament to the versatility and virtuosity of Ellington and Strayhorn as a nonpareil pair of composers and creative geniuses. The gestalt of seeing and hearing the film is a synergistic blend of image and music that creates an unforgettable cinematic classic.

Festival Session: *Idiom '59*

Touring coast-to-coast for the outdoor summer festivals had the Ellington band performing their new works and classic repertoire for thousands of people in tents and stadiums from Newport, Rhode Island, to Monterey, California. After Labor Day, the band was back in New York and in the studio to record their summer hits for a Columbia release to cap the final months of the decade. *Festival Session* begins with the Juan Tizol chestnut "Perdido," which serves as a solo feature for the masterful Clark Terry on trumpet. In fact, most of the repertoire provides a moment in the spotlight for the orchestra's international stars. "Copout Extension" has Paul Gonsalves reprising another tenor saxophone marathon solo, an obligatory crowd-pleaser since Newport. The 1941 standard "Things Ain't What They Used to Be," written by son Mercer Ellington, is all Johnny Hodges in his splendor. The new composition "Launching Pad" was written by Clark Terry, who along with Gonsalves, trombonist Britt Woodman, and clarinetist Jimmy Hamilton constitutes a quartet of the "Duke's Spacemen," who share the spotlight along with soloist Ray Nance. The CD release includes two tracks recorded earlier but not included on the original LP. Jimmy Hamilton's clarinet solo on "V.I.P. Boogie" is so extraordinary, with his circular breathing sustaining the cadential note, that he inspires in-studio commentary from Ellington. "Jam with Sam" is a collective feature, with Ellington introducing each of the soloists taking two choruses each, before Cat Anderson's closing trumpet sends the piece into the stratosphere.

Duael Fuel (Parts I, II, and III) serves as a drum feature for Sam Woodyard and second drummer, Jimmy Johnson, who are presented stereophonically in separate channels. Best known for his singular ability to drive the world's greatest jazz orchestra with his backbeat that sent thousands of people onto their feet dancing and stomping at Newport, Sam Woodyard delivers a drum solo that is, perhaps not surprisingly, a highly musical as well as technically challenging work of creative artistry. He plays melodic motifs across his drums, constructed first in eight-measure phrases, then develops the work into a showcase for his percussive mastery informed by Max Roach's stylistic virtuosity and attention to form, phrasing, and polyrhythms. Woodyard ends his tour de force with his patented, variably pitched tom rolls executed with a stick in one hand and the elbow of the other arm placed in the center of the drumhead, changing the drum's pitch by changing the pressure applied by the elbow to the head. Jimmy Johnson handles the unenviable task of following Woodyard with a solo display of genuine talent and personality executed with technical prowess and acute attention to proportion and variety. The piece ends with an explosive finale that surely exhausted the festival fans as much as the drumming duo; the studio record even includes applause from the band members!

The centerpiece of the recording is the new work composed for the Newport Festival, *Idiom '59.* The annual tradition of an extended work debuted at Newport was brokered by George Avakian to sweeten the enticement for Ellington to return to Columbia in 1956. This was an especially win-win situation for all parties, since Columbia would record subsequent festivals and thereby have a major new Ellington composition to release every year. For the composer(s), this was an annual opportunity to write a new major work with a built-in audience. *Idiom '59* is a tripartite piece composed to capture the open-air joviality and atmosphere of the Newport Jazz Festival. "Part I: Vapor" begins as a light and breezy, bright summer offering. The second section continues in a light, medium dance groove, with a brief minor blues interlude, a laid-back reminiscence of the clarinet and drum dialogue on "Sing, Sing, Sing." "Part III" ends the work as a medium dance piece that is classic Ellington in structure, horn voicings, and phrasing, all serving as a big feature for Clark Terry on flugelhorn. "Part III" begins with a bolero beat that ushers in a contrasting dirge-like introduction, with Ellington foregrounded, before developing into dense, dark, pan-tonal dissonances in the horns, telegraphed by strains in the preceding piano interlude.

Ellington's textural technique here resembles Strayhorn's flexible employment of *Klangfarbenmelodie* (timbre melody) in his earlier treatment of "Polly's Theme" in *Anatomy of a Murder*. Strayhorn's extrapolations of this early twentieth-century musical innovation pioneered by 12-tone composer Arnold Schoenberg were personalized and idiosyncratic, as explained by Strayhorn scholar Walter van de Leur: "Layering independently moving voices, Strayhorn lets the music gradually alter its timbre as instruments drop in and out of the orchestral texture, which is essentially melodyless."[7] Not surprisingly, Ellington evinces in *Idiom '59* a refined development of his personal, post-modern pastiche approach to musical construction, which would incorporate the ideas of Strayhorn as well as others, in the tradition of the best composers who chart new territory. As van de Leur writes:

> Where concepts tended to govern Strayhorn's writing, Ellington seems to have worked case by case, proceeding from chord to chord, from passage to passage, as if designing each sound and phrase separately, without necessarily adhering to a chosen musical technique. As a rule, Ellington kept infusing new and musically unrelated ideas into the musical fabric of a given piece. Numerous Ellington recordings illustrate this practice, including the aforementioned *Sepia Panorama, Harlem Airshaft*, and *I Never Felt This Way Before*.[8]

Coda

Duke Ellington, unparalleled as a composer, bandleader, pianist, arranger, cultural icon, and goodwill ambassador for his country over a half-century-long career, is arguably America's foremost musician. As this chapter makes clear, even during his most challenging times, Ellington maintained his consistent level of artistic excellence, pioneering vision, and creativity.

The arc of Duke's artistic focus in the 1950s began with extended works for concert performances, then shifted mid-decade to shorter pieces (ostensibly to score a hit record and the concomitant remuneration), and finally returned to his passion for commissioned extended works across a variety of disciplines, from Shakespearean theater to a Hollywood motion picture, in addition to his annual extended works premiered and recorded at each Newport Jazz Festival from 1956 to 1959.

Even in his miniatures, Ellington reflected his maturing stylistic craftsmanship in new projects such as the piano-centric album *Piano Reflections*, and in his recasting of his classics in new arrangements. The evolution of *The Mooche, Black and Tan Fantasy*, and other works over decades mirrored his changing sensibilities as a composer, serving as his music barometer of the times. But even his prodigious output could not stem the tide of American tastes towards the youth market. Ellington's career was deleteriously impacted by the quantum shift in the music and new dances of America's teenagers. By mid-decade, Ellington was playing primarily one-nighters; extended engagements were becoming scarce, with big band music losing popularity and audiences to the rise of rhythm and blues, which was marketed as rock 'n' roll to younger mainstream audiences. Ellington was forced by these economic realities to accept tours in the South, which he had previously avoided due to prevalent racial segregation there. Ellington ran afoul of the black press when he agreed to play for segregated audiences, and his comments about racial politics in America were taken out of context by the weekly *Baltimore Afro-American* to portray him as unsupportive of the Civil Rights Movement.[9] Despite his treatment in the press, history clearly documents that Ellington – as a cultural hero and, at times, even a spokesman for the African-American community during the rise of the Civil Rights Movement – represented steadfast adherence to humanistic values and unerring commitment to cultural pride and ethnic valorization in his musical titles and themes, in his actions, and in his words. Ellington was awarded the Spingarn Medal by the NAACP on September 11, 1959, for "the highest or noblest achievement by an American Negro during the preceding year or years."

Ellington proved to be a creative artist no matter what circumstances he faced; his fertile imagination and resourcefulness were engaged even at his career's lowest point. In the summer of 1955, Ellington accepted second billing at the Aquacade on Long Island, where his music accompanied ice skaters, dancing exhibitions and comedians. As Stuart Nicholson writes, "Many fans thought he had reached the end of the road."[10] While working this steady, low-demand engagement, the redoubtable Ellington took the opportunity to write and workshop his play *Man with Four Sides*. Ellington's successes were sometimes so multifaceted and groundbreaking that they set new standards across the various arts and broadcast media. His pioneering work *A Drum Is a Woman* was a musical spectacle blending dance, theater, and song for a television production. This Ellington work not only is recognized as an artistic success but also achieved a first for African Americans: an hour-long TV program that was adventurous in its cultural themes, artistic merits, and messages. Ellington pioneered standards for television by developing the music-theater productions he had been presenting for over a quarter of a century, beginning with his first steady New York engagement at the Kentucky Club.

His tenure with Capitol Records is often viewed as his least artistically successful of the decade. But despite Ellington's occasional penchant to record his versions of popular hits of the day, his Capitol recordings document masterful music performed by an ensemble *sui generis*, with captivating arrangements and themes and great solo features that would be the envy of any other jazz big band of the time. Even Ellington's capitalizing on the mambo craze spreading in the U.S. in the early 1950s has been cited as a low point in his artistic output, as if he had pandered to the meretricious whims of a passing fad.[11] What Ellington crafted in his artful way were sometimes parodies of his own parody of a craze, as in "Bunny Hop Mambo." Also noteworthy of the Capitol sessions is Ellington's pioneering use of the electric piano, as well as Strayhorn's use of the celeste in his arrangement of "Black and Tan Fantasy"; he would feature the instrument again in his music for *Anatomy of a Murder*.

By the close of the decade, Duke Ellington was where he wanted to be, where he had worked hard to be: at the top of his game, at the top of the jazz charts and polls, and on the big screen. It took Ellington all he had to achieve the greatness that came to him in the decade of the fifties and continued up until his death in 1974. Duke Ellington, the consummate renaissance man, undertook the herculean task of leading, inspiring, cajoling, and sometimes scolding the world's most famous jazz orchestra into creating some of the greatest music of the 1950s, including some recordings that will continue to be recognized as among the best he ever made. But as complexly sophisticated, urbane, and indefatigably gifted as Ellington proved to be, he remained – throughout his monumental accomplishments – a man driven by an unfathomable, unquenchable desire to bring beauty into the world.

Notes

1 Smith left after a year, Tizol in 1952, and Bellson in 1953, to become musical director for singer/actress Pearl Bailey, his new wife. Trombonist Tyree Glenn, who replaced Tricky Sam Nanton in 1947, also left Ellington in 1951. Trombonist Britt Woodman and trumpeter Clark Terry joined Ellington's orchestra in 1951.

2 Ellington's son, Mercer, who played trumpet in the orchestra, also managed an independent

record company, Mercer Records, which released self-produced Ellington sessions, several of which showcase the talents of Gonsalves in small-group recordings.

3 The May 1954 *Brown v. Board of Education* Supreme Court decision to integrate public schools reversed the "separate but equal" legislation that had created a segregated nation with the support of the Court's earlier *Plessy v. Ferguson* decision in 1896.

4 Duke Ellington, "The Race for Space," in *The Duke Ellington Reader*, ed. Mark Tucker (New York: Oxford University Press, 1993), 294–95.

5 Ibid., 295–96.

6 Duke Ellington, *Music Is My Mistress* (New York: Doubleday, 1973; reprint, New York: Da Capo, 1976), 112.

7 Walter van de Leur, *Something to Live For: The Music of Billy Strayhorn* (New York: Oxford University Press, 2002), 79.

8 Ibid., 78.

9 See Harvey G. Cohen, *Duke Ellington's America* (Chicago: University of Chicago Press, 2010), 298–308, and Stuart Nicholson, *Reminiscing in Tempo: A Portrait of Duke Ellington* (Boston: Northeastern University Press, 1999), 279–300.

10 Nicholson, *Reminiscing in Tempo*, 301.

11 The mambo craze came to the U.S. years after it had been created and popularized in Cuba by bassist/composer Israel "Cachao" López and his brother, Orestes, and then took root in New York's Palladium ballroom with Machito and his Afro-Cubans, Pérez Prado, and Tito Puente in the late 1940s. Desi Arnaz brought the mambo into mainstream American homes in the 1950s with the immensely popular *I Love Lucy* television show.

10 Ellington in the 1960s and 1970s: triumph and tragedy

DAN MORGENSTERN

When, on April 10, 1972, Duke Ellington entered the impromptu performance space at New York's Whitney Museum for a rare event – a piano recital – his step was as springy, his posture as erect, and his smile as charming as customary. The performance that ensued was a brilliant display of Ellington's piano prowess, with no accompaniment necessary, and his commentary was full of warmth, wit, and wisdom.

Some in attendance – such as his old friend and "Flamingo" lyricist Edmund Anderson, his young amanuensis Brooks Kerr, and his right-hand man, critic Stanley Dance – had been present the night before, when Ellington presided over a performance of his *Second Sacred Concert* at St. Peter's Lutheran Church, not far away. That event took place the day after a seven-week tour of the U.S. – mostly one-nighters, but spelled by a two-week stand in Toronto – that began immediately upon completion of a 36-day odyssey taking the band from Japan to Taiwan to the Philippines to Hong Kong to Thailand to Burma to India to Ceylon to Singapore to Malaysia to Indonesia, back to Singapore, then to Australia and, finally, to Hawaii. The night after the Whitney recital, Ellington and the band were in Portland, Maine, for a joint concert with the local symphony. Eight one-nighters later, he celebrated his 73rd birthday one day late at Newark's Symphony Hall, greeted by 2,000 schoolchildren.

Has any other composer-bandleader-performer in the history of music kept such a schedule? Excepting perhaps the many exotic venues, this cited excerpt from Ellington's travels typifies his extraordinarily active final years. Energy, ambition, financial need, and the always-present desire to hear newly created music performed aside, this hectic pace was made possible by Ellington's conquest of his fear of flying, abetted by his some-time manager-booker, Norman Granz, with whom he had a hot-and-cold relationship. Until the fall of 1958, when Granz persuaded him to take a short flight from London to Berlin (to avoid traveling through East Germany by bus), Ellington had a no-fly clause in his contracts. He had his prayer beads out during the flight, according to trumpeter Clark Terry, but Ellington was an instant convert to air travel and from then on would tease nervous band members during long flights. On shorter hops within the U.S. he continued to let veteran sideman Harry Carney drive him, enjoying his self-appointed role as map-reading guide.

From late 1960 into 1961, Ellington enjoyed what he described in anticipation as "the closest thing to a vacation" he'd ever been able to consider. Not counting an interlude, his time spent away from the band, mostly in Paris, would add up to almost two months. Still it was a working vacation, occupied in the main with scoring the film *Paris Blues*. In Paris Ellington and Billy Strayhorn joined another noted world traveler on a rare leave from his routine, Louis Armstrong, who, unlike Ellington, was to be seen on screen. Strange as it seems, *Paris Blues* was the first collaboration between arguably the two greatest figures in jazz – without the Ellington band, alas, yet Ellington and Strayhorn managed to make an ad hoc assemblage of mostly French musicians, plus some expatriates, sound remarkably Ellingtonian. In Paris Ellington was much in social demand with musicians, show people, and intellectuals; he partied, performed *Come Sunday* at a midnight mass during Christmas season, did a TV piano recital, and scored musical interludes for a revival of a 1709 satirical comedy, *Turcaret*.

In May, 1961, back in New York, Ellington supervised the soundtrack recording of background music for *Paris Blues*, with a considerably augmented orchestra, as I watched from the wings. An extra trumpet (Clark Terry), trombones (Murray McEachern, Britt Woodman), saxophones (Oliver Nelson, Babe Clark), Les Spann doubling guitar and flute, oboist Harry Smiles, and no fewer than five percussionists (incumbent Jimmy Johnson, old friend Sonny Greer, Philly Joe Jones, Max Roach, and Dave Jackson) added new sonic flavors to the mostly brief but very interesting musical interludes. The exact timing required for this synchronization demanded discipline and patience, and it all went down with remarkable ease under Ellington's direction, though he was contractually prevented from conducting the final take, a role assumed by veteran trombonist Lawrence Brown. On playbacks it was disappointing to hear the music obscured by dialogue and other sounds, but the dramatic "Paris Blues" theme emerged at the end, featuring McEachern and Johnny Hodges. Among Ellington's film scores, *Paris Blues* is certainly superior to the later *Assault on a Queen* (1966), and more effective cinematically than the better-known and praised *Anatomy of a Murder* (1959) – if *Anatomy* is perhaps the better picture.

Armstrong, who had interrupted an African tour for his film stint in Paris, was treated to a rare rest after returning to New York, and this set the stage for a much more significant collaboration, albeit again without the Ellington band. Veteran record producer Bob Thiele got wind of the rare joint non-working presence in New York of Armstrong and Ellington, and with all deliberate speed managed to get OKs from both artists and their management, including use of the Armstrong All Stars. Thiele proposed a program of Ellington compositions, and in two sessions on April 3 and 4 – the first from 6 p.m. to 1:30 a.m., the second commencing at 2 p.m. – 17 tunes were recorded, including a new dedication to Armstrong, "The Beautiful American." Armstrong surprised Ellington with a new (and improved) set of lyrics to "Drop Me Off in Harlem," and with his instant recall of the routine of "Black and Tan Fantasy." Armstrong had never recorded this tune but unintentionally upstaged his clarinetist, Ducal alumnus Barney Bigard, who had played it hundreds of times.

I was on hand for the second session, and it was fascinating to observe the ease with which the two protagonists communicated, musically and personally. As was his way, Armstrong gave every take, even rehearsal takes, all he had. Since he'd had an unusual layoff, his embouchure was tender. Ellington arrived complaining of a headache, soon relieved by some Armstrong humor. The key moment came after a marvelous "I'm Just a Lucky So and So," by just the two stars with bass and drums. It prompted Ellington to pull out a lead sheet, pull up a chair, sit down facing Armstrong, and hold it up. Donning his horn-rimmed glasses, Armstrong began to hum and sing. An expert sight-reader, he soon had the melody down. The lyric, with Ellington now at the keyboard, took a bit longer. The tune was "Azalea," inspired many years earlier by *Swing That Music*, Armstrong's first autobiography. Ellington had attempted "Azalea" several times in the recording studio with different singers, but without issuable results. The lyric, baroque even by Ducal standards (rhyming the title with "assail ya," for instance), became poetry in Armstrong's care, and Ellington was soon beaming.

Issued on Roulette Records as *The Great Summit*, the session had unforeseen but musically beneficial consequences. Thiele had not obtained permission from Ellington's label, Columbia, and as a quid pro quo, Columbia asked for Count Basie's band, bringing about the second of Ellington's five 1961–1962 great encounters. Taking place in Columbia's wonderful 30th Street New York studio – a converted church able to accommodate symphony orchestras and thus not troubled by a 32-piece jazz band – the session initially provided a study in contrast between the Basieites and Ellingtonians, the former disciplined and attentive, the latter more relaxed and blasé. It soon became apparent to this observer that Basie would defer to Ellington, even with Basie's own repertory, and when Ellington suggested that the Count join him on the opening pianistics of "Take the 'A' Train," Basie insisted that Billy Strayhorn take this role. As the music unfolded, the Ellingtonians became more involved, even competitive – which the Basieites had been from the start. Throughout, it was Ellington, discreetly seconded by Strayhorn, who guided the proceedings, with his characteristic brand of relaxed authority, establishing order when required. When the concluding "Jumpin' at the Woodside" was called, the Basie trumpets rose for the final brass fireworks. Their Ducal counterparts at first looked askance, but then got up on their feet as well.

The great encounters continued in 1962 with Bob Thiele again the instigator, this time with Coleman Hawkins as Ellington's guest. While the great tenor saxophonist was disappointed that he would not record with the full band, but instead with a septet including Ray Nance, Lawrence Brown, Johnny Hodges, and Harry Carney – the crème de la crème, so to speak – he was pleased with the results, especially "Self Portrait of the Bean," composed by Ellington and Strayhorn for the occasion. Thiele's next idea was more surprising, and a more intimate teaming. *Duke Ellington & John Coltrane* focused on interplay between the protagonists, each with his own customary bass and drums – Aaron Bell and Sam Woodyard for Duke, Jimmy Garrison and Elvin Jones for Coltrane. But on the most successful of the results, Ellington decided to team Bell and Jones. "In a Sentimental Mood," with its haunting piano introduction and shimmering cymbal work, is a Coltrane ballad masterpiece.

Between these Thiele productions came another encounter with modernists, this time with Ellington as the *primus inter pares*, his piano backed by Charles Mingus and Max Roach. As Mingus memorably related in his autobiography, he had been one of the few musicians actually fired by Ellington, whose preferred methodology was to let the unwanted fire themselves. That, of course, was old history, and on this occasion, when Mingus and Roach had a heated argument and Mingus packed up his bass, it was Ellington who took him aside and made some flattering comments about his playing, whereupon the bass got unpacked and the session continued. The album is a sterling example of Ellington the splendid pianist devising musical strategies to cope with a less than ideal situation. The sheer sonic force of his playing, and his unflappable rhythmic thrust, triumph over circumstance, notably on that old warhorse "Caravan."

In the summer of 1963 Ellington created an ambitious show called *My People* for the "Century of Negro Progress" exhibition in Chicago. While always a "race man," supportive of what came to be called the Civil Rights Movement, Ellington preferred to let his music speak for him, and eloquently – one need only think of *Black, Brown and Beige*, subtitled *A Tone Parallel to the History of the Negro in America*, and *New World A-Comin'*, both from 1943. *My People* was in that tradition, if perhaps a bit more overtly political. Strayhorn was in charge of preparations, with a band consisting of several Ellington alumni (and Ray Nance), singers including Joya Sherrill and Jimmy McPhail, a choir, and tap dancer Bunny Briggs. The score – recorded under Strayhorn's supervision, with Jimmy Jones, a frequent associate, conducting – recycled some older pieces, but new ones included "King Fit the Battle of Alabam" and "What Color Is Virtue?" Mixing the sacred and secular, *My People* is of considerable interest as a precursor of the *Sacred Concerts* and indeed premiered the reworking of "Come Sunday" as the up-tempo "David Danced Before the Lord."

The State Department finally discovered Ellington and signed the band for a tour of the Middle East and India, opening in Damascus, Syria, on September 9, 1963, before an audience of 17,000. The next stop was Jordan. Ellington and members of the band seized the opportunity to visit Jerusalem – to appease the Arab and Muslim nations there were no concerts in Israel, one of the few countries where the band never performed. After Lebanon they concertized in Kabul. Then came four weeks in India and Ceylon, nine days in Pakistan, and stops in Iran and Iraq.

Four concerts in Beirut turned out to be the final performances of the tour. A day after arriving in Ankara, Ellington, about to enjoy dinner in his hotel, got a call from the State Department informing him of the assassination of President Kennedy. The remainder of the tour was canceled, though some officials, and Ellington, considered continuing. Despite the tragedy that ended it, the tour was a huge success, especially with Indian audiences, and its lasting legacy will be *The Far East Suite*, completed in 1966. And the State Department would engage Ellington again.

In 1962 Ellington had signed with a new label, Reprise, part-owned by Ellington fan Frank Sinatra. First came an excellent album of new music, *Afro-Bossa*. In April 1964 Ellington recorded, for the first time in many years, a program of current popular material (including Bob Dylan's "Blowin' in the Wind"), issued as *Ellington '65*. On his 65th birthday, Ellington and the band taped a TV show for producer Robert Herridge of *The Sound of Jazz* fame, followed by a surprise party with Lena Horne, Nat Cole, and Patti Page among the guests. Aired as *Portrait in Music – Duke Ellington*, the show includes *Harlem* along with fine versions of chestnuts and an on-the-spot original, *Metromedia Blues*.

On May 22 Ellington made his first of many appearances at the Lyndon Johnson White House, for the annual Correspondents' Dinner, performing his compositions alongside Harold Arlen, Jule Styne, Richard Adler, and Jerry Herman. At a June concert in Venice, California, the band premiered *Impressions of the Far East* (which became *The Far East Suite*) and performed his rarely heard music for a 1963 Canadian production of Shakespeare's *Timon of Athens*. Two weeks later they departed on their first tour of Japan – rather late, considering the great interest there for jazz. It was a rather hectic three-week mixture of concerts, club dates, and two TV shows, with stops in six cities. The tour was partly covered by a CBS camera crew, resulting in the show *Duke Ellington Swings through Japan*. What transpired upon their landing in Los Angeles on July 9 was extreme even for this band: the next day, at 12:30, they played at California State College in Los Angeles, and that evening performed in Ontario, California. Jet lag was apparently not an issue!

An unusual assignment from Reprise, taking on the score to *Mary Poppins*, elicited sighs from the critics, but the result was quite remarkable – Ellington and Strayhorn and the band, at one of its peaks, conjured up a most enjoyable musical flight. The next venture was *Ellington '66*, another compendium of current and recent hits, among them The Beatles' "I Want to Hold Your Hand." It got five stars, the highest rating, from *Down Beat* magazine.

A main event of 1965 was the Pulitzer Prize debacle. The three-man prize jury, having decided that no work that year was worthy, recommended that Ellington be given a special citation for "the vitality and originality of his total productivity" through nearly four decades. When the advisory board rejected the recommendation, two of the jurors – Winthrop Sargeant, author of the first musically literate book on jazz, *Jazz: Hot and Hybrid* (1938), but best known as a classical critic, and Ronald Eyer – resigned and made the issue public. The resultant publicity was almost entirely in Ellington's favor, but typically, he made no statement except the ironic "Fate is being kind to me. Fate doesn't want me to be too famous too young."

In June, Ellington, with the band, was among the luminaries invited to the unprecedented White House Festival of the Arts. Robert Lowell declined attending to protest Johnson's Vietnam policy. Unlike some of the invitees, who followed Lowell's lead yet did show up to express their views in person, Ellington behaved like a gentleman. His band closed a show that featured readings by Saul Bellow and John Hersey, dancing by Gene Kelly and the Joffrey Ballet, scenes from plays by Arthur Miller and Tennessee Williams, and excerpts from films by Alfred Hitchcock, Elia Kazan, and George Stevens, as well as displays of works by Alexander Calder, Edward Hopper, Jackson Pollock, and Jasper Johns. With John Steinbeck and John Updike hanging around the bandstand and making requests, Ellington dispelled the sour notes. Johnson's response included naming Ellington to the National Council on the Arts, awarding him the President's Gold Medal, and inviting him, along with Thurgood Marshall, to the naming of Clifford Alexander Jr. as the first chairman of the Equal Employment Opportunity Commission. Alexander was the son-in-law of Ellington's beloved doctor, Arthur Logan. There were further invitations to the White House, including a state dinner for the King of Thailand. But the most memorable White House appearance leading up to his 70th birthday party was with an octet that performed for the President of Liberia, a country Ellington had celebrated with a suite in the 1940s. "I only wish," he wrote in *Music Is My Mistress*, "I had a picture of Paul Gonsalves coming out the front door of the White House, weaving slightly, his horn in his hand, and just a little bombed."

Ellington was very fond of Gonsalves, always ready to forgive when the tenor saxophonist misbehaved, though he would mete out special punishment, as I once witnessed at a Newport Jazz Festival in the 1960s. "And now," he announced early in the band's set, "Paul Gonsalves," giving the name some extra emphasis, and calling *Body and Soul*, a two-tempoed showcase for the tenorist. For the fast portion, Ellington beat off a killing tempo and kept signaling for another chorus. After a wringing wet Gonsalves (it was a warm outdoor night) returned to his chair, Ellington intoned, "And now [pause] Paul Gonsalves!" With his sad Stan Laurel mien, Paul took his place in front of the band, awaiting the bad news, which arrived in the form of *The Opener*, another racetrack feature. No sooner had he settled in his chair than the leader called his name once more. This time the tempo was kinder, and *Happy Reunion* was the set's final Gonsalves feature. Other leaders levied fines; Ellington had a subtler way of inflicting pain.

If Gonsalves and Ray Nance were the "bad boys" of the band, Billy Strayhorn was an Ellingtonian with an unblemished record. The elegant, diminutive Ducal alter ego was relatively seldom seen on stage or bandstand, though he was often introduced at major events, and he would deputize at the piano whenever Ellington was indisposed, otherwise engaged, or delayed. A concert on June 12, 1965, in New York, was a unique public appearance of Strayhorn as leader of an ensemble – a quintet including trumpeter Clark Terry and reedman Bob Wilber, almost eerily capable of sounding like Johnny Hodges, for whom Strayhorn provided so much inspirational material. Sponsored by the New York chapter of the Duke Ellington Society, the concert revealed a new side of Strayhorn as a charming commentator, in the spirit of Ellington but with his own special voice. That he was a fine pianist was news only to the uninitiated. Ellington was not present but arranged for the quintet to record, paying for and supervising the session a few weeks later – a little-known chapter in their long, close collaboration.

Later that summer Ellington was featured with the Boston Pops, bringing his new young bassist, John Lamb, and his favorite post-Sonny Greer drummer, Louis Bellson. Bellson was also on hand for something much more significant: the premiere of Ellington's *Concert of Sacred Music*, commissioned by San Francisco's Grace Cathedral in celebration of its restoration. The decade had seen a number of jazz masses and other uses of jazz in church services, but Ellington did not want to create a formal mass. While a man of deep faith in God, he was not a member of a congregation or a frequent churchgoer, and he wanted the *Concert of Sacred Music* to reflect his personal, ecumenical belief. The concert mixed adaptations of extant material with new pieces, including what has been called his first choral writing; however, a brief segment in the 1935 short film *Symphony in Black*, titled "A Hymn of Sorrow," in a church setting, was a precursor, as were elements of *My People*.

A bit nervous about how the debut would be received, Ellington was delighted with its resounding success. "I'm sure this is the most important statement we've ever made," he said afterwards, adding that the cathedral's acoustics were "devilish." At Christmas time he brought the *Concert of Sacred Music* to the Fifth Avenue Presbyterian Church in New York, with Lena Horne as a special guest, for two performances that were televised and recorded. With a flexible cast of singers, and choir music that could be prepared in advance, Ellington could perform the work in venues representing many branches of Christianity as well as in synagogues. When he was available, tap dancer Bunny Briggs, featured in "David Danced Before the Lord," was the star of the show – which, while respectful, reflected Ellington's abiding fascination with the theatrical. Its successor, the *Second Sacred Concert*, would be both more serious and more original.

The *Concert of Sacred Music* attracted far more attention than a work for piano (with some assistance by bass and drums) and symphony orchestra, *The Golden Broom and the Green Apple*, unveiled in July 1965, with Lukas Foss conducting the New York Philharmonic and the composer at the piano. In spite of the apparatus, it is not a very serious work, and some authorities suspect the orchestration was done by Mercer Ellington's boyhood friend Luther Henderson, a Broadway theater professional.

In January 1966 the band embarked on a five-week European tour, a highlight of which was a solo recital (the only one of a handful throughout his career that was truly solo, with no bass or drums) at the restored medieval castle in Goutelas, France – an experience later commemorated with Ellington's *Goutelas Suite*. In April Ellington and the band took their first visit to Africa, to participate in the World Festival of Negro Arts in Dakar, Senegal, whose president, the poet Léopold Senghor, Ellington much admired. In anticipation of the trip Ellington unveiled his *La Plus Belle Africaine*, a rare feature for Harry Carney's majestic baritone and one of the composer's most durable works of the decade, at a Paris concert in January. It was the hit of the Dakar concert.

About a month after their return came the second Japanese tour, a two-week affair. *Ad Lib on Nippon*, first heard on the first tour as a piano solo, was this time presented with a role for the band and would be recorded later in the year as an appendage to *The Far East Suite*. Ellington had returned to RCA Victor, and as a condition for recording the suite, not considered commercially viable, the label asked for a program of hits, issued as *The Popular Duke Ellington* and indeed enjoying good sales. While Ellington was less than enthusiastic about this task, he and Strayhorn fitted the tried and true with new clothing, and the band responded with élan, Victor's engineers providing superb sound.

A December performance of the *Concert of Sacred Music* at Constitution Hall in the nation's capital did not meet with the approval of the Baptist Ministers' Conference, taking place in the same city; a resolution from the conference cited jazz as music played in nightclubs, and the "worldliness" of Ellington's music. His response, "Doesn't God accept sinners any more?" was right on target, but the criticism reflected the cultural resistance to jazz in the black middle-class establishment. Around this time, both Fisk and Howard Universities turned down Marshall Stearns's offer to donate the collections of the Institute of Jazz Studies, of which Ellington was a board member.

A *Concert of Sacred Music* performance at Cambridge's Great St. Mary's Church was a highlight of a long European tour in early 1967. The tour included the first performances of Strayhorn's composition *Blood Count*, fittingly a vehicle for Johnny Hodges. The composer had sent the chart to Ellington from his hospital bed; he was suffering from terminal cancer and died on May 31, aged 51. At the funeral service held six days later at St. Peter's Lutheran Church in New York (to which Strayhorn willed his grand piano), Ellington read his moving eulogy. The most frequently quoted passage deals with Strayhorn's four freedoms – "from hate, unconditionally ... from self-pity ... from fear of possibly doing something that might help another more than it might himself, and freedom from the kind of pride that could make a man feel he was better than his brother or neighbor." The service-ending rendition of a slow *Take the "A" Train* by Ray Nance's violin backed by Billy Taylor's piano left few dry eyes.

There was much discussion among Ellington cognoscenti about the effect of Strayhorn's passing, but being left to his own resources stimulated Ellington's creativity. In July he spent two days in Canada, recording works by three Canadian composers, featuring his piano. Typically he had no time to study scores beforehand, and just as typically performed to everyone's satisfaction. Later that month he began a long relationship with a near-ideal Manhattan venue, the Rainbow Grill, on the 65th floor of Rockefeller Center's RCA Building, as it was then known. The band-stand was too small and the room too intimate for the full band, but for five weeks Ellington could present an octet (Cat Anderson, Lawrence Brown, Hodges, Gonsalves, Carney, John Lamb, and drummer Steve Little) while the rest of the band was kept on payroll for recording opportunities and outside bookings on weekends. Best of all, the engagement provided welcome rest from incessant traveling.

Among the recording activities in 1967 was a Strayhorn tribute . . .*And His Mother Called Him Bill*, which included Ellington's solo rendition of "Lotus Blossom." It would become a concert staple. An excellent TV special, *On the Road with Duke Ellington*, was shown on NBC's *Bell Telephone Hour* in October. And in a final effort for Reprise, the band recorded with Sinatra. While the album cover showed youthful portraits of *Francis A. and Edward K.*, as the title read, the arrangements were all by Billy May – though "Indian Summer," with a lovely Hodges solo, made the effort worthwhile.

Meanwhile, Ellington was busy writing the *Second Sacred Concert*, which went into rehearsals on January 15, 1968, at New York City's gargantuan Cathedral of St. John the Divine. To fit the venue, the cast was huge: singers Alice Babs (a former child star in her native Sweden, and as Ellington wrote, "the most unique artist I know"[1]), Trish Turner, Jimmy McPhail, Devonne Gardner, Roscoe Gill, and Tony Watkins; the A. M. E. Mother Zion Church Choir; and the St. Hilda's and St. Hugh's School Choirs. The premiere, on January 19, was attended by some 6,000 people. CBS-TV's lights glared, and the acoustics were less than ideal, but the new work was clearly superior to its predecessor, and soloists, choristers, and band excelled, with Alice Babs the standout.

On April 4, the band was on stage at Carnegie Hall for a fundraiser for Tougaloo College when Ellington was informed of Dr. Martin Luther King, Jr.'s assassination. After intermission, selections from the *Second Sacred Concert* were performed, Ellington telling the hushed audience that the concert's theme was freedom, for which Dr. King had given his life. Soon yet another tragedy struck, the assassination of Robert F. Kennedy. On June 8, a Saturday, CBS-TV aired a jazz tribute to the slain Senator, with Ellington, Hodges, and young bassist Jeff Castleman taking part. Later that month Jimmy Hamilton left the band after 26 years of service, thus breaking up the greatest saxophone section in Ellington (and jazz) history. His replacement was the able Ben Webster acolyte Harold Ashby, who could manage a clarinet part but not a clarinet solo.

An afternoon set at the Newport Jazz Festival joined the two greatest alto saxophonists in classic jazz, Benny Carter and Johnny Hodges, with Ellington, Castleman, and recently returned drummer Rufus Jones. But while Duke uttered accolades for Carter, he gave Hodges more solos and did not include any of Carter's compositions – treatment bordering on rudeness. If Ellington was being protective of Hodges, that seemed entirely unnecessary. But he redeemed himself that evening. Joan Crawford, in her role as a director of Pepsi-Cola, a festival sponsor, took to the podium after a brief introduction from producer George Wein. Visibly nervous (movie stars back then were not accustomed to appearing before large crowds, and more than 15,000 were on hand), she began to read a canned speech, rife with clichés about jazz and its contribution to American culture. The crowd, as was its custom, was inattentive, taking time out for food and drink and friendly chats. Suddenly, Crawford found her voice. "Shut up! You just shut up!" she yelled, eyes blazing, adding some remarks about the audience's manners. It was a fine moment, reminding me of her title role in *Mildred Pierce*. In fact the crowd was quieter than usual. She finished her speech, which turned out to be an introduction to Ellington, in a shaky voice, and as she stepped down to the stage, appeared to lose her composure again. But there was Duke Ellington, resplendent and beaming, to help her down the steps, sweeping her toward center stage, telling her she was gracious and charming and that he loved her madly. He then bussed her twice on each cheek and waltzed her off into the wings. It was a superb rescue, carried out by a complete professional.

The band's first Latin American tour – 16 days in Brazil, Argentina, Uruguay, and Chile – began in September. The reception, notably in Argentina, was so warm and enthusiastic that Ellington was deeply moved, according to Stanley Dance's documentation. A week in Mexico, which was filmed, was tacked on after five days of U.S. bookings. Inspired by the new sights and sounds, Ellington recorded *Latin American Suite* in early November – a delightful work, if more Ellington than Latin.

Ellington's band performed at one of Richard Nixon's inaugural balls, but the White House party for Ellington's 70th birthday was a lot more memorable. The event, well documented on CD and film, was surely one of the best parties ever held there, and also perhaps the longest – at least that was what some happy staffers told us late-departing guests. There was a fine all-star recital, with Earl Hines almost stealing the show. After the presentation of the Medal of Freedom, Ellington kissed Nixon twice on each cheek, Nixon seeming puzzled at the explanation of "one for each cheek." Once the president and first lady had excused themselves to let the good times begin to roll, there was lots of informal music-making, including a brief Ellington–Willie "The Lion" Smith duet. It turned out that Spiro Agnew, the vice president despised by liberals, was a pretty fair piano player – better than Nixon, who offered "Happy Birthday." Ellington's sister Ruth joined him on the receiving line, where his common-law wife

Evie surely would have liked to be. The next day all was back to normal; the band played for a high school prom in Oklahoma City.

A week before the party, Johnny Hodges suffered a heart seizure and was absent for two months. His first replacement was the very young Gregory Herbert, soon relieved by veteran Norris Turney, whose flute doubling brought a new color to the band's palette. He would remain after Hodges returned, boosting the reeds to six. The addition of organist Wild Bill Davis later in 1969 added further depth. Upon the band's return home from a long European tour, Lawrence Brown gave his two-week notice and was replaced by Julian Priester.

A long tour of the Pacific region kicked off in January, 1970. Not long after their return, Ellington was honored at an NAACP benefit concert at Madison Square Garden, hosted by Sammy Davis Jr. The concert lasted six-and-a-half hours, climaxed by the band's appearance with guests Louis Armstrong, Ray Charles, and Jimmy Rushing. Band vocalist Tony Watkins, a favorite of the leader, also got his moments. A puzzle to many critics, Watkins had a gospel background that made him effective in the *Sacred Concerts*, but he was also most useful as a den mother, waking Hodges from his naps, sewing on uniform buttons, ironing, and cleaning up calamities. He gets quite a bit of space in *Music Is My Mistress*.

Ellington worked on the *New Orleans Suite* during an April engagement at Al Hirt's Club in that very city, coinciding with the New Orleans Jazz and Heritage Festival. With Hirt's OK, each night's final set was devoted to rehearsing, much to the chagrin of some well-oiled customers demanding "Sophisticated Lady" and other chestnuts. Ellington, the band members, and busy copyist Tom Whaley were not self-conscious in the presence of an audience, and it was fascinating for me to follow the progress of the suite. A special treat was Paul Gonsalves "strolling" between sets, serenading each table and taking requests – one for "Ramona" yielded results one wishes could be heard again. After five nights at Hirt's, Ellington was ready to unveil the new suite at the festival. Johnny Hodges was at the first recording session for the suite on April 27, but on May 11 he suffered a heart attack and died at his dentist's. His feature in the suite was to have been "Portrait of Sidney Bechet," and Ellington had hopes of persuading him to resurrect the soprano saxophone he played so well until the early 1940s. Gonsalves took his place for the recording on May 13, but it didn't quite work. Fred Stone, a gifted trumpeter who had replaced Willie Cook, was a notable voice in the movement "Aristocracy à la Jean Lafitte."

Ellington's music for the Alvin Ailey ballet *The River* was heard on tape at its New York premiere on June 25. At the Monterey Jazz Festival in September, Ellington debuted *The Afro-Eurasian Eclipse* – a charming work, in particular the movement "Chinoiserie," a feature for Harold Ashby. During a three-week engagement in Las Vegas at Caesar's Palace, starting on Christmas Day, Cat Anderson left the band. There was much more to him than his startling command of high notes, which is why he was in the band for so long despite charges from several colleagues of his kleptomania, another matter Tony Watkins smoothed over. In March 1971 the band played at a very social New York occasion: Joe Frazier's victory party at the Statler Hilton Hotel, following his bout with heavy-weight challenger Muhammad Ali. A few days later Ellington was inducted into the Swedish Academy of Music, one among a multitude of honors bestowed on him at this stage of life. In July Ellington unveiled his *Togo Brava Suite* at Newport; the African nation of Togo had honored him with a stamp (incidentally designed and printed in Israel). When word of Louis Armstrong's death on July 6 reached Ellington, he issued a state-ment: "If anyone was Mr. Jazz, it was Louis Armstrong. He was the epitome of jazz and always will be … he is irreplaceable, and we are going to miss him terribly."

After a month at the Rainbow Grill, Ellington and the band were ready for a big assignment: a month-long State Department tour of Russia. Learning how to say "We love you madly" in Russian, he and the band arrived in Moscow and were treated to a night at the Bolshoi Ballet. In Leningrad, Ellington, once an aspiring painter, made sure to visit the Hermitage Museum, just before the first concert of a hugely successful tour. The biggest problem was finding steaks – a staple of the Ducal diet – so the diplomats had to airlift them from home. In spite of high ticket prices, Leningrad audiences, mostly youthful, filled a 4,200-seat audito-rium for five nights. At a Moscow concert the audience just wouldn't let the band quit. "Four hours and they still want more," said a delighted Ellington. The State Department was delighted as well.

In October 1972 came the weekend fundraiser for the Duke Ellington Fellowship Program at Yale University, which had given Ellington an honorary doctorate in 1967. The Fellows idea was hatched by faculty member, French hornist, and author Willie Ruff to honor the concept of "a conservatory without walls," and to attract attention and funding to an African-American music program at the university. No fewer than 40 musical figures, including Marian Anderson, Paul Robeson, and jazz musicians ranging from Eubie Blake to Jon Faddis, were honored with medals. (When Ruff first told Ellington about his plans, Ellington asked about his white former drummer: "So, Louis Bellson can't be an Ellington Fellow?"[2]) There was much jamming by ad hoc groups, with Dizzy Gillespie, Benny Carter and Charles Mingus on board, and two Ellington band concerts. The most fun for me was to observe Ellington mingling with the students at an unnaturally early hour – a bit past ten. Dressed in a black sweatshirt (with a hole) that he sometimes wore at recording sessions, dark pants, and a bowler hat, he clearly enjoyed himself more than at the formal events.

In January 1973, bothered by a touch of flu, Ellington was obligated to participate in yet another TV "spectacular," *Duke Ellington – We Love You Madly*. Overloaded with talent (Sammy Davis, Jr., Ray Charles, Billy Eckstine, Joe Williams, Sarah Vaughan, Peggy Lee, Aretha Franklin, and then some, plus a band made up of Basie and Ellington graduates), the taping in Los Angeles ended at three in the morning, leaving him bone tired. The next day he was admitted to the hospital for chronic exhaustion and a viral infection. Mercer took over until Ellington returned to activity less than three weeks later.

When Ellington's book *Music Is My Mistress* was finally published, it triggered an instant crisis – the dust jacket was brown, a color he had despised since the day of his mother's death, when he was wearing a brown suit. All the books had to be recalled and outfitted with a new blue dust jacket. Those who expected an autobiography were disappointed – the book is a series of vignettes about people in the author's life, all favorable in tone and reflecting his "love you madly" slogan. There are insights, some good anecdotes, and touches of humor, but for the publisher, the $50,000 advance hardly seemed a bargain.

Norris Turney, who made good contributions to the band, left after a ten-day Miami stand and was not replaced, the reed section reverting to the standard five. Next to quit was Cootie Williams, after coming down with a chest ailment. In Houston the whole band got a checkup, and Ellington and Harry Carney were advised to see their personal doctors. This did not bode well, and six months later Ellington was diagnosed with cancer.

Cootie's replacement was the gifted young Barry Lee Hall, but the band was clearly losing ground. The honors kept coming – doctorates from Columbia and Fisk Universities, and the French *Légion d'honneur*. Four weeks at the good old Rainbow Grill in August were a relief from strings of one-nighters, but Ellington was now focused on his *Third Sacred Concert*, a new work scheduled to premiere at no less than London's Westminster Abbey on October 24.

Ellington and the band arrived in England two days before. At the next day's rehearsal, Gonsalves collapsed and was hospitalized, depriving the band of one of its few remaining great voices. The performance, starring Alice Babs, was respectable, with some recycled material and some fine choral writing. Ellington was too tired to make more than a brief appearance at a dinner in his honor hosted by Prime Minister Edward Heath at 10 Downing Street. The very next day the band, with Babs guesting, performed a concert in Malmö, Sweden. Then the grind continued: 21 days of touring Europe, with a *Third Sacred Concert* performance filmed and recorded in Barcelona, then down to Ethiopia for four concerts, plus two in Zambia. This African visit, sponsored by the State Department, was highlighted by an audience with the aging emperor Haile Selassie I, the "Lion of Judah," who appointed Ellington Commander of the Imperial Order of Ethiopia and gave each band member a gold medallion. Ellington was visibly moved. The concerts were well received, by mostly young audiences hardly familiar with jazz.

On the tour's last day in Zambia, Ellington's trusted friend and doctor Arthur Logan fell to his death from an embankment above the Henry Hudson Parkway near his home in New York City. Mercer and Ellington's sister Ruth kept the news from him until the band reached Dublin, the day of Dr. Logan's funeral, which he most likely would have wanted to attend. "I'll never get over this," he said. "I won't last six months." But he soldiered on, through six more concerts and a TV taping, then flew home and immediately embarked on four one-nighters in Pennsylvania and Maryland. Then, blessed relief, the Rainbow Grill came to the rescue with a month-long stay.

The series of one-nighters that followed, some as far away as South Dakota, did not all include Ellington, whose condition had worsened, but he was on hand at Georgetown University on February 10, 1974, with Jaki Byard assisting at the piano, and at several Florida venues thereafter. Two of these concerts were captured by recordists, March 9 being the last. His final stand with the band was on March 22 for two concerts in Sturgis, Michigan. Three days later he checked himself into Columbia Presbyterian Hospital.

Far from withdrawing from activity, Ellington worked on completing two projects: *Three Black Kings* (a tribute to the black king of the biblical Magi, King Solomon, and Martin Luther King, Jr.) and the opera *Queenie Pie*. Family members, who didn't always get along with each other, were constant presences. His old manager Irving Mills, out of contact in decades, made long phone calls. Granddaughter Mercédes Ellington recalled that he would discuss his love affairs with her. He was aware of at least some of the many international events surrounding his 75th birthday on April 29: a performance of his sacred music at St. Peter's Church in New York; a three-day symposium at Stanford University; the showing of Ellington films at 189 U.S. Information Agency posts in 108 countries; photo exhibits at U.S. embassies in the more than 50 countries he had performed in for the State Department; and concerts by local musicians. Such bad news as the deaths of Paul Gonsalves, on May 15, and Tyree Glenn, on May 18, was kept from him. Duke Ellington died in the early morning of May 24, 1974.

His funeral three days later at the Cathedral of St. John the Divine was front page news in the *New York Times*, as was his obituary. The service, befitting a head of state more than a celebrity, was attended by over 10,000, with a crowd estimated at 2,500 gathered outside. Ecumenical, like the *Sacred Concerts*, the service had readings by Catholic, Lutheran, and Methodist clergy. The eulogy, delivered by Stanley Dance, was worthy of the subject and may have been this writer-advisor-friend's finest moment. There were many musical tributes, among them Ella Fitzgerald's "Just a Closer Walk with Thee" and Joe Williams's "Heritage," the most moving to me. But Ellington had the last musical say. As accompaniment to the processional, the sounds of "Heaven," from the *Second Sacred Concert* – first heard in the very same cathedral, and featuring the voices of Alice Babs and Johnny Hodges – wafted over the crowd like a message from high above.

Notes

1 Duke Ellington, *Music Is My Mistress* (New York: Da Capo Press, 1973), 288.

2 Stanley Dance relayed this quotation to me in a private conversation.

PART III

Ellington and the jazz tradition

11 Ellington and the blues

BENJAMIN GIVAN

In December 1972, less than 18 months before his death, Duke Ellington recorded an album of duets with the bassist Ray Brown in tribute to Jimmie Blanton, whose legendary walking bass lines had anchored Ellington's orchestra over 30 years earlier. Entitled *This One's for Blanton*, the disc debuted a new four-part suite alongside several classic Ellington compositions such as *Do Nothin' Till You Hear from Me*.[1] It also included a rather anomalous medium-tempo blues, part of an original composition called *Mr. J. B. Blues* that Ellington had first recorded in a 1941 duet with Blanton (the first two choruses are transcribed in Example 11.1). Oddly, the album listed the track not by its true name but as the traditional song "See See Rider," which Brown quoted midway through his bass solo (Example 11.2).[2]

Whatever the reasons for it, the discrepant title would surely have had nostalgic connotations for Ellington, who as a young man may well have first heard "See See Rider" on Ma Rainey's famous 1924 premiere recording, shortly after leaving his native Washington, D.C., to settle permanently in Manhattan.[3] In those days the blues was reaching the pinnacle of its popularity, propelled not only by female African-American recording artists such as Rainey and Bessie Smith, but also by influential songwriters such as W. C. Handy, who had been publishing blues songs since 1912. Indeed, by the 1920s sheet music sales and royalties had made the blues a highly lucrative commercial product within the booming entertainment industry, as Ellington was swift to grasp. Upon arriving in New York, he joined half a dozen other songwriters who regularly earned 15 or 20 dollars by writing an original blues lead sheet and selling the publishing rights to Irving Mills.[4]

Unlike the era's jazz, which had been adopted and adapted by high-profile white musicians such as the Original Dixieland Jazz Band and Paul Whiteman, the blues remained largely the province of black artists. "The Negro is the blues," declared Ellington in a 1930 interview. "Blues is the rage in popular music. And popular music is the good music of tomorrow!"[5] Extolled by the younger generation of Harlem Renaissance thinkers as a touchstone of modern black urbanity and an emblem of African Americans' transcendence of oppressive social circumstances, the blues was a richly symbolic creative resource. Ellington's most forthright musical homage to the idiom, a song titled "The Blues" from his 1943 suite *Black,*

Example 11.1. "See See Rider" (public domain), choruses 1 and 2, from *This One's for Blanton* (Pablo PACD2310–721–2), recorded December 5, 1972. Transcribed by Benjamin Givan.

Brown and Beige, dramatized the music's somber expressive dimension with his own lyrics: "The blues ain't nothin' but a cold, grey day, and all night long it stays that way." Still, as he later wrote in his memoir, "the blues are basic to all jazz, and although they are often thought of as sad, they are in fact performed with every variety of expression."

Example 11.2. "See See Rider" (public domain), measures 84–96, from *This One's for Blanton* (Pablo PACD2310–721–2), recorded December 5, 1972. Transcribed by Benjamin Givan.

"In its essential form," Ellington added, "a blues consists of twelve bars divided into three sections of four bars each."[6] His 1972 "See See Rider" recording exemplifies this structure in its opening two choruses (Example 11.1): each 4-bar phrase consists of a short, syncopated piano melody answered by the bass. This same 12-bar chorus form underlies innumerable original compositions spanning his entire career, accounting for the majority of tracks on such celebrated albums as *Ellington at Newport* (1956), *Blues in Orbit* (1958–1959), and the *Back to Back* small-group session with Johnny Hodges (1959). Yet, needless to say, the 12-bar scheme no more limits the possibilities of jazz than – in Ellington's own analogy – the standard sonnet form limits the possibilities of poetry.[7] For one thing, its basic harmonies – four bars of the tonic chord (I) followed by two of the subdominant (IV), two of the tonic (I), two of the dominant (V), and finally two of the tonic (I) – are infinitely variable.[8] Often a subdominant chord (IV) appears in m. 2, a minor subdominant (IVm) in m. 6, a supertonic (II) in m. 9, and a dominant (V) in m. 12. And individual pieces may involve unique alterations, as in Example 11.1's half-step harmonic displacements oscillating above and below the regular chords, and the novel VI chord in m. 10 (B7 in the tune's tonic key of D major).

For another thing, the blues, musically speaking, is not just a matter of form and harmony. It is also characterized by a scale with its third, fifth, and seventh scale degrees lowered (the so-called "blue notes"); microtonal pitch inflections; call-and-response riffs;[9] and heterogeneous timbres such as the wah-wahs, growls, and smears perfected by Bubber Miley, Joe Nanton, Cootie Williams, Clark Terry, and many other Ellington hornmen. All these devices imbue Ellington's entire oeuvre with a blues sensibility regardless of whether 12-bar-blues harmonies are present. Mercer Ellington once remarked of his father that "you'll find the effect of the blues in almost everything he writes."[10] This effect had limitless expressive possibilities. As Stanley Crouch has evocatively written, blues timbres in Ellington's hands "could color any kind of piece, keeping it in touch with the street, with the heated boudoir beast of two backs, the sticky red leavings of violence, the pomp and rhythmic pride of the dance floor, and . . . plaintive lyricism made spiritual by emotion."[11]

Ellington's blues forms and gestures were sometimes comparatively down-home and elemental, especially in certain riff-based compositions of the 1940s (e.g., *Main Stem*, *C Jam Blues*, *Across the Track Blues*, and *Happy Go Lucky Local*) and rhythm-and-blues-inflected works of the 1960s and 1970s (including *Ray Charles' Place*, *Blue Pepper*, *Acht O'Clock Rock*, *Rockochet*, and *Didjeridoo*). Many of these themes pare down the blues's traditional three-phrase poetic structure to merely a thrice-repeated four-bar motive. More often, blues ingredients were served up alongside other popular song idioms, Latin rhythms, or chromatic harmonies and contrapuntal textures redolent of European classical music. The political implications were undeniable. In particular, as John Howland has argued, Ellington's incorporation of the blues within works of symphonic dimensions embodied a "vernacular modernist" (or "Afro-Modernist") symbolic strategy of racial uplift.[12]

Even Ellington's classic contributions to the Tin Pan Alley canon, many of which originated as wordless instrumentals, tend to feature markedly bluesy melodies. The semitonal meandering of *Sophisticated Lady* and *Prelude to a Kiss* recalls blues singing's microtonal sliding, even while complex chromatic chords give both songs a genteel, bourgeois air. Elsewhere Ellington developed a bold harmonic palette by harmonizing blue notes consonantly rather than maintaining their idiomatic minor/major ambiguity. In the refrain of *It Don't Mean a Thing (If It Ain't Got That Swing)*, a lowered-submediant seventh chord ($\flat$VI7) intensifies the first line's straining flat-five blue note on the word "ain't" (Example 11.3). Midway through the bridge of *Drop Me Off in Harlem*, a two-bar tonicization of $\flat$VI is initiated by a melodic blue seventh, which trumpeter Cootie Williams growls avidly on the 1933 recording (at 2′ 31″).[13] And in

Example 11.3. *It Don't Mean a Thing (If It Ain't Got That Swing)*: consonant harmonization of scale degree ♭5. Publishing rights administered by EMI Mills Music Inc. (ASCAP) and Sony ATV Harmony (ASCAP); composition credited to Duke Ellington and Irving Mills.

Do Nothin' Till You Hear from Me, scale-degree ♭3 from the opening key, reiterated through the first half of the bridge, prompts a full-scale modulation to ♭VI. Discussing this song's original instrumental version, *Concerto for Cootie*, Robert Walser notes that composers across the ages have used the same flat submediant key to symbolize a "utopian refuge, illogically related to the main key and fated not to last."[14] In the song's bridge, this key actualizes a single blue note's implicit tonal potential on a grand scale.

Ellington's "See See Rider" recording features not a sweeping, flamboyant modulatory gesture but a swirling kaleidoscope of consonantly harmonized blue notes; in the second half of m. 1, a ♭II13 chord supports a melodic C♮ (scale-degree ♭7), and in m. 2, a VII chord harmonizes F♮ (scale-degree ♭3) in the lower piano line. Expanding the blues's staple three-chord vocabulary was one of Ellington's lifelong preoccupations: as early as the 1930s, with compositions such as *Bundle of Blues* (1933), *Blue Light* (1938), and *Subtle Lament* (1939), he was cloaking blues choruses in harmonies so ornate that their signature formal structure would have been discernible only to the most astute, culturally knowledgeable listeners.

Sometimes a blues number steadily gains in harmonic complexity. A 1934 disc of the song *Saddest Tale*, later sung by Billie Holiday in the short film *Symphony in Black*, follows its opening *Rhapsody in Blue*-like clarinet cadenza with two straightforward blues choruses; next comes a muted trumpet solo (1′ 44″) cushioned by an exquisitely refined saxophone choir that shifts from chord to glowing chord with every beat.[15] Seven years later, singer Ivie Anderson's first chorus on "Rocks in My Bed," from Ellington's 1941 revue *Jump for Joy*, sets a grittier mood, conveyed especially by its V–IV progression in mm. 9–10. The next chorus (1′ 42″), however, delves into a more sophisticated harmonic domain, in stark tension with its archetypically vernacular lyrics ("That mean man o' mine . . . "). Underpinning its first eight bars is a chorale-like horn texture passing through a variety of secondary dominants and modal mixtures at a rate of two chords per bar. Then, at the chorus's climax in m. 9 (2′ 04″), with Anderson singing "That man is lower than a snake in a wagon track," Ellington's horns envelop her in a serpentine series of ninth chords slithering semitonally from ♭V9 down to II9.[16]

Ellington's inspiration for reharmonizing 12-bar blues forms never flagged. On *Transblucency* (1946), co-written with trombonist Lawrence Brown, a *Mood Indigo*-like trio – comprised of Kay Davis's wordless vocal plus a muted trombone and chalumeau-register clarinet – wends through an ethereal harmonic succession that shimmers chromatically into the tonic by way of VII7 (m. 2), II$^{\sharp 11}$ (m. 6), and ♭II (m. 10). Two decades later, on the minor blues "Ad Lib on Nippon," which rounds out *The Far East Suite*, stepwise descending whole-tone chords give the ninth and tenth bars of the contemplative introductory choruses an exotic tint.[17] And "Portrait of Mahalia Jackson," the recessional segment of Ellington's late-career *New Orleans Suite* (1970), includes a loping gospel blues in $\frac{12}{8}$ time with ♭III and ♭VII chords concurrently echoing the parallel progressions of rock music.

Whereas 12-bar choruses are reiterated successively throughout nearly all the above compositions, they can also of course be juxtaposed with other themes. This is the case, more often than not, with early published blues songs, including Handy's 1914 "Saint Louis Blues," which famously complements its 12-bar form with a habanera interlude, and Rainey's rendition of "See See Rider," whose opening verse, though 12 bars long, is not a blues chorus. Ellington's characteristic multi-strain compositions often incorporated blues progressions as subsidiary elements, giving performers a chance to solo over familiar musical ground. *Birmingham Breakdown* (1926) ends with helter-skelter 12-bar choruses that, as Mark Tucker notes, supplant the trio theme (a contrasting melody in a new key) typical of ragtime and marches, and could be extended indefinitely in live performances.[18] Three decades later, Ellington placed another open-ended blues solo section at the end of the song "Hey, Buddy Bolden," from the suite *A Drum Is a Woman*. The effect in each case is of an exuberant, celebratory homecoming to well-trodden musical territory after a distant foray – an emotional release evoking the collective jubilation of a New Orleans second line. When located earlier within a piece, blues forms instead offer a moment to relax and regroup between excursions farther afield, as in "Cycle of Fourths" (from the Shakespearean suite, *Such Sweet Thunder*) and the famous interlude in *Diminuendo and Crescendo in Blue* – both featuring saxophonist Paul Gonsalves.

The several consecutive blues choruses midway through Ellington's 14-minute suite *A Tone Parallel to Harlem* (1950) could be viewed as either a subordinate transition or a primary centerpiece surrounded by the work's curtain-raising prelude and declamatory conclusion. In his earlier compositions of the 1920s, blues forms are often clearly preeminent but, in keeping with Jazz Age conventions, Ellington adorns them with secondary passages. The classic example is *Black and Tan Fantasy*, whose twice-played eight-bar interlude, with its distinctly non-bluesy ♭VI–I progression and a harmonically refined turnaround, creates an elegant diversion between the initial funereal blues melody and the succeeding major-key 12-bar choruses. *Saturday Night Function*, by contrast, hinges on a sacred–secular opposition: framed by a reverent horn choir's spiritual-tinged theme, three of its four central blues choruses are suffused with a churchy diminished-seventh chord (VII°7/V) in their sixth bar.[19] Other early Ellington charts that integrate straightforward blues forms with additional four- and eight-bar phrases include *The Mooche*, which both opens and closes with a darkly dissonant 24-bar theme (itself an expanded AAB structure reminiscent of traditional blues phrasing), and *Harlem Flat Blues*, whose closely-voiced clarinet trio strain recurs three times amid six blues choruses.

Occasionally Ellington weaves blues choruses within elaborate, palindromic multisectional pieces. *Jolly Wog*, from 1930, is structured ABACDCABA, with its recurrent A theme an E-flat major blues scored for muted trumpets plus Barney Bigard's clarinet.[20] *Sepia Panorama*, a collaboration with Billy Strayhorn from a decade later, has an ABCDDCBA design with dramatic sectional contrasts. The riff-based opening and closing theme (A) is a blues, as are the central solo choruses (D); interwoven between them are two episodes pairing lush chromatic textures (B) with a driving unison brass fanfare (C).[21] These balanced patchwork constructions can be compared to traditional African-American quilting patterns or, for that matter, to Romare Bearden's modernist collages: the blues choruses are but one element of a larger assemblage with its own overarching narrative.

Yet Ellington by no means saw the traditional blues form as an immutable, sacrosanct ideal, and he never restricted himself to stitching complete 12-bar choruses together with other musical units. Blues phrasing and harmonies were so deeply rooted in the African-American musical heritage that he could invoke them extremely subtly, and once referenced they stirred in his audiences a set of ingrained expectations that could be just as easily evaded as fulfilled. The blues, in other words, provided a sturdy springboard for musical innovation and experimentation that launched performers and listeners into far-flung realms. Sometimes Ellington secreted intact 12-bar forms beneath jarringly irregular surface-level melodic patterns, as with *Diminuendo and Crescendo in Blue*. At the end of this 1937 chart's third chorus, a four-bar transitional modulation from E-flat to G major sets up a standard 12-bar blues whose increasingly asymmetric call-and-response exchanges between brass and reeds – (2 bars + 2 bars), (2 + 1), (2 + 1), 2 – culminate in a saxophone tutti phrase that extends four bars into the next chorus.[22] One can easily imagine such passages throwing crowded ballrooms for a loop, compelling dancers to listen more closely and rejigger their floor moves.

In many instances Ellington treated 12-bar forms still more malleably, straining the usual three-phrase blues format almost to its breaking point. The first of two 1931 recordings of his early extended composition *Creole Rhapsody* features several complete 12-bar choruses, with solos by Barney Bigard (at 1′ 05″), Cootie Williams (1′ 31″), and Ellington (3′ 28″). But it also contains a 16-bar theme, scored for two trombones, that elongates each 4-measure phrase of a typical blues; its initial tonic phrase is five bars long (4′ 04″), as is the following IV–I succession (4′ 15″), while its final dominant-based progression (4′ 26″) encompasses six measures. After this protracted chorus the music immediately reverts to normalcy with a reassuringly orthodox blues melody stated by muted trumpets (4′ 39″).

In other cases Ellington used blues forms fragmentarily. "Sonnet to Hank Cinq," the fleeting third movement from *Such Sweet Thunder*, willfully toys with his listeners' default 12-bar-chorus expectations. After a 4-measure introduction, trombonist Britt Woodman plays a stentorian melody (in iambic pentameter) that traverses a standard blues progression for 10 bars before being abruptly superseded by a new 16-bar theme in the parallel minor over a double-time rhythm section. The opening theme then returns, but this time the accompaniment halts at its ninth bar while Woodman completes the previously truncated blues form with a rousing rubato cadenza that rises to a final, climactic high A♭. By first sundering the blues progression and then demonstratively tying together the strands initially left hanging, Ellington creates a sweeping dynamic arc of tension and resolution in the space of just 90 seconds.

Elsewhere he references the standard blues form without ever stating it fully. "Flirtibird," from his 1959 *Anatomy of a Murder* film score, has an AAABA thematic structure whose 8-bar A phrase is harmonically identical to the last 8 bars of a 12-bar blues. This sultry, sauntering alto saxophone melody, a leitmotif for the movie's female lead, Laura Manion (played by Lee Remick), gives an impression of drapes parting to reveal an illicit blues-in-progress.

Incomplete blues chord changes are even more closely entwined with popular-song phrasing conventions on the classic 1940 chart *Harlem Air Shaft*. Never deviating from a standard 32-bar AABA song form after its capriciously modulating introduction, *Harlem Air Shaft*'s 8-bar A sections simply jettison the last four measures of a typical 12-bar blues. Rather than encountering the blues form midstream, as with "Flirtibird," the listener (or dancer) is led down a familiar musical route only to arrive at an unanticipated cul-de-sac. Retracing the same pathway, the second A section magnifies the listener's uncertainty as to the eventual destination; only at the bridge does the actual compositional roadmap become clear. The chart's blues sensibility is heightened by the opening chorus's

Example 11.4. *Jazz Convulsions*: harmonic structure of the opening theme. Recorded September 13, 1929.

Time	Phrase	Chord Progression
0:05	A	‖ V/V^9 V^9	IV^9 V^9	V/V^9	⁒	V/V^9 V^9	IV^9 V^9	V^9/II	⁒	
0:14	B		IV	VII^{o7}/V	I	V^7/II	V^9/V	⁒	V^7	⁒	
0:24	A′		V/V^9 V^9	IV^9 V^9	V^9/IV	⁒	
0:28	C		IV	IVm	I	V^7/II	V^7/V	V^7	I	⁒ ‖

muted-trumpet riffs, the saxophones' four-bar send-offs during Cootie Williams's subsequent solo, and Barney Bigard's call-and-response with the trombones in the third chorus.

Partial blues choruses had the practical advantage of enabling Ellington's soloists to improvise on new compositions using the same melodic licks and phrases that they habitually played on the blues. Such incomplete progressions could be concealed ingeniously. The early up-tempo number *Jazz Convulsions*, dating from over a decade before *Harlem Air Shaft*, has a 28-bar ABA′C opening strain (Example 11.4) whose A section contains a tonally ambiguous succession of dominant-ninth saxophone chords with impetuous plunger-mute interjections from Williams.[23] The trumpeter takes center stage over saxophone riffs for the B section, which ends with an inconclusive half cadence. The B section's first five bars correspond harmonically to the fifth through ninth measures of a standard blues chorus – a reference scarcely perceptible to the casual listener. But after the A phrase's abbreviated return, the concluding eight-bar C phrase varies the B section to end with an authentic cadence, making it harmonically identical to the last 8 bars of a standard blues form, just like the partial progression heard 30 years later in "Flirtibird." Even if subliminal to the layperson, this use of blues changes contributes immeasurably to the passage's ebullient, rousing mood, exuding "the irrepressible joyousness, the downright exhilaration, [and] the rapturous delight in physical existence"[24] that, Albert Murray reminds us, are among the blues's vital human dimensions.

Essentially the same chord sequence heard in the C section of *Jazz Convulsions* appears in Ellington's medium-tempo composition *Move Over*, from a year earlier, except that the second chord is a modal-mixture IVm rather than VII^{o7}/V. In this case, though, the interface between standard blues changes and popular-song form is even richer. The first theme, played by Bubber Miley, contains two phrases: an 8-bar A phrase and a 12-bar B phrase whose last 8 measures harmonically resemble the latter two-thirds of a blues. But Ellington furthermore constructs the A phrase from two successive variants of the B phrase's last 4 bars, such that the A and B phrases together contain a smaller-scale "aaba" design.

Example 11.5. *Move Over*: harmonic structure of the opening theme. Recorded October 1928.

Time	Phrase	Chord Progression
0:12	A	a a 		V⁷/V	V⁷	I	V⁷/II	V⁷/V	V⁷	I–IV	I		
0:24	B	b a || V⁷	V⁷/VI	VI	V⁷/IV	IV	IVm	I	V⁷/II	V⁷/V	V⁷	I	∕ ||

Example 11.6. *Merry-Go-Round*: harmonic structure of the closing choruses. Recorded April 30, 1935.

Time	Horns	Chord Progression	Description
2:13	saxes	|| I	∕	∕	∕	IV	∕	I	∕	V	∕ ||	First 10 bars of a 12-bar blues
2:24	tbns	|| I	∕	∕	∕	IV	∕	I	∕	V	∕ ||	First 10 bars of a 12-bar blues • First 2 bars complete previous chorus
2:35	tpts			I	∕	∕	∕			First 4 bars of a 12-bar blues • First 2 bars complete previous chorus • Dovetails with the next chorus
2:39	tpts, saxes	|| IV	∕	I	∕	IV	∕	I	∕	V	∕	I	∕ ||	12-bar blues starting with IV instead of I
2:52	tpts, tbns, saxes			I	∕	∕	∕			Coda

Example 11.5 labels the large- and small-scale phrases with upper- and lower-case letters respectively; the A phrase consists of two four-bar "a" phrases and the B phrase contains an eight-bar "b" (bridge) plus a final "a" phrase. In other words, a listener hearing *Move Over* for the first time could well perceive the opening theme as a 16-bar "aaba" song form, structurally analogous to tunes like Sonny Rollins's *Doxy*, but with its bridge extended by 4 bars. The embedded 12-bar blues segment might pass undetected, but would likely become more tangible when, at the composition's end (2′ 29″), the complete 20-measure opening theme (A+B) returns in the wake of three straightforward blues choruses (1′ 20″). Already, less than a decade into his career, Ellington had found extraordinarily intricate ways to dovetail blues progressions with the phrasing norms of mainstream popular song.

He could even alter blues forms so as to metaphorically evoke an extramusical topic. The blues-based composition *Merry-Go-Round*, heard in *Symphony in Black*'s upbeat final scene, "Harlem Rhythm," shares a basic structural principle with the titular carousel.[25] After an introductory sequence and a central series of 12-bar forms, Ellington's saxophone section, led by Hodges on soprano, cascades through a blues chorus with festive, ascending scalar figures (2′ 13″).[26] This chorus's expected final two bars on the tonic chord are, however, preempted by a new chorus featuring trombone riffs (2′ 24″). Since the tonic chord is typically found at both the end and the beginning of a blues chorus, the two choruses overlap harmonically, paralleling the effect of a revolving carousel – the end of one cycle is indistinguishable from the beginning of the next. As shown in Example 11.6, the end of the trombone chorus overlaps in the same way with what at first sounds like a new trumpet blues chorus (2′ 35″). Then, in a dazzling stroke of invention, Ellington musically depicts the merry-go-round's final vertiginous spinning. Once the trumpets have stated a four-bar phrase on the tonic chord, the saxes enter (2′ 39″) as the harmonies shift to the subdominant for two bars and then back to the tonic for two more; we seem at this point to be eight bars into another blues chorus. Yet the next chord turns out to be a subdominant rather than the expected V (or II), and as the measures whirl by we instead realize that the preceding saxophone entry (2′ 39″) actually began a new blues form with a subdominant chord in place of the usual tonic. If it was Ellington's intent to whip a hall full of discombobulated dancers into a mental frenzy as well as a physical one, this dizzily disorienting congeries of blues choruses seems likely to have done the trick.

The blues, in Ellington's hands, was a musical tool with an extraordinary capacity to affect how people felt and behaved. Blues choruses could be distended almost beyond recognition, as with the amorphous, expressionistic piano solos that open and conclude *The Clothed Woman* (1947). Or they could be unabashedly flaunted in tandem with vibrant blues melodies, textures, and sonorities: *The Shepherd*, a formidable, slow minor-key blues, as wrenchingly emoted by Cootie Williams for the *Second Sacred Concert* (1968), revels in bringing the blues's fire and brimstone to a sacred venue – New York's Cathedral of St. John the Divine. And even without its usual chorus form, the blues idiom, it is worth emphasizing, could be manifested unambiguously by melodic, harmonic, and timbral means. The majestic and largely under-appreciated 1958 suite *Princess Blue* is a perfect illustration, notwithstanding Ellington's enigmatic denial when asked if it was blues. "It's not blues," he replied. "It's a hint of tint. Almost as blue as the blue in the sky; almost as blue as the hue of bye-bye."[27] The suite itself nevertheless tells another story, for its vast, luxuriant tapestry of themes is utterly drenched from start to finish in the blues's sound and spirit.[28]

Yet at the sunset of his career, with an infinite variety of blues transformations behind him, Ellington still saw fit to play blues themes as simple and unadorned as his 1972 "See See Rider" duet with Brown. Perhaps the most curious detail of that succinct performance is that, although it was actually his original composition *Mr. J. B. Blues*, Ellington identified it as a traditional authorless blues in the public domain, forfeiting his right to royalties. As a young man he had learned bitter lessons about the world of music publishing when Irving Mills, his manager, claimed a financial stake, sometimes undeserved, in some of his most lucrative popular songs. Ever since, he had vigilantly guarded his creative output by retaining his own copyrights. For him, at the age of 73, to forgo credit for *Mr. J. B. Blues* by calling it "See See Rider" was to tacitly acknowledge that his ultimate rewards had become more artistic than monetary. With this autumnal gesture Duke Ellington symbolically brought his lifelong journey with the blues full circle, magnanimously offering his own work to the communal blues tradition from whose fertile soil he had reaped a monumental legacy.

Notes

1 Duke Ellington and Ray Brown, *This One's for Blanton* (Pablo OJCCD-810–2), recorded December 5, 1972.

2 On *Mr. J. B. Blues* (Victor 27406-B) the same melody is heard at 1′28″. Ken Rattenbury provides a transcription and analysis in *Duke Ellington: Jazz Composer* (New Haven, CT: Yale University Press, 1990), 154–55. A sheet music version is printed in Duke Ellington, *Piano Method for Blues* (New York: Robbins, 1943), 33. Ellington also interpolates this melody at 0′28″ on his 1960 recording of *Main Stem* on the LP *Piano in the Background* (Columbia CS 8346).

3 Gertrude "Ma" Rainey, "See See Rider Blues" (Paramount 12252), recorded October 16, 1924.

4 Duke Ellington, *Music Is My Mistress* (New York: Doubleday, 1973; New York: Da Capo, 1976), 72–73.

5 Quoted in Florence Zunser, "'Opera Must Die,' Says Galli-Curci! Long Live the Blues!" *New York Evening Graphic Magazine*, December 27, 1930, reprinted in *The Duke Ellington Reader*, ed. Mark Tucker (New York: Oxford University Press, 1993), 45.

6 Ellington, *Mistress*, 417.

7 Duke Ellington, "Defense of Jazz," *American Mercury* 57/241 (January 1944): 124; reprinted in *Ellington Reader*, ed. Tucker, 209.

8 This is the pattern given in Ellington, *Piano Method for Blues*, 6.

9 Ibid., 13, 18.

10 Quoted in Stanley Dance, *The World of Duke Ellington* (New York: Da Capo Press, 1981), 37.

11 Stanley Crouch, "Duke Ellington: Transcontinental Swing," in *Considering Genius: Writings on Jazz* (New York: Basic Civitas Books, 2006), 138.

12 John Howland, *Ellington Uptown: Duke Ellington, James P. Johnson, and the Birth of Concert Jazz* (Ann Arbor: The University of Michigan Press, 2009), 141.

13 For a transcription of this passage, see Gunther Schuller, *The Swing Era: The Development of Jazz 1930–1945* (New York: Oxford University Press, 1989), 59.

14 Robert Walser, "Deep Jazz: Notes on Interiority, Race, and Criticism," in *Inventing the Psychological: Toward a Cultural History of Emotional Life in America*, ed. Joel Pfister and Nancy Schnog (New Haven, CT: Yale University Press, 1997), 284.

15 In *Symphony in Black* the soloist in this chorus is trombonist Joe Nanton.

16 Billy Strayhorn made an uncredited contribution to "Rocks in My Bed"; see Walter van de Leur, *Something to Live For: The Music of Billy Strayhorn* (New York: Oxford University Press, 2002), 283. Unraveling the complexities of Ellington and Strayhorn's collaboration is of course a thorny task; within this chapter I treat van de Leur's determination as definitive, and otherwise attribute compositions to Ellington based on their copyright registration unless there is evidence to the contrary.

17 A transcription of this passage appears in Edward Green, "'It Don't Mean a Thing if It Ain't Got That Grundgestalt! – Ellington from a Motivic Perspective," *Jazz Perspectives* 2/2 (2008): 245. Green relied on a transcription by John Howland.

18 Mark Tucker, *Ellington: The Early Years* (Urbana: University of Illinois Press, 1991), 219–20.

19 *Saturday Night Function* is co-credited to Barney Bigard.

20 *Jolly Wog*'s B section, which tonicizes C minor and then B-flat major, is played first by Joe Nanton and then by Ellington upon its return. The middle of the piece consists of horn solos over a I–IV vamp in C minor: Cootie Williams takes the first C (eight bars) and the D (twelve bars), with Hodges entering for the second C.

21 Discussed by Lawrence Gushee, "Duke Ellington 1940," in *Ellington Reader*, ed.

Tucker, 433; Schuller, *Swing Era*, 130–31; and van de Leur, *Something to Live For*, 34–36.

22 This passage begins at 0′ 34″ on the original 1937 recording of *Diminuendo in Blue*, and at rehearsal letter B (p. 6, m. 30) in David Berger's transcribed score (New York: Jazz at Lincoln Center Library/Essentially Ellington, 2004).

23 I add a prime to letter-name phrase labels when the phrase in question is altered from its original form. Thus the "ABA′C" phrase structure shown in Example 11.4 includes an altered recurrence of the initial A phrase – a truncation of its original form.

24 Albert Murray, *Stomping the Blues* (New York: McGraw Hill, 1976), 20.

25 Ellington apparently considered three alternative titles for *Merry-Go-Round*: *Ace of Spades*, *Cotton Club Shim Sham*, and *142nd Street and Lenox Avenue*. See Eddie Lambert, *Duke Ellington: A Listener's Guide* (Lanham, MD: Scarecrow Press, 1999), 55. It is not apparent how Ellington settled on the final title, or to what extent he considered the piece's musical structure.

26 Track timings refer to the 1935 recording of *Merry-Go-Round* rather than the original 1933 version.

27 Quoted in Irving Townsend's liner notes to the album *Newport 1958* (Columbia CL 1245).

28 *Princess Blue* is discussed in Crouch, *Considering Genius*, 149.

12 "Seldom seen, but always heard": Billy Strayhorn and Duke Ellington

WALTER VAN DE LEUR

When Duke Ellington met Billy Strayhorn in December, 1938, at the Stanley Theatre in Pittsburgh, the former was a composer and bandleader of international fame. Over the course of the late 1920s and 1930s Ellington had developed an unparalleled musical language, played by an unparalleled orchestra. While the swing craze was reaching its peak, Ellington continued to experiment with harmony, orchestration, and form in pieces that boldly ignored the conventions of the swing idiom. His works dealt with orchestral sound and musical narrativity, but this complexity rarely made his music inaccessible: some of these compositions had become hits. He had extensively toured the United States, and had conquered the hearts of his European fans during his first overseas trip in 1933; he was scheduled to return in the spring of 1939. He had been featured in several film shorts. He had successfully shielded off racial stereotypes and positioned himself as an African-American composer seeking to express through his music what it meant to be black. Wealthy and respected, Ellington was by and large personally responsible for all these successes, especially concerning his artistic choices. He collaborated with many – his band members, his agent Irving Mills, recording studios, record companies, radio networks, and venues – but the final artistic responsibility resided with him and him alone. Nearing the age of 40, Ellington was in his prime, and hardly in need of any assistance.

So the young man who was more or less pushed by his friends to look Ellington up at the Stanley did not interest him much at first. George Greenlee, who accompanied Strayhorn to the theater, recounted the event to Strayhorn's biographer David Hajdu:

> Ellington, alone with his valet, lay on a reclining chair in an embroidered robe, getting his hair conked, eyes closed.
>   "I introduced Billy, and we stood there," said Greenlee. "Duke didn't get up. He didn't even open his eyes. He just said, 'Sit down at the piano, and let me hear what you can do'." Strayhorn lowered himself onto the bench with calibrated grace and turned toward Ellington, who was lying still. "Mr. Ellington, this is the way you played this number in the show," Strayhorn announced and began to perform his host's melancholy ballad "Sophisticated Lady" ... "The amazing thing was," explained Greenlee,

"Billy played it *exactly* like Duke had just played it on stage. He copied him to perfection." Ellington stayed silent and prone, though his hair work was over. "Now, this is the way *I* would play it," continued Strayhorn. Changing keys and upping the tempo slightly, he shifted into an adaptation Greenlee described as "pretty hip-sounding, and further and further 'out there' as he went on."

At the end of the number, Strayhorn turned to Ellington, now standing right behind him, glaring at the keyboard over his shoulders.[1]

Strayhorn continued to play and sing some of his own compositions: *Something to Live For* and a work that was yet untitled, but would become known as *Lush Life*. Ellington was deeply impressed with his piano playing, compositions, and lyrics, and, undoubtedly, something in the young man's personality.

William Thomas Strayhorn was born in Dayton, Ohio, on November 29, 1915, the second of what would eventually be six surviving children (James, Jr., Billy, Georgia, John, Theodore, and Lillian). His family moved to Pittsburgh in 1920, where his father had found work in the steel mills. After moving around the city they settled in the Homewood neighborhood, where Strayhorn would remain until he left for New York in 1939. Working conditions for the head of the family, James Strayhorn, were not good, and he took to drinking. He could be violent, and at times took out his rage on young William, now known to most as Bill. During school vacations, Bill stayed with his paternal grandparents in Hillsborough, North Carolina, where his grandmother taught him to play the piano. (She also instilled in him a love for flowers, reflected in many of his composition titles.) Strayhorn decided that he needed a piano back home as well, and set out to earn one, first by selling newspapers. Eventually he climbed up to delivery boy for the local drugstore. In time he managed to buy a broken player piano, and his musical studies progressed well. Drugstore costumers would ask for Strayhorn to deliver their goods so that he could play some piano, which earned him extra tips.

Enrolled in Homewood's Westinghouse High, he took harmony classes (some of his exercises survive), performed piano works with the school's classical orchestra, and played in a piano–trumpet duo. He had also started to compose. One of the surviving works is a remarkable waltz titled *Valse (lento sostenuto)*, possibly as a nod to Chopin, to whom the charming work owes some of its flavor.[2] Strayhorn's waltz shows that he fully understood and controlled formal balance, melodic development, and a mature harmonic language. Though his main interest was classical performance and composition, Strayhorn got involved with a high school musical, *Fantastic Rhythm*, for which he wrote music, lyrics, and orchestral arrangements. For inspiration he seems to have turned to the Gershwins and Cole

Porter, yet the surviving scores are full of original finds and typical Strayhorn touches.

The best-known piece from his teens is undoubtedly *Lush Life*, a through-composed song with exceptionally urbane lyrics. The work displays Strayhorn's ability to "marry melody, words and harmony," as Ellington once said, and it foreshadows the eloquence of his later scores. His text-setting is detailed and smart, closely following the softly ironic and somewhat fatalistic poem, while at times providing commentary. Where the text speaks of "gay places," or when everything "seemed so sure," the harmonic motion suggests something quite different.

Though he had hoped to become a classical piano player – Strayhorn even enrolled at the Pittsburgh Musical Institute for about two months – his focus gradually shifted to jazz. He started gigging around the Pittsburgh area with his trio, The Mad Hatters, modeled after Benny Goodman's group. As with Goodman, the trio grew to a quintet with clarinet, vibraphone, piano, bass, and drums. In addition, Strayhorn was writing compositions (including *Smada*, recorded later by Ellington) and arrangements for a number of territory bands, such as the Moonlight Harbor Band, the Buddy Malone Orchestra, Honey Boy Minor and His Buzzing Bees, the Bill Ludwig Orchestra, and the Rex Edwards Orchestra.

The bespectacled, somewhat small young man who had entered Ellington's dressing room was an experienced pianist and an exceptionally original composer-arranger. Without any clear plan on how to use him, Ellington invited Strayhorn to join his organization, marking the beginning of a remarkably fruitful, complicated, enigmatic, and often romanticized musical and personal relationship. Strayhorn moved to New York early in 1939 and ended up staying in his new employer's apartment. While Ellington was away for his second European trip – from March 23 to May 10, 1939 – Strayhorn had a chance to study Ellington's scores, including *Reminiscing in Tempo, Caravan, In a Sentimental Mood, Solitude, Echoes of Harlem*, and many more highlights of the previous decade.[3] Through the scores he quickly deepened his understanding of Ellington's techniques, including "cross-section voicing" (a unique way of blending instrumental colors) and Duke's trademark "on the man writing." Rather than designing generic parts, Ellington often wrote for particular members of his orchestra; a part might specifically call for Cootie Williams, for instance. In his scores, notes in a chord often have the names of individual musicians attached to them, for instance specifying that the top note is to be played by trumpeter Wallace Jones, the second by tenor saxophonist Ben Webster, the third by valve-trombonist Juan Tizol, and so forth. Throughout his career, Strayhorn would apply these techniques in his own compositions, though in a personalized way.

At first his tasks for Ellington were unclear, but before long Strayhorn was a full working partner. After a couple of months Ellington trusted his protégé with scoring for the so-called small units, recording ensembles formed around the orchestra's main soloists. In addition, Strayhorn took care of virtually all the vocal arrangements for the Ellington orchestra, an easily overlooked yet important task, since the orchestra relied for much of its income on dances where audiences expected to hear the latest hit songs.

Working for arguably the most exciting jazz orchestra of his time, Strayhorn found inspiration to write new pieces, including the emotionally involved ballads *Passion Flower*, *A Flower Is a Lovesome Thing*, and *Day Dream*, all features for Johnny Hodges. In these tunes he worked with carefully crafted "impressionistic" melodies over advanced chromatic chord progressions. Characteristic of these and many other Strayhorn compositions is the economical use of musical ideas. In his personal life he also came into his own, moving in with his lover, the pianist Aaron Bridgers. Throughout his life he would be openly gay, quietly accepting the consequences, including a life away from the limelight.

Artistically, the early 1940s marked an extremely rewarding period in the history of the Ellington orchestra. Jimmie Blanton's innovative bass playing and Ben Webster's warm tenor sound were among the factors that helped Ellington reach new heights. Virtually every recording from the period is a success: *Jack the Bear*, *Harlem Air Shaft*, *Concerto for Cootie*, *Ko-Ko*, *Cotton Tail*, and many more. In the meantime Strayhorn continued to arrange pop tunes and standards, while fleshing out parts of an occasional Ellington score. Though the evidence is not conclusive, one such contribution might be the introduction to *Concerto for Cootie*, which in its chromatic counterpoint points to Strayhorn. In another instance, Ellington reused one of his collaborator's adaptations in a new context: *Sepia Panorama* is built around a segment of Strayhorn's unrecorded *Tuxedo Junction* arrangement. Confounding matters, Strayhorn himself cited *Jack the Bear* as an example of his early adaptation of Ellington's work, but the surviving score is in Ellington's hand (and sounds thoroughly Ellingtonian, too).

Much of Strayhorn's work was still behind the scenes, but this changed with an assignment to adapt a new song by Ted Grouya and Edmund Anderson, titled *Flamingo*. His arrangement is extraordinary, both in form and orchestration. Vocal arrangements of that time tended to consist of some sort of opener, a string of choruses with possibly a short modulation, and a little tag, but over a third of Strayhorn's arrangement contains new material in through-composed transitional and modulatory sections. As in his earlier works, he takes his cues from the lyrics, and develops the form with a keen use of harmonic and rhythmic material. The score is derived from a handful of ideas, which generate the chords and background lines. Atypically for a romantic pop song, the piece travels through remote keys that are seamlessly connected by means of astutely chosen ambiguous chords. *Flamingo* quickly became a hit record and the signature tune for Herb Jeffries, the orchestra's male singer. As Ellington wrote in his autobiography, *Music Is My Mistress*, *Flamingo* was "a turning point in vocal background orchestration, a renaissance in elaborate ornamentation for the accompaniment of singers ... Since then, other arrangers have become more and more daring, but Billy Strayhorn really started it all with 'Flamingo'."[4]

A disagreement over royalties between the radio networks and the nation's largest performing-rights organization, the American Society of Composers, Authors and Publishers (ASCAP), led to the so-called broadcasting ban, blacking out much of Ellington's repertoire from the airwaves in 1941. This development marked Strayhorn's breakthrough, since the band needed new repertoire. Strayhorn contributed *Take the "A" Train*, *Chelsea Bridge*, and *Rain Check* – pieces that introduced him to Ellington's larger audience. Reportedly written in 1939 (with lyrics derived from the directions Ellington gave to his apartment in "Sugar Hill way up in Harlem"), *"A" Train* quickly became the orchestra's signature theme. The piece salutes Fletcher Henderson in its call-and-response writing but has some unexpected touches, such as the metrically shifting modulation at the end of the solo chorus, the rhythmically displaced cross-section bell chord before the final chorus, and the ensuing *wah-wah* brass responses to the theme's repetition (try to tap along). As the opener to virtually every concert, *"A" Train* achieved such a prominent place in Ellington's oeuvre that fans, critics, and musicologists have wondered to what extent the piece was actually Strayhorn's. His autograph score, however, carries all the music except for the piano introduction and an eight-bar background that was rescored in the weeks after the initial recording – and even these minor additions are fully consistent with Strayhorn's writing style.

Chelsea Bridge bespeaks the composer's admiration for the works of Debussy and Ravel. He alludes to works of both; most notably, the theme of *Chelsea Bridge* shares the same parallel-moving opening chords as the second movement of Ravel's *Valses nobles et sentimentales*, although Strayhorn maintained he didn't know the piece until someone pointed out the resemblance. Other new Strayhorn additions to the band book were *Clementine*, *After All*, and *Love Like This Can't Last*. The new voice in the Ellington orchestra did not pass unnoticed. Colleagues, including Gil Evans and John Lewis, expressed their admiration, while others, such as Charles Mingus and George Handy, would find inspiration in these works.

Ellington and Strayhorn's first major joint project was the 1941 theatrical revue *Jump for Joy*, a work that celebrated racial emancipation and civil rights. Strayhorn was deeply involved, though it is impossible to establish to what extent the dozens of surviving scores are his original compositions, arrangements or collaborative works with Ellington. One work that emerged from the show was the Ellington ballad *I Got It Bad (And That Ain't Good)*. Authorship is misty here, too. The piece carries mainly Ellingtonian traits, but Strayhorn was the arranger of the popular recording with Ivie Anderson and of the many versions that followed in the ensuing decades.

In addition to these vocal arrangements, small-band arrangements, original works, and collaborations, Strayhorn composed numerous pieces that were not recorded, and may not have been played by the orchestra at all. Among these are impressive works, such as the 12-minute *Pentonsilic*, or dissonant ballads such as *Blue House*, *Portrait of a Silk Thread*, and *Blue Star*. Some of his 1940s works were recorded eventually: *Allah Bye*, in 1957, or *Lament for an Orchid*, released as *Absinthe* in 1963. Also, part of *Pentonsilic* was used for the first movement of the *Perfume Suite* (1944).

In these works, Strayhorn composed an individual musical world. His approach to form, harmony, counterpoint, voicing, and instrumentation created an unmistakable personal sound, laid down in forward-looking scores, which were repeatedly performed by the Ellington orchestra but often went uncredited. As I wrote elsewhere: "Strayhorn had added, silently and almost anonymously, an entirely new stylistic wing to the Ellington building – a building of which Ellington was still believed to be the sole architect."[5]

Strayhorn's personal sound derives from a number of techniques and approaches, which serve as his musical fingerprints and allow the listener to distinguish his arrangements and compositions from those of Ellington. Form is an important aspect of these fingerprints. As with the aforementioned *Flamingo*, Strayhorn devotes much space to extensive introductions, transitions, modulatory sections, and codas, often built on thematically, rhythmically, or harmonically related musical material. In addition, his pieces often have a ternary form, where a middle section contrasts with the outer sections. Examples are *Hearsay* (from the *Deep South Suite*), *Overture to a Jam Session*, *Blue Heart*, *Portrait of a Silk Thread*, and *Charpoy* (also known as *Lana Turner*), as well as his arrangements of *Can't Help Lovin' Dat Man* and *Where or When*.

Strayhorn's orchestrations, like Ellington's, tend to be full of dissonance, but the flavor is different. He favors chromatic voice leading, often in contrary motion, and in general his chords are more open-spaced; Ellington would write the notes closer together, leading to a thicker sound. In addition, Ellington preferred to use the lower register of the instruments, and often called for lower-register dissonance, as illustrated by his treatment of the baritone saxophone. By contrast, Strayhorn's dissonances are often assigned to the higher voices in the ensemble. An example is his version of *Day Dream* for Ella Fitzgerald, which opens with sharply dissonant chords in clarinet, alto saxophones, and trumpets.

In the years that followed, Strayhorn continued to provide the orchestra with compositions and arrangements, which sometimes became movements or parts of larger collaborative works. A good example is the final movement of Ellington's *Black, Brown and Beige: A Tone Parallel to the History of the Negro in America* (premiered in 1943), which incorporates an earlier Strayhorn work titled *Symphonette-Rhythmique*. For this movement Ellington borrowed from his own stockpile as well, reusing portions from his *Concerto for Clinkers* (written for *Jump for Joy*) and other earlier works. While in *Black, Brown and Beige* the insertion of earlier material was somewhat concealed, in many of the later collaborative suites the two composers simply divided the work between them and wrote separate movements. This became the modus operandi for their joint work on film scores (*Anatomy of a Murder, Paris Blues*), theater shows (*Beggar's Holiday*, and a revised version of *Jump for Joy*), and the so-called suites, including *Deep South Suite, Jazz Festival Suite, Portrait of Ella Fitzgerald, Such Sweet Thunder, Suite Thursday, The Nutcracker Suite, Peer Gynt Suite, Far East Suite*, and others. When they actually collaborated on single works – which did not occur often – the process was usually layered. For instance, Ellington added a new melodic line to Strayhorn's arrangement of *Out of This World*, which became *The Eighth Veil*, while Strayhorn added material to Ellington's *C Jam Blues*, reworked and expanded the unfinished *Blutopia*, and wrote the coda to *Harlem*.

Hence, the famous musical collaboration between Ellington and Strayhorn seems to have mostly involved discussion, mutual inspiration, and collaborative work in the recording studio, but not so much the co-writing of distinct pieces. In the absence of scores and clear composer-arranger credits – and with Ellington and Strayhorn's reluctance to answer the "who had written what" questions – most commentators felt that the work of the two was indistinguishable. During Strayhorn's lifetime, many assumed that he worked in a style largely developed by Ellington, and that his role was mainly to emulate his employer. Yet Ellington would not have been interested in a mere imitator. He was known for seeking out individual voices for his orchestra – if one musician left, his replacement was expected to bring a different musical character.

The differences between the two composers were significant, and they mostly involved the deeper layers of their works, such as musical form.

Strayhorn tended to work mostly from harmonic and melodic development and preferred an economical use of musical material. This led to long musical arches, with integrated transitory sections, smooth modulations, and thematically connected introductions and codas. Ellington's pieces tended to include sharper transitions, and contrasting sections replete with fresh musical ideas. This is also reflected in his scores, where the music often appears in a different order than the recordings. Ellington sculpted the final architecture of his pieces during rehearsals on the bandstand and in the studio, moving segments around and inserting blocks of material from other scores.[6] The resultant music offered contrast and variation, convincingly unified through the unique sound of his orchestra.

By the early 1950s, Strayhorn had distanced himself somewhat from the Ellington organization. Growing frustrations over his lack of artistic recognition, and copyright issues with Tempo Music, the Ellington organization's publishing firm, led him to branch out to independent projects. He wrote music for an off-Broadway theater adaptation of Federico García Lorca's surrealist play *The Love of Don Perlimplín and Belisa in His Garden*. Strayhorn set some of García Lorca's poems to music, resulting in songs that sooner call up the piano works of the French composer Francis Poulenc than jazz. These works sound open and somewhat forlorn, with simple-sounding melodies over calmly flowing piano accompaniment. Another endeavor was a collaboration with his friend Luther Henderson, again intended for the theater: *Rose-Colored Glasses*. This show never left the drawing board, but Strayhorn's cabaret-esque scores for the annual Copasetics dances did. The Copasetics were a group of tap-dance professionals who regularly met in commemoration of Bill "Bojangles" Robinson. Strayhorn was introduced to these "hoofers" by a friend, and became a founding member and president. He also took on the musical responsibilities for the annual one-night shows staged in Harlem. These scores show that Strayhorn maintained his own voice away from Ellington, even if they were written for different ensembles in a different context.

Ellington and Strayhorn renewed their musical partnership late in 1955. During the late 1940s and early 1950s, Ellington had been able to keep his orchestra working through commercially difficult times. Thanks to a new contract with Columbia and renewed interest from audiences (the jitterbug generation was now nearing 40), the band was on the verge of a new peak period. Collaborative high-profile projects centered around various LPs, such as *Ellington at Newport, Ella Fitzgerald Sings the Duke Ellington Songbook, Ellington Indigos*, and *Blues in Orbit*; suites such as *Such Sweet Thunder, Suite Thursday*, and *The Nutcracker Suite*; and a one-hour TV show called *A Drum Is a Woman*. In addition, the band recorded a number of somewhat more commercial albums, such as *At the Bal Masque, Ellington Jazz Party, Recollections of the Big Band Era, Will the Big Bands Ever Come Back?, All American in Jazz, Midnight in Paris*, and *Mary Poppins*. Strayhorn contributed extensively to all these projects: he often arranged more than half the music.

Such *Sweet Thunder*, based on Shakespeare, stands as one of the more successful suites of the 1950s. Though the work was largely Ellington's (*Such Sweet Thunder, Sonnet for Caesar, Lady Mac, The Telecasters, Sonnet for Sister Kate, Madness in Great Ones*, and *Circle of Fourths* can positively be ascribed to him), Strayhorn's contributions were no less relevant. His breathtaking Johnny Hodges feature *Pretty Girl* was recycled as *The Star-Crossed Lovers*, and another earlier piece called *Lately* became *Half the Fun*. Inspired by a line from *A Midsummer Night's Dream*, Strayhorn also added *Up and Down, Up and Down*, a virtuoso display of contrapuntal writing. Cross-section instrumental groups represent the various quarreling couples that are misled by Puck, the mischievous fairy. A comparison between the suite's sections reveals that Ellington's movements tend to be more gutsy and to rely more on improvised ideas.

Strayhorn continued to compose originals recorded by the orchestra, including *Upper Manhattan Medical Group, Ballad for Very Tired and Very Sad Lotus Eaters, Star-Crossed Lovers, Northern Lights, Blues in Orbit, Sweet and Pungent*, and *Cordon Bleu*, along with *Satin Doll*, co-written with Ellington. As before, not all these works were properly credited on records or even copyright files. Strayhorn also wrote pieces that remained shelved, such as the remarkable *Cashmere Cutie*. Over 50 of these unused compositions were recorded in the 1990s by the Dutch Jazz Orchestra and issued on four compact discs by Challenge Records. These works show that the sound and repertoire of Ellington's orchestra now fully relied on the creative forces of both Ellington and Strayhorn. "Billy Strayhorn is one of the most important people in our group," Ellington said while introducing his musical partner on a 1964 BBC television program. "Very seldom seen in public appearances, but always heard."

In 1963 the Ellingtonians traveled through the Near and Middle East on a tour sponsored by the U.S. State Department. Ellington and Strayhorn translated their impressions into *The Far East Suite*, one of their most convincing collaborative works. Directly inspired by the trip were Ellington's *Amad, Depk, Tourist Point of View, Mount Harissa*, and *Blue Pepper*, along with Strayhorn's *Agra* and *Bluebird of Delhi*. The work's success owes to the relatively long time the composers took to write it, drawing inspiration from the rich musical cultures they had visited. The suite smartly incorporates non-jazz elements, such as drones and non-Western scales, into idiosyncratic Ellington-Strayhorn music. Strayhorn's earlier composition *Elf*, now retitled *Isfahan* after Persia's former capital, filled out the suite. The piece was composed with the unsurpassed Johnny Hodges in mind, as were many other Strayhorn ballads: *Day Dream, Passion Flower, A Flower Is a Lovesome Thing, Ballad for Very Tired and Very Sad Lotus Eaters*, and *The Star-Crossed Lovers*.

Strayhorn's works for *The Far East Suite* were among his final contributions to the orchestra's repertoire. Early in 1964 he was diagnosed with cancer of the esophagus. He underwent operations and radiation therapy, but over the course of 1966 his condition quickly worsened. Although the exact date of composition remains unclear, the harrowing ballad *Blood Count* – one of the few pieces Strayhorn ever wrote in a minor key – is closely identified with this period, and resounds with sadness and frustration.

In his final works, composed when he was terminally ill, Strayhorn returned to a more classical style. He wrote a multi-movement work called *The North by Southwest Suite* for the piano–French horn duo of Dwike Mitchell and Willie Ruff, recorded after his death as *Suite for the Duo*. According to Ruff, the piece "thunders with highly autobiographical overtones; the moods of a vibrant musical career, shutting down."[7]

Strayhorn died at the age of 51, on May 31, 1967. Ellington was devastated. As a tribute, he and his orchestra recorded *...And His Mother Called Him Bill*, an album of Strayhorn originals. The final track of the original LP has Ellington playing Strayhorn's gracious waltz *Lotus Blossom*, unaccompanied and caught on tape as an afterthought; the orchestra was packing up to leave the studio. Ellington's *Lotus Blossom* is full of grief and frustration – he had lost the only person he ever allowed into his musical inner circle. As he later wrote in his autobiography,

> Billy Strayhorn was always the most unselfish, the most patient, and the most imperturbable, no matter how dark the day. I am indebted to him for so much of my courage since 1939. He was my listener, my most dependable appraiser, and as a critic he would be the most clinical, but his background – both classical and modern – was an accessory to his own good taste and understanding, so what came back to me was in perfect balance.[8]

Strayhorn's importance lies first and foremost in his massive work for Duke Ellington and his orchestra: close to 600 scores can be positively linked to recordings, and hundreds more were used in concerts, dances, and broadcasts. With a collaborator shouldering part of the daily workload, Ellington had more time for his personal musical endeavors. Not only did Strayhorn's work free his hands, but Ellington also found a musically kindred spirit, and drew inspiration from the radically different musical language he brought to the orchestra.

Strayhorn's work was outstanding in terms of harmonic and melodic invention, orchestration, and structural ingenuity. He managed to fuse compositional strategies that stemmed from European classical music with more American idioms. Still, his music was firmly rooted in his African-American heritage. Strayhorn sought to express a complex emotional life through his music, and left us some of the most sophisticated and meaningful works in the entire history of jazz.

Notes

1 David Hajdu, *Lush Life: A Biography of Billy Strayhorn* (New York: Farrar, Straus & Giroux, 1996), 50.

2 For detailed musical analysis of Strayhorn's works, and a listing of the works he wrote for Ellington, see Walter van de Leur, *Something to Live For: The Music of Billy Strayhorn* (New York: Oxford University Press, 2002).

3 Original autograph scores for these works are housed in the Duke Ellington Collection, Archives Center, National Museum of American History, Smithsonian Institution.

4 Duke Ellington, *Music Is My Mistress* (New York: Doubleday, 1973; New York: Da Capo, 1976), 153.

5 Van de Leur, *Something to Live For*, 64.

6 See Walter van de Leur, "People Wrap Their Lunches in Them: Duke Ellington and His Written Music Manuscripts," in *Ellington Studies*, edited by John Howland (Cambridge University Press, 2015).

7 Willie Ruff, *A Call to Assembly: The Autobiography of a Musical Storyteller* (New York: Viking, 1991), 10.

8 Duke Ellington, *Mistress*, 156.

13 Duke Ellington and the world of jazz piano

BILL DOBBINS

Duke Ellington's place in the world of jazz piano is just as unique as his place among jazz composers and bandleaders. Although his prominence as the leader of one of the most popular and influential jazz orchestras often overshadowed his pianistic abilities, his contributions to jazz piano playing were truly enormous.

In all spheres of creativity the term "innovation" is often overrated and misunderstood. Innovation can rarely be attributed to a single person. Moreover, the way an artist utilizes a particular technique or sound is ultimately of more significance than the technique or sound taken in isolation. Just as Ellington the composer was not the originator of the growls, moans, and other expressive devices that jazz musicians developed from European instruments, neither was he the inventor of the particular techniques he used at the piano. It was the wealth of possibilities he uncovered for combining, simplifying, expanding, or even distorting the common jazz piano vocabulary of the day that put Ellington in a class by himself. He always had his ears open to what was happening in the jazz world, and could always adapt whatever was in the air to his very particular tastes.

Perhaps Ellington's greatest contribution to jazz piano was that of a master consolidator, who brought together the music of his time in ways that other well-known pianists could not have imagined, and made recordings from the 1940s to the 1970s that still sound fresh and modern today. In this respect his place in jazz might be compared to the place of J. S. Bach in the music of eighteenth-century Europe. Although some of Bach's contemporaries were considered more innovative, his ability to consolidate the musical vocabulary of his time in a uniquely creative manner was without equal. Just as European composers of the late nineteenth century rediscovered and built upon Bach's unsurpassed use of chromaticism and tonal counterpoint, many of today's jazz pianists are realizing how far ahead Ellington was in developing the language of jazz piano.

Ellington's early education as pianist

It seems too perfectly ironic that the first piano teacher of this jazz giant had the name of Mrs. Clinkscales, but Ellington always swore that was, indeed, her name.[1] While she insisted that he learn to read music, his other musical instruction while growing up in Washington, D.C., was of a more informal and aural nature. Ellington absorbed everything he could from local pianists Claude Hopkins, Roscoe Lee, Doc Perry, Louis Brown, Les Dishman, Clarence Bowser, Sticky Mack, and Blind Johnny. There was a stimulating and fruitful exchange between those who read music and those who didn't, and Ellington continued learning in this practical and proactive manner after moving to New York City in 1923.[2]

Ellington also had some harmony lessons from Henry Grant, a high school teacher who taught classical piano. Jazz pianist, composer, and author Billy Taylor, who studied with Grant during the late 1930s, noticed a peculiar design to most of his lessons. It seemed the telephone would usually ring at some point midway through the lesson and Mr. Grant would excuse himself to take the call. It was Duke who would call, never hesitant about getting musical advice from his old mentor, or perhaps just wanting to pay his respects from time to time. Whatever the content of Taylor's lesson up to that point, the remainder was about Duke Ellington.[3]

Of course, the real schoolhouses of jazz piano in the 1920s were the after-hours clubs, where the best players held regular competitions or "cutting contests." In New York at that time, the Hole in the Wall and Mexico's were two of Harlem's most regular venues for these events. A favorite contest piece was James P. Johnson's *Carolina Shout*, and Johnson himself was often at hand when the best were being tested. In the stride piano style the left hand usually alternates between bass notes or octaves in the low register and chords in the middle register, while the right hand plays the themes and improvised variations. Stride piano is very technically demanding, and the piano often sounds like a one-man jazz band.

Ellington said that he adopted the wisest strategy in these contests: be the first to play. He had learned *Carolina Shout* by slowing down the piano roll on a player piano until he could figure out the intricate patterns. While basically a romantic personality, Ellington was also a master at finding practical solutions to aesthetic or technical problems. After playing *Carolina Shout* and then buying the first round of drinks, he could sit back and enjoy hearing New York's jazz piano masters trying to outdo one another.[4]

Ellington's solo piano version of his composition *Black Beauty*, recorded for the Okeh label on October 1, 1928, illustrates his approach to medium-tempo stride piano.[5] It also shows his incorporation of the harmonic vocabulary used by contemporaries such as Fats Waller, Willie "The Lion" Smith, and George Gershwin. The contrasting moods, the variations of stride style, and the use of dissonances – especially half-step grinds involving blue notes – reveal an Ellington aesthetic that is already

Example 13.1. *Black Beauty* (Duke Ellington), "A" theme improvisation, measures 1–2, recorded October 1, 1928. Released on *The Okeh Ellington*, Columbia C2K46177 (CD, 1991) and transcribed by Bill Dobbins. Publishing rights administered by Sony ATV Harmony (ASCAP).

distinguishable from that of his peers. The use of the whole-tone scale, as in his improvised variation of the opening theme (Example 13.1), was heard in Bix Beiderbecke's 1927 piano piece, *In a Mist,* and became a common element in the music of bebop pianists, especially Thelonious Monk.

While most of America's jazz pianists were honing their skills through incessant practice and performance, Ellington was more and more occupied with writing his orchestra's shows for the Cotton Club, especially from 1927 through the early 1930s. From such classic compositions as *Mood Indigo, The Mooche,* and *Black Beauty,* it is clear that his work as a composer was making great advances, and his piano accompaniment and occasional solos perfectly complemented the orchestra's musical personality. It seems likely, however, that Ellington had little time for practicing the piano during these years.

In spite of this, he came up with his own stride piano tour de force, entitled *Lots o' Fingers.* It was included in a medley, recorded for the Victor label on February 9, 1932, sandwiched between orchestral versions of *East St. Louis Toodle-O* and *Black and Tan Fantasy.* For Ellington piano aficionados this recording is well worth tracking down, as it reveals influences of Fats Waller, Willie "The Lion" Smith, and James P. Johnson, among others. Ellington displays his mastery of all the common tricks of the trade, including rapid, repeated bass note figures that were forerunners of the later boogie-woogie style; left-hand octaves that mimic the energetic quarter-note lines played by the string bass in small and large jazz bands; and three-beat cross-rhythms that sprawl out over the underlying $\frac{4}{4}$ meter in exciting bursts of rhythmic tension. *Lots o' Fingers* is infused with Ellington's individual brand of pianistic bravado, proving he could play stride at a breakneck tempo with the best of the best.

Ellington in the 1930s and 1940s

If there is one thing that distinguishes Ellington from his contemporaries, as well as his successors – in both his piano playing and his big band

Example 13.2. *Uptown Downbeat* (Duke Ellington), measures 1–2, recorded July 29, 1936. Released on *The Complete 1932–1940 Brunswick, Columbia and Master Recordings of Duke Ellington and his Famous Orchestra*, Mosaic MD11–248 (CD, 2010) and transcribed by Bill Dobbins. Publishing rights administered by Sony ATV Harmony (ASCAP).

arranging and orchestration – it is his keen sense of balance between dissonance and consonance, tension and resolution. The manner in which he harmonized his thematic material was familiar enough not to put off the general audience, yet the music was sprinkled with colorful and dissonant harmonies that perked up the ears of musical sophisticates. A great example in relation to Ellington's piano style is the July 29, 1936, Brunswick recording of *Uptown Downbeat*. The piece begins with brief call-and-response phrases between the orchestra and the piano (Example 13.2). Ellington's response sounds melodically similar to something Count Basie might have played, but the subtle dissonance in the voicings is pure Ellington.

In one of Ellington's early extended compositions, the two-part *Diminuendo and Crescendo in Blue* (1937), his short solo at the end of the first part combines edgy, syncopated rhythms with dissonant right-hand chords and especially colorful notes in the left-hand melodic lines. The material is derived mainly from the diminished scale, alternating whole steps and half steps, for example: F–G–A♭–B♭–B–C♯–D–E–F. These sounds were still very new to jazz, even though twentieth-century classical composers such as Stravinsky and Bartók had used them. Ellington was certainly among the first jazz musicians to incorporate them into his musical vocabulary.

In the years from 1938 to 1941, generally considered the most fruitful period of his career up to that point, Ellington's piano interjections and short solos demonstrate his deep understanding of the piano's potential in a big band context. Of special interest are *Subtle Lament* (1939), *Jack the Bear* (1940), *Ko-Ko* (1940), and *Blue Serge* (1941, composed by Ellington's son, Mercer). In *Subtle Lament*, the piano solo that follows the opening theme makes effective use of parallel ninth chords and descending chromatic arpeggios, both of which were relatively common sounds in jazz piano at the time. Ellington, however, uses these sonorities to create short conversational statements that play a specific role in an organized

Example 13.3. *Blue Serge* (Mercer Ellington), last four measures of Duke Ellington's solo, recorded February 15, 1941. Released on *The Blanton-Webster Band*, RCA Bluebird 5659–2-RB (CD, 1986) and transcribed by Bill Dobbins. Publishing rights administered by Tempo Music Inc. (ASCAP).

composition for jazz orchestra. *Jack the Bear* and *Ko-Ko* include dissonances that later became key ingredients in the style of Thelonious Monk. These include percussive major-second jabs, which answer the unison saxophone theme in *Jack the Bear*, and powerful left-hand cluster chords and rapid right-hand runs derived from the whole-tone scale, both heard prominently throughout his short solo in *Ko-Ko*. Although Basie and other swing-era pianists also used the accented, staccato right-hand tenths heard near the end of this solo, Ellington hammers them out just as Monk would nearly a decade later.[6] The closing chords of the solo in *Blue Serge* must be listened to more patiently, since the tempo is slow and the mood is more reflective and subdued (Example 13.3). Upon close attention, these chords reveal a beautiful, bittersweet harmonic tension that resolves just before Ben Webster's soulful tenor saxophone states the closing theme. The melody note that creates this tension is, characteristically, a blue note. More than any other jazz pianist, Ellington took advantage of blue notes in melodies in order to create tension with the harmony. Because the ear clearly hears how such melody notes lend a blues feeling to the music, it accepts strong tensions with the accompanying harmonies, provided there is a convincing resolution.

It was also during this period, 1939 to be exact, that Ellington's composing and arranging partner and musical alter ego, Billy Strayhorn, joined the Ellington organization. Also a fine pianist with a considerable background in classical music, Strayhorn certainly encouraged Ellington to follow his natural inclinations in developing new formal structures and expanding his musical vocabulary with regard to harmony, orchestration, and piano playing. Ellington and Strayhorn sometimes played four-hand piano at parties just for fun, including both informal improvisations and impressive but obscure compositions such as Strayhorn's *Tonk* (1940). Their mutual influence and their parallel and

Example 13.4. *In a Mellotone* (Duke Ellington), measures 1–3, recorded September 5, 1940. Released on *The Blanton-Webster Band*, RCA Bluebird 5659-2-RB (CD, 1986) and transcribed by Bill Dobbins. Publishing rights administered by Sony ATV Harmony (ASCAP).

collective musical achievements represent a truly singular phenomenon in twentieth-century music.

In addition to looking for unique and unconventional sounds, Ellington also pioneered voicings and textures that became basic stock in trade for jazz pianists from the 1950s onward. A great example is the introduction to the 1940 Ellington hit *In a Mellotone*. The opening voicings have rootless ninth chords in the left hand with the right hand playing the root as an octave with the fifth in the middle (Example 13.4). Billy Taylor said he was so intrigued by these voicings that he developed a whole style from them.[7] Indeed, the particular "block chord" style used by Ahmad Jamal in his classic trio arrangement of *Billy Boy* – later popularized by Red Garland's playing with the Miles Davis quintet in the late 1950s and Garland's cover of the Jamal arrangement on Davis's influential 1958 album *Milestones* – is derived, I believe, from voicings similar to those heard at the beginning of *In a Mellotone*. The point here is not that Ellington was the first jazz pianist to use such voicings but, rather, that he was every bit as much a solid craftsman as he was an enigmatic artist and innovator.

Ellington's fascination with the myriad elements of stride piano, blues, American popular song, and the chromatic harmony and dissonance of early twentieth-century classical music reached a new level of synthesis in *The Deep South Suite* (1946). Two movements from the suite showcased Ellington's piano playing more than any previous works.

The third movement, "There was Nobody Looking," is a miniature tone poem for solo piano. As Ellington explains in his autobiography, *Music Is My Mistress*, it is about the trials of a playful puppy attempting to make contact with a pretty little flower. Every time he reaches out, a breeze comes along and blows the flower away. Ellington points out that there is no antagonism between the puppy and the breeze; each is simply following its natural tendencies. The title, as Ellington explains, had a significant connection to the story: "'There Was Nobody Looking' illustrated the theory that, when nobody is looking, many people of different extractions

Example 13.5. *There Was Nobody Looking* (Duke Ellington and Billy Strayhorn), "A" theme, measures 13–16, recorded November 23, 1946. Originally issued as V-Disc 759. Transcribed by Bill Dobbins. Publishing rights administered by Billy Strayhorn Songs Inc. (ASCAP), Reservoir Media Music (ASCAP), The Duke Ellington Heritage LLC (ASCAP), and Tempo Music Inc. (ASCAP).

are able to get along well together."[8] It also illustrates his ability to address America's racial issues in an imaginative, winning manner, without being preachy or confrontational.

After a four-bar introduction, the piece displays a rondo-like design: ABACA. It is the A sections that convey the story line in musical terms, with the sudden rubato, the surprising left-hand C7 with a lowered fifth, and the right-hand triplet quarter-note blue notes suggesting the puppy's disappointment as the flower is suddenly whisked away by the breeze. The B and C sections provide suitable contrasting themes. Ellington's masterful use of a variety of articulations, dynamics, and slight shifts in tempo suggests the plot so clearly that the listener can easily picture the whole scene being played out, although the piece can also be appreciated purely on its musical merits by those not familiar with the story. There may be no other solo jazz piano piece coming from the stride tradition that is so successful on both musical and narrative levels of entertainment. And Ellington's use of blue notes, dominant seventh chords with fifths and ninths lowered, strident dissonances involving minor ninth intervals, and inventive, chromatic harmonic sequences (Example 13.5) shows a highly personal pianistic approach that would continue to develop in the decades ahead.

The final movement of the suite, "Happy Go Lucky Local," is one of many Ellington compositions inspired by trains and train travel. In creating some of the instrumental effects that simulate train sounds, from clanging bells to powerful steam whistles, Ellington continued to stretch the piano's percussive and harmonic potential in ways that, even today,

Example 13.6. *The Clothed Woman* (Duke Ellington), "A" section, measures 1–4, recorded December 27, 1947. Released on *The Duke Ellington Carnegie Hall Concerts – December 1947*, Prestige 2PCD24075–2 (1991), and transcribed by Bill Dobbins. Publishing rights administered by Sony ATV Harmony (ASCAP).

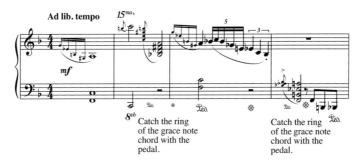

have not yet been fully explored by jazz pianists. From his percussive chords in the opening measures, through the brilliantly conceived solo passages, to the thundering mid- and low-register dissonances answered by Cat Anderson's stratospheric trumpet screeches near the end, the piano's role in telling this train's musical story is something only Ellington could have conceived. Although similar sonorities can be heard in early recordings of Monk from the mid-1940s, it would be another decade before Monk would use them with the functional precision and authority heard in *Ko-Ko* and *Happy Go Lucky Local*. Interestingly, while touring England with Ellington in 1948, Ray Nance played Ellington a new Monk recording on a portable gramophone. "Sounds like he's stealing some of my stuff," remarked Ellington.[9]

Ellington's anticipation of future trends

The Clothed Woman, from 1947, is probably Ellington's most innovative piano piece. It also illustrates his special ability to blend opposites in an amazingly convincing manner. Within the space of a relatively short ABA structure, Ellington anticipates the piano style of Cecil Taylor in the beginning and ending sections and, after a bop-like interlude, harkens back to stride pianist Willie "The Lion" Smith in the middle. In addition to the unusual dissonances and percussive effects in the A section, Ellington uses special pedaling techniques, which, combined with the rapidly alternating chords in the right and left hands, imply the "wah-wah" effects of brass instruments with plungers.

Although the solo piano A section has been described as atonal or bordering on atonality, it is actually a chromatic abstraction of a basic blues progression (Example 13.6). In the two-bar introduction of the studio recording from December 30, a characteristic Ellington arpeggio using notes from the E diminished scale leads to a low G♭, setting up the key of F. The first four measures of the A section clearly emphasize an F triad, decorated with blue-note arpeggios or passing C7 implications, moving to F7 with a lowered fifth in the fourth measure of the phrase. Just as in a basic blues, measures 5 and 6 emphasize the subdominant chord (B♭7), with the right hand adding the lowered fifth and lowered ninth in a brief tremolo, followed by the blues color of the raised ninth. The "wah-wah" effect is used only briefly in measures 2 and 4, but is heard prominently following the B♭7 chord in measure 6, leading back to the F tonic chord in measures 7 and 8.

Measures nine and ten consist of highly chromaticized voicings of G7 to C7 and B♭6 to C7, respectively. These voicings are further abstracted with grace-note chords in the right hand that suggest harmonies either a half step above (A♭13 coupled with G7^{-5}) or a half step below (AMaj7 coupled with B♭6) the primary chords stated in the left hand. Instead of completing the blues form with the usual tonic chord in measure 11 and the dominant in measure 12, Ellington returns to the first four-bar phrase, extending the form from 12 to 14 measures. The F7 chord in the fourteenth measure leads to the key of B-flat for the boppish transition and the more substantial B section. This transition features a small group of instruments and consists of lower-register left-hand piano figures that set up a repeated eight-bar section of call-and-response phrases between Ellington's piano and either Shorty Baker's squeezed trumpet notes or Harry Carney's baritone saxophone. A four-bar piano solo then leads to the B section.

The main theme of the B section is in the spirit of Willie "The Lion" Smith, with a jaunty, eight-bar right-hand melody accompanied by repeated left-hand staccato chords in brisk march tempo.[10] The colorful line in the bottom voice of these chords begins on the major seventh of the B♭ chord, creating a subtle dissonance with the root next to it. The line then marches down in half steps to the fifth of the chord and back up, making a two-bar vamp pattern that continues until the harmonic cadence in measures 7 and 8 (C7, F7, B♭). After a repeat of this section, an eight-bar bridge is fashioned from fragments of the same material, with the left hand alternating pairs of second-inversion B-flat major and A diminished triads in a one-bar vamp. Then comes a return to the initial eight-bar phrase of the B section, followed by a variation of the eight-bar bridge. Here the left-hand vamp alternates two beats of second-inversion B♭ triads with two beats of first-inversion C7 voicings, with the melodic material derived from the earlier four-bar piano solo that led from the boppish transition to the B theme. In the studio recording, the first eight-bar phrase of the B section then recurs for a fourth time, and the earlier four-bar piano solo section leads back to a recap of the A section and the coda. However, on the Carnegie Hall concert recording, just three days before the studio session, Ellington develops an extended piano improvisation from the vamp consisting of alternating pairs of second-inversion B♭ triads and first-inversion C7 voicings. As this one-bar vamp is based on a simple embellishment of a C7 chord, Ellington's improvised statement deserves to be considered an early forerunner of modal jazz improvisation.

In fact, *The Clothed Woman* was recorded before the earliest modal efforts of George Russell and far in advance of the Miles Davis and Gil Evans collaborations and Cecil Taylor's jagged and expressionistic first recordings. Even if Ellington's contribution to jazz piano should be viewed mostly in terms of consolidation, he was also experimenting on a regular basis, often in advance of those who were viewed as innovators. Some critics and listeners considered Ellington old-fashioned by the end of the 1940s; perhaps this is because Ellington, by the time a new trend had been around long enough for critics to notice it, had already extracted what suited his purposes and moved on. Moreover, he had an extraordinary ability to incorporate just about anything into his music in such a natural and organic manner that it never stood out as bizarre or freakish.

Ellington the Impressionist

Before Ellington entered the next important phase in his development as a pianist, he composed what is generally considered his most successful extended composition, *Harlem*, recorded by the Ellington orchestra on December 7, 1951. In sharp contrast to the *Deep South Suite*, which featured generous stretches of Ellington's piano, *Harlem* excluded the piano altogether. Perhaps it was just such an extensive focus on his composing for the orchestra alone that suggested, as a kind of aesthetic equipoise, the need to showcase his piano playing afterwards. *Piano Reflections*, a 1953 Capitol release, was the first of several Ellington trio outings for different labels over a ten-year span, representing some of his finest piano work. The Capitol sessions contain three compositions that draw heavily from impressionistic harmonies associated especially with French composers Debussy and Ravel.[11] While *Retrospection* seems slightly unfocused, *Reflections in D* (Example 13.7) and *Melancholia* are true jazz milestones in their incorporation of impressionistic harmonies and in Ellington's touch, phrasing, and dynamic nuances.

Willie "The Lion" Smith's 1939 solo recordings, including *Echoes of Spring* and *Morning Air*, include harmonies heard in early impressionism,

Example 13.7. *Reflections in D* (Duke Ellington), measures 4–6, recorded April 13, 1953.
Released on *Piano Reflections*, Capitol CDP-7 92863–2 (1989), and transcribed by Bill Dobbins.
Publishing rights administered by Sony ATV Harmony (ASCAP).

but Smith used these harmonies in the context of simple, often pentatonic
melodies and danceable rhythms associated with swing music. Only Bud
Powell's revolutionary *Dusk in Sandi*, from a 1951 Verve solo piano
session, can be considered a close jazz precursor to these Ellington pieces.
All three are played in a relatively free, rubato manner, with bowed bass
accompaniment and no drums. The melodies are chromatic but sparse,
somewhat like recitatives. Interestingly, Bill Evans recorded *Reflections
in D* in 1978 on the LP *New Conversations*, the final recording in his
"conversations with myself" series, and it was the only piece done simply
as a piano solo, with no overdubbing of "conversational" piano tracks.
Unaware of Ellington's version, Evans learned the piece from a Tony
Bennett recording, and remarked on how strange it was for so extraordinarily beautiful a piece to have remained obscure for so long. Listening
to Evans's interpretation after Ellington's reveals just how far ahead
Ellington was at exploring the piano's expressive potential in such a
context. In Ellington's original performance, some particularly colorful
moments are provided in the A sections as the right hand's diatonic triads
are approached chromatically by half step from below.

Ellington returned to this "impressionistic" style later in his career.
Many of the suites he composed from the mid-1960s to the early 1970s
have at least one movement featuring Ellington the pianist, and he often
used these opportunities to take his impressionism into previously
unexplored sonic realms. The strongest examples include "The Single
Petal of a Rose," from *The Queen's Suite* (1959), the third section of
Ad Lib on Nippon (1965), and *Meditation* and *T.G.T.T.* from the *Second
Sacred Concert* (1968).

The Queen's Suite was written especially for Queen Elizabeth II, after
she was unable to attend an Ellington concert at an international arts
festival in Leeds in October 1958. Ellington was so moved by her apologies
that he recorded the suite entirely at his expense and had only a single copy
pressed, for the queen's ears alone. It has been reported that "The Single

Petal of a Rose" came about spontaneously during a party that Ellington's friends Renee and Leslie Diamond gave for him at their new apartment in Leeds. Supposedly, while improvising late in the evening on a piano that he had just sent to the Diamonds as a housewarming gift, Ellington noted that one petal had fallen from the vase of roses on the piano. He then played the material that became known as "The Single Petal of a Rose," although it might have already been occupying his imagination.[12] In any case, it illustrates Ellington's uncanny knack for the dramatic public gesture.

Although *Ad Lib on Nippon* is included in *The Far East Suite* recording, it was originally a separate, one-movement suite, inspired by the orchestra's first trip to Japan in 1964. Clarinetist and tenor saxophonist Jimmy Hamilton collaborated on the final section. The opening themes feature Ellington's piano, fusing oriental-like modal melodies with minor blues forms. But it is the lengthy, rubato piano solo leading to Hamilton's concluding clarinet theme that is one of Ellington's more eloquent impressionistic statements, and it shares some thematic and harmonic connections with the orchestra's up-tempo finale.

Meditation, from the *Second Sacred Concert*, seems closely related to the pieces from the *Piano Reflections* sessions. *T.G.T.T.* adds the angelically lyric vocal abilities of the Swedish singer Alice Babs, who was featured throughout the concert. Especially impressive is her almost nonchalant perfection in executing the difficult chromatic leaps in the vocal lines, a common characteristic of Ellington's ballads. In both pieces, the range of sonority and expressive power in Ellington's piano playing is worth noting, as well as his exceptional sensitivity as an accompanist in *T.G.T.T.*, which stands for "too good to title." In the concert's program notes Ellington added, "It violates conformity in the same way, we like to think, that Jesus Christ did. The phrases never end on the note you think they will."[13]

The final decades

Through the last two decades of his life Ellington continued to explore the piano's expressive potential. Of all the pianists in the history of jazz, he best understood, and most colorfully employed, the specific sonorities of every register of the instrument. This was obvious already in *Ko-Ko* and *Happy Go Lucky Local*, but even more apparent in the *Piano Reflections* material, especially *Dancers in Love* (originally included in the 1945 *Perfume Suite*), *Who Knows?* (an Ellingtonian view of bebop piano), and *Kinda Dukish*, which later became the introduction to the ebullient, crowd-pleasing rearrangement of his 1930 masterpiece *Rockin' in Rhythm*.

Example 13.8. *Night Creature* (Duke Ellington), part two, measures 1–3, recorded March 16, 1955. Released on *Les Suites Sinfoniche*, Musica Jazz 2MJP-1021 (LP) and transcribed by Bill Dobbins. Publishing rights administered by G. Schirmer Inc. (ASCAP).

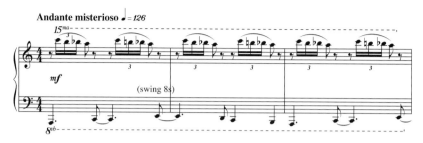

Perhaps the most imaginative use of the piano's extreme registers can be heard in the second movement of *Night Creature*, his evocative symphonic work written in 1955 for the Symphony of the Air. A sinister melody in the lowest register is accompanied by grace-note figures that use the four highest notes of the piano (Example 13.8). The grace notes lead to the off beats of each measure, creating the perfect rhythmic reference point for the loping melodic figures far below. In Ellington's liner notes, he makes it clear that this movement represents death. Cleverly avoiding a predictable, melodramatic mood, Ellington portrays the grim reaper in a lighter vein, as a slow-motion boogie-woogie in a minor key.

Ellington had a superb sense of humor. One of the most wry and subtle instances is documented on videos from the 1960s of trio performances of the band's theme song, Billy Strayhorn's *Take the "A" Train.* When played in the original key of C, the third note from the end of the second phrase is a Db, outside the key, resolving to C and E. Most singers were unable to find this note, singing the easier to locate D♮ instead. Even instrumentalists who learned the melody by ear often failed to notice this chromatic note, and also played a D♮ instead of the Db that Strayhorn obviously intended. In a clip from the wonderful PBS American Masters documentary, *A Duke Named Ellington*, Ellington is featured in a trio performance of Strayhorn's classic. When this tricky phrase comes up for the last time, Ellington stops on the Db, sustaining it instead of ending the phrase. Still not content, he makes a tag of the last phrase, stopping each time on the Db. By the last couple of times he turns his head toward the camera, chewing gum with a totally deadpan expression. Only those who know the comic history of that note really get the joke.[14]

In the later suites Ellington never hesitated to dip into some current pianistic vocabulary, finding what suited his highly discriminating musical taste and incorporating it in a manner that, somehow, simply sounded like more Duke Ellington. The opening theme of "Mount Harissa," from *The Far East Suite*, clearly shows his awareness of Horace Silver and the many pianists who followed a similar direction. Ellington's playing on the *Latin American Suite* and *The Afro-Eurasian Eclipse* acknowledges modal jazz developments, chords built in fourth intervals, exotic scales, and bass register ostinatos using fifth intervals, but all in a manner that sounds entirely Ellingtonian. In a curious way, it seemed as if each new trend represented just another minor tributary that had already been a part of Ellington's great stream of pianistic vocabulary.

Of course Ellington's pianistic skills included those of a superb accompanist, a fact best substantiated by the testimony of legendary bassist and composer Charles Mingus. Mingus complained that with most pianists he started hearing some of the same comping figures by the second chorus of a performance. He remarked that with Ellington, however, there was not only a limitless repertoire of comping figures, but also a great variety in texture. In one chorus Ellington might use five-note voicings, then in the next chorus thicken the texture to seven-note voicings or thin it down, even to single notes.[15] At times Ellington and the soloist would have a dialogue rather than assuming the traditional roles of soloist and accompanist. This can be clearly heard in the closing chorus of *Mood Indigo*, especially recordings from 1950 on, where Ellington often improvised a dialogue with the clarinetist Russell Procope or whichever soloist played the closing theme.

Ellington was also the perfect accompanist of his orchestra. He played a lot of piano when the music called for it, none when none was needed, and in other situations always seemed to find just the percussive chord, tasteful trill, or interjection that sounded tailor-made for the situation. The manner in which Gil Evans played piano in his own orchestra from the early 1950s through the late 1960s owed much to his keen awareness of the Ellington orchestra and the way Ellington's piano contributed to so many special moments. On perusing the many Ellington and Strayhorn scores that are preserved in the Ellington collection at the Smithsonian Institution, it is striking that, with very few exceptions, there is not a single note written for piano. As though the hundreds of compositions Ellington wrote were not enough, he somehow maintained enough of a connection to them all that he never needed even a sketch of a piano part.

Thus Ellington's piano playing, as soloist or accompanist, always involved improvisation. Often the improvising was simply a fresh embellishment of a given melody or accompaniment, a creative form of "shadowing the melody" that has been largely neglected in recent decades, as pianists have focused more on the accompanying harmonies. As Ellington advised the young pianist Billy Taylor, as they got to know one another in New York during the late 1940s, "Whatever music you choose to play, play it your own way."[16]

Improvisation should cover everything from the varied manner in which Russell Procope embellished the melody of *Mood Indigo* nearly every night for 26 years to Paul Gonsalves's freewheeling, 20-plus choruses on *Diminuendo and Crescendo in Blue* and everything in between. Ellington's comments in his autobiography, *Music Is My Mistress*, from the chapter "The Mirrored Self," are worth reading and pondering: "Anyone who plays anything worth hearing knows what he's going to play, no matter whether he prepares a day ahead or a beat ahead. It has to be with intent."[17]

In the end Ellington's piano playing deserves his own highest compliment: it is "beyond category." The same could be said of his orchestra. Because the Ellington orchestra continued to play some of the early pieces and a medley of their hit songs right along with the most forward-sounding new works, it was virtually the only orchestra from which the attentive listener could learn about the origins of jazz, its immediate past, its present, and its possible future all in one program. Similarly, Ellington's piano playing as soloist and accompanist was always a personal expression of the origins, past, present, and future of jazz piano. There were many peers who were more fashionable or more experimental, but none who consolidated more of the rich legacy and musical vocabulary of jazz piano in such a deeply personal manner. Johann Sebastian Bach would understand!

Notes

1 Duke Ellington, *Music Is My Mistress* (Garden City, NY: Doubleday, 1973; reprint, New York: Da Capo, 1976), 9.

2 "I went on studying, of course, but I could hear people whistling, and I got all the Negro music that way." Ibid., 33.

3 Telephone conversation between the author and Billy Taylor, August 2007.

4 Ellington relates this story in his own words in the Terry Carter film *A Duke Named Ellington*, which aired on PBS Television's American Masters series in 1988 and was released on DVD in 2007.

5 The piece was also known as *Portrait of Florence Mills*, in reference to the black singer and entertainer.

6 Monk's first recordings as a sideman appeared in 1944, but his mature style is more clearly identifiable in his first recordings as a leader from 1948 to 1950.

7 Telephone conversation with Billy Taylor, August 2007.

8 Ellington, *Mistress*, 184.

9 Derek Jewell, *Duke: A Portrait of Duke Ellington* (Toronto: George McLeod, 1977; reprint, New York: W. W. Norton, 1980), 107.

10 Smith uses a similar left-hand march style with attractive left-hand voicings in the middle section of his 1939 solo recording, *Morning Air*. Eight unique, original piano solos were recorded at this session, his first extended outing as a solo pianist. He preferred to record what he considered more lucrative material with singers and instrumental groups.

11 Strayhorn's admitted interest in the music of Debussy, as evidenced in his 1941 masterpiece, *Chelsea Bridge*, certainly encouraged Ellington's interest in such colorful harmonies, even if only through Strayhorn's own contribution to the orchestra's repertoire.

12 Jewell, *Duke*, 133–34.

13 Ellington, *Mistress*, 276.

14 From the film *A Duke Named Ellington*, cited above.

15 Mingus talks about Ellington the accompanist in the film *A Duke Named Ellington*, cited above.

16 Telephone conversation with Billy Taylor, August 2007.

17 Ellington, *Mistress*, 465.

14 Duke and descriptive music

MARCELLO PIRAS

Painter to composer

Like most children, Edward Ellington showed little enthusiasm for piano exercises. He dreamed to be a painter; he even showed early signs of talent in the field. Then, one night at a party, he discovered that the pianist drew the girls' attention, and soon found piano practicing worth the effort. He learned to play, read, and write music, and eventually acquired enough command of the keyboard to perform intricate rags. Music became his profession; art was seemingly downgraded to hobby.

As a matter of fact, Ellington was one of those rare birds endowed with multiple gifts. He also proved a fertile narrator. He was an endless source of short stories, fables, and funny moral tales, sometimes set to music in later years (e.g., *Monologue*, 1951). His mind was busy watching, describing, and depicting all the time.

Ironically, composing music turned out to be the toughest task. In his early years, what he had was a miniature band made up of friends, plus some talent for business, but little compositional skill. His earliest pieces (such as *Soda Fountain Rag*, from 1914), mostly surviving as fragments from later recordings, show that Duke could passably ape current fads. His first records are also surprisingly unpleasant. Instrumental parts overlap and clash; naïve sound effects are interspersed. *Choo Choo* and *Wanna Go Back Again Blues* contain train whistle imitations, hardly an original idea back then.

Listeners familiar with Ellington's full-fledged masterpieces and their rich tonal palette, lush, sensuous melodies, and daring harmonies may expect to find signs of gradual growth across the body of his work. Surprisingly, those ugly early records and Duke's first acknowledged masterpiece, *East St. Louis Toodle-O*, are separated by a mere five months. What had happened?

By 1924–1925, Ellington began taking lessons from a composer of stature, Will Marion Cook (1869–1944). A seminal figure in the development of black music in the U.S.A., Cook had studied in Berlin, been a protégé of Antonín Dvořák at the New York Conservatory, and written theatrical plays – not operas, but classy musical comedies. He furnished Ellington with a legitimate composer's basic vocabulary. Also, he knew how to write music for the theater, connected to the plot by commenting, describing, or suggesting events, characters, environments, moods. Some time later, Will Vodery (1885–1951), an authority on Broadway, began teaching Duke orchestration and advanced harmony.

Being an eclectic talent, Ellington was a natural candidate for musical theater, a verbal/visual/musical medium. Moreover, as a pianist, he was a geographically peripheral offspring of that Northern ragtime school whose leading figures – Eubie Blake, James P. Johnson, Thomas Waller – were virtuoso pianists who also wrote show music. As early as 1925, Duke tried his hand at it. Not only did he write songs for a revue that toured Europe, *Chocolate Kiddies* – he began going to theater as often as he could, following rehearsals, watching productions. Once he declared: "I am a man of the theater."[1]

Theatrical success always escaped him, at least in theaters. Despite box office failures, however, Duke's output includes three incomplete operas, eleven musical comedies, six revues, five ballets, incidental music for six plays, and four pieces with narrator, plus eleven movie soundtracks.[2] Even more interestingly, he conceived much of his "pure" instrumental music as synesthetic fusion of image and sound.

Except for a few cases, such as train imitations, Ellington did not do so to make his music easier. Songs are his easy music. Descriptive pieces often rank among his most enigmatic creatures, especially when Duke himself gave no clue. Yet, missing such extramusical elements he associated with his compositions amounts to a vital loss in the appreciation of his art.

Sound to image

Music is fundamentally an abstract art. Its easiest link to the physical world is onomatopoeia, which has been in use since the Stone Age. Keyboard pieces such as William Byrd's *The Battle* often hosted imitation of rattling drums, anthems, or cannonades. Music based on bird calls is also common in many cultures.

Within a more sophisticated approach, music can describe, suggest, or evoke external reality by analogy. In a renaissance madrigal, "rise" could be suggested by an upward scale, "trembling" by a trill. This is fairly direct. But when the idea of "white" is suggested by whole notes and half notes, and "black" by quarter notes and eighth notes, the link escapes the attention of everyone but the music reader.

Opera, born around 1600, inherited some of those usages. It soon hosted descriptive devices, which developed over time into a panoply of recurring musical symbols. For instance, a storm was depicted by a fast orchestral episode with frantic string tremolos and chromatic scales running up and down. This topos survived into the twentieth century; it is still found in Gershwin's *Porgy and Bess*.

By 1760, onomatopoeia had almost disappeared from European keyboard music, yet it crossed the ocean and found a haven in the English colonies, where local audiences, untrained in the intricacies of sonata form, welcomed naïve sound effects they "understood." Catalogs of North American composers, from Benjamin Carr onward, list dozens of battles, bird calls, wind- and water-inspired pieces. By 1850, Europe saw Liszt's invention of the tone poem, an orchestral piece following a detailed literary program. In the U.S.A., John Philip Sousa conceived entire suites, such as *Dwellers of the Western World* (1910), as fragmented tone poems for which he wrote down a story. With the surviving onomatopoeic tradition and the new tone-poem vogue overlapping, descriptivism became a staple of American Romantic music.

Nobody was to commission a tone poem from the young Duke. But he was rooted in ragtime, where descriptivism was common fare – water imagery, for instance, from Joplin's *The Cascades* to Luckey Roberts's *Ripples of the Nile* to Gershwin's *Rialto Ripples*. Duke's early solo-piano piece *Swampy River* (1928), an entirely notated irregular rag, forms his contribution to the genre. It springs in terse ripples to a lively Charleston rhythm (A section); gets broader as it flows, in a mix of Cuban *danza* and Harlem stride bass (B), with an occasional vortex (release of B); forms new ripples (A); calms down in the swamps of an Alberti bass (C), with its little cascade (release of C); then resumes its main course (B), to make its final effluence into the sea (the closing *rallentando*).

Rags to Cotton (Club)

From 1923 to 1927, Duke's home base was a cabaret known as Club Kentucky. Its Lilliputian stage hosted floorshows with singers, entertainers, and dance numbers, all backed by the house band. When Duke's Washingtonians were not there, they were usually booked to appear in musical comedies in nearby theaters.

Working for floorshows must have encouraged Duke to shape his pieces around a story. Certainly he did so in later years. In 1966, he was interviewed at home and asked about his working methods; Duke, lying in bed in his pajamas, said that sometimes a story came to his mind and then he worked on it.[3]

As he said in retrospect, "Painting a picture, or having a story to go with what you were going to play, was of vital importance in those days. The audience didn't know anything about it, but the cats in the band did."[4] He also explained the title of *East St. Louis Toodle-O* (1926): "Those old Negroes who work in the fields for year upon year, and are tired at the end of their day's labour, may be seen walking home at night with a broken, limping step locally known as the 'toddle-O'."[5] All this looks more like a vague inspiration than truly descriptive music, yet it is revealing of Duke's mentality. About *Immigration Blues* (1926), one scholar warily suggested that it depicts "an uprooted black southerner living in the North ... The opening section suggests the folk culture of the southerner, steeped in religion and expressed through the spiritual. The second section might have represented the southerner after relocation – now with a case of the blues."[6]

Alas, music is more ambiguous than language. It can express sadness, but not specify whether it stems from an ended love affair or a dry bank account. As with a Rorschach test, we are left with impressions that many different stories fit equally well. To stay on solid ground, an extramusical interpretation needs a clincher: a detailed, section-by-section correspondence to the music, or a quotation, or a recurring formal solution – or Duke's word, if any.

A piece that has long elicited sundry (and mutually incompatible) decipherments is *Black and Tan Fantasy* (1927). Mercer Ellington once asked his father about its origin, but got a typical Ducal answer, clouding rather than clarifying. Duke was nicknamed "the Artful Dodger" from his ability to find a way around direct questions on private matters.[7] According to Mercer – who was eight in 1927 – Duke said it commemorated the death of his affair with Fredi Washington, the main actress in Dudley Murphy's movie *Black and Tan*.[8] This makes no sense, as the movie was produced two years later. Other explanations have been attempted, but they only fit sections of the piece.[9] A new one is offered here.

Black and Tan Fantasy "was written in a taxi cab on the way to a recording session,"[10] and recorded three times in 1927. Comparison of versions shows that, in fact, it didn't require much paper. The piece is a blues with a verse, conflating two of Ellington's favorite forms: the verse-and-refrain song format, and the blues format with different reharmonizations for each section, following this structure: R-V-R-R-R-R-R. It begins with a plaintive melody in minor, based on Stephen Adams's sacred song "The Holy City," and ends with a final tutti quoting Chopin's "Marche funèbre."

What was really staged at the Kentucky and then at the larger Cotton Club is only vaguely known. Black was supposed to be synonymous with savage, and exotic foils abounded. Dancers, male and female – two or three per routine, given the narrow space – were often as scantily clad as decency would allow. Also, Harlem cabarets were not opera houses, where people get detailed program notes; plots had to be simple and easy to grasp.

Now, the reader is invited to think of a very famous story, set in a primitive location, and requiring little tailor work.

Please take your time to guess.

Yes, Genesis. Adam and Eve chased away from Eden. A story anybody recognizes, set in the primitive scenario par excellence. Compare point by point the music with the biblical verses.

1. *Adam and Eve are God-fearing and live in unity* (Gen. 2:24, "and they shall be one flesh"): Cornet and trombone, in parallel harmony, play a simple melody, lifted from the refrain (in major) of "The Holy City," where it says "Jerusalem! Jerusalem! Lift up your gates and sing: Hosanna in the highest! Hosanna to your King!"
2. *The serpent tempts Eve* (3:1): The mellifluous alto sax plays a winding, seductive six-bar melody. *Eve says no* (3:2–3): The band "waves its head" – a semitone motif going alternately in opposite directions. *The serpent tempts Eve again* (3:4–5): Same alto sax melody. *Eve agrees*: An assertive two-bar cadence.
3. *Eve bites the apple*: A long, sustained high B♭ (the crux of the piece, notated). *She is happy and invites Adam as well* (3:6): A talking (with plunger mute) cornet solo on the major blues, also featuring laughter (a descending scale played staccato) on bar nine.
4. *Adam and Eve suddenly acquire knowledge* (3:7: "And the eyes of them both were opened"): Piano solo on a new blues progression, now suddenly replete with sophisticated harmonic knowledge.
5. *God asks and curses* (3:8–15): Harsh trombone solo. Notice the "cursing" downward glissando on bar nine (found in all early versions).
6. *Adam and Eve beg for mercy*: Cornet plea. *But they are chased away*: Abrupt band chord (3:24, the "flaming sword." All this twice). *As a punishment, death enters humankind* (3:19, "for dust thou art, and unto dust shalt thou return"): "Marche funèbre."

Readers may want to estimate the odds that it is all coincidental.

If this is the plot, no wonder Duke shrouded it in silence. He must have felt embarrassed about using the Bible for a sexy floorshow, and his returning to the subject in his *Second Sacred Concert* takes on a flavor of atonement.

A different case is *Black Beauty* (1928), a piece meant not for an actual theatrical routine, but as a musical depiction thereof. It portrays the talented actress/singer/dancer Florence Mills (1896–1927). Its 1943 remake bore a subtitle, *Portrait of Florence Mills*, never attested before, and scholar Mark Tucker assumed the dedication had been invented *a posteriori*.[11] Analysis shows the opposite.

Soon after Florence's unexpected death, a few lugubrious records were hastily put together to thrive on the grief. Duke had a hand in a couple. But then he felt the need for a less passing homage. The painter in him conceived the idea of a "portrait" in sound. But how can such a thing be done? Duke found here the solution he was to resort to in virtually every portrait – drawing from a melody associated with the portrayed person.

Florence was endowed with a petite, supple body, a shrill voice, and a natural talent for acting and dancing. She appeared in revues, often performing duo routines with a male partner (Ulysses S. Thompson, Johnny Nit). Her hit was "I'm a Little Blackbird Looking for a Bluebird," from *Dixie to Broadway* (1924), a song that can be interpreted as hinting at interracial love. She was largely identified with that tune, which quickly sank into oblivion after she passed away.

In order to suggest a blackbird, songwriters George Meyer and Arthur Johnston used a common bird-call motif: a repeated note followed by an upward jump. Its first two instances are found right at the beginning of the chorus:

Such a pattern is not hard to notice on the original edition – it appears 15 times.

But which bird is this? No blackbird for sure.[12] Bird-call motifs in ancient music had to be very specific (in times when anybody could tell a nightingale from a sparrow, an art largely lost to us moderns) and at the same time adhere to a fixed musical pattern. For instance, a downward minor third meant "cuckoo," as in Bernardo Pasquini or Johann Kaspar Kerll. One can also find the nightingale (François Couperin), finch (Vivaldi's famous flute concerto), dove (François Dagincourt), and so on. Now the sad news is, the bird in this song is the *hen*. The clearest example is Jean-Philippe Rameau's *La poule* (1728); the oldest one, possibly Alessandro Poglietti's *Capriccio und Canzona über das Henner- und Hannergeschrey* (c.1680). Meyer and Johnston may have known the hen motif from Gottschalk's *La gallina* (1863) or perhaps, brutally but effectively, resorted to inverting a motif from "Listen to the Mocking Bird."

Oblivious of ornithology, Duke picked up this pattern as the song's trademark and changed *two* pitches,[13] from

to

This appears in the first theme; the intro is made entirely from another variant of the same motif. Also, a rhythmic pattern is picked up from the verse. A new melody is born, in pure Ducal style, out of fragments of "I'm a Little Blackbird," prompting identification from period listeners. (The following generation needed the subtitle.)

Black Beauty has two themes, A (32 bars) and B (16), appearing in ABAA order. In the above-described A, the showgirl, with her seductive aura, shrill voice, and supple movements, is depicted not only by Ellington's melody but also by Arthur Whetsol's tone and phrasing. His muted trumpet *is* Florence. Then, both the bridge from A and the entire B apparently introduce a male character, played by Joe Nanton's trombone. On B, we hear the dancing of some chorus girls behind him, rendered by three high-pitched reeds performing close steps in staccato fashion, like the patting of heels and toes on the stage – actually an inversion of the "modified hen" motif:

In the second occurrence of A, a tap-dancing duo routine is depicted by a (largely notated) dialogue in the rhythm section. First, drummer Sonny Greer and Duke's right hand portray the light-footed Florence, then Wellman Braud's slapped bass impersonates her more muscular partner – then her again, then him, and so forth. Finally, in the third occurence of A, Florence's theme reappears, played by Barney Bigard on the clarinet – she wouldn't sing soon after dancing, as she would be out of breath. She (that is, Whetsol's muted trumpet) only returns for the final eight bars, ending up with a little *rallentando* bow. We have been exposed to a three-minute sketch of Florence Mills's stage art.[14]

Mimicry to dictionary

Over the years, Duke's experimenting with the descriptive resources of his band formed a rich tool kit. Being as fertile and as pressured by deadlines as the old opera masters, he reused and refashioned old solutions, while also trying new ones and exchanging them with Billy Strayhorn. Tried-and-true tricks piled up in what we might call *Duke's Daunting Database of Depictions*. A few tentative entries are offered below.[15]

America

A trumpet fanfare that seems to stand for either the nation or the continent in at least two compositions. In the *Liberian Suite* (1947), it bursts at the end of "Dance No. 2," apparently disjointed from the rest of the movement (a miniature concerto for clarinet, vibraharp, and band). As I have suggested elsewhere,[16] the piece depicts the Middle Passage on a slave ship, and the fanfare means "destination reached." (The following "Dance No. 3" reveals that the ship landed in Cuba.) In *Harlem* (1951), a similar fanfare rounds up the entire tone poem. After depicting various corners of Harlem in an imaginary promenade, it proudly reaffirms that such a human microcosm entirely belongs in the American mold. This was a significant statement by which Ellington distanced himself from the Marxist left à la Paul Robeson, from separatists, and from Marcus Garvey's "Back to Africa" movement.

Ascension to Heaven

Climbing up to the *altissimo* register. In the "Dance No. 3," Ray Nance's violin impersonates an African who comes out of the ship barely alive, feebly sings a sad song, and dies. Death is depicted by the solo violin cadenza, which ends up on a barely audible high pitch: the poor prisoner's soul flies to Heaven. Similarly, when Ellington wrote *In the Beginning God* (1965), he gave his trumpet marvel, Cat Anderson, a cadenza at the end of the third section. In the live recording made at the Fifth Avenue Presbyterian Church in New York, soon after Anderson squeezes his most piercing screech out of his trumpet, Duke says: "That's the highest we got!"

Birds

Motifs resembling bird calls, played by a reed instrument. None have been found in Duke's early years, when his descriptions were mostly confined to Harlem and to people. Only later, as he began traveling extensively, were his painter's eye and composer's ear drawn to new visual and sound landscapes; then bird calls appeared. Known examples are "Sunset and the Mocking Bird," from *The Queen's Suite* (1959), and a Strayhorn contribution, "Bluebird of Delhi," from *The Far East Suite* (1964). In a symphony orchestra, such calls are typically scored for flute or oboe. Having neither instrument, Duke and Strayhorn systematically resorted to Jimmy Hamilton's immaculate clarinet. It is therefore reasonable to suspect that some contrapuntally independent clarinet parts in other pieces hide hitherto unidentified birds – the final bar of "I Like the Sunrise," for instance.

Dancers

A duo/trio section with piano exchanging rhythmic patterns with bass, drums, or both, suggesting foot-tapping. The *Black Beauty* routine is the prototype. The same idea opens and closes *Bojangles* (1940), a portrait of the great dancer Bill Robinson, and is then expanded into a formidable cutting contest in *Pitter Panther Patter* (1940), a tour de force duo with Duke, the older dancer, challenging young bassist Jimmie Blanton to perform several steps, some already out of fashion (James P. Johnson's *Charleston* is quoted). In the *Perfume Suite* (1944), the third movement, "Dancers in Love" ("Stomp for Beginners"), depicts naïveté; its sparse texture and small melodic intervals sketch the hesitating steps of a young couple. The foot-tapping was originally introduced by the plucked bass, then – in later versions – by finger-snapping. That emphatically wrong F♯ (in F major) on the V-Disc version may symbolize a wrong step. A still later example is *Tap Dancer's Blues* (1966).

Ellington himself acknowledged that Will Marion Cook taught him such common compositional techniques as retrograding (right to left) and inverting (up to down) motifs.[17] Whenever such motifs were finalized to depict, suggest, or accompany dance movements, Duke had a chance to display his obsession for symmetry. In fact, his penchant for palindromes – symmetric motifs that are identical played backwards – peeps out everywhere. Examples include the opening cell from *Azure* (1937):

a variant of which occurs in "Autumnal Suite" from *Paris Blues* (1961); Duke's left-hand line from *Fragmented Suite for Piano and Bass* (1972), third movement;[18]

or the opening five tones

from *Blue Feeling* (1934), by the way a piece entirely symmetrical in form.

Obviously, palindromes, as motifs pointing to gestures, are useful in dance numbers, for whatever you do on stage, sooner or later you must either do the opposite or walk out. Palindromes also effectively underline circular movements of limbs or torso. An early case seems to be *Hop Head* (1927), a Charleston clearly intended not for flappers but for professional dancers, who apparently got specific clues to body movements from the music (or vice versa). Here, as elsewhere, Duke suggests footwork by repeating a close interval:

Also, the title is period jargon for "opium taker." Those who consume opium will probably feel their heads spinning; hence the "revolving" opening pattern

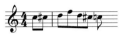

likely suggested circular head movements. Both motifs are palindromic. The latter comes from a Cook song, "Bon Bon Buddy." Ellington knew the song well – he had quoted another motif from it in *Li'l Farina* (1925).[19]

Finally, the association of palindrome and dance gesture shows up in a ballet, *Night Creature* (1955). Its opening motif has five notes followed by their retrograde:

Diversity

Abruptly juxtaposed or superimposed snapshots of music depicting a heterogeneous humankind. The intro from *Harlem Air Shaft* (1940) is a case in point – a jigsaw puzzle of sharply contrasting musical blocks with distinct identities, tone colors, and keys: a trumpet motif redolent of a field holler (in A-flat), a sax motif perhaps evoking a church organ (in C), and a trombone motif suggesting a gramophone playing a Count Basie record, *Swingin' the Blues* (in E).

Diversity boasts a respectable ancestry in American music. Way before "melting pot" and "multi-kulti" were coined, New World composers strove to convey an image of their nation hosting different cultures – think of Gershwin's *"I Got Rhythm" Variations*, Gottschalk's symphony *La Nuit des Tropiques*, and most of Ives's output. Their forefather was Mexican chapel-master Gaspar Fernandes (1566–1629), with his kaleidoscopic *Cancionero de Oaxaca*. However, those composers focused on ethnic diversity; Ellington's air-shaft diversity is rather about individuals – people walking, dressing, cooking, dancing, singing, and praying in various ways. It is found from the extended opening of *Merry-Go-Round* (1933) all the way down to the convulsive *Traffic Jam* (1967). At first, it was an image of Harlem. Then, as Ellington acquired a taste for globe-trotting, he broadened his views, only to discover that the Earth is nothing but a larger Harlem, which he looked at from above, as it were, taking colorful, bizarre, moving, witty musical snapshots he then combined in geographic suites, such as *The Afro-Eurasian Eclipse* (1971).

Faith

A Negro spiritual paraphrased or emulated to mean "God," "church," or "prayer." On occasion the original is recognizable: the first theme of "Dance No. 1" from the *Liberian Suite* (1947) is redolent of "Wade in the Water," and the opening theme from *Echoes of the Jungle* evokes "Go Down, Moses" but comes from the first movement of Dvořák's "New World" symphony, bars 148–151. Other themes sound original. "Come Sunday" (1943), in particular, might be called "Duke's plainchant" as he used it from *Black, Brown and Beige* (1943) to *David Danced Before the Lord* (1963). But "Come Sunday" is untypical. Most of Duke's religious themes are opened by the major triad arpeggio, as in *Echoes of the Jungle* or the church theme in *Harlem*.

One of the Artful Dodger's best kept secrets was his being a Freemason. He had attended Masonic venues since 1919,[20] and in 1932 was affiliated with Washington's Social Lodge No. 1 of the Prince Hall (black) Freemasonry. His major, or only, Masonic work is the *Liberian Suite*, commissioned for Liberia's centennial. President William V. S. Tubman was also a Mason, and Masons had a major role in Liberia's history. When Duke had his suites premiered at Carnegie Hall he loved to explain their underlying stories. On the *Liberian Suite* he only spent few, and actually misleading, words. The Masonic double entendre peeps out in the opening "I Like the Sunrise," where an African (singer Al Hibbler) delivers a hymn to the Sun. As a Christian, Ellington does not portray his African ancestor as a pagan or polytheist, but as a forerunner of monotheism. Actually monotheism was invented in Africa by the pharaoh Akhenaton, who, in his ill-fated revolution, forced the replacement of the old pantheon with the Sun. Of course, identifying the Christian God with an Egyptian one is very Masonic. Again, the opening theme is built on the major triad, C–E–G.

This writer's interpretation of the piece had stopped here for years, until an incredible confirmation dawned on him. In both the studio and live recordings, Hibbler sings the words "I like the sunrise" seven times.[21] The word "sunrise" is increasingly smoothed out. He gradually obliterates "–se" and pronounces "sun ray," then obliterates "–y" and says "I like the Sun Ra." The real meaning of the piece is thus exposed to the initiated and veiled to laypeople.

Fear

An emotion rare in Duke, but usually related to the whole-tone scale. In Ellington and Strayhorn's *Perfume Suite* (1944), the second movement, "Strange Feeling" (that is, violence) has a theme by Strayhorn, who also

orchestrated the sung part. The instrumental first half, scored by
Ellington, has a recurring whole-tone scale at the end of each A section.[22]
In "Dance No. 2" from the *Liberian Suite*, the solo clarinet, playing an
African in chains on the slave ship, expresses his terror in up-and-down
whole-tone scales. The prototype is perhaps the ghostly clarinet–banjo duet
in *Echoes of the Jungle* (1931), where the clarinet has a repeated up-and-
down pattern, which, albeit blurred in a quasi-glissando, is whole-tone
upward (not downward). Shivers of fear are in tenor banjo tremolo-
glissando effects.

Man/Woman

Two contrasting musical ideas depicting the conflict/attraction of sexes. In
Cotton Club floorshows, concise stories of seduction, courtship, attrac-
tion/refusal, and runaway/pursuit, performed by a male and a female
dancer, were simple and universal enough to be grasped without words.
Duke translated such dualities into music by assigning each character one
theme. Cook probably taught him the common bithematic forms in
classical music. Some, such as the ABA *Lied* form, would soon come in
handy for three-minute records (*Awful Sad*, *The Mooche*). Others, such as
sonata form, were less suitable. Ellington also used folk-like alternating
bithematic forms, as in ABABAB (*East St. Louis Toodle-O*), or could raise
the verse of a song to the dignity of a second theme, as in ABAAAA (*Black
and Tan Fantasy*, *Old Man Blues*, *Mood Indigo*, and more, up to *Suite
Thursday*). Pieces from any category may display a male/female polarity.
This is subtler than just scoring for high and low registers; rather, it often
seems to express a basic idea Ellington associated with women – attrac-
tiveness. Apparently he was fascinated not only by actual women, but also
by women as a source of an invisible essence, drawing men like the smell of
a rose draws a bee. It is this essence that he repeatedly tried to express in
sound. In fact, most of his female themes are associated with a *call*, and not
only in bithematic pieces. The earliest case is *Creole Love Call* (1927), with
its elementary two-note motif (picked up from King Oliver, but first of a
series of similar motifs in Duke) and Adelaide Hall improvising over it.

A masterpiece in the genre is *The Mystery Song*. Again, the title alludes
to a call, again stemming out of a two-note motif, this time apparently
coming from a remote horizon. Gunther Schuller stressed the "distant,
muted tone color" of that A strain for the brass choir (although he
dismissed the rest of the piece).[23] To get this effect, Ellington chose the
D major key, rare in jazz and unlikely for brass, followed by a male B strain
(in C major) – one of those warm, seductive reed obbligatos Ellington was
capable of. The man is soft-spoken but articulate – all sorts of intervals are
found in the melody. The two get closer in the following A section, an

intimate, nocturnal, whispered dialogue. Here Ellington picks up the high clarinet and the low baritone sax, but gives the low instrument the high register and vice versa, so that they come closer – the sweet baritone plays the woman's role and theme; it even laughs on bar 29. The deep clarinet improvises the man's answers. And then comes the finale, where the two themes embrace and reach fusion: melodic cells from B are placed over the chord structure of A. A four-bar tag-ending quickly switches the lights off.

Yet the apex of Ellington's work in the genre is probably *On a Turquoise Cloud* (1947), starring classical soprano Kay Davis for the mysterious female call, and Lawrence Brown's trombone in a masterful rendering of an elegant, handsome seducer. Duke no longer worked at the Cotton Club, yet he still saw a stage in his mind. His piano intro is a curtain raiser. In A, Kay Davis sings her call; B follows, played by Brown (who actually composed this melody). Then A and B merge, like in *The Mystery Song*, but in reverse pattern: A motifs (voice and clarinets) on B chords. Finally – and symmetrically – she sings A again, with the trombone discreetly in the background. Now the two elements fuse: we can almost *see* the final embrace, in the exceedingly long fermata with its astonishing blend of tone colors. This languid finale is like a long, never-ending kiss. And simultaneously (not afterwards!) we hear Ellington's piano intro, which had raised the curtain and now lowers it, wisely veiling the two lovers' privacy. As if Duke would no longer describe, but rather wink: "You can imagine the rest."

Message

A musical episode focused on percussion and/or hosting a drum solo, associated with the traditional image of talking "jungle drums" (which ought to be properly called "savannah idiophones"). One example is the opening from *Black, Brown and Beige* (1943). Ellington's own typescript plot of *Boola*, the unfinished opera this suite was extracted from, begins:

> A message is shot through the jungle by drums
> Boom! Boom! Boom! Boom!
> Like a tom-tom in steady precision . . .[24]

which fits the opening bars. The idea of message is again conveyed by tympani in "Dance No. 4" from the *Liberian Suite*, where the message is one of liberation – ships will carry freed blacks back to Liberia.

Portrait

A piece depicting somebody by means of a motif that listeners associate with that person. The earliest example is the cited *Black Beauty*. Another is

Portrait of the Lion (1939), based on the B theme from Willie "The Lion" Smith's composition *Passionette*.

River

Decades after *Swampy River*, this idea resurfaced as a ballet, *The River* (1970). For this piece, as choreographer Alvin Ailey discovered, Duke did "meticulous research on water music from various musical periods, including Handel's *Water Music*, Debussy's *La mer*, Britten's *Peter Grimes*, and Smetana's *Moldau*."[25] Most of the episodes illustrating parts of the river ("Spring," "Vortex," etc.) expand those already detectable, in embryonic form, in the 1928 piano solo.

Speech

A soloist emulating the human voice. Famous examples are the two-note opening motif from *Harlem*, with the muted trumpet pronouncing the word "Har-lem," and several occurrences in *Such Sweet Thunder*, co-composed with Strayhorn: the four "sonnets," with a soloist delivering a melody cast in sonnet format – 14 phrases of (more or less) 11 pitches – or musical sentences that fit an actual line from Shakespeare, as with Puck (trumpeter Clark Terry) delivering "Lord, what fools these mortals be" in "Up and Down, Up and Down."[26]

Train

Onomatopoeia of train noise. This runs the gamut from the whistle interpolation in *Choo Choo* (1924), to the happily running locomotive in *Lightnin'* (1932), to the astonishingly detailed and virtuosic *Daybreak Express* (1933), to a further transformation into a social-political symbol in *Happy Go Lucky Local*, the popular finale to the *Deep South Suite* (1946), to the abstract *Track 360* (1958).

Matter to spirit

Duke aimed higher as he grew older. In later years his writing, like in Beethoven's third style, took on a somewhat disembodied quality. Accordingly, his imagery delved more directly into abstract matters, giving old images a spiritual meaning.

In his three *Sacred Concerts* Duke gathered most entries of his descriptive dictionary, pushed to maximum intensity and turned into powerful metaphors. His musical descriptions rise from outer nature to inner nature, as Arnold Schoenberg would put it, in a sort of *Summa Theologica* of his art for faith's sake.

In the final section from *In the Beginning God*, Jesus' salvation message starts its run through the world. The chosen metaphor is of course the train. We hear a speaking chorus starting slowly and speeding up while calling the four Evangelists, then *Acts*, then the epistles of St. Paul, faster and faster, until the piece explodes in an infectious drum solo – in Duke's code, the greatest message a drum could ever spread – finally pointing to Heaven with Cat Anderson's trumpet. The imagery of diversity reappears in the *Second Sacred Concert*, as the final gathering of all humankind, "the place where all ends end," the Judgement Day, here called "The Biggest and Busiest Intersection." And, in a more contemplative form, in a collection of musical prayers in contrasting styles – "Every Man Prays in His Own Language" (*Third Sacred Concert*).

In Ellington's last creations, the trip from worldly imagery to supernatural imagery is completed. Now, the trip into the meanings of his oeuvre is up to us.

Notes

1 A. H. Lawrence, *Duke Ellington and His World: A Biography* (New York: Routledge, 2001), 45.

2 Marcello Piras, "Works" section of "Duke Ellington" entry in *The Grove Dictionary of American Music*, 2nd edn. (New York: Oxford University Press, 2013).

3 Ruggero Orlando, interview with Ellington in *Duke Ellington: Jazz e simpatia*, RAI documentary, 1966. Ellington was composing *The Golden Broom and the Green Apple*. RAI is Italy's public radio and television company.

4 Duke Ellington, *Music Is My Mistress* (New York: Doubleday, 1973), 47.

5 Duke Ellington, "My Hunt for Song Titles," *Rhythm*, August 1933, 22–23. Reprinted in *The Duke Ellington Reader*, ed. Mark Tucker (New York: Oxford University Press, 1993), 88.

6 Mark Tucker, *Ellington: The Early Years* (Urbana: University of Illinois Press, 1991), 233.

7 Derek Jewell, *Duke: A Portrait of Duke Ellington* (London: Elm Tree Books, 1977), *passim*.

8 Mercer Ellington with Stanley Dance, *Duke Ellington in Person: An Intimate Memoir* (Boston: Houghton Mifflin, 1978; reprint, New York: Da Capo, 1979), 48.

9 Mark Buselli, in "Duke's Use of Visual Imagery" (formerly published on the Internet, but no longer online) correctly focuses on the Man/Woman duality but places it in the wrong piece (as this writer, too, has done for years). David Metzer's article "Shadow Play: The Spiritual in Duke Ellington's 'Black and Tan Fantasy'," *Black Music Research Journal* 17/2 (1997): 137–58, has pure speculation.

10 Stanley Dance, *The World of Duke Ellington* (New York: Charles Scribner's Sons, 1970; reprint, New York: Da Capo, 1981), 271.

11 Mark Tucker, private letter to Bill Egan, author of *Florence Mills: Harlem Jazz Queen* (Lanham, MD: The Scarecrow Press, 2004), c. 1999.

12 As can be verified at www.garden-birds.co.uk/birds/blackbird.htm#Voice.

13 Here transposed in G to facilitate comparison.

14 Reference to an earlier stage of this analysis is in Egan, *Florence Mills*, 285.

15 Descriptive devices found only once in Ellington's oeuvre are not included.

16 For a detailed deciphering of this major work, see Marcello Piras, "Ellington narratore di storie: la *Liberian Suite*," *I Quaderni – Trimestrale dell'Istituto Gramsci Marche* 32 (1999): 41–67.

17 He said that Cook "would give me lectures in music. I'd sing a melody in its simplest form and he'd stop me and say, 'Reverse your figures'." *Ellington Reader*, ed. Tucker, 241.

18 Syncopated variants not notated.

19 This quotation was first noticed by Randy Sandke, to whom I am indebted. I subsequently discovered that Cook's motif, too, is a manipulated quotation from Franz Lehár's "Vilja's Lied." The teacher had passed on to his pupil not only the specific melody, but also the general trick.

20 See ad reproduced in Tucker, *Early Years*, 60.

21 Some (inconclusive) evidence suggests that Hibbler himself might have been a Freemason.

22 Walter van de Leur, *Something to Live For: The Music of Billy Strayhorn* (New York: Oxford University Press, 2002), 94.

23 Gunther Schuller, *Early Jazz: Its Roots and Musical Development* (New York: Oxford University Press, 1967), 356.

24 Quoted in Maurice Peress, *Dvořák to Duke Ellington* (New York: Oxford University Press, 2004), 181. From the original typescript housed at the Smithsonian Institution.

25 John Franceschina, *Duke Ellington's Music for the Theatre* (Jefferson, NC: McFarland, 2001), 161.

26 Only in one of the two known takes.

15 Sing a song of Ellington; or, the accidental songwriter

WILL FRIEDWALD

Let me start at an angle: an Ellington song, but no singer. On first hearing, you might assume the 1956 recording by Eddie Condon's band of "Don't Get Around Much Anymore," from the album *Treasury of Jazz*, is just one of innumerable mainstream instrumental covers of a Duke Ellington vocal classic. But there are things to note here. First and foremost, it's a singularly beautiful performance; trombonist Cutty Cutshall chose the song as his solo feature, and plays it more movingly than any other soloist I can imagine – with the exception, perhaps, of Ellington's own hornmen. Cutshall's performance is filled with the kind of vocalized nuances, sighs, moans, and gasps that would do these players proud; yet, to his credit, he doesn't sound as if he's imitating any of Ellington's trombonists.

Cutshall and Condon treat the tune as a ballad. This was surprising in 1956. Ellington had taken it more like a danceable foxtrot, and even its earlier instrumental version, *Never No Lament* (1940), was in medium tempo. "Don't Get Around Much Anymore" already has an implicit contrast of tempi – a contrast built into the relation of words and music. The lyrics are the slow element. Melancholy, they describe a broken romance, or at least a protracted separation (it's possible to view the words in the context of other separation songs of the World War II era). On the other hand, there is the tune, simply as tune, and it had always been performed by the Ellington band (and others in the jazz world) in a more upbeat manner. At least until Condon and Cutshall.

As to "standard" tempo, let's consult the song's most definitive singers. They are likely Al Hibbler, Ellington's own long-running male soloist, and Ella Fitzgerald – who wasn't about to leave it out of her 1957 *Duke Ellington Songbook*. Each sang it as more or less upbeat but with just a hint of regret and remorse: a dash of pepper in the stew. It wasn't until Tony Bennett's 1999 Ellington centennial album that a major vocalist gave this song a slow and thoughtful, a sadly intimate, interpretation.

Yet here we are, back in 1956, with instrumentalist Cutty Cutshall playing it as a ballad.

The Ellington song catalogue had arrived at an interesting junction, with implications for how the Maestro's songs – and those of other jazz composers – were subsequently done. The curious part is that for generations – even by 1956 fans could be counted in generations – it had been taken for granted that jazz musicians could take a pop song or a show tune and play it any way they wanted. It was considered basic practice to "personalize" the tempo. In a famous example, the pioneering jazz singer Lee Wiley in 1951 boldly slowed down "I've Got a Crush on You" from a foxtrot to a ballad. Radical as this interpretation was, it went on to become the enduring template for how to perform the Gershwin brothers' standard. Even the extremely conservative Ira Gershwin approved. But this is precisely why Cutshall's slow version of "Don't Get Around Much" is so noteworthy. While it was permissible for a singer, arranger, or instrumentalist to take liberties with a pop song or a show tune, a completely contrary tradition had evolved when it came to songs that were written by jazz musicians and taken directly as jazz.

Jazz musicians felt they had an obligation to preserve the composer's central rhythmic intention. No one made a waltz out of Jelly Roll Morton's *King Porter Stomp*, nor were there red-hot recordings of Ellington's "In My Solitude." Up to that point in jazz history, you were allowed, even encouraged, to change the core rhythmic design of a written melody *unless* it had been written by a jazz composer. Since Ellington was the most accomplished composer in the world of jazz, in terms both of instrumentals and song, he inadvertently had more to do with establishing this "tradition" than anyone else.

If all this seems familiar, it's because Ellington, the foremost jazz performer-composer of the twenties, thirties, and forties, anticipated a more common recent phenomenon: the singer-songwriter. If the composer is also his own interpreter, it seemed then (and seems now) to lock a song into a fixed design. In this regard, Ellington joins Bob Dylan and John Lennon; it is rare to rewrite their songs as well. (No tangos, no heavy funk, for "The Times They Are A-Changin'.")

The "instrumental" songwriter

That Ellington was, at once, bandleader, pianist, and composer, sheds light on the most crucial fact about his songwriting: The great majority of his most celebrated songs were not conceived as songs originally, but rather as "absolute music" – as pure instrumentals. It's one thing to place Ellington in the pantheon of jazz composers such as Jelly Roll Morton and Thelonious Monk; quite another (and just as right) to see him in the company of Jerome Kern, Irving Berlin, Cole Porter, George Gershwin, Richard Rodgers, and Harold Arlen: the "Big Six" theater-based writers whose work forms the cornerstone of "The Great American Songbook."

Benny Carter, Benny Golson, Don Redman, Tadd Dameron, and other writers from the jazz world certainly wrote the occasional pop hit, but it's safe to say that Ellington – with the possible exception of Fats Waller – was the only major jazz composer who likewise was seen as a major pop songwriter. The flip side of the coin is that, of major American popular songwriters, he was the only first-rank jazz musician.

To drive home Ellington's unique position, consider: He was the only major American popular songwriter whose life's work was overwhelmingly instrumental. Richard Rodgers, it is true, had a few instrumentals, and also a few songs that began as instrumentals and later had lyrics added, but only the merest handful.[1] "Beneath the Southern Cross" comes swiftly to mind; a cue from his score to the 1952–1953 television documentary *Victory at Sea*, a few months later it emerged as the song "No Other Love" for the show *Me and Juliet*. One tune serving for both war and love!

Then there is Gershwin, whose brother, Ira, added a lyric to one of the melodies from George's celebrated tone poem *An American in Paris*. Of the "Big Six," only Gershwin created a respectable body of instrumental music, including a piano concerto and a "Cuban" overture, as well as *Rhapsody in Blue*. But none had a second lease on life in pop-song format, something which happens over and over again with Ellington. And Gershwin was obviously at ease in the vocal idiom, writing together with Ira, often in measure-by-measure collaboration, literally hundreds of songs that were from the outset conceived as songs. Even with Gershwin's intense desire to prove to the world that he was not merely a writer of pop hits and could write "serious" long-form works, the fact remains: He is still remembered at least as much (if not more) for his songs than for his purely instrumental catalogue.

It is different with Ellington. He generally seemed more "himself" when writing in the purely instrumental idiom, and his instrumental music still forms the center of scholarly – and fan – interest. Yet if, as his career unfolded, it would be fair to call Ellington "The Accidental Songwriter," he began that career on quite a different footing. The youthful Ellington was impelled towards song, well aware that African-American composers were likely to make their largest mark through songwriting – especially through hits in musical theatre, as were had on Broadway by Will Marion Cook and Eubie Blake. As Mark Tucker makes clear in his masterful biographical study, *Ellington: The Early Years*,[2] most of his earliest works were songs, written largely in collaboration with lyricist Jo Trent. Nor was the Ellington/Trent team lacking in ambition; as early as 1924–1925 they had written several songs for *Chocolate Kiddies*, a revue produced in Europe.

Throughout his career Ellington hoped for, yet never achieved, a major stage success, despite efforts such as *Jump for Joy* and *Beggar's Holiday*. The irony is that when he finally got his wish, the success was posthumous: the 1981 Broadway sensation *Sophisticated Ladies*. Yet what was its score? A medley of his greatest hits, many (or even most) of which were conceived in a purely instrumental manner first.

It is impossible to give anything approaching a complete account of Ellington's vocal output in this short chapter, so I'll restrict myself to a sample of what I see as his best work in the field. I'll proceed chronologically, with observations along the way about some celebrated performances of these songs.

"Mood Indigo" (1930/1931)

This work grew out of a melody brought to Ellington by Barney Bigard, who had earlier obtained it from his New Orleans clarinet teacher, Lorenzo Tio.[3] Thanks to a lyric by Mitchell Parish, "Mood Indigo" became in 1931 Ellington's first full-fledged "pop-song" hit. (It was an instrumental hit a year earlier.) Technically it is a compound song consisting of two fully developed, and strikingly different, tunes. The first, apparently, is entirely by Ellington; the second is the reworked Tio-Bigard melody. Yet these 16-bar "sub-tunes" complement each other beautifully. Counting in 4-bar units, the overall structure is AA'BA; CC'DC''. Altogether we have 32 bars, which is standard for American pop. Still, this is hardly a "standard" way of going about it.

In terms of melody, "Mood Indigo" contains many chromatic tones in each of its two parts. For example, the song starts with a two-bar phrase ("You ain't been blue") in which the word "ain't" falls on a blues third (out of key), while the word "blue" lands perfectly within the key, on its uninflected major third.

Now isn't that charming? That solidly diatonic major third "*ain't* been blue." Too pure to be blue. And there's another subtlety at work: "blue" is harmonized as the ninth of a B♭9 chord, an unexpected and lovely touch.

The next two bars set only a single word repeated three times: "no." By themselves, these bars comprise a mini-drama. From a harmonic point of view, the first "no" is very surprising. A moment earlier we heard that B♭9, and with it came the unconscious expectation that an E-flat major chord would follow. Instead, in comes E-flat *minor*. Protest is implied. The second "no" uses the blue note we heard earlier on "ain't," only now harmonized as the sharpened fifth of the dominant chord. The result is a

Example 15.1. Two measures from "Mood Indigo." Adapted from *Duke Ellington: American Composer* (Hal Leonard, 1995). Publishing rights administered by Sony ATV Harmony (ASCAP), EMI Mills Music Inc. (ASCAP), and Indigo Mood (ASCAP) with composition attributed to Duke Ellington, Irving Mills, and Barney Bigard.

quizzical quality. For the third "no" we resolve at last to the tonic (A-flat major), making this a curiously affirmative "no."

To recap, the first "no" – which falls with melodic intensity on the top note of the song, a high E♭ – has an attitude of dissent. The second "no" has a distinct feeling of puzzlement, as it seems to ask, "What's going on here?" By contrast, the third "no" says "yes" in the clearest possible manner, as it falls on the bright major third (C) of the most secure of chords: the tonic major. One might say these three presentations of "no" illustrate the classic emotional pattern identified by Elisabeth Kübler-Ross: first a resolute "no," then a "maybe," and lastly, an acceptance.

It's simply amazing how Ellington gets so much drama here; it could be called a "novel in three notes." But does the credit not go in equal measure to the lyricist who, listening hard to Ellington's "abstract" musical design, found words appropriate to the emotions embodied in it? This question can't simply be evaded in any study of Ellington as songwriter.

Other than sharing the key of A-flat major, the two "sub-tunes" of "Mood Indigo" seem to have little in common. In a general melodic/thematic sense, they say "No" to each other, contradict each other. Yet there would have to be elements of agreement as well, if the thing is to hold together artistically. And there are; for example, both parts share the words "mood indigo." The settings appear quite different melodically, yet a little analysis (Example 15.1) reveals that each features a three-note chromatic slide on the word "indigo" – in opposite directions.

When we reach measure 17 (the first measure of the second "sub-tune"), the words "Always get" likewise receive an upward slide, but there are subtle changes (Example 15.2). The slide is transposed down a step and shifted metrically to a different position in the measure. Add to this a sense

Example 15.2. Motivic figure in "Mood Indigo." Publishing rights administered by Sony ATV Harmony (ASCAP), EMI Mills Music Inc. (ASCAP), and Indigo Mood (ASCAP) with composition attributed to Duke Ellington, Irving Mills, and Barney Bigard.

of "tonic" harmony – rather than the "dominant" harmony with which the figure was set earlier – and the surrounding lyrics, and a very different musical effect results. Still, at heart, it is the same motivic figure. Ellingtonian sophistication – ease, finesse, and boldness with the purely "abstract" elements of music – is manifest here.

No official credit was given to Parish for lyrics to the song, nor to Tio for its original melodic impetus. On the sheet music we see only Ellington, Irving Mills, and Bigard. As to who actually wrote the words, there has been controversy. Mills (Ellington's business manager) implied that he did by having his name on the published sheet music. Meanwhile, Parish, a long-time employee of Mills, asserted that his boss never wrote so much as a syllable. The controversy takes a stranger turn as we learn that Charlotte Austin, daughter of crooner Gene Austin, insisted that her father was responsible for the lyrics. (Incidentally, he recorded what might be the first "pop" version of the song.) Meanwhile, as Parish told me at a meeting of The Duke Ellington Society in New York, Ellington himself acknowledged publicly that it was "Mike Parish's words" that made the song a hit. And the words have had a surprising history. For example, the Three Keys, in their 1932 recording – not long after Ellington's – give the second half of the song an entirely different set of lyrics, beginning with "When I'm in this mood it seems . . . " and ending with "mood indigo lingers on." Indeed.

"It Don't Mean a Thing (If It Ain't Got That Swing)" (1932)

The recording session of February 2, 1932, was remarkable. As Ivie Anderson sang "It Don't Mean a Thing (If It Ain't Got That Swing)," Ellington introduced to the public the greatest of all the singers who would ever work with his band, and preserved on acetate a permanent impression of one of his most memorable musical inspirations. Now, this was hardly the first song to use "swing" in its title. Back in 1903, Ellington's mentor Will Marion Cook had composed the all-black Broadway musical *In Dahomey*, which opened with the jubilant choral number "Swing

Along." There was also "Swinging Along" (1927), a song of British origin. Yet neither had made the term memorable; it was that infectious combination of Ellington's words and music that did the trick. This song of 1932 christened an entire era of popular music: Swing.

In some ways, "It Don't Mean a Thing" is an outgrowth of earlier "wordless songs" by Ellington for improvising female vocalists. The 1927 classic "Creole Love Call" is the most famous of these. Yet in its own unforgettable "doo-wot, doo-wot, doo-wot" manner, "It Don't Mean a Thing" is more compositionally ambitious. Ellington blends pre-set lyrics (his own) with scat singing, resulting in improvisatory sections for both singer and instrumental soloists. In later years, Ellington used the song as a vehicle for Ray Nance. Ellington also used it as a basis for instrumental jamming, as did many other "mainstream" jazz groups; the way the song moves from relative minor to relative major makes it particularly appropriate and exciting for improvisation.

About this tonal design, Edward Green, in his essay "Duke Ellington and the Oneness of Opposites: A Study in the Art of Motivic Composition," observes:

> Boiled down to its essential tonal drama, this work is a "large scale" attempt to achieve a clear diatonic cadence in the key of A-flat after struggling (delightfully) through the "shifting sands" of chromaticism. On a melodic level, it takes the form of an effort to fix the note C firmly in one's ears: to have this diatonic major third overcome the tendency of the music to fall to the bluesy C♭.[4]

And, he notes, it is only in the coda that these goals are fully achieved. That is to say, Ellington – like Beethoven, Brahms, or any other solid composer of whatever musical tradition – sets up a musical premise at the onset of a work and follows its implications through its entire course. Like any first-rate mind (musically or otherwise), he doesn't get distracted.

That amazing coda, moreover, which seems to presage musical minimalism by half a century, is purely instrumental. This further illustrates the point I made earlier: Ellington was far more characteristically himself in instrumental territory than in the field of purely vocal composition. In any case, "It Don't Mean a Thing" was the most successful "Ellington/ Ellington" collaboration – the best song he ever wrote with himself as lyricist.

As a historical aside, it's worth noting that the tonal trajectory (vi → I) found in this song apparently caught the ear of Ellington's contemporaries. It is employed, for example, by Irving Berlin in "How Deep Is the Ocean?" (also 1932), and by Richard Rodgers in "My Funny Valentine"

(1937). Each of these songs, however, takes the tonal journey at a far slower pace.

Ellington's lyrics almost appear a throwaway, yet the song has a serious purpose: It is a follow-up to the Gershwin brothers' huge hit of 1929, "I Got Rhythm." Both are clarion calls to take up the cause of swinging, part of a long parade of songs – stretching back to Irving Berlin's "Alexander's Ragtime Band" and moving on to Bill Haley's "Rock Around the Clock" – asserting that something fresh and alive is taking place in American music, and we should pity those who can't get with it. There's even a kind of special Zen to Ellington's message: those who do not swing will find all things meaningless.

"Sophisticated Lady" (1932)

If Mitchell Parish went uncredited for "Mood Indigo," he may well have written the words to other Ellington songs – only we don't know which. But for at least one Ducal masterpiece, he did receive clear credit: "Sophisticated Lady," first recorded in an unissued master from an RCA session in 1932.[5] There have been all sorts of stories concerning the title. Ellington himself said it referred to a school teacher – or a composite of several – from his youth in Washington, D.C. On the other hand, his son, Mercer, insisted that the "sophisticated lady" was the Maestro's own first wife (and Mercer's mother).[6]

Musically, the song is remarkable. Lots of pop songs modulate upward in the bridge, but "Sophisticated Lady" is one of the very few that modulate downward; in this case from A-flat to G. Likely, Ellington was influenced by "Body and Soul" of 1930, the most prominent earlier example of precisely this modulation, though the keys are E-flat and D. And since Ellington recorded "Body and Soul" on several important occasions – including his classic 1940 set of piano–bass duets with Jimmie Blanton, and the albums *Ellington '55*, *The Cosmic Scene* (1958), and *Piano in the Foreground* (1961) – it is hardly unreasonable to assume his familiarity with it when he wrote "Sophisticated Lady."

With no disrespect to "Body and Soul," Ellington's song is arguably far more integrated in terms of strict composition. Not only is the descending semitone the basis of its overarching tonal design – that same interval is likewise central to its melodic structure. As Edward Green shows in the essay previously cited, the song literally hinges on the descent from G♭ (F♯) to F. This descent is present – but artfully varied – at every crucial point in the evolution of the melody.[7]

"Solitude" (1934)

First recorded in January, 1934, "Solitude" is the one hit Ellington song with lyrics by Eddie DeLange. Like Parish, DeLange was an employee at Mills Music. Later he led his own band (both on his own and in conjunction with fellow arranger-composer Willie Hudson) and collaborated on a number of classic songs with Jimmy Van Heusen, including "Darn that Dream" and "All This and Heaven Too."

Since Ellington's compositional palette was so colorful, we often think his melodies must be love affairs with chromaticism. Often they are; a clear example is "Prelude to a Kiss" (1938), which I'll get to presently. But just as often we are fooled: the melody is fairly simple, and it is the accompanying harmonies that are richly chromatic. This is the case with "Solitude." Its melody is utterly chaste: diatonic all the way. Even the bridge is purely diatonic. The melody thus has a stark quality, appropriate to the lyrics and the sense of the solitary life.

As the song begins, we meet the word "solitude" set on the leading-tone of the major scale; it is high, yearning. When it resolves to the upper tonic on the word "you," that resolution is undercut through harmonization by a minor chord (vi). All this enforces the idea of an intense, unfulfilled yearning: "In my solitude you haunt me." Throughout the song, the "you" isn't really present; it's just the thought, the ghostly idea of the you. And here again is Ellington's subtlety: never once does the melody present the tonic pitch simultaneous with a root-position tonic harmony. In a sense, there is never full closure in this song, which fits the meaning perfectly. Again, who should we credit for this coordination of purely "absolute/abstract" musical design and "verbal/psychological" meaning? Ellington? DeLange? Separately? Together?

Sometimes listed as "In My Solitude," the song has been sung by nearly everybody over the last 75 years. To me, it will always be a signature of Billie Holiday, who recorded it at least three times (not counting live versions), most definitively in 1947. She makes it even more haunting by concluding on the sixth degree of the scale, rather than the third, as written by Ellington. More than anyone else, she conveys the blue feeling of abject loneliness – as if it were not 32 bars, but a hundred years, of "Solitude."

"In a Sentimental Mood" (1935)

The obscure Manny Kurtz, another Mills employee, provided the lyrics to this song. I say "obscure" because most of his other lyrical work from this period is undistinguished. (Later, in the rock 'n' roll era, Kurtz wrote "Let It Be Me," which was widely recorded, including by Elvis.)

Near the end of his life, Ellington wrote a piece called *A Mural from Two Perspectives*. "In a Sentimental Mood" operates this way; we sense a double perspective, not in terms of words, but in terms of strictly "musical" elements. In his use of melody, harmony, and rhythm, Ellington makes us feel something stable and something agitated at once. I'll give some examples.

First: the melody of the opening eight bars is almost entirely diatonic.[8] It is stable. Most of it, in fact, uses the calmest of scales: the pentatonic. But simultaneously, the accompanying harmony has a contrary perspective, shot full of agitated chromatic tones. Second: nearly every melodic phrase outlines, from its lowest to highest tones, a dissonant interval: either a ninth or a seventh. One phrase, however, containing the words "while your loving attitude," outlines a pure octave; D is the highest note of this phrase, and the lowest. But it is precisely in this phrase, with its completely consonant outline, that we get for the first time a dissonant melodic note: the bluesy A♭ on the second syllable of "loving." Again, Ellington is making us feel two contrary things simultaneously. My third example occurs at the end of the opening A section. Now, for the first time harmonically, we reach the most restful of chords: the tonic chord, F major. But where is the melody at this point? On the ninth of that chord: an agitated position, on the word "gloom."

The lyrics, on their own account, also thrust forth the relation of stability and agitation, though here of course we have to credit Manny Kurtz. For example, in the opening eight measures we hear the "oo" sound again and again: "In a sentimental *mood* / I can see the stars come *through* my *room* / while your loving att*itude* / is like a flame / that lights the *gloom*." The repetition makes for stability, but rhythmically speaking, the asymmetrical appearances of the vowel create the opposite effect – of something off-kilter and uncertain.

All of the foregoing is very technical.[9] Meanwhile, as the philosopher Eli Siegel (a close contemporary of Ellington) has pointed out, nothing happens in artistic technique, no matter how seemingly abstract or even "mathematical," without direct human emotional significance. As he explained, "The resolution of conflict in self is like the making one of opposites in art."[10] Who among us has never had conflicts about calm and agitation? The desire for stability and yet also for excitement? So who wouldn't want, for their lives, the parallel of what Ellington (and DeLange) are achieving here on strictly artistic grounds? Who wouldn't want a oneness of rest and motion, security and adventure? And this song is a perfect exemplification of what Siegel described elsewhere as the very basis of happiness: the state of "dynamic tranquility."[11] Nor is this the only work by Ellington to embody and express this state of mind. Hardly.

In the well-nigh philosophic depth of its artistic achievement, "In a Sentimental Mood" seems to come from an entirely different planet than other pop or show tunes from 1935; you won't hear anything like it in *Jubilee*, *Jumbo*, or *Top Hat*, the major productions that year by Cole Porter, Rodgers and Hart, and Irving Berlin, respectively. The song became an even more significant Ellington milestone in 1962 after it was included on his epic collaboration with perhaps the most consciously philosophic of jazz musicians, John Coltrane. It is the one tune that everybody remembers from that classic album.

Edmund Anderson, who was a close friend of Ellington and wrote the English lyric to "Flamingo" (a big hit for the band in 1941), told one of the great stories about "Sentimental Mood." He once asked Ellington, in the parlance of the day, what was the "most Negro" tune he had ever written, and was surprised when the answer was "Sentimental Mood." Anderson replied that most people weren't even aware that this song was "written by a Negro." Answered Ellington slyly, "Ah, that's because you don't know what it's like to be Negro."[12]

"Prelude to a Kiss" (1938)

Ellington introduced this work as an instrumental in August 1938, but came back to the studio a few weeks later to re-record it as a vocal number with singer Mary McHugh, then little-known. The lyrics are by Irving Gordon, who later had quite a notable career as a hitmaker, including his 1950 song "Unforgettable." (Gordon lived to see it win a Grammy when it was re-recorded in 1991 by Natalie Cole.)

Overall, "Prelude to a Kiss" is extremely chromatic. The lyrics of the bridge say (with conscious humor?): "Though it's just a simple melody / with nothing fancy, nothing much / you could turn it to a symphony, / a Schubert tune with a Gershwin touch." That phrase, "just a simple melody," brings to mind "Play a Simple Melody," a 1914 song by Irving Berlin, which Ellington surely would have heard growing up. How complex Ellington's song actually is can be illustrated by a technical detail: At the very end of the bridge we hear a set of rising semitones (G–G#–A–A#–B) on the words "Gershwin touch. Oh! How ..." and then an exact mirror (B–Bb–A–G#–G) as the A section returns with "How my love song gent[ly] ... "

It's an extraordinary moment, rarely paralleled in jazz composition of the time. It brings to mind, instead, two other Ellington contemporaries:

Bartók and Webern. Its mathematical sophistication befits a song that began as a pure instrumental.

"I Got It Bad (And That Ain't Good)" (1941)

Ellington's 1941 stage production, *Jump for Joy*, is sometimes dismissed as a flop because it never made it to Broadway. However, from the point of view of the Ellingtonian song canon, *Jump for Joy* can only be considered a monumental success. It resulted in five widely recorded standards: "Jump for Joy," "Rocks in My Bed," "Subtle Slough" (which became "Just Squeeze Me"), "Just a-Sittin' and a-Rockin'," and "I Got It Bad (And That Ain't Good)" – all of which made it onto Ella Fitzgerald's *Ellington Songbook* project. Few scores by Irving Berlin or Richard Rodgers resulted in as many standards. *Jump for Joy* also included "Bli-Blip," "The Brown Skin Gal in the Calico Gown," and "The Chocolate Shake" – also excellent Ellington songs.

By far the best-known song from the show is "I Got It Bad (And That Ain't Good)," with a lyric by future multiple Academy Award winner Paul Francis Webster. Sadly, it is also notable as the last Ellington standard to be introduced on record by Ivie Anderson. It's also unfortunate that *Jump for Joy*, for which the lyrical assignment was divided between Webster and comedy writer Sid Kuller, would be Webster's only collaboration with Ellington – though part of the composer's modus operandi was never to settle into a sustained partnership with a lyricist.

Webster was doubtlessly inspired by Ellington's melody. His lyric is masterful, and fully captures a distinctly Ellingtonian mood: sad but not without humor, saturated with the spirit of the blues (and even a suggestion of religion), but also, to use that favored Ducal adjective, "sophisticated." The structure of the piece reveals a highly organized, profound composer at work. The melody can be broken down into a motivic cell of four notes that is repeated and varied over the course of the composition (Example 15.3). (The cell itself is slightly reminiscent of *Clementine*, a Billy Strayhorn instrumental recorded by the band around this time.) The first time we hear the cell is in the opening measure ("never treats me"), where it takes the form C♯–D–E–D, with an octave displacement between the low-register C♯–D ("never") and the high-register E–D ("treats me"). This is its primal form: a collection of three consecutive scale steps (C♯–D–E), expressed by four notes, so that one pitch (D) is stated twice.

The cell is disguised a bit by that octave displacement. Its next appearance, to the words "sweet and gentle," is easier to hear since there is no displacement. Meanwhile, it is transposed up a fourth to F♯–G–A–G.

Example 15.3. "I Got It Bad (And That Ain't Good)" (Duke Ellington and Paul Francis Webster), melodic cell. Publishing rights administered by Sony ATV Harmony (ASCAP), EMI Robbins Catalog Inc. (ASCAP), and Webster Music Co. (ASCAP).

The third presentation (to the words "the way he should") stretches the cell into two measures, with "should" emphasized by getting a full whole note. Here the cell is slightly altered. There is still a collection of three scale steps, only we meet them in a different order: high, low, middle, high (B–G–A–B). A further development of the cell can be heard on the words "I got it bad": we hear B–G–A–B again, only set to a different rhythm. Ellington then concludes the A section with yet another development of the cell. Now he alters the size of the intervals within the cell. Earlier, it was a three-note group of conjunct scale steps; now it is widened to a grouping of thirds (G–B–D). The actual configuration we hear (to the words "and that ain't good) is D–G–B–G.

Note this subtlety as well: Ellington varies the cell over the course of the A section by adjusting which of the "three-note pitch collection" will serve as the repeated tone. In the first two presentations, it's the middle tone (two Ds, then two Gs); then it's the top tone (B); and then, for "and that ain't good," the bottom tone (G). An analysis of the bridge section would reveal even further, and more subtle, developments of that core musical cell.

Biographers often overstate – ad nauseam, in my opinion – how Ellington, in his personal life, was somewhat disorganized and afraid of closure, not to mention reluctant to commit. But as an artist, as one of the twentieth century's greatest composers – American or European, from high classical to low-down vernacular – it is obvious that he was organized to the nth degree.

"Don't Get Around Much Anymore" and "Do Nothin' Till You Hear from Me" (1942–1943)

In the early 40s, Bob Russell (born Sidney Keith Russell) was responsible for a double miracle. He adapted a pair of Ellington instrumentals – already hits – into what would be, quite independently, two of the band's most successful songs. *Never No Lament* was transformed into "Don't Get Around Much Anymore" (1942), and *Concerto for Cootie* into "Do Nothin' Till You Hear from Me" (1943). In each case, Russell freely adapted the original instrumental melody.[13] In the first instance, he and his wife Hannah (a competent pianist) virtually rewrote the bridge; the one they came up with is, for vocal purposes, much stronger and more melodic. They also made "Do Nothin' Till You Hear from Me" into something far more song-like than the original, which, as its title implied, was a vehicle for trumpeter Cootie Williams.

"Don't Get Around Much Anymore" is one of the most striking songs of Ellingtonia, a true "meeting of the minds" between the Maestro and Russell. Each phrase of the A section runs a full octave, until we get to the payoff on the words "don't get around much anymore." Here the intervals and harmony become much tighter, moving in a mostly chromatic way within a smaller range. After the freedom of those earlier swooping octaves, the notes suddenly feel constricted, as if, quite literally, the song itself is not getting around much anymore. It's a brilliant feat of verbal/musical coordination, all the more remarkable in that the music wasn't conceived as a song to begin with.

Another sign of the song's instrumental origins is in the very strange way the melody drapes itself over the 32-bar form. A typical song is 8+8+8+8, but upon close examination, this one is actually grouped 8+9+7+8. A composition that began life as a "pop song" would be very unlikely to be designed that way, and it is to Russell's credit that he pulls it off, lyrically, in such a graceful manner that we hardly notice the bold asymmetry.

"Do Nothin' Till You Hear from Me," on the other hand, is shaped very differently from its instrumental forebear. It has a perfectly standard 32-bar AABA structure, with every section a conventional eight bars – despite its origins in the wildly irregular phrase lengths of *Concerto for Cootie*. From a harmonic point of view, both pieces are relatively conventional – far more conventional, in fact, than is usual for Ellington. It's worth noting that this song, which derived from a composition honoring Cootie Williams, was recorded twice by Cootie's own inspiration, Louis Armstrong – once with a big studio orchestra and once with Ellington himself. These two treatments are about as definitive as it gets.

Ellington and Russell wrote another classic song together, "I Didn't Know About You," adapted from the instrumental *Sentimental Lady* (earlier known as *Lost*). However, curiously enough, when they wrote one song together apparently from scratch, the result was "Ring Around the Moon" (1943), a completely forgotten piece of work that never went anywhere. A pity, since it's not bad at all.

Bob Russell's granddaughter is a fashion designer who works under the name Savannah Spirit. According to her family lore, it was the combined success of the two Ellington-Russell blockbuster hits that saved the band from bankruptcy. That's obviously a bit of an exaggeration, since the

Ellington band was flying high during the mid-forties when these songs were introduced. But there's no doubt that over the long run Ellington's songwriting produced a far richer revenue stream than his bandleading or even his purely instrumental recordings. Had his song hits from the thirties and early forties not continued to bring in ASCAP royalties in the late forties and early fifties (mainly from covers by other artists), Ellington would have had to disband his orchestra, so little revenue was it then pulling in on its own.

As an aside, but relevant to the question of the band and money, *Never No Lament* / "Don't Get Around Much Anymore" undoubtedly began its musical life as a brief "hot lick" improvised by Johnny Hodges. Apparently Ellington bought it from the saxophonist, as he did with dozens of his sidemen's musical phrases, developing them into full compositions. Since a lick is not a composition, the credit quite fairly goes to Ellington. Even so, according to historian and observer James Maher, whenever Ellington, at a performance, would call for "Don't Get Around Much Anymore," Hodges would turn toward him and pantomime the act of counting money.

"Satin Doll" (1953)

"Satin Doll" might figuratively be called the daughter of "Sophisticated Lady." In this later song, the team of Ellington and Strayhorn (we don't really know who wrote which aspects of this tune) begin with a ii chord – a commonplace enough gesture, frequently used in pop songs. It is a perfect choice of harmony for conveying an action already in progress, as one feels with this song. It gives the sense that we are entering a scene midway. The lyrics, by Johnny Mercer, appropriately present what seem like random snatches of slangy verbs, objects and subjects, rather than well-rounded, classically full sentences. Together, the lyrics and melody give us a collection of hints which eventually add up to a substantial portrait of the title character. As in several other of Mercer's classic songs, the words proceed in a manner akin to cinematic cross-cutting. Finally we get the lady in full view at the end of each A section, where, not coincidentally, we hear for the first time both the tonic major chord (on the word "doll") and the song's title phrase.

Some of Ellington's tunes are rangier than others. "Satin Doll" may be the Ellington song with the most miniscule range – and yet it is incredibly effective. The melody of the whole A section fits neatly between G and D, a perfect fifth. The bridge likewise spans the same gamut; in fact, the very same fifth, G to D. (This is why "Satin Doll" is virtually the only Ellington

Example 15.4. Measure from "Satin Doll" (Duke Ellington, Billy Strayhorn, Johnny Mercer). Adapted from *Duke Ellington: American Composer* (Hal Leonard, 1995). Publishing rights administered by Sony ATV Harmony (ASCAP), Tempo Music Inc. (ASCAP), and W B Music Corp. (ASCAP).

song I was ever able to play on my saxophone. Just be glad you weren't there.) The song is also a sterling example of how closely linked are the melody and the harmony in Ellington and Strayhorn's best songs; if you were to rewrite the harmony, and put a different chord behind the phrase "satin doll," it would totally change the song's character. You might wind up with a cotton doll, or a polyester doll, but you most certainly will no longer have a satin one.

"Satin Doll" has a tactual sense of richness and fullness while still being smooth and sleek, as exemplified in the measure containing the words "that satin doll." In that measure, Ellington and Strayhorn manage things so as to present every one of the 12 chromatic tones that make up the pitch structure of Western music (Example 15.4). As a result, the music feels as rich as it can be, and with a melody that is gentle, smooth. There is none of the roughness that comes with either jumpy, large intervals or strange, melodic dissonances.

I'm hardly the first to complain about the tragedy that Johnny Mercer only wrote one song with Ellington. Yet this is a pattern Duke repeated with nearly all his lyrical collaborators. Even with Bob Russell and Don George, Ellington only wrote about ten songs each. He was, in other words, lyrically promiscuous and non-committal, not wanting to settle down with any one songwriting partner. That is why we have only one major song apiece with Mitchell Parish, Manny Kurtz, Eddie DeLange, Irving Gordon, and Henry Nemo, the lyricist for "I Let a Song Go Out of My Heart" (1938). One gets the feeling (sadly enough) that Ellington wanted to assert sole authorship of his catalogue, and therefore took preventative measures so that no partner could lay claim to any significant part of his songwriting canon. "Satin Doll," for instance, is almost always included in Ellington songbook albums but rarely in Mercer tributes. To this day, when you think of "Don't Get Around Much Anymore" or "I'm Beginning to See the Light," you don't think of Bob Russell or Don George, you think exclusively of Ellington.

The "accidental" songwriter.

Notes

1 With many Rodgers songs the music came first and the lyrics were added later, particularly in partnership with Larry Hart. But the songs were released to the public *as* songs, rather than in a "two-step" process, instrumental first, song later, as was so often the case with Ellington.

2 Urbana: University of Illinois Press, 1995. See in particular chapter 8: "The Songwriter: From 'Jim Dandy' to 'Yam Brown'," 119–39.

3 Barney Bigard with Barry Martyn, *With Louis and the Duke* (New York: Oxford University Press, 1986), 64.

4 *Ongakugaku: Journal of the Musicological Society of Japan* 53/1 (2007): 9.

5 Lawrence Brown maintained that the opening phrase of *Sophisticated Lady* was his, and that the bridge was by Otto Hardwick. The first recording gave credit to them both, as well as to Ellington and Irving Mills. In any event, the cohesion of the song should be credited to Ellington.

6 Mercer Ellington with Stanley Dance, *Duke Ellington in Person: An Intimate Memoir* (Boston: Houghton Mifflin, 1978), 48.

7 Ibid., 5–8.

8 There is reason to believe the opening eight measures of *In a Sentimental Mood* were created by Otto Hardwick.

9 This technical analysis (and several others in the chapter) along with their wider aesthetic implications, emerged from conversations I had with the editor of this volume, Edward Green – for which I thank him.

10 Cited by Chaim Koppelman in his essay "I Believe This About Art" in *Aesthetic Realism: We Have Been There: Six Artists on the Siegel Theory of Opposites*, ed. Sheldon Kranz (New York: Definition Press, 1969), 55.

11 Eli Siegel, *Self and World: An Explanation of Aesthetic Realism* (New York: Definition Press, 1981), 165.

12 Derek Jewell, *Duke: A Portrait of Duke Ellington* (New York: W. W. Norton, 1977), 58.

13 Johnny Hodges contributed significantly to the melody of *Never No Lament*, and *Concerto for Cootie* begins with a phrase from Cootie Williams.

16 The land of suites: Ellington and extended form

DAVID BERGER

Write what you know

Starting with its premiere at Aeolian Hall in New York City in 1924, the popularity of George Gershwin's *Rhapsody in Blue* sent a shock wave throughout America. Was Gershwin America's answer to Beethoven? Irving Mills was one person who was not willing to concede that. In early January of 1931 he announced that Duke Ellington was about to record a new long work that would rival Gershwin's monumental tour de force. He might have given Ellington some advance notice so that the Maestro could at least have some time to write the piece, but maybe Mills knew that Ellington would rise to the challenge of an extreme deadline. Thus was the origin of *Creole Rhapsody*. Ellington recorded it on two sides of a 78 rpm disc on January 20. After performing, honing, rewriting, more performing, and more honing, he recorded a second (and vastly different) version five months later.

With no formal education in composition, Ellington was learning on the job how to create three-minute compositions and, now, a seven-minute multi-themed piece. The opportunity to tell a longer story and to compete in the world of serious composition with Gershwin and the European masters certainly must have stirred the 31-year-old Ellington, who years earlier expressed his desire to be a great composer to Will Marion Cook. Ellington asked Cook if he should go to Europe to study. The world owes Cook a big thank you. His response was that the European classics evolved out of European folk and popular music and that if Ellington wanted to be great, he should do the same thing in his own way with the music of his culture. What we can sense, in retrospect, is that Cook was alert, in a way that was highly unusual for his day, to the fact that aesthetics transcends culture. For any small- or large-scale work, no matter what musical vocabulary it uses – European or African-American – a composer has to solve the problem of how to satisfy opposing values.[1]

Ellington's writing for his band had practical uses: shows, dancing, and backgrounds for singers. Records were basically limited to three minutes in duration, and so Ellington became the master of the three-minute miniature. No sooner was he getting started when along came Gershwin with his higher aspirations. Although Gershwin and Ellington learned from the same great stride pianists, most notably Willie "The Lion" Smith and Luckey Roberts, Gershwin brought jazz colors to his otherwise Tin Pan Alley and European orchestral pieces; Ellington, on the other hand, infused Tin Pan Alley and European devices and colors into his jazz arrangements and compositions in such an integral way that they grew of one cloth.

And so, when we listen to *Creole Rhapsody*, we are struck by the primitive energy and wholly American jazz approach. Although Ellington's band of the 1920s was heavily influenced by the New Orleans style of King Oliver, by 1931 Ellington had evolved into a first-class composer and arranger whose work was tightly constructed and evoked picturesque short stories with the most provocative characters played by his own repertoire company – Duke Ellington and his Famous Orchestra. The ensemble sound was made up of unique solo voices. Ellington built the individual roles out of his musicians' musical personalities. Even at this early juncture in his career we hear proof of his future collaborator Billy Strayhorn's famous statement that Duke Ellington's instrument is his orchestra.

Because of Ellington's lack of formal study, he used trial and error to develop his three-minute creations and similarly extended this to longer forms. The two versions of *Creole Rhapsody* give us a great deal of insight into Ellington's creative process. As he reshapes the piece over a period of months, he keeps the essential theme and also uses it for transitions.

Both versions suffer from sameness/difference and continuity/discontinuity issues. This would prove to be the central challenge that Ellington would deal with in his longer works over his entire career. Where his short works mainly use repeated chorus forms to develop and create length, the longer works constantly push the boundaries of form in jazz. The lack of the continuity of the repeated song form (so important for dance) forces Ellington to find new avenues of development. It's ironic that the beboppers are generally thought of as taking jazz out of the dance hall and giving it artistic pretentions; by the time they came around, Ellington had been doing this for over a decade and would continue to do so for another 30 years.

Almost 40 years after *Creole Rhapsody*'s original recording Ellington recorded new arrangements of the opening theme (*Neo-Creole*, Example 16.1) and the gorgeous spiritual theme (*Creole Blues*, Example 16.2). One can only surmise that he saw great value in those two themes, but found the rest of the piece problematic or at least not fitting for his late band to record.

Gershwin was delighting the critics and fans by the tens of millions with his concert pieces, but *Creole Rhapsody* received comparatively little notice. In 1931 jazz was music for dancing. Few jazz lovers were ready for something that deviated from that function, but Ellington would not be deterred. He frequently spoke of his dream to write a piece about the

Example 16.1. *Neo-Creole* theme. Transcribed by David Berger. Publishing rights administered by Tempo Music Inc. (ASCAP).

Example 16.2. *Creole Blues* theme. Transcribed by David Berger. Publishing rights administered by EMI Mills Music Inc. (ASCAP).

history of the American Negro. In 1935 he got his chance. He was approached to compose the music for a film short in which he would act and the band would perform his masterpiece. It would be called *Symphony in Black*.

Although there are some wonderful moments in this nine-and-a-half-minute film, ultimately the score falls far short of Ellington's dream. Apparently he ran out of time to compose and wound up filling in most of the piece with numbers that the band was currently playing (*Ducky Wucky*, *Merry-Go-Round*, and *Saddest Tale*). What is notable is the young Billie Holiday singing the blues in her first film performance, and a plaintive *Hymn of Sorrow*: Arthur Whetsol's muted trumpet playing at the funeral for a child.

Apparently, Ellington didn't figure out that the history of the American Negro was too big a story to be told in a single piece of music, no matter how long, because he would come back to this idea time and again and never with complete success.

1935 also saw the death of Ellington's beloved mother, sending the Maestro into a tailspin. He was overcome with a grief like none other in his entire life. So he turned to music for solace and put his feelings into *Reminiscing in Tempo*, which spans four sides (two complete 78 phonograph records). Although heartfelt and beautifully harmonized and orchestrated, the piece, unfortunately, stays in the same slow tempo for over 12 minutes, ultimately lulling the audience to sleep. *Reminiscing in Tempo* is really a beautiful three-minute story that didn't know when to quit. Although there is plenty of rich harmony and many interesting key changes, the most important element of change in longer works is that of tempo. And this brings us to the heart of the technical problem jazz musicians – Ellington included – have faced in creating extended jazz pieces.

Jazz, having evolved from dance music, almost always comes in the form of short pieces that establish and remain in a constant tempo.

Example 16.3. Motif for *Diminuendo and Crescendo in Blue*. Transcribed by David Berger. Publishing rights administered by EMI Mills Music Inc. (ASCAP).

Variations on this are double-time, half-time, and more abstractly (and more rarely used), third-related times (metric modulations based on the triplet). Most often, the mood of the piece stays constant as well. In order to keep interest in music, we need change, and in a long piece, we need big changes, which almost always necessitate changing tempo.

It's somewhat ironic that in the early 1930s Ellington was quoted as saying that he feared for the future of jazz once it left the dance hall. After all, he was, if not the first, then one of the first jazz composers and bandleaders to go beyond the boundaries of dance. Adding to the irony, he said this a few years before the great American swing dance craze really hit.

In 1937 Ellington wrote one of his most unusual pieces, *Diminuendo and Crescendo in Blue*. *Diminuendo* occupied side A and *Crescendo* side B of a 78. The piece does exactly what it says: *Diminuendo* starts loudly and gets softer, then you turn over the record and *Crescendo* starts softly and gradually builds to a ferocious climax. Both pieces are beautifully crafted out of a single motif (Example 16.3) that is sounded by the reeds in the very first measure of the piece. There was no precedent in all of jazz for a composition that built such an abstract structure out of a mere snippet of such common material. It satisfied both the dancers and the intellectuals, or at least the hip members of both camps.

In 1939 Ellington composed two somewhat extended works: *Blue Belles of Harlem* and *Blutopia*. The former is a piano feature that uses typical song form, but adds out-of-tempo sections to extend the form. The piece lacks contrast and thus doesn't sustain sufficient interest or feel all that satisfying upon its conclusion. *Blutopia* (commissioned by Paul Whiteman) utilizes two contrasting themes: one a pseudo-gospel with blues lines and triadic harmony, and the other a more typical Ellington blues-oriented form with the requisite five- and six-part harmonies including ninths, elevenths, thirteenths, and their chromatic alterations. The lack of development of the primary theme and its recapitulation leaves the listener frustrated and wondering why Ellington bothered to create a second theme when he had already written hundreds of single-theme pieces that develop so much more. Although Ellington is never at a loss for melodic material of first-rate quality, it is his ability to weave fascinating stories with a minimum of material – transforming a measure or two into three to five minutes of music – that at once feels surprising and inevitable.

Black, Brown and Beige

Curiously, during the ensuing three years (1940–1942) – Ellington's most prolific and arguably his most creative period – he wrote no extended works. He and Orson Welles planned a movie about the history of jazz, which never got beyond the planning stage. Ellington also wrote pages of initial libretto for an opera he planned to call *Boola*, but it too never materialized. He became fascinated with the history of black Americans. According to his sister, Ruth, he bought and read every book on the subject that he could lay his hands on. He still had this dream of writing the great American Negro Symphony that would tell the story of his people. *Symphony in Black* was merely a trailer to the epic piece that he kept talking about.

As 1943 dawned, the world of jazz was abuzz with the news that Ellington was writing a symphony and would premiere it with his orchestra at Carnegie Hall (New York City's shrine to European classical music) on January 23rd. As usual Ellington scurried to complete and rehearse the work, titled *Black, Brown and Beige*. Billy Strayhorn was pressed into service to arrange a few sections (including "Cy Runs Rock Waltz," which Ellington edited fairly extensively).

Ellington and the band performed a dry run the night before in an out-of-town theater. The Carnegie Hall concert was a benefit for Russian War Relief (at the time the Russians were our allies courageously fighting the Nazis). Despite the blizzard that night, Carnegie Hall was sold out. Extra seating was created on the unused parts of the stage to accommodate the overflowing crowd.

Ultimately Ellington ran out of time to finish composing the last movement. He hastily threw in a reprise of the "Come Sunday" theme before his over-the-top patriotic ending. Actually, he planned the last section to be even more patriotic, with Jimmy Britton singing lyrics about the Black, Brown and Beige fighting for the Red, White and Blue. He had the good sense to delete the vocal, but kept the pompous music in an instrumental form.

The audience's reaction to the premiere was ecstatic. This was clearly jazz's finest moment. Jazz appeared at last to have shown itself equal to the European symphonies in no less a venue than Carnegie Hall. Ellington was elated. Everyone went home on cloud nine. Everyone, that is, except record producer John Hammond and the music critics. Hammond and the jazz press thought *BB&B* was pretentious. They resisted jazz leaving the dance hall. The classical critics likewise panned *BB&B* because it seemed too rooted in dance music and was not abstract enough for their taste. Race may also have played a part. The white classical world was hardly about to welcome this upstart Negro with open arms – especially when the subject matter of the piece was about the dignity of the American Negro.

When Ellington read the reviews the next morning, he went into a terrible funk. His most challenging work – his American symphony – was not hailed as a masterpiece. He felt blindsided. This was the first of many yearly Carnegie Hall performances by Ellington and his orchestra. He composed a new extended work for each performance, but never again did he attempt to write a symphony. In fact he would not record *BB&B* commercially in its entirety until the 1960s. Due to the American Federation of Musicians' recording ban, Ellington didn't record in 1943 and most of 1944 (except for transcriptions, V-Discs, and a film sound-track). He finally took the band into the studio in December of 1944 and recorded excerpts from *BB&B*. These excerpts stand as some of the finest Ellington on record – even though by this time two of Ellington's greatest stars (Ben Webster and Barney Bigard) had left the band, and Webster had been replaced by a good player, though much his inferior (Al Sears).

It is very curious that Ellington would be so insecure as to believe the critics. This was definitely not a common occurrence for him. His career was about going his own way regardless of the current fads. He performed excerpts from *BB&B* at Carnegie Hall in December 1944, and at other venues over the next few years, eventually pulling it from the band's repertoire after a performance at the Hollywood Bowl in August, 1947.[2] His dream of this being his *Rhapsody in Blue* just wasn't working out.

In 1958 the band made a record with Mahalia Jackson singing and the band playing much of *BB&B*. Ellington wrote lyrics for "Come Sunday." Although America never really got hip to the greatness of *BB&B*, "Come Sunday" remains to this day the greatest piece of sacred music to come out of jazz. Its subsequent inclusion in hymnals in churches across America would make Ellington very proud. Ellington recorded excerpts of *BB&B* one more time in 1965. Although the recording is clean, the performance suffers from the lack of personalities present in the original performance. It feels a bit like putting on a suit that was tailored for your father when he was your age.

Each time Ellington came back to *BB&B* he tried to fix the continuity problems (transitions, cadenzas, et al.) and the ending. Ultimately, he couldn't quite do it. And so here is perhaps the greatest flawed masterpiece in all of jazz. Parts of this piece are as great as any music. The opening "Work Song" theme (Example 16.4) has an epic sweep that far surpasses its predecessor in *Symphony in Black*. In fact every theme is truly inspired.

Example 16.4. "Work Song" theme. Transcribed by David Berger. Publishing rights administered by Tempo Music, Inc. (ASCAP) and G. Schirmer Inc. (ASCAP).

Example 16.5. "The Blues" theme. Transcribed by David Berger. Publishing rights administered by G. Schirmer Inc. (ASCAP).

Example 16.6. "Come Sunday" theme. Transcribed by David Berger. Publishing rights administered by Tempo Music Inc. (ASCAP) and G. Schirmer Inc. (ASCAP).

Example 16.7. "Sugar Hill Penthouse" theme. Transcribed by David Berger. Publishing rights administered by Tempo Music Inc. (ASCAP) and G. Schirmer, Inc. (ASCAP).

One great melody follows another. "The Blues" (Example 16.5) is what American opera could be if it were truly American. "Come Sunday" (Example 16.6) is the most tender spiritual moment in jazz. "Sugar Hill Penthouse" (Example 16.7) is the ultimate in sophistication and refinement. Ellington's ability to write music that brings out the individual personalities of his players contributes to making this piece such a personal statement. In terms of rhythm, melody, harmony, and orchestration, *BB&B* was by far the greatest piece of jazz music written in the first half of the twentieth century.

But once again Ellington's lack of experience with larger forms rears its ugly head. The transitions, the extraneous dances that stop the forward motion of the piece, and the lack of a successful ending ultimately detract from the absolute genius in the scope and details. It would be five years more before Ellington reached perfection in the long form.

The Gershwinesque piano concerto *New World A-Comin'* (1943) and *Frankie and Johnny* (the 1945 version, basically a piano fantasy based on the well-known blues) both lack strong development. The seemingly frivolous four-movement *Perfume Suite* (1944) depicts the effect that four different perfumes have on the women who wear them, but ultimately lacks continuity. The four-movement *Deep South Suite* (1946) falls short on unity. The first movement lacks a clear point of view; the second ("Hearsay") is a renamed Strayhorn piece (originally *Orson* – for Orson Welles) that was pressed into service; the third is a marvelous solo piano piece in the stride tradition; and the final movement is the monumental train classic *Happy Go Lucky Local* – the main theme of which was appropriated by tenor saxophonist Jimmy Forrest for his rhythm and blues hit record, renamed *Night Train*. The three-movement *Tonal Group* (1946) yielded the concerto grosso gem *Jam-a-Ditty*. *The Beautiful Indians* is notable for its gorgeous melodies written for classical soprano Kay Davis and Ray Nance's violin. The *Blue Skies*-ish tenor feature for Al Sears is a warm-up for the second movement of Ellington's next and most integrated suite.

Liberian Suite

1947's *Liberian Suite* (commissioned for the centennial of Liberia) tells the story of a young Liberian man waking up in the bush and traveling to the city for the centennial celebration. Consisting of a song and five dances, this piece, unlike so many of its predecessors, was carefully developed out of the first sounds we hear. No extraneous compositions were inserted. "I Like the Sunrise" is a heartfelt melody whose fresh harmonies and orchestration would be emulated in Broadway show scores for generations to come. Ellington's brilliant use of the talents of his musicians (talking plunger trombone, high-note trumpet, heroic baritone saxophone) including their ability to double (violin, vibraphone, and tympani) combined with creative and courageous composition that firmly sits in the concert hall, but never abandons the dance impulse. A few later suites may rival the *Liberian Suite* in terms of rich and original music, but none come close to matching its integrity and powerful feeling of hope and awe.

The Tattooed Bride (a comical titular reference to Smetana's *The Bartered Bride*) is a fantastic tone poem that is built on a motif of major seconds in the shape of the letter "W," and moves seamlessly through various moods, styles, and tempi ("W" for woman; see, as core motif, notes 5–9 of Example 16.8).[3] The exhilarating forward motion is capped by Jimmy Hamilton's cool clarinet sound and impressive virtuosity. As terrific as this tone poem is, it was soon completely overshadowed by its successor, Ellington's greatest masterpiece.

Example 16.8. Motif of major seconds in *The Tattooed Bride*. Transcribed by David Berger. Publishing rights administered by Sony ATV Harmony (ASCAP).

Harlem

Harlem (also known as *Harlem Suite* and *A Tone Parallel to Harlem*) was commissioned by Maestro Arturo Toscanini for the NBC Symphony and composed for Ellington's band in January 1951 while he traveled by ship back to New York from Europe. Ellington enlisted an orchestrator to translate his jazz band piece for the Ellington band plus symphony orchestra. Ellington's band version was a staple of his repertoire for the next 23 years. The orchestral version was played in conjunction with orchestras all over the United States and Europe – but never by Arturo Toscanini. As a symphonic piece, it lacks sufficient participation and idiomatic material by the orchestral players, but as a jazz piece, it is the pinnacle of jazz composition.

Designed as a travelogue, *Harlem* roams the streets of Ellington's beloved adopted city within a city, covering the various activities of its citizens and ultimately uncovering the soul of a people. The opening half is a kaleidoscopic, upbeat tour that abruptly runs into a funeral procession. In typical New Orleans fashion the funeral march begins in a somber tone, but grows into a joyful celebration of life. The bombastic, Tchaikovskyesque coda following the tom-tom roll was written by Billy Strayhorn.

Beginning with Ray Nance's two-note enunciation of the word "Har-lem" on plunger-muted trumpet, the entire piece is defined. This descending minor-third interval is the source of all the melodic material. The succeeding call-and-response patterns provide the rhythmic motifs. As Wynton Marsalis so brilliantly explained in his National Public Radio show *Making the Music*, the trumpet sounding the "Harlem" descending minor-third interval is answered by the saxes, first with one chord, then with three chords in a half-note triplet (Example 16.9), and then with four chords in quarter notes. Throughout the entire piece we have dozens of Harlems and responses that follow the patterns set up here. The half-note triplet is used to set up the changes in tempo later in the piece. These initial six measures provide the inspiration for the next 14 minutes in this tightly structured opus. Ellington's imagination is working full force to transform these initial sounds through the use of traditional compositional techniques (inversion and retrograde, augmentation and diminution, truncation, etc.) in the service of his

Example 16.9. Trumpet interval answered by saxophones in *Harlem*. Transcribed by David Berger. Publishing rights administered by G. Schirmer Inc. (ASCAP).

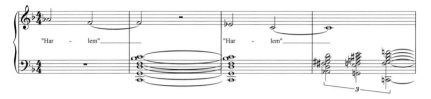

programmatic theme. The way that the music flavors the program makes us feel that our tour guide and all the people we encounter on our trip are genuine Harlemites in their environment. They let us in on how they really behave at home – no editing, no politeness, just people, or as Ellington said, "my people." And when asked who his people are, he responded, "My people are *the* people."

Harlem is made up of two large sections. The first is a tour that we enter as outsiders, and we gradually get pulled into the rhythm and guts of life. The pace and intensity build up through a series of constantly modulating blues choruses, rising to a steep climax and an abrupt halt as a funeral procession crosses our path. In this second section Ellington's spiritual theme captivates us and we are drawn into the inner life of *the* people. The everyday business and even pleasures of the flesh are experienced, but now they are seen from a deeply spiritual point of view. The spiritual theme reaches its climax with a long falloff into a tympani roll. At this point Ellington handed over the score to Billy Strayhorn to write the spectacular coda.

Harlem is the only extended work that Ellington continued to play throughout the rest of his career. Its power comes from the incredible integrity and scope of expression. At the conclusion we feel exhilarated, exhausted, and satisfied like no other jazz piece before or since. This is jazz's grandest 14 minutes and all without improvisation. A few small liberties are taken in the solo passages and the bass and drums are free to accompany with some latitude, but the story is told by Ellington, the composer. Although Ellington was 51 when he wrote *Harlem*, and he lived (and composed) for another 24 years, he never attempted another piece with symphonic dimensions. Perhaps he knew that he achieved perfection, and so he turned in another direction – loosely connected suites that featured the individual soloists in his band.

The *Controversial Suite* (1951) is a cute oddity in the Ellington oeuvre. It consists of two distinct parts: "Before My Time" (a tongue-in-cheek pastiche of New Orleans jazz) and "Later" (a brilliant, modernistic, dissonant, and abstract view of the future of jazz that has sometimes been described as Ellington poking fun at Stan Kenton). In 1955 Ellington wrote *Night Creature* for his band and symphony orchestra. Where the concerto grosso version of *Harlem* left no room for the symphony orchestra to play on its own, *Night Creature* succeeded in providing independent music for both groups of musicians.

Whereas Ellington composed a new suite for his yearly appearances at Carnegie Hall in the 1940s, starting in 1956 his new venue for premieres moved outdoors to summer jazz festivals. *Jazz Festival Suite* was premiered at the 1956 Newport Jazz Festival only to be overshadowed by the far superior, 19-year-old *Diminuendo and Crescendo in Blue*. *Jazz Festival Suite* sounds hastily written and rehearsed. Although the writing has fine moments (including a luscious Strayhorn saxophone section soli in the second movement), the entire work is disjointed and features aimless blues improvisations from the sidemen. Ellington's piano work would appear two years later at Newport in *Princess Blue*, which for all the gorgeous writing ultimately suffers from the tedium of staying too long in a slow tempo.

Other jazz festival suites include *Toot Suite* (which lacks cohesion), *Suite Thursday* (which sets up a recurring motif, but fails to develop it sufficiently), and the underrated *Idiom '59* (which was written around the same time as Ellington's first major motion picture score, *Anatomy of a Murder* – and bears a strong kinship).

Ellington never had much success at movie scoring. He and Strayhorn wrote and recorded a pile of music for *Anatomy of a Murder*, most of which wound up on the cutting room floor. That which does survive is so engaging that it upstages the action on screen. Although Ellington was the greatest accompanist in all of jazz, he failed to understand his supportive role in films. *Anatomy of a Murder* is frequently shown on TV in New York City, and the schedule listing in the *New York Times* always says something very complimentary about the film, ending with "the one catch, Ellington's music doesn't fit." Oddly enough, the music should have fit since Jimmy Stewart plays a lawyer and amateur jazz pianist who sits in with Ellington in one scene.

A few years later Ellington received a similar offer to score *Paris Blues* (1961), a minor movie about two expatriate American jazz musicians. Louis Armstrong appears in two scenes playing Ellington's music. The excitement and power of jazz is captured beautifully in film and music. Ellington's underscore also has some fine moments.

Frank Sinatra got Ellington involved in *Assault on a Queen* (1966), a heist film he was starring in. Neither the film nor Ellington's music succeed. Ellington was put in the awkward position of writing for a few of his soloists in the midst of a Hollywood studio band.

Another film project that Ellington got involved in was a documentary about Degas and horseracing. Although the film was never released, the 1968 recordings of Ellington's music were released posthumously as *The Degas Suite*.[4] As usual there is some interesting and beautiful writing, but it certainly doesn't hold together as an entity. The ballad (played separately by Johnny Hodges under the title "Race" and by Harold Ashby under the title "Drawings") along with "Promenade" show Ellington's spark of inspiration, but by the time this piece was written Ellington was losing the patience to complete the compositional/orchestrational process.

Such Sweet Thunder

In 1957 Ellington was commissioned to write a suite for the Shakespeare Festival in Stratford, Ontario. Rather than base it on plot lines, he chose to write 12 pieces about Shakespearean characters (Romeo and Juliet, Othello, Julius Caesar, Cleopatra, Hamlet, and so on). Premiered in New York's Town Hall in a series entitled "Music for Moderns," *Such Sweet Thunder* contains some of the most challenging and beautiful music ever written for big band.

Ellington's title piece about Othello is a reharmonized blues that moves back and forth between major and minor. Strayhorn's "Lady Mac" is a waltz with blues pretensions. "The Telecasters" is a development of *Fuzzy*, a previously written but unrecorded piece that Ellington conceived for Harry Carney and the three trombones. He added an ominous intro and coda to portray the prophecies of the three witches in *Macbeth*. "Up And Down, Up and Down" is Strayhorn's homage to the second movement ("The Play of the Pairs") of Bartók's *Concerto for Orchestra*. These are the romantic couples in *A Midsummer Night's Dream*, with Clark Terry playing Puck right up to the final "Oh, what fools these mortals be!" Strayhorn's excruciatingly beautiful "The Star-Crossed Lovers" was previously written as *Pretty Girl*. Johnny Hodges plays Juliet to Paul Gonsalves's Romeo. Ellington's "Madness in Great Ones" is Hamlet feigning insanity. What seems to be a series of musical non sequiturs is in reality highly structured motivic development. The use of Cat Anderson's stratospheric trumpet in the coda is more than spectacular. Strayhorn's *Lately* is turned into "Half the Fun," with Johnny Hodges playing the seductive Cleopatra. Ellington's "Circle of Fourths" is the only disappointment. The band is under-rehearsed and the movement is too short and doesn't reach a big enough climax to make a satisfying conclusion to the suite.

After recording the eight big band movements, Ellington wrote and interspersed four portraits composed in sonnet form as small-group solo features: Jimmy Hamilton is Caesar, Britt Woodman is Henry V ("Sonnet to Hank Cinq"), Jimmy Woode is Othello (the only character to appear twice in the suite), and Quentin Jackson is Kate from *The Taming of the Shrew*.

Although there isn't much thematic relationship between the 12 movements, there is a consistency of mood. Each movement is so compelling that we get lost in the sheer beauty and creativity. This is Ellington and Strayhorn at their peak.

In *Portrait of Ella Fitzgerald* (1957) Ellington and Strayhorn split the writing (the first three movements are Strayhorn and the final blues riff is Ellington), the piano interludes, and the narration. Strayhorn's charts are very good, but there is little to hold the piece together. The most interesting parts are the piano/narration interludes.

The Queen's Suite (1959) is six pieces composed for Queen Elizabeth II of England. Although there is no motivic development between the movements, Ellington sustains a feeling of regal dignity, strength, and beauty throughout.

The Nutcracker Suite and *Peer Gynt Suite* (both 1960) successfully avoid the usual superficial jazz treatments of European classical themes by finding the corresponding American rituals and describing them in American terms; thus the "Dance of the Sugar Plum Fairy" becomes the sexy "Sugar Rum Cherry."

The *Girls Suite* (1961) is Strayhorn arrangements of older songs with girls' names in the title (*Diane*, *Sweet Adeline*, et al.) along with some new originals from Ellington written for friends and colleagues – *Lena* (Horne) and *Mahalia* (Jackson). The latter was further developed as part of the *New Orleans Suite* nine years later.

The recent advent of the long-playing phonograph record changed the way artists were marketed in the 1950s. Instead of putting out a 78 rpm record with a three-minute song on each side, now as much as 46 minutes was available (23 minutes per side). Ellington issued a number of theme albums (*Mary Poppins*, *All American in Jazz*, *Midnight In Paris*, *At the Bal Masque*, *Afro-Bossa*, etc.). Surprisingly, these albums, although conceived by record companies as commercial vehicles, stand up artistically as extended works.

Impressions of the Far East

1964's *Impressions of the Far East* (a.k.a. *Far East Suite*) stands alongside *Such Sweet Thunder* as one of Ellington's greatest suites. Written during and following a tour of the Middle East and India, the first title is actually more descriptive of the work. Each movement of the suite is a rare and

beautiful postcard home from Ellington. Although there is a consciousness of Middle Eastern music in the suite, neither Ellington nor Strayhorn
(nor the players in the band) were trying to imitate the local music that
they heard. Instead they found the common ground and let the music
follow its natural course.

By the mid-1960s jazz was increasingly influenced by popular music
and moving away from swing. The opening "Tourist Point of View" deals
with modality and manufactured grooves in an original, purely
Ellingtonian way. Strayhorn's "Bluebird of Delhi" (a.k.a. *Mynah*) was
suggested by Ellington, who heard the bird's song outside his hotel room
and phoned Strayhorn so that he could hear it. Strayhorn's incredibly
beautiful and delicate feature for Johnny Hodges, "Isfahan," originally
entitled *Elf*, was written previous to the tour but is much better served as
"Isfahan." "Depk" is an unusual Middle Eastern rhythm in three-bar
phrases. "Mount Harissa" has an ABA structure – piano, band, and
piano with the band playing a *Take the "A" Train* chordal variant over
a bossa nova beat. "Blue Pepper" is a simple three-chord blues over a rock
'n' roll beat. "Agra" is Strayhorn's homage to the majesty of the Taj Mahal.
Ellington's tower of strength, Harry Carney, is featured. Notice the sensitive underbelly of Carney's call-and-response with the other saxophones
just before the recapitulation. The wild "Amad" is another version of
Ellington modality – this time featuring Lawrence Brown playing the
Muslim call to prayer. "Ad Lib on Nippon" was not originally intended
as part of the suite but was included as the last piece on the LP, and so has
become the last movement of the suite. Ellington pieced together some of
his piano themes with a spectacular clarinet feature composed, arranged,
and played by Jimmy Hamilton to make an incredibly exciting conclusion
to this forward-looking masterpiece.

The *Latin American Suite* (1968) began its life as *Mexicanticipation*.
Although there is much great writing for the band, there is far more
emphasis on the piano and the rhythm section than on the horns.
Perhaps this is due to the loss of longtime major voices in the band
(Jimmy Hamilton's clarinet, Ray Nance's trumpet, and Lawrence
Brown's trombone). The rhythm section has also deteriorated from its
incredibly high level. Rufus "Speedy" Jones lacks the innate swing and
subtlety of Sam Woodyard on drums, and the bass chair would never again
regain the prominence in jazz that it enjoyed with the succession of
Wellman Braud, Billy Taylor, Jimmie Blanton, Oscar Pettiford, Jimmy
Woode, Aaron Bell, and Ernie Shepard.

The *Little Purple Flower* (1968) is an unusually rich, overlooked two-
movement work. The first movement bears some resemblance to *The
Queen's Suite* and is a precursor to *The UWIS Suite* in its chromaticism

and modernistic approach. The piano is the centerpiece along with Ellington's witty and urbane narration. The second movement is a shuffle blues that alternates major and minor. Although the writing is superb, the performance on the the album *Yale Concert* suffers from substandard playing and recording.

The *New Orleans Suite* is Ellington at the end of his life and career looking back on his roots and musical heritage, from the exuberant parade of "Second Line" (which provides a great solution of the age-old problem of how to orchestrate the New Orleans three-horn front line for the twelve horns of a big band) to the tributes depicting the city's favorite sons and daughters, both musical (Louis Armstrong, Sidney Bechet, Mahalia Jackson, Wellman Braud) and historical (the pirate Jean Lafitte). Each gets a fitting and original tribute – modern and yet stylistically appropriate and spiritually evocative. Conspicuously missing are King Oliver (Ellington's early influence) and Jelly Roll Morton (Ellington's early rival and arch-enemy).

The Afro-Eurasian Eclipse is a short collection of totally unrelated and uneven miniatures. The influence of John Coltrane and 1960s pop music (rock 'n' roll) can be heard in the pseudo-African sections (which have their Ellingtonian origins going back to the Cotton Club).

By this time Ellington was on in years and had diminishing attention span and patience. The combination of under-rehearsing, very few takes, and the loss of key personnel account for the poor performance and recording of this and later suites. The band had been in decline for a decade, but the loss of Johnny Hodges, Jimmy Hamilton, and Sam Woodyard proved to be more than Ellington could deal with. Both the solos and the section playing are substandard.

The Goutelas Suite (1971) was written shortly after Ellington received a great reception during his visit to a recently refurbished castle in France. His development of the opening fanfare is oddly fitting for the subject matter. He captures the nobility and formality along with the power and sensitive artistry that made this restoration a labor of love. Do not be misled by the bad intonation on the recording. This is indeed one of Ellington's finest suites.

Togo Brava Suite (1971) is Ellington at his least inspired. Even geniuses have bad days. There is little to no melodic material to mine. Relying on the blues and soloists doesn't work like it used to.

The UWIS Suite (1972) came out of a two-week residency for the band at the University of Wisconsin in Madison. The opening movement has some interesting and unusual writing (the use of flute and piccolo, angular melodies, etc.) but is marred by an awkward transition (or lack of one) from $\frac{4}{4}$ to $\frac{3}{4}$. The second movement ("Klop") was intended to be a polka (spelled backwards), but actually sounds more like a march. The final movement ("Loco Madi") is a combination of a train blues and a reworking of *Blue Tune*, an Ellington piece from 1932. Unfortunately, neither bassist was informed that the bridge was from *Honeysuckle Rose*.

Ellington wrote *Three Black Kings (Les Trois Rois Noirs)* on his deathbed. "King Solomon" has an African groove and includes a thumb piano; "King of the Magi" has a gorgeous ballad written for trumpeter Money Johnson; and "Martin Luther King" has a simple pop groove. Ellington only wrote a preliminary sketch for the third movement. After his death Luther Henderson wrote the arrangement, which, unfortunately, is totally out of character with the other two parts.

During the last decade of his life, Ellington wrote three *Sacred Concerts*. Although he said that this was his most important work, it is far from his best. Most of the lyrics are sophomoric, and the choir tends to be poorly integrated into the work as a whole. Ellington (who lacked experience working with choirs) delegated the arranging and conducting of the choir to young men from the choral world with little knowledge of jazz or Ellingtonia. On the bright side there are some wonderful tunes ("Come Sunday," "Heaven," "Almighty God Has Those Angels," "Is God a Three-Letter Word for Love?" et al.) and engaging arrangements ("The Shepherd," "Praise God and Dance," "Don't Get Down on Your Knees to Pray Until You Have Forgiven Everyone," et al.). The ambitious opening number of the first concert ("In The Beginning God") is a bit rambling but contains some excellent concert writing.

The beauty of Ellington's extended works is that the longer forms gave him more space to do what he did best – develop his ideas. Conversely, the weakness of many of the longer works is the lack of focus and consistency that the best of his smaller pieces had. Some of this is due to advancing age. Roger Rhodes, who worked with Ellington frequently in his final decade, told me that the Maestro exhibited diminished patience and energy. And then there is the age-old difficulty of removing jazz from its dance roots.

We shouldn't judge Ellington too harshly though, since he was a pioneer (or more properly – *the* pioneer) in long-form jazz. He was and continues to be the inspiration for most composers working in that area of jazz, from Charles Mingus to Wynton Marsalis. Even Ellington's flawed works have much beauty and point the way for others to follow. His influence increases exponentially with each succeeding generation and with ever more and more attention given to his longer works. When you consider that so much of his time and energy was devoted to the creation of these pieces, it seems fitting that this should be a major part of his legacy.

Notes

1 As the American philosopher Eli Siegel was to show, among the crucial opposites in art are those of continuity and discontinuity, and in an essay he asked, "Is there to be found in every work of art a certain progression, a certain indissoluble presence of relation, a design which makes for continuity? – and is there to be found, also, the discreteness, the individuality, the brokenness of things: the principle of discontinuity?" From Siegel's essay "Is Beauty the Making One of Opposites?" in *Aesthetic Realism: We Have Been There; Six Artists on the Siegel Theory of Opposites*, ed. Sheldon Kranz (New York: Definition Press, 1969), 103–8.

2 For more detail, see Andrew Homzy, "*Black, Brown and Beige* in Duke Ellington's Repertoire," *Black Music Research Journal* 13/2 (Fall 1993): 87–110.

3 In his verbal introduction to *The Tattooed Bride* at the Carnegie Hall premiere on November 13, 1948, Ellington informed the audience, "The bride was tattooed all over with the letter 'W'." This can be heard on issued recordings of the concert.

4 On the CD *The Private Collection Volume Five: The Suites, New York, 1968 & 1970* (Saja 91045–2).

17 Duke Ellington's legacy and influence

BENJAMIN BIERMAN

Duke Ellington was a composer, an arranger, a pianist, a bandleader, an entertainer, an entrepreneur, and an important public figure, all at the highest level. After his astonishing body of music, it is Ellington's remarkable and unmatched ability to integrate these various areas of expertise in both his music and his public persona that is his greatest legacy, and it is unrivaled in modern American music. In the broadest possible sense, Duke Ellington stands alone as America's most complete musician. Miles Davis expressed this clearly and succinctly: "I think all the musicians should get together one certain day and get down on their knees and thank Duke."[1]

Celebrations of Ellington's impact can be seen in many areas. His archives have been carefully tended at the Smithsonian Institution. The Essentially Ellington program at Jazz at Lincoln Center spreads his music throughout America's high schools. His face is on a United States postage stamp. Songs are dedicated to him by musicians in many genres. Critical discussion of Ellington's music and life has reached well beyond jazz discourse since his early career. West 106th Street in New York City is named after him. He received numerous honorary degrees and international high honors, including France's most prestigious award, the Legion of Honor. The list can go on and on. There is no parallel to his level of achievement in jazz or in American music.

Ellington's breadth is not unique in the history of music, however, and is reminiscent of past musical stars such as Haydn, Johann Strauss, Jr., Liszt, Verdi, and Puccini. These artists were composers, instrumentalists, orchestrators, showmen, and terrific entrepreneurs, and they were extremely prolific, leaving legacies of artistic and commercial success. They understood what the public wanted, and with very personal and artistic voices produced some of the greatest music of the day in such a way that the public clamored for their works. This accomplishment is extremely rare, and is central to Ellington's legacy and influence.

With all of this in mind, it is intriguing that though many composers and arrangers have something recognizably Ellingtonian in their work, no one actually sounds like Ellington, and the influence of his specific sound and style upon others has not been particularly prevalent or strong. In fact, other early jazz composers and arrangers were perhaps more directly influential upon the field of jazz writing. Jelly Roll Morton was writing at a very high level before Duke, and was crucially important to the field of jazz arranging and composition. Fletcher Henderson, Don Redman, and Benny Carter were important early arrangers with their own distinct style, independent of anything Ellington was doing at the time, and all of them powerfully influenced jazz arranging. Later composers and arrangers such as Charles Mingus, Gil Evans, Thad Jones, and Oliver Nelson were certainly influenced by Duke, but again, each had a distinct and individual approach, and none would ever be mistaken for Ellington.

This chapter examines why Ellington maintains his lofty position at the top of the jazz canon. To this end, I consider how Duke's unique qualities, remarkable accomplishments, and unequaled stature have influenced five important musicians – Charles Mingus, Gerald Wilson, Clark Terry, Cecil Taylor, and Quincy Jones – who have in turn created legacies of their own. All of them greatly admired Ellington, and each exemplifies his legacy and influence in a particular area of expertise. They managed to absorb much of what Duke had to offer, embrace their own abilities (and their short-comings), and forge a unique path that builds upon the Ellington legacy.

Composer: Duke Ellington and Charles Mingus

50 years of Ellington's full-time composing and constant recording, the consistently remarkable quality of his work, and the range of his craft – he was as comfortable writing a popular tune as he was an extended compo-sition or suite – all contribute to his legacy and influence as a composer. In addition, hundreds of Ellington's compositions are an integral part of the fabric of American music.

Bassist Charles Mingus (1922–1979), another of jazz's major compos-ers, idolized Ellington. It appears, however, that their times together were not charmed. Mingus had an extremely brief stay with Ellington's band in 1953, but after Mingus was involved in racially charged physical confrontations with the white saxist-clarinetist Tony Scott and the Puerto Rican valve-trombonist Juan Tizol, he was either fired or pressured to leave the band. More importantly, Ellington and Mingus later recorded a fascinating trio album, *Money Jungle*, along with drum-mer Max Roach. Apparently, though, Duke's powers of persuasion were again called upon to thwart Mingus's attempt to leave in the middle of the record date.

Mingus was an excellent composer in the broadest sense of the word. He wrote in short and long form, and composed music that was fully notated, primarily improvised, or somewhere in between. His early works that were fully notated, such as *Half-Mast Inhibition*, highlight his interest in classically oriented composition. When I think of Mingus, however, I think of the dramatic music beginning in the mid-1950s with his group, the Jazz Workshop. In this period he made a crucial switch from notated music to communicating the parts to the musicians by rote. His compositions took on an entirely new character and signaled Mingus's arrival as an innovative composer who also harkened back to the earliest of jazz traditions. Through this new process he created exciting and varied compositions and performances that are some of the most important in jazz.

Simple riff-based tunes such as *Better Git It in Your Soul* and *Boogie Stop Shuffle* avoid the standard jazz format of melody-solos-melody in favor of ever-changing musical landscapes, perhaps reminiscent of Ellington's *Creole Rhapsody* and *Black and Tan Fantasy*. Mingus is certainly one of the most successful at creating extended compositions in the jazz idiom, as can be seen in works such as *Pithecanthropus Erectus*, *Cumbia & Jazz Fusion*, and *Haitian Fight Song*, following in the tradition of Ellington's *Black, Brown and Beige* and his dynamic *Harlem*. *Revelations*, a Mingus work included in a concert featuring so-called "third stream" compositions, combines fully notated, classically oriented composition and more jazz-oriented sections employing both improvisation and notated parts.[2] *Goodbye Pork Pie Hat* shows Mingus at his most lyrical. This hauntingly beautiful composition is as lovely as any work in jazz, and stands proudly alongside such Ellington compositions as *Sophisticated Lady* and *In a Sentimental Mood*.

There are a number of similarities between Ellington and Mingus. The strength of their musical visions demanded they have a band to articulate their musical aesthetic. Ellington realized this and became a leader early in his career. Mingus spent considerable time as a sideman, but fronting a band was clearly his destiny. They also shared a desire for self-reliance, which led both men to assume more control of their own business affairs by, for example, establishing record companies, Mercer (Ellington) and Debut (Mingus).

The most crucial similarity between the composers is also an essential and defining difference. Mingus, with the concept of his Jazz Workshop, continued the legacy of Ellington by involving his sidemen in the creative process, featuring and building upon their strengths and characters both in the ensemble and as soloists. Neither Ellington's nor Mingus's sidemen were nameless – the musical personality of the players was an inextricable ingredient in the music. That being said, both composers had strong voices that also transcended their players, and their sounds remained clear and definite through all of their various personnel changes.

Mingus's spin on this is a wonderful adaptation, and his compositional and bandleading methods – such as singing the parts to the players rather than using notation – created an intentional ensemble looseness. And where Ellington at times created tunes from phrases gleaned from his soloists, Mingus actually conceived whole arrangements based on the musical dialogue of his players.

Mingus's signature sound emphasizes improvisation and individual expression, yet – like Ellington at the piano – he was always a dynamic force very much in control of the aesthetics of the music, driving the band with his powerful bass playing and constant vocal prodding. This made for an exceptional and unusual quality in a jazz composer: the ability to make a fully realized composition sound spontaneous and organic. This style necessarily places less emphasis on harmonic voicings and often limits the orchestration to who is or is not playing at a given time, separating Mingus from the carefully coloristic approach of Ellington. As a result, Mingus has certainly claimed a place as one of jazz's most important composers while absorbing and building upon the Ellington legacy.

Bandleader: Duke Ellington and Gerald Wilson

It is impossible to separate Ellington's compositional output from his bandleading. The orchestra's constant touring forced Ellington to continually create new music, and, conversely, his musical ambition necessitated his maintaining a working band. More importantly, he excelled in his ability to maintain a steady core of essential musicians. For example, Harry Carney was with the band for 45 years and Johnny Hodges for 38.

Gerald Wilson (1918–2014) had a long and illustrious career as a trumpeter, bandleader, composer, and arranger. He wrote for, or played with, a long and impressive list of the great big bands, including those of Duke Ellington, Count Basie, Jimmie Lunceford, Lionel Hampton, Benny Carter, Benny Goodman, and Woody Herman. By 1944 Wilson had his own band, and as early as 1945 he shared a bill with Ellington and Lunceford at the Apollo Theater in Harlem, and had a number of recordings to his name. He went on, in the spirit of Ellington's longevity, to lead his own big band for over 65 years. Wilson also wrote extensively for television and film (as did Ellington), as well as for symphony orchestras, and was an educator, most recently at the University of California, Los Angeles.

Wilson was direct regarding Ellington's influence: "From the time that I was ten years old, I knew that I was going to be a bandleader . . . because I was already a great admirer of Duke Ellington. And listening to their records and listening to them on the radio, I knew that I was going to be a bandleader and I was going to be an orchestrator, an arranger, composer."[3] Wilson continued: "I wrote for Duke Ellington for many years . . . Duke was one of my favorite musicians. Actually, he was my favorite. He was my number one man."[4] Yet even with this powerful influence, Wilson carved his own path in the relatively narrow world of the jazz big band.

From his experience arranging for Ellington, Wilson came to understand the importance of the musical personalities in a band as well as an individual arranging style: "Well, actually writing for Duke Ellington was easy because he had all those great people there. They are the sound of his band. It's not just the music that he writes. And so once you write [an arrangement], it sounds like Duke Ellington wrote it. In fact, he didn't put on the record that it was orchestrated and arranged by Gerald Wilson. He just let the people think he wrote it. I kid about it all the time. He didn't want me to try to write like him. 'I want you to write like you. You write like you want to write for me'."[5]

Wilson managed, in his own fashion, to have similar opportunities to write for players he knows well, but in his case they were part of the studio and jazz scene in Los Angeles. (More recently Wilson recorded with studio musicians in New York City.) Being based in L.A. did not allow Wilson to keep a steady band, as only constant touring can do that, but it did offer him a consistent pool of some of the greatest players in the country who cut their teeth on constant playing on the road. Their ensemble skills and reading abilities make them perfect studio musicians, and their solo styles – largely honed in the disciplined context of the big band – also lend themselves well to the recording environment that Wilson primarily used to articulate his music.

Love for Sale (from the 2005 CD *In My Time*) is an excellent example of Wilson's harmonic approach, which builds on Ellington's harmonic sense, and is perhaps his most recognizable accomplishment. Wilson's harmonies are thick and colorful to the extreme, including as much as eight-part harmony. The final ensemble in *The Diminished Triangle – Blues For Manhattan* (from *In My Time*) also displays this intense harmonic richness, creating a sometimes harsh but always satisfying dissonance. Additionally, Wilson's hard-driving vocal arrangement of *You're Just An Old Antidisestablishmentarianismist* (1947) for the Ellington band gives an early picture of his powerful writing for brass as well as his penchant for fat, colorful, and edgy voicings for the horns.

Wilson's attitude towards the profession of bandleader was in tune with Ellington's: "I don't have just a band. I have an orchestra, really. A band is a commercial business. I'm not in it for the commercial business. I'm a musician. The music is what is important to me."[6] Ellington, with his constant writing, rewriting, and tinkering, clearly shared the same joy in the process, yet the profession of bandleader came to him easily and was a way of life that he appeared to savor. Contrastingly, Wilson quickly became weary of the road life and the demands of the bandleading business. He settled in Los Angeles and found his own way through the life of a professional arranger-composer while continuing to consistently write for his band. With his large discography of recordings and an important career as a jazz educator, Wilson offers a distinctive and musically rewarding example of carrying on the legacy of Ellington while forging a unique path as bandleader.

Showman: Duke Ellington and Clark Terry

Ellington had a wonderful stage presence. He was a consummate entertainer, able to handle the bandleading chores and play the piano, all the while making the audience feel they were honored guests and part of the show. This type of showmanship was an essential job requirement for the swing-era big band leaders. While many post-swing bandleaders have either lost or eschewed this skill, perhaps barely taking time to introduce songs and band members, some artists, schooled in the entertainment-focused world of the big bands, continue to bring the skills of the dance band leader to the listener-oriented music world.

Clark Terry (b. 1920), recently honored with a 2010 Grammy Lifetime Achievement Award, has long been one of the premier trumpet and flugelhorn players in jazz, and his playing is instantly recognizable. His style is a captivating and entertaining blend of serious trumpet and jazz soloist skills and a fun-loving and joyful attitude towards life and music. When you hear Terry play you cannot help but smile, which is surely part of what makes him a wonderful bandleader and entertainer. He was an in-demand sideman as well, with important bandleaders such as Count Basie and Quincy Jones, and was a vital member of the Duke Ellington orchestra from 1951 to 1959, featured on such important records as *A Drum Is a Woman* and *Such Sweet Thunder*. Describing Ellington, Terry says he was a "fantastic person. If I had to name a person who inspired me the most and the one man in this world whom I figured to be the *most* important, the most influential, and the greatest person that ever lived, I would say Duke Ellington."[7]

This association, among others, propelled Terry to jazz stardom, but he was most visible to the general public as a member of the NBC Tonight Show Orchestra for ten years. Terry was at times a featured soloist on the show, and his humor and signature numbers, such as *Mumbles*, were a part of his entertainment value.

Terry's long tenure in the Ellington orchestra contributed to his understanding of showmanship and how to entertain an audience. As Terry states, "I learned an awful lot about establishing a rapport between the bandstand and the audience. How to handle men psychologically, how to read audiences, how to program music. It's very important to someone in front of a band. You've got to *know* your audience, you've got to know what kind of music to choose. Just from being around Duke, these things would rub off on you."[8] While Ellington was welcoming to his audience, his "cool" demeanor created a certain level of remove. In many ways Ellington was an enigmatic figure who carefully controlled his relationship with the public. Clark Terry, on the other hand, has an ebullient and outgoing way of relating to his audience.

This carries over to his trumpet playing, as his playful sense of humor is a crucial element of his style. This wit is also a central element of his relationship to the audience. For example, in a 1964 recording with pianist Oscar Peterson, Terry introduces *Mumbles*, a very funny novelty number that became a regular part of his performances.[9] He plays the role of a blues vocalist, and acts as if he is singing lyrics and speaking to the audience, but he is "mumbling" unintelligibly, actually scat singing. His scat singing is extraordinary, very much akin to his trumpet style.

Terry's other bits are equally entertaining as well as highly skillful. He will hold a trumpet in one hand and a flugelhorn in the other, trading phrases from horn to horn, gradually speeding up until he is quickly trading brief phrases with himself. He will also at times employ circular breathing – playing long, continuous phrases by breathing in through the nose while blowing out through the mouth, using air stored in the cheeks – which is always a crowd pleaser.

What makes it all work, of course, is the extremely high level of musicality that even the casual listener can appreciate. That, in conjunction with his sense of humor and his obvious desire to embrace and entertain his audience, has made him a consummate musician and entertainer. Artists like Terry continue to show us that entertainment and high art can work together in an extremely effective and appealing manner – another important element of the Ellington legacy.

Pianist: Duke Ellington and Cecil Taylor

While fronting his band Ellington was featured as pianist, both as a soloist and as an integral part of the ensemble sound. We will not fully understand Duke's level of artistry as a pianist, however, until we examine his wonderful and enlightening small-group recordings such as *The Duke*

Plays Ellington (1953, later released on CD as *Piano Reflections*), *Money Jungle* (1962), and *Duke Ellington & John Coltrane* (1962). These showcase Ellington's outstanding piano artistry both as an accompanist and soloist, and add depth to our understanding of his almost self-effacing playing in the context of his orchestra.

Pianist-composer Cecil Taylor (b. 1929) has been a shining example of a creative artist with a fierce commitment to his art, and he states that Ellington is a primary influence. Taylor is in the midst of his own hugely influential 50-year career, and is an intriguing branch of the Ellington legacy. There is little on the surface to indicate this, and Ellington had limited involvement with the avant-garde, but Taylor speaks candidly about Ellington's influence on his playing: "I learned more music from Ellington than I ever learned from the New England Conservatory." Taylor adds that he "never would have thought of playing the piano without thinking it out along Ellington's lines, and that's the base."[10] Consequently, alongside profound differences, there are many similarities between the two.

While a night at an Ellington concert made you feel as if you were his guest for a night of art and entertainment, a Taylor concert is an exhilarating yet challenging experience. He integrates his passion for dance and poetry by often imbuing his performances with movement and recitations, and his playing is marked by an extreme and engaging physicality as he often hunches over the piano, his hands furiously flying across the keyboard. This type of playing does not fit Ellington's reputation, but their piano touch has much in common, as both often have a percussive approach. For example, the fierce clusters and bass notes that Ellington pounds out during much of his intense minor blues *Ko-Ko* (1940) are a precursor to Taylor's dissonant clusters and flurries in his version of Ellington's classic blues *Things Ain't What They Used to Be* (from the 1961 LP *New York City R&B*).

Taylor and Ellington also share an orchestral, compositional sensibility in their pianism, harkening back to the Harlem stride piano style, in which unaccompanied piano fills the roles of bass, chordal accompaniment, and horn-style melody. Taylor speaks to this when he states, "It's Ellington who influenced my concept of the piano as an orchestra, which meant that the horn players and all of the other layers other than the piano were in a sense soloists against the background of the piano. It's like studied improvising."[11]

In addition, both men, like all of the artists I place in the Ellington legacy in this chapter, were natural leaders, and their strong musical concepts generally demanded they become bandleaders in order to control their musical settings and articulate their musical visions. A major difference between the two men, however, is in their ability, or inability, to adapt to a variety of musical situations.

On *Money Jungle*, Ellington blended seamlessly with bassist Charles Mingus and drummer Max Roach, both innovators from a younger generation. *Duke Ellington and John Coltrane*, another album that matched Ellington with a younger innovator with a seemingly contrasting style, demonstrates what a wonderful and sensitive accompanist Duke could be. Duke also brought an orchestral and arranging sensibility to the small group, as evidenced by his lovely motivic introductions, endings, and accompaniments on this record. In contrast, when Taylor combined with John Coltrane, trumpeter Kenny Dorham, bassist Chuck Israels, and drummer Louis Hayes for the 1958 album *Stereo Drive* (later released under Coltrane's name as *Coltrane Time*), the results were quite mixed. The group never quite jelled; for example, Taylor and Dorham, a more mainstream player, found little vocabulary in common. Similarly, a planned performance with Ornette Coleman's Prime Time fizzled when Coleman's musical requests eventually proved unacceptable to Taylor and he ended the collaboration.[12]

Taylor has had many strong musical relationships, however. Some of Taylor's strongest music was made in collaboration with alto saxophonist Jimmy Lyons over the course of 25 years, including the recordings *Conquistador* (1966) and *Dark to Themselves* (1976). The cool approach of Lyons was an exceptionally effective foil for the all-out, fiery physicality of Taylor. This brings to mind the long-term relationship of Ellington with his perennial lead alto player, Johnny Hodges. Interestingly, both Hodges and Lyons were imperturbable and somewhat expressionless on the bandstand, and both were more successful in these collaborations than on their own. In addition, both Lyons and Hodges were extremely expressive and lyrical players.

A major difference arises when examining the positions of Ellington and Taylor in the music business. Ellington consistently worked to maintain a place in the commercial mainstream. For example, he continued to play dance jobs late in his career when he could have played only concerts. Contrastingly, Taylor deliberately and forcefully challenges artistic conventions in both his playing and his performance style. His art is an uncompromising one, and he remains essentially unknown to the general public. Yet, interestingly, his concerts nearly always play to packed houses, even though his style and business model have proven difficult in commercial terms. For example, the performance of a single composition, often well over a wildly intense hour, can tax even the most avid fan.

Finally, a crucial element in Ellington's music is the blues, and while it may not be as easy to hear, Taylor considers his music to be blues-based as well:

> [This] again brings us back to Ellington, from whom I derived most of my
> approach to structure and music, even down to the mannerisms, which
> are personal with me as they are personal with Ellington . . . There are
> certain values here. If you listen to Ellington's records, particularly his blues,
> you can determine these values, and they can be found in the life that he
> lived. This is particularly true of the music that he wrote in the forties,
> and relates to the whole organization of the band.[13]

Like Ellington, Taylor is acutely aware and appreciative of classical compositional approaches, yet proudly and firmly considers his music a
product and expression of his African-American heritage. This is essential
to the work of both men, and to the Ellington legacy.

Entrepreneur: Duke Ellington and Quincy Jones

Along with his musical skills, Ellington was also a terrific entrepreneur,
carving out a unique place in the American musical landscape. He took
control of his own business affairs; handled the media effectively with a
measured aplomb; self-published and recorded his music; and provided a
wonderful and consistent musical product to the world with an irresistible,
debonair charm that appealed to audiences of all ages, races, and nation-
alities. Owning and controlling his own business as an African American
is a crucial element of his legacy, though he made entrepreneurship look
easy and did not trumpet his success in this area. This is a remarkable
achievement, particularly considering the time period.

Quincy Jones (b. 1933) has absorbed and built upon many aspects of the
Ellington legacy. In his autobiography Jones states: "Duke very rarely let anyone get too close to him, but I loved and admired him as the greatest."[14] Jones
began his career as a big band trumpeter, playing alongside such trumpet
greats as Clifford Brown and Art Farmer. His arranging skills quickly came
to the fore, and he has long been established as one of the top arrangers in
jazz. He fronted his own big band for a brief period, and periodically
resurrected it for recording and short tours. But Jones never allowed himself
to be limited to the conventional notion of what it means to be a jazz
musician. His musical and business ambitions seem to know no bounds,
and his media empire is one of the most important models for black-owned
entrepreneurship. All the while he has embraced Ellington's adage: "There
are two kinds of music. The good kind, and the other kind." Jones is perhaps
contemporary American music's single greatest entrepreneur, in terms of
his social consciousness as well as his business and artistic success.

In addition, like Ellington before him, Jones has his finger on the pulse
not only of high art, but also of popular music, and he consistently

produces music that successfully bridges these two supposedly separate genres. His number one hits as producer began with Lesley Gore's 1963 "It's My Party." Michael Jackson's *Thriller*, also produced by Jones, became the largest selling record in history for a reason: the music is unequivocally excellent in all regards. Of course Michael Jackson was one of popular music's greatest stars, yet it takes a musician and businessman such as Jones to put a star in the right settings, including conception, arrangements, performance, production, and marketing.

The jazz world has bred many musicians who equate financial success with selling out and being less of an artist. Critics and the media also have popularized this notion at times. For example, many musicians and critics have vilified jazz stars such as Miles Davis and Herbie Hancock for their early use of electronic instruments and their employment of popular music styles. Fortunately, musicians such as Ellington and Jones have provided models for music and music businesses that are both artistically and commercially viable. The landscape is perhaps slowly advancing in this regard, as the over-romanticized portrait of the struggling artist slowly fades. In addition, with the advent of the Internet as a forum for artists and small businesses to grow outside large corporate structures, these kinds of independent models are even more important.

Jones also comports himself in a manner reminiscent of Ellington – proud, calm, debonair, personable, articulate, and outspoken. More importantly, he carries the torch of African-American music, and American music in general, in the spirit of the Ellington legacy, pushing borders and resisting categorization. He has taken entrepreneurship to new levels with his involvement in print media, cable television, and record labels, and is currently actively lobbying for the creation of a presidential cabinet position of Secretary of Culture.

Conclusion

In this chapter I have focused on established musicians who, while embracing Duke's legacy and influence, have each created their own powerful and important legacies. Yet all players, composers, arrangers, and bandleaders in the jazz field feel the immensity of Ellington's influence, and his spirit lives on and thrives in contemporary musicians. Bandleaders with important commissions and large ensembles playing a wide range of original compositions that stretch traditional notions of jazz include, among many others, Bob Brookmeyer, Muhal Richard Abrams, Maria Schneider, David Berger, John Hollenbeck

(Large Ensemble), Arturo O'Farrill (Afro Latin Jazz Orchestra), and Darcy James Argue (Secret Society).

Musicians with smaller ensembles that embrace tradition and a broader vision of jazz also continue to expand jazz's palette. Pianist Jason Moran is rethinking the piano trio, and his occasional use of a turntablist to augment it is cunning and effective, adding a mysterious and enthralling quality. Guitarists Kurt Rosenwinkel and Bill Frisell speak to and articulate young musicians' appreciation of a multitude of styles. The energy and stylistic breadth of the trio The Bad Plus also give insight into a broader view of jazz today. And saxophonist Steve Coleman and the M-Base Collective have a long track record of encouraging the rethinking of the creative process. In fact, most successful contemporary musicians in the jazz field currently embrace and exemplify this expanded vision. This is a crucial element of Ellington's legacy and influence – however counterintuitive it may seem, given his place in the standard jazz canon – and it continues to shape the vibrant, ever-changing jazz and American music scene.

Notes

1 Leonard Feather, "The Blindfold Test," *Down Beat*, September 21, 1955, 33–34.
2 *Revelations* was initially performed at the 1957 Brandeis Jazz Festival of the Arts, but recorded shortly afterwards at a New York studio for the Columbia LP *Modern Jazz Concert* (reissued on the CD *The Birth of the Third Stream*, Columbia CK 64929).
3 Clora Bryant et al., eds., *Central Avenue Sounds: Jazz in Los Angeles* (Berkeley: University of California Press, 1988), 333.
4 Gerald Wilson interview by Molly Murphy for the National Endowment for the Arts, October 25, 2006.
5 Ibid.
6 Bryant et al., eds., *Central Avenue Sounds*, 337.
7 Wayne Enstice and Paul Rubin, *Jazz Spoken Here: Conversations with Twenty-Two Musicians* (Baton Rouge: Louisiana State University Press, 1992), 278.
8 Gene Lees, *You Can't Steal a Gift* (New Haven, CT: Yale University Press, 2001), 134.
9 The LP is titled *Oscar Peterson Trio + One Clark Terry* (Mercury MG20975).
10 A. B. Spellman, *Black Music: Four Lives in the Bebop Business*, 4th edn. (1966; reprint, New York: Limelight Editions, 1994), 55, 60.
11 Ibid., 72.
12 Howard Mandel, *Miles, Ornette, Cecil: Jazz Beyond Jazz* (New York: Routledge, 2008), 225–26.
13 Ibid., 71–72.
14 Quincy Jones, *Q: The Autobiography of Quincy Jones* (New York: Doubleday, 2001), 214.

Select bibliography

It would be impossible to list here the thousands of magazine and newspaper articles, liner notes, reviews, oral history sources, and websites of interest to Ellington scholars and fans. However, special mention should be made of the collection of online links at http://ellingtonweb.ca. The holdings of the Duke Ellington Collection at the Smithsonian Institution are itemized at http://american history.si.edu/archives/d5301.htm.

Books and dissertations

Bigard, Barney. *With Louis and the Duke: The Autobiography of a Jazz Clarinetist.* Edited by Barry Martyn. New York: Oxford University Press, 1986.

Cohen, Harvey G. *Duke Ellington's America.* Chicago: University of Chicago Press, 2010.

Collier, James Lincoln. *Duke Ellington.* New York: Oxford University Press, 1987.

Cooper, Matthew J. *Duke Ellington as Pianist: A Study of Styles.* Missoula, MT: The College Music Society (Monographs & Bibliographics in Music, 24), 2013.

Dance, Stanley. *The World of Duke Ellington.* New York: Scribner, 1970; reprint, New York: Da Capo, 1981.

  The World of Swing. New York: C. Scribner's Sons, 1974; reprint, New York: Da Capo Press, 1979.

Denning, Michael. *The Cultural Front: The Laboring of American Culture in the Twentieth Century.* New York: Verso, 2000.

Dietrich, Kurt. *Duke's Bones: Ellington's Great Trombonists.* Rottenburg N., Germany: Advance Music, 1995.

Dinerstein, Joel. *Swinging the Machine: Modernity, Technology, and African-American Culture between the World Wars.* Amherst: University of Massachusetts Press, 2003.

Ellington, Duke [Edward Kennedy]. *Music Is My Mistress.* New York: Doubleday, 1973; reprint, New York: Da Capo, 1976. An index to this book can be found online at http://roundaboutjazz.de/depages/IndexToMiMM.htm.

Ellington, Mercer, with Stanley Dance. *Duke Ellington in Person: An Intimate Memoir.* Boston: Houghton Mifflin, 1978; reprint, New York: Da Capo, 1979.

Erenberg, Lewis A. *Swingin' the Dream: Big Band Jazz and the Rebirth of American Culture.* Chicago: The University of Chicago Press, 1998.

Faine, Edward Allan. *Ellington at the White House 1969.* Takoma Park, MD: IM Press, 2013.

Franceschina, John. *Duke Ellington's Music for the Theatre.* Jefferson, NC: McFarland, 2001.

Gammond, Peter, ed. *Duke Ellington: His Life and Music.* New York: Roy Publishers, 1958; reprint, New York: Da Capo Press, 1977.

George, Don. *Sweet Man: The Real Duke Ellington.* New York: G. P. Putnam's Sons, 1981.

Hajdu, David. *Lush Life: A Biography of Billy Strayhorn.* New York: Farrar, Straus & Giroux, 1996.

Haskins, Jim. *The Cotton Club*. New York: Random House, 1977.

Hasse, John Edward. *Beyond Category: The Life and Genius of Duke Ellington*. New York: Simon & Schuster, 1993.

Howland, John, ed. *Duke Ellington Studies* (Cambridge: Cambridge University Press, scheduled for 2015).

   Ellington Uptown: Duke Ellington, James P. Johnson, and the Birth of Concert Jazz. Ann Arbor: University of Michigan Press, 2009.

Jewell, Derek. *Duke: A Portrait of Duke Ellington*. Toronto: George J. McLeod, 1977; reprint, New York: W. W. Norton, 1980.

Knauer, Wolfram, ed. *Duke Ellington und die Folgen*. Hofheim, Germany: Wolke Verlag, 2000. [All essays in German.]

Lambert, Eddie. *Duke Ellington: A Listener's Guide*. Lanham, MD: The Scarecrow Press, 1999.

Lavezzoli, Peter. *The King of All, Sir Duke: Ellington and the Artistic Revolution*. New York: Continuum, 2001.

Lawrence, A. H. *Duke Ellington and His World: A Biography*. New York: Routledge, 2001.

Lock, Graham. *Blutopia: Visions of the Future and Revisions of the Past in the Work of Sun Ra, Duke Ellington, and Anthony Braxton*. Durham, NC: Duke University Press, 1999.

McLaren, Joseph. "Edward Kennedy (Duke) Ellington and Langston Hughes: Perspectives on Their Contributions to American Culture, 1920–1966." PhD diss., Brown University, 1980.

Morton, John Fass. *Backstory in Blue: Ellington at Newport '56*. New Brunswick, NJ: Rutgers University Press, 2008.

Nicholson, Stuart. *Reminiscing in Tempo: A Portrait of Duke Ellington*. Boston: Northeastern University Press, 1999.

Peress, Maurice. *Dvořák to Duke Ellington: A Conductor Explores America's Music and Its African American Roots*. New York: Oxford University Press, 2004.

Rattenbury, Ken. *Duke Ellington: Jazz Composer*. New Haven, CT: Yale University Press, 1990.

Schiff, David. *The Ellington Century*. Berkeley: University of California Press, 2012.

Steed, Janna Tull. *Duke Ellington: A Spiritual Biography*. New York: Crossroad, 1999.

Stewart, Rex. *Boy Meets Horn*. Edited by Claire P. Gordon. Ann Arbor: University of Michigan Press, 1991.

Stratemann, Klaus. *Duke Ellington: Day by Day and Film by Film*. Copenhagen: JazzMedia, 1992.

Teachout, Terry. *Duke: A Life of Duke Ellington*. New York: Gotham Books, 2013.

Timner, W. E. *Ellingtonia: The Recorded Music of Duke Ellington and His Sidemen*. 5th edn. Lanham, MD: The Scarecrow Press, 2007.

Tucker, Mark, ed. *The Duke Ellington Reader*. New York: Oxford University Press, 1993.

   Ellington: The Early Years. Urbana: University of Illinois Press, 1991.

Ulanov, Barry. *Duke Ellington*. New York: Creative Age Press, 1946; reprint, New York: Da Capo, 1972.

Vail, Ken. *Duke's Diary: The Life of Duke Ellington, Part One; 1927–1950*. Lanham, MD: Scarecrow Press, 1999.

Duke's Diary: The Life of Duke Ellington, Part Two; 1950–1974. Lanham, MD: Scarecrow Press, 2002.

van de Leur, Walter. *Something to Live For: The Music of Billy Strayhorn.* New York: Oxford University Press, 2002.

Book chapters and journal articles

Balliett, Whitney. "Celebrating the Duke." In *Collected Works. A Journal of Jazz 1954–2000,* 806–12. New York: St. Martin's Press, 2000.

"A Day with the Duke." In *American Musicians: 56 Portraits in Jazz,* 319–23. New York: Oxford University Press, 1986.

"Duke Ellington." In *Goodbyes and Other Messages: A Journal of Jazz, 1981–1990,* 23–30. New York: Oxford University Press, 1991.

Bañagale, Ryan Paul. "Rewriting the Narrative One Arrangement at a Time: Duke Ellington and *Rhapsody in Blue.*" *Jazz Perspectives* 6/1–2 (2012): 5–27.

Barg, Lisa, and Walter van de Leur. "'Your Music Has Flung the Story of "Hot Harlem" to the Four Corners of the Earth!': Race and Narrative in *Black, Brown and Beige.*" *Musical Quarterly* 96 (2013): 426–58.

Baumgartner, Michael. "Duke Ellington's 'East St. Louis Toodle-O' Revisited." *Jazz Perspectives* 6/1–2 (2012): 29–56.

Bellerby, Vic. "Duke Ellington." In *The Art of Jazz: Ragtime to Bebop,* edited by Martin T. Williams, 139–59. New York: Oxford University Press, 1959; reprint, New York: Da Capo Press, 1981.

Berish, Andrew. "Leisure, Love, and Dreams in Depression America: Duke Ellington and Tin Pan Alley Song." *Musical Quarterly* 96 (2013): 339–68.

"A Locomotive Laboratory of Place: Duke Ellington and His Orchestra." In *Lonesome Roads and Streets of Dreams: Place, Mobility, and Race in Jazz of the 1930s and '40s.* Chicago: University of Chicago Press, 2012.

Burrows, George. "*Black, Brown and Beige* and the Politics of Signifyin(g): Towards a Critical Understanding of Duke Ellington." *Jazz Research Journal* 1 (May 2007): 45–71.

Caine, Daniel C. "A Crooked Thing: A Chronicle of 'Beggar's Holiday'." *New Renaissance* 7/1 (Spring 1987): 75–100.

Charters, Samuel B., and Leonard Kunstadt. "The House That Mills Built." In *Jazz: A History of the New York Scene,* 207–21. New York: Doubleday, 1962; reprint, New York: Da Capo Press, 1981.

Cohen, Harvey G. "Duke Ellington and *Black, Brown and Beige*: The Composer as Historian at Carnegie Hall." *American Quarterly* 56/4 (Dec 2004): 1003–34.

"Duke Ellington on Film in the 1930s." *Musical Quarterly* 96 (2013): 406–25.

"The Marketing of Duke Ellington: Setting the Strategy for an African American Maestro." *The Journal of African American History* 89/4 (Autumn 2004): 291–315.

Cooke, Mervyn. "Jazz Among the Classics, and the Case of Duke Ellington." In *The Cambridge Companion to Jazz,* edited by Mervyn Cooke and David Horn, 153–73. Cambridge: Cambridge University Press, 2002.

Cox, Felix. "Duke Ellington as Composer: Two Pieces for Paul Whiteman." *Jazz Perspectives* 6/1–2 (2012): 57–74.

Crawford, Richard. "Duke Ellington (1899–1974) and His Orchestra." In *The American Musical Landscape: The Business of Musicianship from Billings to Gershwin*, 184–212. Berkeley: University of California Press, 2000.

Crouch, Stanley. "Duke Ellington: Transcontinental Swing" and "Come Sunday: Duke Ellington, Mahalia Jackson." In *Considering Genius: Writings on Jazz*, 133–52, 258–70. New York: Basic Civitas Books, 2006.

Davis, Francis. "Surviving Ellington" [subject: *Queenie Pie*] and "Ellington's Decade." In *Jazz and Its Discontents: A Francis Davis Reader*, 55–67, 68–75. New York: Da Capo Press, 2004.

DeVeaux, Scott. "*Black, Brown and Beige* and the Critics." *Black Music Research Journal* 13/2 (Fall 1993): 125–46.

Dietrich, Kurt. "Joe 'Tricky Sam' Nanton: Duke Ellington's Master of the Plunger Trombone." *Annual Review of Jazz Studies* 5 (1991): 1–35.

"The Role of Trombones in *Black, Brown and Beige*." *Black Music Research Journal* 13/2 (Fall 1993): 111–24.

Domek, Richard. "Compositional Characteristics of Later Ellington Works." *Jazz Research Proceedings Yearbook* [IAJE] 19 (1999): 127–45.

"The Duke as Impressionist: Another Look." *Jazz Research Papers* [IAJE] 14 (1994): 55–64.

"Ellington's Development as a Background Artist." *Jazz Research Proceedings Yearbook* [IAJE] 17 (1997): 6–29.

"The Late Duke: Ellington's and Strayhorn's Music for *Anatomy of a Murder* Considered." *Jazz Perspectives* 6/1–2 (2012): 75–121.

Edström, Olle. "Ellington in Sweden." *Musical Quarterly* 96 (2013): 478–512.

Edwards, Brent Hayes. "The Literary Ellington." *Representations* 77 (Winter 2002): 1–29. Reprinted in *Uptown Conversation: The New Jazz Studies*, edited by Robert G. O'Meally et al. New York: Columbia University Press, 2004.

Ellison, Ralph. "Homage to Duke Ellington on His Birthday." *Washington Sunday Star*, April 27, 1969. Reprinted in *Living with Music: Ralph Ellison's Jazz Writings*, edited by Robert G. O'Meally. New York: Modern Library, 2001.

Feather, Leonard. "The Duke." In *From Satchmo to Miles*, 45–64. New York: Da Capo Press, 1972.

"Duke." In *The Jazz Years: Earwitness to an Era*, 62–70. New York: Da Capo Press, 1987.

"Duke Ellington." In *The Jazz Makers: Essays on the Greats of Jazz*, edited by Nat Shapiro and Nat Hentoff, 187–201. New York: Rinehart, 1957; reprint, New York: Da Capo Press, 1979.

Fitzgerald, Sharon. "To Love Him Madly." *American Visions* 14/2 (April 1999): 16–25.

Fox, Charles. "Duke Ellington in the Nineteen-Thirties." In *The Art of Jazz: Ragtime to Bebop*, edited by Martin T. Williams, 123–38. New York: Oxford University Press, 1959; reprint, New York: Da Capo Press, 1981.

Gabbard, Krin. "Duke's Place: Visualizing a Jazz Composer." In *Jammin' at the Margins: Jazz and the American Cinema*, 160–203. Chicago: University of Chicago Press, 1996.

"*Paris Blues:* Ellington, Armstrong, and Saying It with Music." In *Uptown Conversation: The New Jazz Studies*, edited by Robert G. O'Meally et al., 297–311. New York: Columbia University Press, 2004.

Gaffney, Nicholas L. "'He Was a Man Who Walked Tall Among Men': Duke Ellington, African American Audiences, and the Black Musical Entertainment Market, 1927–1943." *The Journal of African American History* 98/3 (Summer 2013): 367–91.

Gaines, Kevin. "Duke Ellington, 'Black, Brown, and Beige,' and the Cultural Politics of Race." In *Music and the Racial Imagination*, edited by Ronald Radano and Philip V. Bohlman, 585–602. Chicago: University of Chicago Press, 2000.

Giddins, Gary. "Duke Ellington: The Poker Game," "Duke Ellington: The Enlightenment," and "Duke Ellington: At the Pulpit." In *Visions of Jazz: The First Century*, 102–17, 233–52, 490–501. New York: Oxford University Press, 1998.

"Not for Dancers Only." In *Rhythm-a-Ning: Jazz Tradition and Innovation in the '80s*, 250–59. New York: Oxford University Press, 1985.

Gleason, Ralph J. "The Duke." In *Celebrating the Duke*, 153–266. Boston: Atlantic Monthly Press, 1975.

Green, Edward. "Did Ellington Truly Believe in an Afro-Eurasian Eclipse?" *International Review of the Aesthetics and Sociology of Music* 43/1 (2012): 227–35.

"Duke Ellington and the Oneness of Opposites: A Study in the Art of Motivic Composition." *Ongakugaku (Journal of the Musicological Society of Japan)* 53/1 (2007): 1–18.

"'Harlem Air Shaft': A True Programmatic Composition?" *Journal of Jazz Studies* 7/1 (2011): 28–46.

"'It Don't Mean a Thing if It Ain't Got That Grundgestalt!' – Ellington from a Motivic Perspective." *Jazz Perspectives* 2/2 (2008): 215–49.

Harrison, Max. "Reflections on Some of Duke Ellington's Longer Work." In *A Jazz Retrospect*, 121–27. London: Quartet, 1991.

Hasse, John. "'A New Reason for Living': Duke Ellington in France." *Nottingham French Studies* 43/1 (Spring 2004): 5–18.

Hentoff, Nat. "Diminuendo and Crescendo in Blue" [six articles on Ellington]. In *Listen to the Stories: Nat Hentoff on Jazz and Country Music*, 3–24. New York: HarperCollins, 1995.

"The Man Who Was an Orchestra." In *Jazz Is*, 21–39. New York: Random House, 1976.

Hodeir, André. "A Masterpiece: Concerto for Cootie." In *Jazz: Its Evolution and Essence*, 77–98. New York: Grove Press, 1956.

Hoefsmit, Sjef. "Chronology of Ellington's Recordings and Performances of *Black, Brown and Beige*, 1943–1973." Edited by Andrew Homzy. *Black Music Research Journal* 13/2 (Fall 1993): 161–73.

Homzy, Andrew. "*Black, Brown and Beige* in Duke Ellington's Repertoire, 1943–1973." *Black Music Research Journal* 13/2 (Fall 1993): 87–110.

Horricks, Raymond. "Classic Ellington." In *Profiles in Jazz*, 55–91. New York: Transaction, 1991.

Howland, John. "Ellingtonia, Historically Speaking." *Musical Quarterly* 96 (2013): 331–38.

"Ellingtonian Extended Composition and the Symphonic Jazz Model." *Annual Review of Jazz Studies* 14 (2009): 1–64.

Hudson, Theodore R. "Duke Ellington's Literary Sources." *American Music* 9/1 (Spring 1991): 20–42.

Jackson, Travis A. "Tourist Point of View? Musics of the World and Ellington's Suites." *Musical Quarterly* 96 (2013): 513–40.

Jaffe, Andy. "An Overview of Duke Ellington Composition Techniques." *Jazz Research Papers* [IAJE] 16 (1996): 71–90.

James, Burnett. "Johnny Hodges," "The Impressionism of Duke Ellington," and "'Such Sweet Thunder'." In *Essays on Jazz*. London: Sidgwick and Jackson, 1961; reprint, New York: Da Capo Press, 1990.

Johnson, Aaron J. "A Date with the Duke: Ellington on Radio." *Musical Quarterly* 96 (2013): 369–405.

Knauer, Wolfram. "'Simulated Improvisation' in Duke Ellington's *Black, Brown and Beige*." *The Black Perspective in Music* 18 (1990): 20–38.

Lees, Gene. "The Enigma: Duke Ellington." In *Meet Me at Jim & Andy's: Jazz Musicians and Their World*, 45–57. New York: Oxford University Press, 1988.

Levine, Mark. "Notes on Ellington. The Clave and Piano Strategies." *Musica Oggi* 19 (1999): 18–22.

Lomanno, Mark. "Ellington's Lens as Motive Mediating: Improvising Voices in *The Far East Suite*." *Jazz Perspectives* 6/1–2 (2012): 151–77.

Lyttelton, Humphrey. "Duke Ellington." In *The Best of Jazz*, 143–52. London: Robson, 1978; reprint, New York: Taplinger, 1982.

Marsalis, Wynton, and Robert G. O'Meally. "Duke Ellington: 'Music Like a Big Hot Pot of Good Gumbo'." In *The Jazz Cadence of American Culture*, edited by Robert G. O'Meally, 143–53. New York: Columbia University Press, 1998.

Martin, Henry. "From Fountain to Furious: Ellington's Development as Stride Pianist." *Musica Oggi* 23 (2003–2004): 55–68.

McCarthy, Albert. "Duke Ellington: Apex of the Big Band Tradition." In *Big Band Jazz*, 328–46. New York: G. P. Putnam's Sons, 1974.

McManus, Laurie. "Ambiguity of Identity in the 'Global Village': Ellington, McLuhan, and *The Afro-Eurasian Eclipse*." *Jazz Perspectives* 6/1–2 (2012): 179–96.

Metzer, David. "Shadow Play: The Spiritual in Duke Ellington's *Black and Tan Fantasy*." *Black Music Research Journal* 17/2 (Autumn 1997): 137–58.

Morgenstern, Dan. "The Duke and His Men." In *Jazz People*, 99–124. New York: H. Abrams, 1976; reprint, New York: Da Capo Press, 1993.

Living With Jazz: A Reader. Edited by Sheldon Meyer. New York: Pantheon, 2004. Contains twelve pieces on Ellington.

Murray, Albert. "Duke Ellington Vamping Till Ready," "The Vernacular Imperative," "Storiella Americana as She Is Swyung: Or, The Blues as Representative Anecdote," and "Armstrong and Ellington Stomping the Blues in Paris." In *The Blue Devils of Nada*, 21–28, 75–82, 83–96, 97–113. New York: Vintage, 1996.

Peress, Maurice. "My Life with *Black, Brown and Beige*." *Black Music Research Journal* 13/2 (Fall 1993): 147–60.

Priestley, Brian, and Alan Cohen. "*Black, Brown, and Beige*." *Composer* 51 (1974): 33–37; 52 (1974): 29–32; 53 (1974–1975): 29–32. Revised edition in Tucker, ed., *The Duke Ellington Reader*.

Roeder, Michael Thomas. "Ellington Exposed: *Back to Back* and *Side by Side*." *Annual Review of Jazz Studies* 9 (1997–1998): 339–49.

Schiff, David. "Symphonic Ellington? Rehearing *New World A-Comin'*." *Musical Quarterly* 96 (2013): 459–77.

Schuller, Gunther. "Duke Ellington: Master Composer." In *The Swing Era: The Development of Jazz 1930–1945*, 46–157. New York: Oxford University Press, 1989.

"Ellington in the Pantheon," "Ellington vis-à-vis the Swing Era," and "The Case for Ellington's Music as Living Repertory." In *Musings: The Musical Worlds of Gunther Schuller*, 47–50, 51–59, 60–64. New York: Oxford University Press, 1986; reprint, New York: Da Capo Press, 1999.

"The Ellington Style: Its Origins and Early Development." In *Early Jazz: Its Roots and Musical Development*, 318–57. New York: Oxford University Press, 1968.

Shapiro, Nat, and Nat Hentoff, eds. "Ellington Plays the Piano, But His Real Instrument Is His Band." In *Hear Me Talkin' To Ya*, 224–38. New York: Rinehart, 1955.

Simon, George T. "Duke Ellington." In *The Big Bands*, 187–96. New York: Macmillan, 1967.

Stewart, Rex. "Ellingtonia." In *Jazz Masters of the Thirties*, 80–142. New York: Macmillan, 1972; reprint, Da Capo Press, 1982.

Teal, Kimberley Hannon. "Beyond the Cotton Club: The Persistence of Duke Ellington's Jungle Style." *Jazz Perspectives* 6/1–2 (2012): 123–49.

Tucker, Mark. "Duke Ellington." In *The Oxford Companion to Jazz*, edited by Bill Kirchner, 132–47. New York: Oxford University Press, 2000.

"The Genesis of *Black, Brown and Beige*." *Black Music Research Journal* 13/2 (Fall 1993): 67–86.

Ulanov, Barry. "The Ellington Programme." In *The Jazz Cadence of American Culture*, edited by Robert G. O'Meally, 166–71. New York: Columbia University Press, 1998.

Vogel, Shane. "Madam Zajj and US Steel: Blackness, Bioperformance, and Duke Ellington's Calypso Theater." *Social Text* 30/4 (Winter 2012): 1–24.

Wall, Tim. "Duke Ellington, Radio Remotes, and the Mediation of Big City Nightlife, 1927 to 1933." *Jazz Perspectives* 6/1–2 (2012): 197–222.

Ward, Geoffrey. "Like His Music, The Duke Was Beyond Category." *Smithsonian* 24/2 (May 1993): 62–71.

Waters, Charles H., Jr. "Anatomy of a Cover: The Story of Duke Ellington's Appearance on the Cover of *Time* Magazine." *Annual Review of Jazz Studies* 6 (1993): 1–46.

Welburn, Ron. "Duke Ellington's Music: The Catalyst for a True Jazz Criticism." *International Review of the Aesthetics and Sociology of Music* 17/1 (June 1986): 111–22.

Wiedemann, Erik. "Duke Ellington: The Composer." *Annual Review of Jazz Studies* 5 (1991): 37–64.

Willard, Patricia. "Dance: The Unsung Element of Ellingtonia." *The Antioch Review* 57/3 (Summer 1999): 402–14.

Williams, J. Kent. "Hodges at Newport: The Rhetoric of 'Jeep's Blues'." *Jazz Perspectives* 6/1–2 (2012): 247–63.

Williams, Katherine. "Improvisation as Composition: Fixity of Form and Collaborative Composition in Duke Ellington's *Diminuendo and Crescendo in Blue*." *Jazz Perspectives* 6/1–2 (2012): 223–46.

Williams, Martin. "Duke Ellington: Form Beyond Form." In *The Jazz Tradition*, 100–21. New York: Oxford University Press, 1983.

Zenni, Stefano. "The Aesthetics of Duke Ellington's Suites: The Case of 'Togo Brava'." *Black Music Research Journal* 21/1 (Spring 2001): 1–28.

Index

Cambridge Companions to Music